I0663546

DEATH THIEVES

Also by Julie Wright

Spell Check
Swimming in a Sea of Stars
The Art of Us
Wendy's Ever After
Four Chambers
Loved Like That

Discover more great books on
Juliewright.com

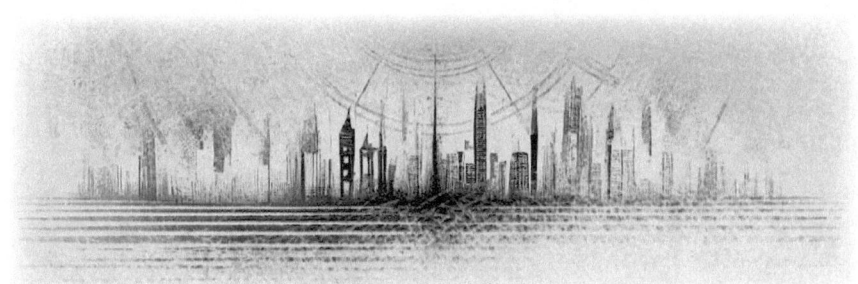

DEATH THIEVES

JULIE WRIGHT

HEART
STONE
PRESS

Death Thieves

Print Copyright © 2016 by Julie Wright

All rights reserved. No part of this book may be reproduced or transmitted in any form or by any means, electronic or mechanical, including photocopying, recording, or by any information storage and retrieval system, without permission in writing from the publisher.

This book is a work of fiction. Any reference to historical events, real people, or real locales are used as fiction in the work. Other names, characters, places and incidents are all a product of the author's imagination and any resemblance to actual events, locales or people, living or dead, is purely coincidental.

Interior Design by Jules Hartman

Cover image by Jules Hartman

Published by Heart Stone Press

St. George, Utah

Printed in the United States of America

First printing: August 2016

Second Printing March 2025

ISBN: 978-1-941849-04-0

To Merrik,
The kind of fabulous son who would visit me via time
travel if he knew I was having a bad day . . .
you know . . . if he had access to time travel.

ONE

I stumbled in the dark, trying to get out without alerting anyone to my escape. The window stuttered open, sticking in various places from serious lack of use. With a quick glance behind me to see if anyone noticed, and a deep breath, I heaved myself out the window, my feet dangling off the side searching for footholds—anything to keep me from falling to my death.

A few more feet and I'd be free. A few more feet and—

"Where exactly do you think you're going?"

I cursed under my breath and looked up. "Are you going to tell Mother Theresa?"

My twin sister scowled at my nickname for our aunt. "Summer, don't. Don't ask me to lie for you."

"I'm not asking you to lie. I'm asking you to not tell. It's totally different."

"So where are you going?"

I couldn't see her gold-flecked hazel eyes that were mirrors of my own, but knew she was irritated with me. "Caving. It's for a good cause. We're cleaning up the cave walls from all the graffiti." Surely a good cause was reason enough to break out of my prison. My fingers cramped as they clung to the lattice work on the side of our Aunt Theresa's house.

Winter sighed but said, "Fine. I won't tell. But don't get caught." She shook her head, making her dark brown hair look wild as she stared down at me from the window. I began my descent again, jumping the last few feet.

I blew a kiss up at her. With a twist of her mouth that landed somewhere between a smile and grimace she said, "I love you too. Be back before *you*."

I saluted, chuckling softly at her joke over my name, Summer Dawn. Reminders on when to be back weren't needed. If our aunt found me gone, my current three-month grounding would be extended to a year or more—maybe a life sentence. But it couldn't be helped. I *had* to get out. She had grounded me for three months of my senior year of high school. What kind of person did stuff like that?

Mother Theresa, that's who. The woman wasted no time to dole out punishments like grounding or taking away privileges when she felt things weren't going her way. And even when I tried really hard to let her have her way, she'd say my attitude needed work, and I'd end up grounded . . . again.

I stuck to the shadows, feeling nervous as I headed to the street. I'd had the insanely creepy feeling that someone was watching me all week. Winter laughed when I told her about it and told me to stop getting hysterical on her.

The street light glowed over Nathan's car a half a block down. I shook off the feeling. A half a block wasn't enough distance to walk alone to merit getting all jumpy.

"You made it!" His long, thin frame shoved off from where he'd been leaning against his dad's car. He caught me in his arms. I breathed in the rich scent of mud and water that never seemed to wash out of his clothes. "I didn't think you'd come."

"If we don't get out of here now, she'll catch us."

He nodded and slid in behind the driver's wheel. Mother Theresa terrified Nathan.

Easy breathing didn't happen until we were ten blocks down the road and pulling onto the highway heading out of the city of Orting, Washington and up into the mountains. I willed myself not to look in the rear view mirror, fearing I'd see the glare of her headlights coming after me.

"This is getting ridiculous," Nathan said as if reading my thought.

"We're almost through it." The impossibility of keeping the tired out of my voice overwhelmed me.

He flicked his glance from the road to me. "Three months is a life sentence in high school years. She's not even your real aunt. What is she? A cousin three times removed or something? Can't you put in a call to someone? Tell them Theresa is a psychopath and you need a different foster home?"

"Are you kidding? Alice nearly held a parade for the entire state of Washington when she found out we had any relatives willing to take us in: aunt, cousin, or otherwise." Alice had the unsavory job of being my social worker. She felt like more of a mother figure to me than the crack-addict-mother she took Winter and me away from when we were five years old. Alice had worked hard to keep Winter and me together. Aunt Theresa's house was a last-chance opportunity, and we all knew it. There were no different foster homes. There was only the freedom that would come on our eighteenth birthdays.

Nathan pulled off the road next to several other cars. His headlights slashed into the dark maw of the cave. Just as he cut the lights, a face appeared from within the shadows, disappearing as his lights went out. "Hey!" I pointed to the cave. "Did you see—?"

Nathan was already out of his seatbelt and half-hanging out of the door as he reached behind us for the duffel. "See what?"

"I saw someone, in the cave, before you turned your lights out." I pointed some more, though he wasn't looking at me.

"Yeah? And?"

"I just . . ." I trailed off, wondering how to explain in a way that didn't make me sound like a mental patient.

"Relax, Summer. Everyone else is already here. So if you saw someone, it was just one of the guys. You're getting so axe-murderer paranoid lately."

He'd hefted out the duffel and headed to the cave.

I scrambled to catch up. "I am not!" My defense sounded hollow, even to me. The truth, when forced to admission, was that I'd been paranoid all week. But that face didn't belong to one of the guys. The face wasn't anyone we knew. I gave myself a hard shake back to reality. The stranger looked close to my age, maybe a bit older. One of Nathan's friends might have brought an older brother, cousin, or someone from a different high school. And what did it matter? A stranger wouldn't know Theresa. A stranger couldn't get me into trouble.

Nathan fastened his headlamp on with Velcro straps and slung the duffel over his shoulder. The dark of the cave swallowed him. With a grunt, I followed—bumping into him just past the entrance. He laughed when he heard my cry of alarm. "Scared ya!"

I punched his shoulder.

"Ow! Summer! Don't get mean!" He flipped on his headlamp and handed me mine.

The cave went deep, ending abruptly at a yawning hole in the ground. A frayed climbing rope wound around a boulder and disappeared into the dark of the throat.

We strapped ourselves into the harnesses, clipping the carabiner into the eye hook. "Ladies first." Nathan's grin glowed white in the low light from my headlamp.

"Whatever. You go first. That way, if I fall I have something soft to land on."

"There's nothing soft about me." He flexed his muscles before hooking himself to the ropes. After several minutes he called up to me. "Down already.

My hands shook as I clipped the carabiners together. "What is my damage?" I muttered. Lots of girls were skittish; my own sister was still afraid of the dark, but me? Never. Voices filtered up from below, indicating Nathan's friends were gathered and ready to go. Likely the new guy would be among them. Everyone would be waiting on me.

I started my descent, going faster than normal. I looked up just as I passed the lip into the lower caves and gasped.

DEATH THIEVES

The whites of his eyes flashed in the glimmer of light that passed over him from my headlamp.

The face again.

Not a new guy below me, but a stranger looming above me.

With a panicked cry, I let go of the rope.

TWO

Before I could muster the sense to grab the rope and catch my fall, I'd bounced against the wall several times, sending jolts of pain through my body. My fingers burned hot through the climbing gloves as I finally caught the rope. "Stupid!" I yelled, not entirely sure what I meant by that, just grateful I'd found my voice.

"What are you doing?" Panic laced Nathan's voice, and several lanterns shined up at me blinding me to anything but the bright spots. I looked up to the top, my headlamp illuminating the lip of the hole, but saw nothing there except the shadows cast by my own movement and light.

"Stupid!" I shouted again, still not sure what I meant by the word. "I swear, Nathan—if this is some prank, I am so going to kill you a hundred different ways!"

"Whoa, whoa, whoa! You think I want you to break that pretty neck? Huh?"

His friends laughed, making me grateful I'd missed whatever comment they may have made about my neck or any other body part. I hurried to the bottom.

Nathan moved quickly to grab me and hold me. I allowed myself to all but collapse against him—allowed him to be the force holding me on my feet.

"It's okay. I got you." He smoothed his hands over my hair. "Don't be pulling stunts like that though, right? It'd mess me up bad if something happened to you."

"I don't know what happened." And I didn't. It couldn't have been a prank with Nathan acting so protective. Could someone really be lurking in the high cave? But no. Too impossible. I saw the face as we pulled in. No one ever came out. But we didn't pass anyone on our way to the throat, and hiding places within the cave didn't exist. The sheer walls made it all impossible.

"I don't know what happened," I repeated. Telling him about the face again would sound lame. They'd think I was crazy and that was without telling them that I felt like someone had been following me for over a week and that sleeping at night had been close to unbearable due to the irrational fear that someone watched me. I shook my head. "I'm fine. Just tired probably."

"Then let's get going!" Shawn, Nathan's best friend, cried out.

They all pulled out various cans from their back packs and duffels. "Wild world reclamation project! Begin!" Tony shouted. They were smart enough to bring face masks so the propellant from the paint cans didn't make anyone sick.

Over the many decades people had been coming down into the cave, people had also been leaving their mark. Graffiti littered most of the stalactite and stalagmite formations. Nathan and his art class friends had bought a bunch of various colored spray paint cans and decided to paint the cave back to its natural beauty. I couldn't miss the craziest art project I'd ever heard of. Which was how I found myself shimmying down the lattice work of Mother Theresa's house.

Nathan threw a can to me, my still-shaking hands making a clumsy catch. Then he got down to business. I spent more time watching Nathan than painting. He understood how to mix the browns and whites into something earthy and natural. I loved watching him work.

He was the reason Mother Theresa grounded me for three months. She said it would protect my virtue and keep me from becoming a crack-head like my mother. She made lots of little jibes at me like that. Everything she did, she did to keep me virtuous and to keep me from creating little crack-babies like my momma did. She even used the word momma, as if Winter or I would ever call our mother *momma*.

So when Nathan brought me home late one night, accompanied by the police for getting kicked off the roof of a family-operated motel in Parkland, she went into tirades on soul saving. She wouldn't hear my explanation that we hadn't been doing anything *bad*—no crack-baby-making or crack consuming. We were just throwing ice cubes off the roof.

Nathan emptied his first can and threw it into his duffel. He tossed me over a wink and went back to work. So cute. I tried to focus on the flutter he caused in my stomach rather than the flutter caused by thinking on who might be at the top of the throat. *Just my imagination.* I repeated that phrase often while pretending to smile and enjoy myself. And when everyone finished with the first room and had moved on down the tunnel and into the second room, I stood there alone for the briefest of minutes while I finished painting out the words "true love always" from the sidewall.

The tingling in my gut made me stiffen and suck in a stuttering breath. The hairs on my arms and the back of my neck vibrated with the sense of someone's eyes on me, I didn't look back towards the tunnel leading to the throat, fearing what might exist there. I fled to the second room, rushing to the combined light of the others, hurrying away from the absolute knowledge that if I turned, that pale, passive face would be the only thing to see.

***

"Someone's watching me." I didn't have to wait long for Winter to wake up. It was as though she sensed my need for her, and so pulled herself from deep slumber. A perk of being twins. We couldn't read each other's thoughts, but emotions were so much more than thoughts. I'd have felt guilty about waking her up, but her alarm would have gone off in another eighteen minutes anyway.

She blinked several times before focusing on me. "Aunt Theresa was in her room all night. She didn't follow you."

"I don't mean her. A guy. Our age. He's following me. He looks like a ghost."

"You don't believe in ghosts." She stretched and pushed back her covers.

"I don't." And I didn't, not like other people perceived them anyway. I believed the dead had better things to do than hang around living people rattling chains and wearing sheets. "But it wasn't like poltergeist-ghost. It was like creepy-axe-murderer-stalker ghost."

Winter went to the window to look out past our curtains. I didn't dare follow, fearing if I looked, he'd be there—his eyes wide and his face the ashen grey of the undead. "No one's outside." She turned to me with her arms folded over the red Drug Free t-shirt she always wore to bed. Sometimes I wondered if, by wearing that shirt, she was labeling herself so everyone would know she had nothing in common with our mother. "Maybe he's the parole ghost, haunting you for breaking out last night."

"You're so not funny. I had to go last night. It was a good cause. We're reclaiming the wild." I willed her to come away from the window—which she did, as though pulled by my thoughts.

"You're off ground in another two weeks. You couldn't reclaim the wild then?"

"The art club had it already planned. They weren't going to change their plans just because Theresa's a Nazi."

"Theresa isn't a Nazi."

I narrowed my eyes at her, and jabbed a finger her direction. "You're going Stockholm on me, aren't you?"

"No." Her turn to be defensive. "Stockholm Syndrome is for people being held hostage, not for people whose relatives are providing food and shelter for them."

"You *are* going Stockholm." I couldn't believe she'd gone over to the dark side, defending Mother Theresa. She'd accused me of the Stockholm syndrome once, back when we were ten and living with the McCoy's. She'd heard the phrase mentioned by a teacher at school and applied it to our situation with the couple who acted nice enough when other people were around, and not so nice when it was us alone with them. She felt like I saw too much from their point of view and had forgotten the fact that they often failed to feed us. She'd begged me to get us out of there.

For whatever reason, the state never left us with nice people very long, and forgot about us when we were with people who were at best neglectful, at worst . . . far worse.

"I am not. It's us and just us. Wonder twins forever." She put her fist to mine and smiled. "Wonder twin powers . . ."

"Activate." I finished the phrase and dropped my hand.

"Anyway," she said, turning to the closet to rummage for clothes. "We're not in a hostage situation. You'd save us from that if we were— like last time."

I joined her at the closet, looking for something to change into so the signs of mud and errant spray paint could be hidden away until they could be washed without Theresa noticing. "Yep. I'll save us. And you'll save everyone else." It always worked that way. I'd get us out of a home where we were either being starved or beaten or treated like slaves or worse.

After we were out of danger, Winter spoke loudly of our mistreatment. She complained to anyone who would listen, until the state would be left with no other choice but to investigate the foster home. That way she knew she protected whatever child might have come after us, protected them from what is worse. For us, it seldom actually came to the worse part—the real blessing of being twins. We recognized the signs and banded together to keep worse at arm's length until the case worker, Alice, would come in her Civic with the missing arm rest and rusted passenger door to pick us up.

There were times when I went to great lengths to get Alice's attention. Sometimes it meant breaking the law so the police would get involved. That always got her attention, but I had to stop doing that because Alice threatened to split Winter and me up. Keeping family units together was hard enough without me making it so no one wanted us. The one thing we had going for us was being twins. The state hated to separate twins. I resorted to simple phone calls and the threat we'd run away. We never actually ran. Runners *always* got split up. They hated runners more than they hated law-breakers.

Alice didn't like me much, but she loved Winter. Everyone loved Winter, which explained why she made captain of the cheerleading team, why she was the star-lead-role in every single play. Everybody loved her. But no one loved her as much as I did. I'd go to the ends of the universe for my sister.

Changing clothes turned out to be slightly painful. My jeans had fused to the dried blood from the cuts which fused to my leg. I felt bruised and battered everywhere.

"You look worse than I've ever seen you." Winter winced as I pulled off my jeans.

"That's saying something considering—"

"Considering you've got a hickey on your neck." Winter pointed.

My hand automatically went up to feel if she was right at the same time I denied any making out. "I totally do not! He only kissed me goodnight, on the lips, nothing more!" But when my hand went to my neck, I felt a slight lump there. The spot felt tender as my fingertips traced the perimeter of the lump. "Oh." I groaned and dropped to the bed, cringing with the motion, since there were bruises all over me. "I fell through the throat and bounced into the wall. Lots of rocks were sticking out. I guess one of them got me here, well I mean, they got me *everywhere*. They used me as a punching bag." I met her eyes. "But it definitely *isn't* a hickey."

"You don't have to convince me. But how are you going to convince Aunt Theresa you weren't making crack-babies?" She smirked. "Because it *really* looks like a hickey. It looks like someone squashed a tomato against your neck."

I went to the mirror to check it out. "No, no, no!" No amount of cover-up would *ever* cover it up. "Would a turtleneck look suspicious?" I stretched my neck to inspect the bruise better in the mirror.

"With Theresa? Everything looks suspicious." Winter rummaged on her side of the closet, which looked a lot more organized than my side, until she pulled out a light blue blouse with a high ruffled collar. "Try this on."

I smiled gratefully. "And what about tomorrow?"

She laughed. "You can try the turtleneck then. Maybe you'll be abducted by aliens today, and you won't ever have to worry about tomorrow."

Winter finished getting ready, and talked while I stared at the wall, feeling the energy drain from me with every moment.

"Mr. Williams says I have a good chance at the acting scholarship from UW."

"That's great." Keeping my tone light took effort. How would *I* ever pay for school? A scholarship hung above me, too high for me to ever reach. My grades weren't bad, but they weren't anything to applaud either. There were government programs, but I wanted to shake off the need for government assistance as soon as I turned eighteen and Theresa put me out of the house.

"You should apply for a scholarship, too." Winter's words echoed my own thoughts as she wriggled her head through the top of her shirt.

I rolled my eyes. "Yeah, whatever. You're the smart one, not me."

Winter took her turn to roll her eyes. "No one thinks of the actress as smart. I could never get a biology scholarship, but you could."

"Whatever."

She made noise in her throat that sounded like those voice exercises before a performance. "You've played dumb for so long, I'm starting to worry you believe you *are* dumb." She flattened down the little static frizzes of hair all over her head. "Anyway, we should go to Seattle and check out the campus sometime in the next month, once you're done with being grounded." She turned to face me, forcing me to open my heavy eyes and smile back at her beaming face. "A scholarship would totally rock, wouldn't it?"

"Definitely. And it'd be nothing less than you deserve."

"And I, um . . . need to borrow some money from the pot of gold." She looked at me, her eyes filled with apology.

Of course she brought up the scholarship first because she knew I was a sucker when it came to her going to school. "For what?"

"I want to take a few acting classes—outside of school drama class. I really think I could be a lot better with a little direction. And then, when I audition for the scholarship, the professional classes might make me stand out."

"How much?" Because Winter had tons of after-school activities, she couldn't ever get a job. But I worked washing dishes and mopping floors at a dodgy little dinner just off the main highway. The pot of gold was for any just-in-case situations where we found ourselves on our own. We hid the money inside a hole we'd made in the closet floor that we kept covered by padding and carpeting.

"The classes are sixty dollars an hour, and there are six one hour classes." She had her smile turned all the way up, though not bright enough to erase the shame in having to ask. She hated borrowing from the pot, knowing I worked hard to keep it full. Though honestly, working was a relief. It got me out of the house several days a week—even when Theresa grounded me.

"Yeah sure. Go ahead."

She hugged me tight. "I'll pay it back when I get my first job."

I waved her off, yawned, and groaned. "I'm too tired to shower and go down for breakfast."

She tucked in her shirt and stomped her feet into her tennis shoes. "That happens when you're out all night. Hey, go back to bed. I'll tell Theresa you feel sick."

"I already promised not to make you lie for me."

"Not a lie. Every time you go without sleep, you *do* get sick. It's a verifiable fact. Besides, you cover for me all the time."

This statement was not strictly true; Winter never did anything wrong. But I covered her in other ways, like providing money for acting classes so she didn't have to ask Theresa. Theresa and Paul were living off their retirement, which wasn't much. Asking for anything felt akin to mugging a homeless person.

I finally shrugged and put on the ruffle-necked shirt, just in case Mother Theresa came in to check on me. Then I sank back into bed and wrapped myself in the luxury of my blankets. When we were seven, someone donated handmade quilts to the state for kids in the foster care system. By giving us the quilts, it allowed us to have something familiar as we moved around from place to place . . . something we could call our own. The square patches on my quilts all had suns on them. Winter's was covered in various phases of the moon. The quilts worked exactly as they were meant to. Everywhere we went, the quilts went with us. We would cut off our own hands and leave them behind before we ever left one of our quilts.

I woke up several hours later, the bruising on my body almost hurting more than before I went to sleep. My stomach rumbled a reminder of missed breakfast while I showered. If we weren't on time at Theresa's table, we didn't eat until the next meal.

I stood for several minutes longer, letting the hot water run over me until it turned tepid, and grabbed a towel and my robe. I met Theresa in the hall on my way back to my room.

"Oh good, you're up, which must mean you're feeling a little better." She had a hawkish sort of nose, and eyes too small and spaced too close together to make her comfortable to look at for any length of time.

"I'm feeling a little better." I pretended to shiver and pulled the worn collar of my bathrobe higher so it covered the bruise on my neck. "I'm just really tired and have a lot of body ache." No lies there. I ached. Oh, how I ached.

She put her hand to my forehead. "Hmm, maybe the flu. We'll do soup for dinner and see if that helps. Make sure to drink plenty of water so you stay hydrated."

I nodded. And shivered again. Theresa believed soup cured disease. The black plague wouldn't have stood a chance against her garlic soup. Theresa really did seem nicer when she thought we might be sick.

Once in my room, I heard the garage door opening and closing. The low whine in Theresa's car engine that made it easy to identify as it backed out of the driveway. Saturday errands. The perfect time to get my painted, bloody clothes cleaned up before she noticed.

I hurried to the closet, flipped on the light, and shoved aside the hamper lid to dig around in the basket. I frowned and dug deeper, finally removing every stitch of clothing, piece by piece until the hamper was empty.

Panic.

The clothes were already gone.

She found them. While I showered. She came in here and found them. She knows I'm faking. "I'm so busted." Talking to the hamper didn't help.

I made my way back downstairs. "Wineve?" I called Winter by the pet name I'd given her when we were barely old enough to talk.

"What's wrong?" She turned.

"My clothes!" The words came out in a hiss between my teeth since I had to keep my voice low. Theresa's husband, Paul, could have been anywhere, and having him hear my confession of sneaking out guaranteed Theresa would also hear about it. Paul was a good guy, and he definitely liked Winter and I, but his ultimate loyalties went to Theresa.

Winter shook her head—not understanding. "Your clothes?"

"Missing. Gone. She must've found them."

Winter snorted. "She hasn't been in our room this morning. You are so paranoid sometimes. She didn't even come upstairs all morning except for that once to check on you. If she'd have found them, you would've heard—she'd be mad enough the whole neighborhood would've heard."

All this made sense. Theresa never put off scolding or punishment for later. She believed swift action helped us understand the importance of penance. "I put them in the hamper, but they're gone."

"Well don't look at me. I didn't take them. It's *your* week for laundry." She turned me toward the stairs and walked with me, keeping her voice low as well. "They're probably still there. You just didn't look hard enough."

She helped me look when we got back to the room. Together, we tore the room apart. The clothes were missing.

I expected war when Theresa came home, but she bustled about the kitchen, humming and making garlic soup.

The clothes were missing, but no one took them.

THREE

Monday at school, Nathan nearly tackled me in his excitement to see me. "You gotta talk to your aunt. Three months being grounded is lame."

I pulled myself away from him so I had a view of something more than his Orting High Cardinal Pride shirt and shrugged. "It's almost over," I said. Talking to Theresa about loosening her rules would be like asking a lemon to produce grape juice. Besides, after her mothering me with my fake sickness over the weekend, I felt a little softened towards her. She really could be a decent person when she set her mind to it.

"Isn't that Winter's shirt?" he asked.

"Yeah, so?"

"Ruffles aren't your thing." He picked up one of the ruffles between his two fingers and gave it a little flip as though amused by my choice of clothing.

I didn't explain about the bruise looking like a hickey, feeling pretty certain he'd take it as a challenge to give me something real. Growing up the way I had made me wary of guys who marked up their girlfriends like a dog would mark his territory. Too many men had marked up my mother.

"Makes me wonder if I've got the right sister, that's all."

"Trust me. We don't pull switches like that. Besides you're not her type." The last time Wineve and I pulled a switch turned into a full blown disaster. The same day the cheer team did pictures for the year book, Winter had found an open audition for some acting company in town. Hollywood had come to Washington. She asked me to cover for her so she could do the audition. After all, the cheer team was only taking pictures, and I did have her face. At a technical level, the switch should have been easy. And it was—right up until they decided to do the picture in a pyramid with the cheer captain on top.

Yeah, easy. It looked like a demolition car pileup full of red cheerleader skirts and arms and legs. As everyone untangled themselves, no one doubted my true identity. Aunt Theresa received a phone call, and I got into big trouble for trying to be someone I wasn't. Winter ducked out of trouble since she got the part and with it, her Screen Actor's Guild card. Theresa and Paul took us to dinner to celebrate.

Nathan hung his arm over my shoulders as we walked to lockers. "We're meeting everyone at the Corner Cafe for lunch. Come with." He crossed his arms over his school pride shirt and leaned against Winter's locker.

"It's risky. I'm so close to being not grounded." I pulled out my biology book, and stuffed my English book onto the shelf. "And I usually eat with my sister." He knew this, which is why it bugged me to have to remind him.

"There's room in the car. Bring her."

"I'll think about it." I slammed my locker shut and swirled the combination dial so it wouldn't open for random sluffers who raided lockers during class time. "Gotta go." I swept a quick kiss on Nathan's lips and hurried to class, sliding into my seat just as the bell rang. Winter shot me a look and flexed her arm while she crossed her eyes. This was sign language for, "The brain-dead-monkey-man made you late, didn't he?"

Before I could defend Nathan or ask about lunch, Mr. Ware started class.

Biology. We were learning about genetics and DNA. It was the only class that interested me lately. I liked the nature versus nurture argument, and hoped that not everything depended on either nature or nurture since both were in short supply in my life. I hoped, somehow, my own free will factored into the equation too.

"Want to go to lunch?" I asked as soon as the bell rang.

"Go? Where?" She stuffed her book into her already bulging bag.

"Nathan and a few of his friends are meeting at Corner Cafe for lunch. He said we could ride with him. We won't be late coming back because he has art class right after lunch. You know how he is. He'd never miss that." I tried to make it sound fun and non-trouble-making.

Winter stood and slung her bag over her shoulder, making me cringe just imagining lugging all that weight around. "I don't—"

"Aw, c'mon, Wineve. Just come with me."

She shook her head. "I just don't think we should today."

I raised my eyebrows. "What makes today different from tomorrow?" I followed her as she filed out of the room behind the rest of the class.

The crowd of teenagers buffeted against us as we made our way to Winter's next class. My next class was on the other side of the school, but I couldn't wait until lunch to debate on whether or not to go. Time would be short enough as it was.

"I just have a bad feeling about it, that's all." Her face looked determined. "I'm not going. You shouldn't either."

"Okay, now you're being weird. It's five blocks. What's gonna happen?"

She'd arrived at her classroom door. "I don't know. I just don't feel good about it." She faced me, her eyes fixed on mine. "Don't go, Summer. It feels wrong."

I snorted. "Don't get all mystical on me, Wineve. It's just lunch." Still . . . she looked so worried and terrified, I gave her a hug. She held me longer than normal, and when I tried to break away, she held a little tighter. "Stay with me, Summer," she whispered.

"I'm fine. Five blocks can't kill me." I laughed and pulled away.

She called after me from down the hall. "Please!"

I turned around, walking backwards, since I couldn't afford the time to stop altogether. "You're being paranoid! But I love you! Wonder Twin Powers!" I didn't wait to hear if she answered back "activate."

Winter's worry worried me too. The curse of twins–what bothers one of us will bother both of us, whether we want it to or not. Still, I held firm that five blocks couldn't kill me. Unless Theresa found out, then it would as good as kill me.

Nathan had already pulled up to the curb by the door leading to student parking. He revved his engine when he saw me. I got in and buckled my seatbelt, giving an extra tug to make sure the strap held tight, grumbling about Winter's paranoia.

We were off. I let out a small breath of relief when we got to the Corner Cafe without anything catastrophic happening, and chastised myself for giving in to Winter's delusions. Half the art club filled nearly every seat of the diner.

Nathan kept a close eye on the clock while we ate and rushed us out exactly on time. I stared out the car window as we drove back, trying not to feel drowsy from the full stomach, when I sat up straight. My throat closed off, choking out any noise I might have made. I pointed at the window, my fingers tapping violently against the glass trying to get Nathan's attention.

It was the face, the grey guy—he stood pale and ominous on the sidewalk, his long black cloak swirling around his legs in the wind, his eyes locked on mine. He gave a small nod.

"Nathan—" I turned to tell him about the guy. That's when I saw something far more alarming. Barreling towards the driver's side was a canary yellow truck. It had run the red light. I screamed. "Nathan! Look out!"

Everything went quiet. Nathan's mouth moved, yet no sound came out. The guy in grey suddenly appeared by Nathan's window. I wanted to yell at him to move, but couldn't. As I threw my hands up in front of me to brace myself against the impact, the guy's face shimmered through my vision again, only this time it was right in front of me. He unclipped my buckle, and I felt a pulling from my midsection.

My heart thumped faster in the mire of the moment. The pulling sensation stopped, and I found myself outside the car, standing on the sidewalk.

The crunching of metal and shattering of glass filled the silence, making me jump in alarm, and shock. Nathan's car flipped and skidded across the road. Pieces of windshield rained down, glittering in the sun as they fell to the ground. My hands ran over the length of my body. *How am I staring at Nathan's car? I'm supposed to be inside that car.* I'd yelled to Nathan about the truck. It was going to hit us. We didn't have time to avoid it, but I'd yelled—yelled and stared at the oncoming truck, unable to close my eyes to the horror of impact. Yet, here I stood, *not* in the car.

"Nathan!" I screamed. "Nathan!" I tried to run to the car, but something held my arms, making any forward motion impossible.

My breath came in sporadic bursts. My head spun as if I'd been turning in circles for an hour. I looked down at my arms, trying to comprehend what held them pinned at my sides. *Hands* held me.

I turned, every inch of me shaking and convulsing with shock. And there he was—the face. "Wh—what happened?" My voice sounded foreign and hollow.

He stared me down, his ashen features hard with lack of emotion, measuring me before he took a deep breath. "You're dead, Summer Dawn Rae."

That was it. His entire explanation swept over me in an icy wave of five words.

"No. I'm not—" I couldn't say the word. *Dead.* My legs buckled, and I fell to my knees. In an odd moment of detachment, it occurred to me that the action hurt me. Blood pooled under my right knee. The wound from the cave ripped open on impact of the cement. *Yes. That hurts. Do dead people hurt?*

I tried to stand, but my watery legs refused to obey my brain's commands. "If I'm dead, why am I bleeding?"

He did look concerned then, and swiftly bent to pick me up. His muscles tensed under my weight. "I'll get you medical care for your wound." In the movement of being picked up, I felt a pulling at my middle again. I squeezed my eyes shut against the vertigo. When I opened them, he appeared to have actual color in his face. He no longer looked like a human made of grey thunderclouds. His eyes seemed like hard blue ice crystals, chipped from glacial ice. His brown hair was darker than mine, something Winter would have called henna-brown. Compared to the pale ghost of a person he'd been before, he now looked like he might have been blushing.

"What are you?" I'd meant to say, *who are you*, but *who* didn't sound right. "The angel of death?"

He looked down into my face again. His blue eyes flickering with a warmth so brief, it could have been imagined. He jerked his head back up and began walking, seeming entirely unhindered by carrying a girl around. "I am the furthest thing from an angel that I know. Your heart still beats. You're only dead to everyone who knows you."

At these words, and with the realization that his movements took me away from the car and Nathan, I freaked. I struggled to release myself from his grip, but he held firm and didn't act bothered by my attempts to escape. "What are you? Some sort of psycho kidnapper? Let me go!" Sirens wailed in the distance, coming because of the accident. "What about Nathan?" Tears streamed down my cheeks.

"He *is* dead."

"Why didn't you pull him out?" I kicked and flailed with greater fervor, desperate to get away. "What is going on here?"

Again the flash of warmth—of compassion. "He's already infected. I'm sorry."

I screamed.

I screamed long and loud, stopping only long enough to draw in another breath and scream some more. People walked past us—me screaming. No one paused or took notice. I'd become invisible, like the ghost I still half-believed this guy to be.

The sobs came from lack of oxygen and the irrepressible fear tightening all around me. I shuddered and heaved. "They can't see me!" I said. "They can't hear me!" I looked over my abductor's shoulder, back to the car wreck. The entire scene behind me looked hazy. "I *am* dead. Nathan! I'm dead! Nathan—No!" My breath caught with a realization that swept beyond the car holding the shattered remains of my boyfriend, beyond any thought of myself. "Winter!

FOUR

No matter what I did, the grey man's grip never loosened. His strength seemed superhuman. No one on the street saw me. Paramedics, fire trucks, and police cars all raced past with no notice of this ghost stealing me away. No one heard my cries. Every step took me farther from the world I knew.

He stopped several blocks away and looked at the sun as though trying to tell time from its position in the sky. He stood there several long moments. Impulsively, I bit into his wrist. With a yelp, he released me, which landed me hard on the ground. Adrenaline took over as I hopped to my feet and sprinted away. I still screamed—screamed and ran—until I found someone out changing the letters in the sign outside a bookstore. I grabbed the person's shoulders and spun him around, trying to force him to see me. The guy looked maybe twenty, his face the ashen color that the grey man's used to be. His eyes swiveled everywhere as though a demon had caught him and he didn't know what to do about it.

"Help me!" I yelled in his face, but he gave no indication he'd heard me. He whimpered and his jeans turned dark at the crotch. Bewildered, I let him go. He stumbled back, falling to the ground, where he crab-walked backward until he could get his feet under him. Then he ran back into the bookstore.

I spun in a circle, taking in the world around me all at once. Everything had gone grey as though a wet newspaper had been wrung out over the city, leaving a colorless film over everything.

The grey man was now the only thing that had color. He caught up to me and took a firm hold of my arm. "You made us miss our window." His tone indicated his irritation.

"He didn't see me." I glared at the man. My breathing came too fast, making it hard to move oxygen to my brain. "He acted like a ghost had him. If I'm not dead, why can't anyone see me? Why can't anyone hear me? *What* is going on?"

The man looked at his wrist and sighed. "You're outside of this dimension, but inside the same time. You don't exist on the same level as these people."

"So I am dead?"

"No." He moved us off the sidewalk so the mother with her little boy could pass without bumping into us as they headed to the bookstore. "Dead means something else. No one knows what happens to the dead. Lots of research, but no conclusions." He lifted up his shirt sleeve, revealing what looked to be an arm shield for people who did archery. It had a screen like my phone. The grey man manipulated the screen with his fingers, making information appear. "This has enabled us to move outside of this dimension. We're here, but outside of it. Does that make sense?"

"No. Who are you? And when are you going to let me go, so I can go home?"

"My name's Tag. I can't let you go."

As I breathed in to start screaming again, he put his hand—the one not gripping my arm like a tourniquet, to my mouth. "Let's start over. Let me explain. I'm not going to hurt you. But I know I've handled this badly." He sat us down, his grip on my arm strong enough to leave me no choice but to sit with him, even though I wanted to stay standing, to stay in a position that allowed me to run.

"You've been following me for days." I accused. "You were at the cave. And you've been outside Theresa's house."

He nodded. "I worried you would damage yourself in the cave. I had to make sure that didn't happen."

"By what? Scaring me enough I let go of the rope? Thanks for the assist."

He ignored my sarcasm, but instead looked confused. "You saw me? That's why you let go of the rope?"

"I'm not blind."

"But I was outside of time. You shouldn't have seen me. I should have been invisible to you."

"Nice try on being sneaky. You will never be invisible to me."

He smiled as if I paid him a compliment. "I shouldn't be surprised. That was one of the things I noted about you in my research: you see things when all others cannot."

"Notes? Who are you?"

"I'm from the year 2113, sent to save you from your death and bring you back to a place where you'll have great influence. Had I not pulled you out, you would be dead along with your boyfriend."

"So, great. You pulled me out. Now let me go home."

"You're dead to everyone who knew you." He looked irritated to have to repeat this information.

"But I'm here. They're going to know I'm not dead when they don't find my body." The surreal slant of the conversation made me feel sick. My muscles trembled. Blackness edged into my vision.

"There's a body there. One who matches you in most respects. The coroner has no reason to delve too deeply, because it's known you were with Nathan in his car." The words sounded far away in my ears.

"I *am* dead."

I blacked out.

***

I had no idea how long I'd been unconscious. A soft, thin sheet slipped off of me when I stood. The cold air bit into my skin once the sheet no longer offered me protection from the elements.

The sun setting far to the west meant that a lot of time had passed, and we'd traveled outside of Orting, Washington and into Mount Rainier National Park. Tag sat in front of a fireless fire pit. The tang of charred wood, ash, and pine clung to the cold air. He looked like a shadow—all huddled into himself in front of the dark pit. I'd been laid out in a clearing next to a picnic table. My first instinct was to run, but in what direction? He watched me closely through the long shadows cast by the sun's waning presence. I moved a step to the right and two more steps behind me. *In what direction should I run?* The panic started immediately upon seeing him.

I ran my hands over me, wondering if he'd taken advantage of my inability to fight back while I'd been unconscious, and wondering if—somehow—my blacking out had been his fault. Had he drugged me? I didn't know and couldn't tell.

My clothing looked undisturbed aside from the hole in my jeans at the knee. He'd cut the hole open larger and a white bandage now lay over where I'd cut myself. The tank top worn under Winter's ruffled blouse remained tucked in. My shoes and socks were still on and my laces were tied the way I always left them. Could he remove my clothes and put them back on exactly the way I'd had them? I didn't know and couldn't tell on that either. "You drugged me." The accusation hung in the air between us.

"I didn't touch you," he said finally.

Could he read my mind? How could he know I was thinking that?

"How do I know you didn't? How do I know you're not some pervert preying on high school girls?"

He stood, but stayed on the opposite side of the fire pit. "I didn't touch you." His words came through clenched teeth. I kept my hands at my side to keep them from double checking all buttons and zippers on my clothing. After holding his gaze for several long moments, I determined he just might be telling the truth. But if not to take advantage of me, kill me, and leave me in the forest so some Boy Scout troop could find my body in six or seven years, why bother kidnapping me?

"You have to let me go home."

He let out a breath of exasperation. "The future is in a crisis situation. You're going to be like a—a queen. You'll be honored and very nearly worshipped for the service you'll perform for humanity."

"Service? What service? What crisis? Do you have any idea how Hades-in-the-underworld you sound right now?"

"Hades?"

"He's a Greek God, bonehead!"

He cringed when I shouted and let out another deep breath of exasperation.

"I know who Hades is. I just don't understand how this compares. We don't need to be enemies—"

"Well don't expect me to be your friend. I just want to go home! My sister needs me!" I kicked some old leaves into the fire pit.

He pulled out a small metal box looking thing and turned his back on me as he dropped packets into his box. I examined him good and hard for several long moments to make sure I could pick him from a lineup when the police caught him. He wore a long black jacket—like something Indiana Jones would have worn— only with better style and cut, and I preferred black to khaki any day. It had a utility look, filled with pockets. Those pockets bulged slightly from whatever they contained. The jacket itself hung loosely over his medium build. He was taller than me, but not so tall as to be remarkable in any way. I was 5'8" and I guessed him to be a few inches above that, 5'10' or 5'11". His black hair was short on the sides and in the back and just long enough to comb back on the top. No scars or tattoos or anything that made him stand out were readily visible with him all bundled up. His black jeans and jacket cast silver glimmers in the fabric as he moved. He ignored me with the same intensity that I inspected him. That bothered me.

"Didn't you hear me? I want to go home!" I moved in front of him to keep from being ignored. If he waited much longer, I fully planned on going back on my own—even being lost on Mount Rainier had to beat being a kidnap victim.

"I heard you." His soft voice almost made me feel guilty for all my shouting. Almost. He finally looked up from his box. "Dinner's ready." He handed me a spoon and lifted the lid to the box. Without waiting or saying a blessing on the food like Theresa did, he pulled out a pouch and dug into the contents of the pouch with his own spoon.

"What is that? A little heater or something?" I peered into the box.

"It's a hydrator. It'll heat too on solar power, but as you can see—" He looked up to the darkened sky. "We have no solar power at the present, so we'll have to make cold pasta work."

"How does the hydrator work?" I didn't really care, but wanted him to think I had an interest in his stuff. My mind raced with ideas for things I should do—things I might say, how I might get myself out of this nightmare.

"It pulls moisture out of the air. They don't work so well in arid climates. Some of the other soldiers have reported troubles, but I've been lucky so far."

Small talk failed me. I couldn't pretend. Winter was the actress, not me. My mind pulsed with plans and confusion, and keeping the anger under the surface proved impossible. "So what happens after we eat? You rape me and bury my body under the leaves?"

His mouth clamped shut so hard, his teeth made a clicking noise. He turned his back on me. He poured something else into his hydrator and pulled out a knob, pumping it several times before pushing it back in. "I would be violating my guard honor to even *think* of touching you," he finally said.

"Oh yeah, we wouldn't want to violate that."

"Exactly." He'd apparently missed my sarcasm.

My stomach growled, but I refused to eat any food from his little gadget. If he wanted to be Hades and drag me to his underworld, then I would be Persephone and not eat.

"Were I to touch you in any way that would harm you, I would be executed."

"I thought you were taking me to the future, not the dark ages."

He smiled. "Executions aren't as they once were. There is no guillotine, no mass audience to take delight in the fact that their head isn't on the chopping block. The death sentence is quick, private, and . . . seldom anticipated." His face darkened with every word as though he'd gathered together a black hole and consumed it. He shivered and inhaled deeply. "The future is dark, but you will change all that."

"No, because you're going to make a decision to do the right thing and take me back to my sister." Though I'd determined to not eat anything, I couldn't handle the cold anymore. I grabbed the little sheet–blanket thing and wrapped myself up. I sat on a boulder near the fire pit as though the non-existent fire might contribute warmth.

"When you died in that car wreck, you became lost to her."

"But I *didn't* die in that car wreck," I reasoned. "You said so yourself."

"To her, you did."

My throat constricted against the sob that fought its way to the surface every time Winter came to my thoughts. Since Winter always stayed in my thoughts, the sob sat like a cancerous lump in my throat. I tried to swallow it down to keep my kidnapper talking.

"So what exactly does the future need from me?" I didn't really believe his claims to be from the future. Sure the hydrator was kind of cool, but not outside the realm of the unusual. I felt pretty certain the military had things just like that. I made a mental note to do a Google search once home again. I'd do it now, except my phone had been on the seat between Nathan and me when our lives exploded.

"Your blood."

I sat up straight, instinctively grabbing the thermal blanket to keep it from slipping off again. "What?"

"No. Not like that. Your blood is pure. You have no disease. You can bear children within your own body without the help from labs and testing."

"How do you know if my blood is free from disease? A doctor once told me I had anemia." Did he really just say *bear children?* I had no intentions of bearing any children for at least another decade. Maybe not ever. "For all you know my blood isn't pure at all." I thought I had him on that point, though I scooted farther away from him in case he decided to stick me with a needle to get proof. When he stayed quiet and didn't meet my gaze, I paused. "*You.* You took my jeans after the cave. You stole my blood."

"I had to be certain you were what the records stated." He shifted as though he felt uncomfortable. Well, he should feel uncomfortable, going into a girl's room uninvited and stealing her pants. I glared at him, not that I'd ever really stopped glaring. I took several deep breaths. *Keep him talking. Make him your friend.*

"So you have a blood sample. What does that mean?"

"You can bear children."

I shook my head. My heart rate went up. Was he seriously discussing having babies? What kind of psychopath was I dealing with? "*Lots* of people can have children. It's not exactly a superpower."

"It is to some people. In the year 2113, no one can have children. All women and men are sterile due to HTHBI. All newborns are born sterile due to the infection passing from one genetic subject to another."

"HTHBI?"

"Human to human birthing infection."

That actually sounded bad. Like a zombie apocalypse infection. "So what? The world is dying off?" His continual references to having babies freaked me out. I wanted to run away screaming, but couldn't think of how to get away without getting caught again. I darted furtive glances to the woods around me. The trees stood like dark sentinels refusing me safe passage through them.

He shook his head. "Of course not. Scientists have formed alternative methods to create life. But those methods are—" He frowned. "Not always stable." He finished eating the contents of his pouch, crumpled it, and put it in the small silver knapsack near his hydrator. "We're lucky in many ways. There's a scientist with extraordinary talent and intelligence. He could see patterns of time and dimension. Because he could see those patterns, he was able to find ways to pass through the windows of time and into other places. Because of this, he found a way to mend the future." Tag gave me a meaningful look. I snorted at him and then chastised myself. Snorting at a crazy guy wouldn't make him my friend. It wouldn't get me home.

Tag glanced at his wrist band. "The next window to our destination won't open for several more days." He picked up his hydrator. "We don't have enough food to last that long with any comfort. We'll need to skip."

"You want me to skip?" Oh great. I'd been abducted by the hopscotch killer.

"Skip through time. Calculate what windows we could take that will allow us to skip in and out until we get where we want to go." He fiddled with his little wrist screen. "The next window will take us back two years but allow us to jump eighty. That's why I had to bring you here. This is where the most viable window will be. From there we'll only have to wait an hour until the next jump, which will take us exactly where we want to go. We'll leave in thirteen minutes." He hurried to his feet and packed the hydrator into his knapsack. He looked as though he might take the thin blanket I'd kept wrapped around me to stave off the cold, and turned away, apparently thinking better of it.

"Changing dimension is easier than changing time," he said. "Time shifts are disorienting. Hang on to me, and I'll help you adjust."

Hang onto him? As if! After all his creepy comments about bearing children and being a queen? I wouldn't touch him to scratch his face off. We stayed silent for several long minutes while he cleaned up, making sure we didn't leave anything behind.

"My sister will worry if I don't get home soon. We're twins. Twins need each other. If I don't go home, it'll be like killing her." Would he care if he killed her?

"She'll survive it."

His bitter tone and scoffing grunt infuriated me. "She won't survive anything! She needs me! Don't you get it? If someone takes a swing at her, I catch the fist. If someone tries to hurt her, I get her somewhere safe. I protect her, and she takes of everyone who might come after. That's the way we work. But she's not strong enough to protect herself. She'll shrivel into a submissive mass of nothing! You're wasting the most incredible potential humanity has ever created. Just let me go back. You want me to go to the future with you and be some alien experiment, let me bring her with." Not that I had any intentions of allowing him anywhere near Winter. But if I could get him to take me home, I could sic Aunt Theresa and the police on him.

The way he packed things up and then seemed to be waiting on some miraculous window to the future to open had moved me to a new realm of freaking out. Would he wait the full thirteen minutes and then shoot me or stab me? So far, no evidence of a gun or a knife had presented itself, but that didn't mean it wouldn't. That jacket had a lot of pockets.

"I can't take her. You're the one not getting it. You *died* in that car wreck. If I hadn't pulled you out, you'd be lost to her anyway—except you'd be really dead. Your sister had to learn to be her own person on the day of your accident. I didn't change anything for her."

"Then just go get her. I'll go with you if she comes with me."

"I can't pull her life out of history. I won't chance the chaos that could arise from ending the influence she has on the world around her. She has her part to play in history. And you have yours."

"Oh yeah! Great part I'm playing. I get to die! You know what? Just don't talk to me anymore. I hate you, you know that. Hate you!" So much for making him my friend.

"I know." His whole response—two words that seemed as heartless and cold as a machine. He knew I hated him and didn't care. I turned away, scrubbing my hand hard over my cheeks to clear away the tears. I got up which brought Tag abruptly to my side, his hand on my arm.

"I thought you weren't allowed to touch me." I let the hate ooze into my words.

"I am allowed, and required, to detain you. But I would never violate you."

Him even saying the word violate made my skin crawl. The thought of Winter facing the world alone filled me with a pain so deep, the back of my throat burned and my whole body shuddered.

What would Winter be doing right now? Would she be huddled in a corner of our room lost in a depression so deep, no one would be able to pull her out? Would she be scrambling through Theresa's medicine cabinet trying to pull a stunt like Mom, and drug herself into numbing relief? I couldn't conceive of how I would handle it if anything ever happened to her. *I'm so sorry, Wineve . . . so sorry . . .*

More minutes passed; Tag continually checked the time. His hand stayed on my arm, but as the minutes ticked away from us, he settled his hand firmly around my wrist. "It will feel uncomfortable at first, like trying to wear a shirt that's too tight. But if we stay in contact, you'll be fine."

His waiting for some imaginary time warp to whisk us away drove me insane. Without letting go of my wrist, he moved to press his fingers into his screen. Out of irritation and outright anger, I reached my own fingers out, and swiped them over the screen. The pulling sensation gripped at my middle at the same time Tag shouted, "Nooooooooooo!"

His shout echoed and vibrated in my ears and the tugging sensation gave way to the feeling that someone squeezed the air out of my lungs. The world around me blurred away in a spinning funnel of color and texture.

FIVE

In a panic I tried to pull away, but Tag tightened his grip on my wrist. When the pressure at my chest let up a little, the spinning color slowed enough I could almost make out the images within the swirl.

Cold wet drops splattered down on my face and hands. I looked up to the rain beating down from thick clouds. There was enough light to prove it was no longer night, yet the clouds made everything seem dark and dismal. I pivoted, or *tried* to pivot. Tag still had a mean grip on my wrist. When I finally looked at him, mostly to question what in the world had just happened, his eyes flashed. "You did it again! We missed the window to the proper time. Now we're in—" He checked his wrist thingy. "In the middle of a rain pour in 1572! 1572!" His grip tightened, cutting off the blood supply to my hand.

Disoriented, I tried to blink the raindrops from my vision and really *see* around me, tried to get my bearing as to where I was, *when* I was.

Not only had the weather and time of day changed, the fire pit had disappeared. The clearing where the picnic table had been had also vanished. I blinked some more. A mist rolled through the trees.

"Do you have any idea how easily you can kill us with time travel? Of all the stupid stunts to pull. We could end up in the middle of a war zone!" He started undoing the binding clips that held it to his wrist. I wasn't sure what taking it off would accomplish, but felt dazed enough not to be able to comment, make observations, or ask questions beyond the involuntary squeak my voice made.

The wind howled, ripping Tag's words away as he cursed and muttered about me and my stupidity. He looked up and seemed to be cursing the sky too, something about needing solar power.

Trees creaked and swayed under the slashing wind, their shadows mournful and disturbing. Then I looked closer, some of those swaying shadows were *advancing*. I found myself gripping Tag's jacket, trying to position him between me and whatever moved towards us.

Tag's head shot up from where he'd been focusing on his wrist thing. It hung by one binding clip, dangling from his arm. He took a sharp breath. "Takhoma Indians." Instead of undoing the last binding, he picked up the dangling part and rested it back against his arm, though he didn't take the time to re-hook it. His fingers moved deftly over the screen. He reached around and pulled me in by the waist, since I still held onto his jacket and was too terrified to let go, we ended up in some odd version of an embrace.

He tapped his screen.

The tugging at my gut again, the tightening of my chest until breathing became a miraculous feat. I buried my head into his jacket, not wanting the disorientation that came with the world swirling around me. His arms stayed around me, holding me close to him. Under his jacket, the solid mass of muscles felt like a cage's iron bars holding me in. I didn't care. I just wanted away from the torrential rain and the shadows moving with the trees—moving towards me.

How had he done that? How had he made everything different? He changed the weather, the time of day, *everything*. How? He was like some sort of magician, some sort of psycho sorcerer. I'd seen a rerun of Darren Brown the Hypnotist where, in the middle of daylight, he hypnotized some guy into a catatonic state and then left him that way until the sun disappeared into the horizon and the only light came from the stars. He changed the guy's watch time and then woke the guy up.

The guy was totally messed up. He believed the hypnotist had altered time. He completely freaked. Had Tag done this same thing to me? Was I trapped in illusion?

After what seemed an eternity, Tag released my waist, lifted my chin, and looked me directly in the eyes. I held the intensity of his gaze. My fingers wound tightly into his jacket still refused to let go. I had to force myself to pry each individual finger free.

The world around us had stopped spinning. The sun hung at its zenith. The only clouds in the sky were the ones of the huge white fluffy variety, and none of them dropped rain on us.

"You're safe." The words came out with the heat of his breath, warming my face, which was still cold and wet from the rain.

I shoved away from him. "Safe?" I spat. "I'm not safe! First it was nighttime in early autumn, then it was raining and there were *Indians*!" I dropped the blanket to the ground.

He picked it up and stuffed it into his knapsack. "They were probably friendly."

I jabbed him in the shoulder. "You don't know that! They could have been headhunters! And now we're . . . and now . . . now it's the middle of the day in—" I cast a cursory glance to the trees surrounding us. The fiery leaves shivering on their branches announced the autumn season we stood in. "What is this? October?"

He looked at his wrist band thing. "Good guess. 2058, October 21st."

I fell to my knees and threw up.

I stayed on my knees, detached thoughts swimming to my consciousness, then diving back down to be replaced by something equally detached. I left my life almost fifty years ago. Winter would be sixty-four years old. Would she be married? Would she have children and grandchildren? Was Aunt Theresa dead? Odd that I thought about Theresa, odd that it bothered me to think she might not be in the world anymore and to feel so exposed by that fact.

A piece of cloth appeared in front of my vision. "Here, you can clean your mouth off with this." He jiggled the cloth in front of me to entice me to take it.

I moved away from the mess I'd made in the dirt and took his cloth. He handed me a water bottle too. I thought once more about being like Persephone and not eating or drinking anything offered by my captor but had lost my will somewhere in the years. "I didn't even like Theresa," I said after taking a sip of the water.

He didn't ask who Theresa was or why I would say such a thing. He just sat next to me and watched me.

"Is this real? Is this a trick, like some stage hypnotist making a girl flap her arms like a chicken? Are we really in the year 2058?"

He nodded, the action seeming almost apologetic. He looked worried, whether about me, or the year, or whatever, I had no idea.

I stared at the ground, seeing nothing. "Winter's an old woman. Old without me. Her face wouldn't be my mirror anymore." Tears started falling again.

"You're going to get dehydrated if you keep crying and sicking out like that."

I lifted my head to gawk at him. "And you think I care? I have nothing to live for without her. Nothing." My voice cracked, and I felt my chin quivering. I scratched my fingers into the dirt and, in a moment of clarity, formed a plan. I rolled back from my knees so my feet were under me. Tag didn't really notice the change in the movement and was completely unprepared when I picked up fistfuls of dirt and debris and flung it into his face.

His hands flew to his eyes as I clawed for the wrist thing still hanging on by a single binding clip. He tried standing up and batting me away, but I yanked and jerked with all my might on his time traveling wrist watch. I fell back when it finally broke free from his arm.

I jumped to my feet and ran.

Branches tangled in my hair and tore at Winter's shirt as I shoved my way through the trees. Tag crashed through the trees after me. I tried to look down at the little screen on the time travel thing and almost tripped.

Tag's feet thumping behind me sounded closer. He'd catch me within minutes if I didn't get this thing to work. An exact time and date could be a later concern; anything different than being stuck in

2058 with a kidnapper would be good. I pushed my finger against the screen. Nothing happened.

"Stupid!" I pushed it again, swirling my finger over the screen in the hopes it would change something. Nothing happened.

"Stupid! Stupid!" And with these words I went down, falling face first into the dried out leaves and dark soil. I spat out the dirt stuck on my lips and tongue. My fingers tapped at the screen desperately trying to make *anything* happen.

Tag's face appeared through the underbrush. I army-crawled while continuing to swipe my fingers against the screen. "Please, get me outta here!" The tugging-at-my gut feeling came at exactly the same instant hands grabbed at my legs. The world spun as I kicked to make Tag let go. "Leave me alone!" I screamed. The words rolled around the bowl of the swirling funnel, echoing back to my ears again and again.

But he didn't let go. When the world slowed to the speed of a merry-go-round, I'd grown too tired to fight him. My body felt drained and weakened with no food and little water for at least a day, *had it been a day?* Persephone would've scoffed my weakness.

Tag climbed over me as soon as the world stopped and grabbed the time travel device. He was crazy if he thought I'd give up the device that easily. I rolled again, knocking him off balance and over to the side of me, though he still clung to a strap of the time thing. I moved to press the screen again, but stopped when my brain finally registered the world around me. We sat in a pile of *ashes*. Ash fell from the sky like snow. I would have thought it *was* snow except the smothering heat indicated otherwise. Mount Rainier was on fire.

Confused, I sat up. "Where are we?"

Tag shook his head, making the ash fall off his hair, only to be immediately replaced by more. "I'd tell you, but you won't let go of the Orbital." His low voice could have been a shout for all the anger it possessed.

"You won't let go either." I countered.

"That's because it's mine. Your entire plan is to take the Orbital and leave me stranded in an unspecified time and space. I *can* not and *will* not allow that."

As if to punctuate his declaration, the earth shuddered beneath us. Old leaves shivered off the tree branches. Impulsively, I reached out and grabbed Tag around the neck, trying to hold on to anything more stable than I felt. With my motion I yanked his hand, still holding onto the strap, back behind his head. Our faces were so close, our noses almost touched. It seemed almost the early stages of a kiss, except, in my fear, the only thoughts in my head were ones of panic. When the shaking stopped, he looked down at me as though he might kiss me. He must've seen my look of revulsion because he gave himself a violent shake, and shoved me away. In my moment of surprise, he nearly pulled the time device out of my grip. *Idiot.* I'd had the upper hand before, now I was stuck clinging to a corner.

He tugged sharply once more and reclaimed possession of his "Orbital."

"You . . . you . . . absolute crack-head! I need to go home!" I coughed, inhaling a few flakes when drawing a deep breath to yell at him further. I lunged for Tag. He dodged and pivoted from my reach sending out puffs of ash from under his feet.

"None of the others were this difficult!" he shouted as I lunged again.

"Others? You're a serial kidnapper?" I grunted, putting my arm over my mouth to keep from inhaling more ash. My fingers grazed over his jacket as he danced out of my way.

"I thought you wanted to know where we are. I can't look if you're attacking me."

"I don't care where we are. I just want to go home!" We circled each other, kicking up ash with more falling over us—each of us covering our mouths with our shirtsleeves. The exertion made the unbearably hot environment a lot worse. Sweat slicked between my shoulder blades sticking Winter's shirt and my tank top to my back. The fat flakes of ash stuck to my face where sweat streamed down the sides. I pulled Winter's shirt as far as I could over my mouth to keep from inhaling any of the falling debris, but the shirt's narrow neck didn't offer much for protection.

The future boy, Tag, didn't fare much better. He looked gruesome with the grey flakes hanging on his face like mottled skin. I advanced at the same time the earth shuddered under our feet.

The pitching ground knocked both of us to our knees—well, Tag to his knees, me to my backside. Boulders and rocks cascaded down the sides of the mountains, thundering as they smashed into each other and broke apart into smaller pieces. It came to the point that I didn't know which was more horrifying, the shaking that felt like I was sitting on a trampoline while dozens of other people jumped around me, or the noise of the mountain breaking apart and crashing all around me. When it stopped, I breathed into the sleeve of Winter's shirt and tried not to cry.

"Summer?" Tag's frown creased the ash on his face into wrinkles. He looked from the Orbital to the ground under us, and then up to the top of Mount Rainier, though its top was obscured by the falling ash and smoke.

Would forest firefighters be nearby? Could I try to run away again and hope that someone close battled the cause of all this smoke? I didn't have the energy to run. Maybe I'd be better off burning up in a blaze of flame. The chances of getting the Orbital back again seemed too dismal to try to calculate.

"Summer!"

"What?" I mumbled through my shirtsleeve.

"We landed in July, 2102!" He looked back towards Mount Rainier's peak.

"So what," I mumbled and shifted my body so I didn't have to see him.

He jumped to his feet, his steps soft thuds in the ashes as he positioned himself directly in front of me. "Mount Rainier blows its top off this month! I was only seven when it happened, but I wouldn't ever forget the date. All civilization was nearly lost after that. That was the year without summer!"

"Yeah. A year without me really is a tragedy."

His eyes narrowed, the fat flakes in his eyelashes making him look as though he'd closed them altogether. He ignored my joke. "It's a volcanic winter. When a volcano erupts, it changes the atmosphere. The global cooling that followed caused famine throughout half the world. The food shortage crisis killed a third of the population. A *third!* People died, so have some respect. My sister got so hungry, she—" He cut off, gaping at me in horror. "You landed us in the middle of a volcanic eruption! The greatest disaster known in my time!"

I shrugged. "I care? You don't like it? Then blink us outta here, future boy. I'm done trying to be nice to you."

"Right. Because you've been so charming up to now." He tapped on the screen of his little time warp machine "I *would* jump us out, but you broke it!"

My head snapped up. "What?"

"You broke it! And we have no idea what stage the eruption is in. How many earthquakes are left? Has the landslide already occurred? How will we get water and oxygen?" He ticked off these points on his fingers and waved them in my face.

I swiped his hand away. "Well, fix it!"

"Do I look like I have a lab with tools on me?" He threw his arms in the air, coughing with his words.

"You look like an idiot!" I stood up, my legs shaky from lack of nutrition and decent oxygen. "Give me that stupid time warp thing!" I snatched it from his grasp.

It must've really been broken or there was no way he'd have let me take it.

"It's an Orbital."

His correction of what to call the thing fueled my fury. "If you would have just taken me home, none of this would have happened," I muttered, trying to breathe through my sleeve and look at the time warp thing at the same time. It didn't look broken. It looked exactly like it did before—with the exception that instead of flashing numbers and words on the screen, the screen remained blank.

"Did you turn it on?" I asked him.

He took his turn to glare at me. "Of course I turned it on. You're as helpful as texup." He snatched the time warp thing back and fiddled with it for several moments while I turned to take in the world around me. My mountain . . . erupting? How unlikely it seemed that Mount Rainier would explode. We'd had drills at school, so that we'd all run to higher ground due to the river of mud, melted snow, and lava that would bury the town of Orting. Aunt Theresa lived on a high hill overlooking the town which gave me some comfort when I worried about eruptions after the drills. As we grew older, it became apparent to all of us that running might not do any of us any good if the eruption and subsequent mudslide took us by surprise. But the drills made the administration feel like they were taking an active part in our protection. What good would Nathan's wild reclamation project mean if it were just going to be buried over with volcanic debris?

"I hope Nathan's work in the cave survives this." I uttered my thoughts out loud and instantly wanted to call them back.

Tag looked up from his precious Orbital long enough to do a raspberry with his lips, his mouth looking funny and odd, exactly like a red raspberry against the ash grey face. "I do not understand that at all."

"Understand what?"

"You go to paint rock walls in a cave to prove that painting rock walls in a cave is wrong? What's the difference between your graffiti and the graffiti of the generations who came before you? Nothing. That's what." He coughed rather violently before yanking off his backpack and finding the thin blanket I'd used before. He wrapped the blanket around his head like a turban, then used the tail end to cover his mouth. "This is big enough for us to share if you would like." I considered his offering before shaking my head and continuing the use of my shirtsleeve. He slipped his pack on his shoulders.

"Nathan wanted to improve the world around him. His "graffiti" returned the cave to its natural state so when people came down, they could see the stone in their original, natural colors."

"And how does he know what they were originally? Did he have photos with him so he could replicate it?" He glanced up, the challenge evident in his eyes.

"You shouldn't speak ill of the dead, you know." My throat caught at the word dead. *Nathan dead?* My stomach roiled with nausea again. "Especially when you could have done something to save him. By not saving him, that almost makes you a murderer."

"Murderer? By not pulling him from that wreck, I was being merciful. He was already tainted. He had a level one infection. By allowing history to play its part, I saved you both from a hellish future of disease."

"Oh yeah, because *this* future is so neat!" I turned in a circle motioning to the ash falling like a quiet snowfall around us.

"This future is *your* fault, not mine." He shrugged and went back to his Orbital. I stomped a few feet away, not going too far for fear he might zap away with his time warp thing and I'd be left here in the eerie silence of falling ash.

"I can force it to work for a few seconds at a time. I think the volcanic eruption is somehow interfering with the electrics. But I don't know what would happen if we tried to jump and it shut off in the middle of a jump."

"What do you think would happen?"

His eyes blinked away the ash building up on his lashes. "Bad things."

I didn't press him to give better detail on what bad things might be.

He muttered through his makeshift scarf, and paced around a little while staring at the Orbital thing.

The silence shattered with the ground rumbling under my feet. It felt nothing like the earthquake we'd experienced before. It was more like the grumbling from heavy machinery driving down the road. It grew and with horror, I whirled around. "Tag—Oh no!" Behind us, farther up on the slopes, it sounded as though a monster had taken a fall and was now careening down the mountainside, collecting debris, trees, and boulders as it flew past. I'd been to enough drills on what to do should Mount Rainier ever pop. I knew what that sound meant even without the air-siren and the teachers leading us out of the school.

That sound meant run.

I tapped his arm as I flew past him. "Mudslide!" The rumbling had grown loud enough to drown out my yell. Tag seemed to be figuring it out without my instruction as he'd started running too. We ran for all our lives were worth.

SIX

Tag twisted his head to look back. I didn't look back. Those drills had taught me to head for higher ground, and we were running down. Going against all instinct, and wondering how I moved at all in my weakened condition, I changed direction and ran to the side—up the steep embankment—up to where I might find myself out of the reach of the wave of mud and debris.

Once up a good distance, I chanced looking towards where the mudslide swallowed every other noise in the canyon. My breathing through the sleeve of my shirt made it impossible to fill my lungs properly. My lungs felt like they were on fire. Things moved along with us through the haze of the smoke and ash—animals, most likely. Tag grabbed me around the waist and tucked his head into my shoulder.

"What are you doing?" I asked. He'd said the thing was broken and that if we jumped while it had a short in it, bad things could happen.

Tag didn't answer me.

The wall of mud shoved its way to the Puget Sound. We hadn't climbed nearly high enough. The time to run had been spent. "We're going to die!"

As I braced myself for impact, the tug pulled at my middle and the wall of mud swirled away around me only an instant before it should have slammed into me.

When the world stopped spinning, I refused to open my eyes to look, but I could taste the sweet oxygen as it ran pure and clean into my lungs. Tag hugged me tight, laughed, and kept shouting the words,

"We're alive!" When he released me, I couldn't move. My body ached, my lungs ached, my eyes burned.

"Water." I croaked, sounding strangely like the skinny guy crawling around the desert in cartoons. I heard noise and then felt the cool relief of water against my lips. I took in a mouthful and swished it around before spitting it out. I grabbed the bottle from his hand and dropped a little bit of water into each eye and then took several swallows clutching the bottle as though it were a lifeline.

Tag followed my ritual with a bottle of his own, and only then did I think about the fact that he'd taken care of me before caring for himself. I pushed that small act of kindness out of my mind so that it wouldn't get in the way of me hating him. *I won't go Stockholm on you, Wineve.*

I took several deep breaths and looked around. We were still on the mountainside of Mount Rainier. The sun shone down on newly blossoming flowers as though there had never been a mudslide through this canyon—as though there never would be.

"When are we?" I asked after several moments of drinking in sweet oxygen. I wondered at the words falling so readily from my mouth. *When* are we? How quickly I had acclimated to the fact of time travel when only yesterday, *was it yesterday,* I'd never believed such a thing could be possible.

The grin still smeared across his ash covered face, Tag glanced at his Orbital. "2097. We'll have to stay here awhile though. We need food and some rest from that last little adventure." He turned and gave me a long look as though to make certain I knew who was to blame for that "last little adventure."

I had a hard time feeling even a little bad. "I thought you were in a hurry to get back and feed me to your queen."

He shook his head and shrugged his pack off his shoulders. "I'm not feeding you to my queen; I'm making you a queen."

"Whatever."

He settled down on the ground, using a big rock as a makeshift table. He pulled out his humidifier thing and a couple of packets.

The thought of food made me lower to the ground beside him. My legs shook with exhaustion. No matter what Persephone might have thought of me, I needed to eat.

"It'll be warmed this time since we have solar power." He glanced to the sky and smiled at it with a nod to the sun as though it had done him a personal favor by being out.

Within only a few minutes of dropping the packets into the machine, he pulled them back out, each one filled with a steamy mixture of vegetables.

I snatched mine from his hands, cringing at my desperation for nourishment. He ate as greedily as I did, slurping down the broccoli and carrots that only tasted slightly off. We made short work of the vegetables, the small meal only adding to my hunger rather than diminishing it. Tag sifted through his bag and produced a few other packets.

Ultimately, he cooked up everything he had. And not a drop or crumb remained when we were through. My stomach still growled.

We drank through his scant supply of water as well. Too tired to care about still being thirsty, I fell back on the ground and closed my eyes. Tag's voice came through the fog of sleep curling around my head. "Summer? Summer?"

I muttered something unintelligible to indicate he was bugging me, and I wanted him to go away.

"Summer, I need to find us water and food. I'll try to be back before you wake up, but if you wake before I return, then STAY! Wait. If you wander off, you could get hurt."

I grunted and swatted my hand in front of me to shoo him off. He must've left, or at least stopped talking, because the fuzz of sleep came uninterrupted after that.

When my eyes fluttered open again, the sun hung low in the sky. I reached up to rub my eyes, which felt extraordinarily dry and scratchy, and winced as I ground dirt and ash into them. My hands were nearly black, and my clothes hadn't fared any better. Without a mirror to check out what the rest of me looked like, I could only guess that my tangled, matted mess of hair had an equal amount of filth.

I couldn't see Tag anywhere, but that didn't mean he wasn't around. "Tag?"

No answer.

"Stupid, good-for-nothing kidnapper." I staggered to my feet, feeling wobbly, and unbalanced. My head pulsed as though a small tribe were beating drums and dancing around in my grey matter. I nearly sank back to the ground for more sleep, but managed to keep my feet underneath me.

"Tag!" I yelled it this time, wincing with the headache.

Still no answer.

That decided it. I needed a bath, food, and water—though not necessarily in that order. If Tag had ditched me—oh, he better not have ditched me! What was I supposed to do with myself nearly a hundred years into the future with all my family and friends dead? The pain of that loss struck me like a slap to the face. "Winter, Winter, Winter . . ." her name crossed my lips again and again, like a prayer that would never be answered.

Sniffing, and wiping tears from my face which only smudged the dirt around worse, I started off down the mountainside alone. Tag had likely been eaten by bears or kicked in the head by a moose. He got me into this mess and sitting around waiting for him to help was like asking the devil to give me a ride to the Pearly Gates.

The setting sun determined which direction to go. With luck I'd find one of the tributaries that emptied into the Puget Sound.

Or not.

After what felt like an hour, my wobbly legs gave out on me. My tongue felt fat in my cottony mouth. Every so often, a cough exploded from my chest, likely a result of breathing in all that ash and whatever noxious gases the earth belched out in the volcano eruption. I sat on the ground and tried not to cry, knowing how desperate my situation had become and how crying would only dehydrate me further.

I fell asleep again, drifting in and out as the discomfort of my body tried to pull me to action—to feed it and water it, but sleep won over those other needs. I dreamed of Winter. We held hands and walked on the beach. My hand slipped out of hers. She cried out my name over and over as something unseen yanked me away from her. "Summer!" she screamed.

"Summer, you have to wake up. Summer!" He jostled my shoulder. My eyes popped open. Tag's light shone on the ground next to us. He slid something cold and wet into my hand—my water bottle. He'd found water and refilled it.

"I told you to wait." He sounded tired. I didn't care. I popped the lid open on the bottle and drank in gulps.

"Slow down!" He pulled the bottle from my hand, or tried to. I had no intention of giving it back. "You'll make yourself sick again."

He was right. I tried to slow down.

He looked off towards the darkened trees. "Orting City isn't too far. We should be able to walk there and get some food. We need rest. The next jump window from this area isn't for another four days. It's best to wait it out than keep jumping ourselves into trouble."

"Orting is not walking distance. I live there, remember? I drove up here all the time. It'll take us four days to walk."

His eyes reflected the light from his flashlight still on the ground near us. His face looked cleaner; so did his hair. He must've found a stream or a river. "Things have changed in the last eighty years. Orting's a big city. But even if they hadn't changed, it would *not* take four days to walk. When you feel up to it, we'll go."

It crossed my mind to be stubborn and never be ready to go, but the need for food overwhelmed my desire to irritate my kidnapper. I tried hard not to think about the fact that I'd only had food and water because he'd given it to me. I was only still alive because he got us out of the mudslide before it swallowed us whole. And though I hated to consider it, I was still alive because he pulled me out of a fatal car accident.

I got up and let him lead. He didn't bother to try to hold me captive; he must've sensed my waning ability to run away. Honestly, where would I go? Who would I run to for help in the year 2097? Winter would be dead by now, my whole world was lost to me, and there wasn't anything I could do about it.

"The next jump window isn't for several days," he repeated. "The Orbital looks like it might be working right now, but I can't tell. I think it needs a break, or who knows when we'll end up? The last thing either of us wants is to be dinner to a T-Rex in the Jurassic period. When we're settled, I'll see what can be done for it." He took my hand when I stumbled over a dried up tree branch sticking out of the ground.

"How are you going to fix it? Didn't you say you were a soldier? What would a soldier know about a computer watch time travel thing?"

"I helped invent it."

"Oh." Smart soldier kidnappers. Just my luck. "I thought you said you couldn't fix it earlier."

"I'll need to makeshift some tools."

"Wineve is dead now." I spoke my thoughts aloud, as I tromped along behind him, yanking my hand out of his.

He didn't respond.

"She's dead, and I don't even know where she's buried to put flowers on her grave. Do you have any idea how much that hurts me?"

He whirled around. "Yes." The one word uttered through gritted teeth stopped me in my tracks. "I do know exactly how that feels. I've lost people I've loved, too. People I can't mourn. So yes, I understand. But you remember that, even without me, she would have lost you. You died in that car wreck. Don't forget that."

You're dead, Summer Dawn Rae. Those had been his first words to me. I felt dead, and yet kept up with him in some self-serving need to not be dead. In spite of everything, I wanted to survive this situation. I didn't want to be dead.

Tag turned out to be right about how far we had to go. Not long into our trek down the mountain, lights appeared through the trees of houses. "This was National Forest land," I said, marveling at the fact that houses existed in the middle of the woods where they couldn't possibly be.

"It still is. These are renters. The government needed money to subsidize several social programs that were failing. They improved much of their more desirable properties and rented them out to people who had the means to pay the overpriced rent. The rental bailout saved a lot of people from losing medical care."

"Says who?" The need to argue blanket statements of government loyalty came from years of living under the government's foster program.

"Says the history plugs."

I didn't ask what a history plug might be. "Yeah, well, fat lot of good it'll do them. When Mount Rainier blows, all of this will be mowed over by lava and mudslides."

Tag didn't argue, which validated my point. We skirted around the first several houses until we came to the main road.

Instead of taking the road, which would have been easier to walk on given my tired, weakened state, Tag insisted on weaving in and out through the trees while keeping the road within our sight.

"Why are we acting like spies?" I asked after several minutes of tripping over rocks and getting dried leaves in my tennis shoes.

"Curfew. I can't remember the year they implemented curfew, but we don't want to get caught out if it happened to be in force this year."

"Aren't we old enough to be out after dark?"

He held a tree branch for me so it didn't swat me in the face. "Age isn't a factor. Curfew is for everyone. They thought it would keep the crazies in line."

"That's not exactly nice to call people crazies, is it?"

He turned to give me a quizzical look, shrugged, and picked his way through an overgrowth of scrub oak. He seemed intent on not talking, which added to my own personal paranoia. "So what happens if we get caught out after curfew?" I whispered, since we'd edged closer to several more large houses in the middle of the forest. Tag kept waving

51

his hand in front of the windows as we passed them. Then he'd frown and we'd move on.

He didn't bother to turn around when he uttered the two words I was getting tired of hearing him say. "Bad things."

We kept on in silence for a long time until Tag found whatever it was he'd been looking for. He led me to a house just off the road. He checked a window, shining his own light in through the darkened pane to make sure it was empty and started jimmying the window open with a wicked looking knife he'd pulled from his backpack.

"Are you breaking in? We can't break in!" I darted furtive glances to the road, certain the police would be showing up any minute. The foster care system might have improved over the decades, but I wasn't in the mood to try it out. Trying out the local prison seemed an even worse idea.

"No one's here. And this house isn't equipped with entry sensors."

"How would you know that? You can't know that!" *Entry sensors?* I tugged at his jacket, but he ignored me.

"This is a bad idea. I don't want to go to jail." I may as well have been talking to a rock for all the good it did me to reason with him. "You're doing that wrong." I yanked the knife out of his hand. "Haven't you ever broken into anything before?" I slid the knife so the tip of the blade pressed against the latch and twisted. The window opened with a pop. I handed it back to him before it occurred to me that I'd had a weapon and then given it back. I was such an amateur. His legs were already dangling out the window as he scrambled to climb inside.

Against all my better judgment, I followed his really bad example and entered the house.

SEVEN

"I t's dark." I stated the obvious as my hand went to the wall to feel for a light.

"It's better that way." He took my hand. "Leave the light off. No one's here right now, but there are still neighbors, and we aren't that far off the road. If anyone's watching, they'll notice the light."

"What are entry sensors? How do you know we didn't trip an alarm and that cops aren't on their way here right now?" He didn't answer but led me farther into the dark. I didn't pull away, needing the security of another human being. The house furnishings weren't weird like I expected them to be. I'd expected chairs made of bubbles and steel cabinets—something future looking, but I ran my hand over the couch and felt the plush fibers of the cushions. I could make out the faint outline of real books in the bookshelves. I didn't think books would have a place in the future. I thought everyone would read books on their cell phones.

Tag took us to the kitchen and closed the big slatted shutters over the windows before pulling out his flashlight and turning it on. He was careful with his light, careful to keep the sweeping beam away from the windows, careful to shine it towards the ground where it would be less likely to leak out through those big slats and offer evidence that the house had some uninvited visitors.

"What if the police are on their way?" I asked again, feeling certain cops were surrounding the house as we stood unaware inside.

He let my hand go and shoved his hand into the beam of his light. "See this ring?"

A thick silver band sat on his left hand, on the finger where a wedding band would traditionally go. The ring's surface was ornately worked with grooves and scrolls in intricate patterns.

"It's a nice ring," I offered lamely, wondering if he was trying to propose. With all that talk about being able to have babies, it was the only thing that seemed logical to me. My mind had been fried beyond the ability to string together any rational thought.

"It's an IDR. Everyone has one. Even people who can't afford one. The government offers basic models to the pov's."

"Pov's?"

"Poor people. You know—poverty. Rich people can afford the nicer models, ones with comms and drives. Mine's a 420b." He puffed out his chest as though this meant something important. I stared at him blankly, wondering when he'd switched from English to this alien language.

He shook his head, recognizing how I'd become more baffled than impressed. "What it means is that each ring is a like a fingerprint to the person wearing it. No one uses keys like they do in your time." His face twisted up as if keys were one of the dumbest ideas in the world. "The IDR scans the entrance to the house and unlocks for the people keyed in as approved for entry. If a non-approved tried to break in, the entry sensors would spark and notify the authorities."

His explanation only made me more nervous. There was no way his ring would be programmed as approved for this house. "That doesn't answer my question. How do you know the cops aren't about to throw in gas bombs through the windows?" Every sci-fi movie I'd ever watched flashed through my mind. Paul had liked old science fiction movies. We watched them together. I could only think of Terminator and how the future was this horrible place where people lived in the smoking ruins of a technological wasteland while robots hunted them down. I suddenly felt that Hollywood had done me a huge disservice not to give me better information on how to protect myself in such a future.

"Look." He moved towards the window and waved his hand in front. Nothing happened. "Did you see?" he asked.

I shook my head.

"The ring would glow red if the sensors felt I was not approved. It would glow green if the sensors had approved me." He waved his hand over the window once more. "But see how it doesn't glow at all? No entry sensors yet. We're fine."

"That doesn't mean they don't have an alarm system that tripped when you opened the window." I peeked out to check for cops. The trees swayed softly in the breeze, but nothing else moved in the shadows.

He shook his head again. "Technically, you opened the window. But alarm systems aren't what they were. Ring law was instated in 2090. Everyone has to have an IDR. By 2095, every other form of contact for emergency service was discontinued. If you didn't install entry sensors on your home or business, then it's your problem."

I looked out. Nothing. I relaxed. The police weren't coming. Once Tag felt I was under control, he nodded and led us back to the kitchen. He inspected the pantry, pulling out cans of things that might be edible. There were bulk sized cans filled with beans, rice, and flour. I watched as Tag mixed some of the beans up with the rice and put them in his humidifier. "Sorry it's taking so long. The dehydrated foods work better because they were designed for the humidifier. Real foods work differently."

"Isn't there running water here? Why are you using that when there's a stove right there?" I pointed at the stove.

He grunted and looked abashed. "Habit, I guess." He maneuvered over to the stove, trying to get the pilot light to catch. When it wouldn't, he pulled a plastic bottle from his jacket and tapped out a match. Blue flame sparked to life around the burner when he touched the match to it.

I turned my hands over and really looked at them for the first time in hours. I was filthy. I got up and moved to the kitchen sink. But simple hand washing wasn't enough for me. I wanted a bath. The idea of walking through the dark house alone to find a bathroom made my heart quicken with fear. "Tag?"

He looked up from the stove.

"Will you help me find a bathroom?" I guess I should have felt guilty for making him be responsible for the food. I should have felt some need to pitch in and do my part. But he was the kidnapper. This was his party and his responsibility. If he didn't like it, he could take me home and be rid of me. Even as I thought these things, I had to force down the twinges of guilt that *did* bubble up. It wasn't in my upbringing to be served.

He guided me through the house until we found a bathroom bigger than the master bedroom in Aunt Theresa's house.

A huge fluffy towel that could have been used as a blanket hung over the side of the tub. It was too dark to make out any colors, but the bathroom had the feeling of being elaborate and posh. Tag pulled a couple of sticks from his jacket and snapped them in half, giving them a brief shake and dropping them on the counter by the mirror.

"Glow sticks?" I let out a nervous laugh.

"What about them?"

"I'd expected something high tech like your ring."

"Some things don't change. If an idea was perfect to begin with, why alter it? If you keep them by the mirror, you'll get the light from the reflection too. It will make the room brighter." He gave a slight bow, like a butler being dismissed. "I'll leave you to clean up. Food will be ready when you come out."

He left the bathroom, very deliberately pulling the door closed tight so the latch caught with a click. I hurried to cross the room and lock the door, feeling grateful the door did have locks.

I wondered if Tag was outside—if he'd heard me lock the door. Would he be offended by my not trusting him? I snorted at my image in the mirror. Did I care if I offended him? I frowned. Unsure why some part of me *did* care.

Giving myself a good shake for the insanity of such thoughts, I yanked off my clothes and stepped into the tub. I turned the shower to hot and scooted back from the spray so the cold water in the lines could warm up. I waved my hand in the water, but the water remained icy cold. Muttering curses about water heaters, I stepped back out, wrapped the blanket sized towel around me, and poked my head out from the bathroom door.

The empty dark hallway reminded me of the horror films I'd seen, the one where the evil guy's blade glimmers at the end of the hallway as he walks toward the terrified teenager wrapped in a towel. "Tag?" My shaky voice made my face flush. What a baby I'd turned out to be.

He called out from the kitchen. "What?"

"There isn't hot water. Do I have to do something to make hot water come on?"

"The heating unit must be broken. I don't know anything about flash heaters. Sorry. My training was history, politics, and soldiering, with a slight emphasis in physics." His voice moved closer and his faint form moved at the end of the hallway. "I'll heat some on the stove." With that his shadow moved away again. I shut the door, trying to shake the respect I had for the space he seemed so willing to give me. A *slight* emphasis on physics? He helped invent a time-travel watch and considered his abilities to be slight?

After a fairly long wait, he tapped at the door. "I'll leave the pot here. You can get it when you feel comfortable. I've already started several smaller pots so you'll have enough."

I held my breath and listened as his footsteps whispered away on the hall carpet. I edged the door open and found a large pan of water. I felt vulnerable standing there in a towel, but Tag had thus far been a perfect gentleman.

I hefted the pan into the bathroom and up onto the counter, hoping it didn't burn the countertop for the owner. "A perfect gentleman?" I looked in the mirror. "Perfect gentlemen don't steal girls from their time zones."

"But you'd be dead if he hadn't," I argued with my image, green in the glow-stick-light.

It comforted me to argue with my mirror image, almost like arguing with Winter. Except Winter had never been so dirty and travel-worn.

If I tried getting into the tub while covered in volcano droppings, I'd be bathing in a swamp of black, sooty water. I sighed and glared at the bathtub. The warmth could be enjoyed after a quick rinse cycle.

I jumped into the shower and clenched my teeth against the shock of cold against my skin. The soap and shampoo came from two smaller curvy looking faucets that released a small squirt in my hand once placed under the nozzles. I soaped up outside of the spray then stepped back in for the final rinse. A small cry against the cold erupted.

Tag knocked on the door again. "Is something wrong?"

"Just c-cold." I stuttered.

"There are three more pans of water ready for you. I can bring them in . . . if you trust me. Just close the curtain. I can pour the water through the curtain. I won't look."

I hesitated. Even the most altruistic boy would have trouble keeping that promise. A kidnapper? But I hadn't relocked the door, and he hadn't tried to enter. "Leave them by the door."

"How about I leave them on the counter. Then you won't have to leave the bathroom at all."

When I didn't argue the idea, he said, "Okay. I'm coming in."

Standing outside the cold shower spray, almost without feeling the backsplash of the cold droplets, I waited.

The door clicked open. I held my breath and listened to him heft pans in and place them on the counter, one by one. The oddity and danger of the situation did not escape me. Only a thin sheet of cloth stood between me and the person who'd ripped me from my life. If he wasn't to be trusted, now would surely be the time he would attack. His shadow moved against the shower curtain, causing me to cast a quick glance around for a weapon I could defend myself with. Nothing looked very weapon-like in the tub. Thinking of the dirt I'd thrown in his eyes, I put my hands under the shampoo dispenser and filled them with shampoo—the most pathetic weapon ever.

His shadow stopped moving. He faced me—I could tell by his silhouette on the curtain. We stood there, facing each other in silence on opposite sides of the curtain for several long moments. "I'm leaving," he said finally. The door clicked shut again.

I inhaled sharply, relief flooding over me that there had been no need for me to defend myself. I rinsed my hands off, pulled the towel from the top of the rod and peeked around the curtain. True to his word, he'd gone. I tied the towel off around my chest and used the pans to fill the tub until the steam rose up in little curls of comfort. I added cold water so as not to scald myself and got in.

Everything seemed like they did in my time. The way the tub worked, the mirror in the bathroom, the towels. I wasn't sure what I expected to be different, but nothing really was. Tag's words came back to me, "If an idea is perfect to begin with, why alter it?" Bathrooms must have been close to perfect before. The only real differences existed in the curves of the ornate handles on the faucets and the palatial size of the room.

Once settled into the water, my mind calmed enough to consider the implications of my situation. Tag hadn't looked—hadn't even tried. Nathan might have tried. *Nathan's dead.* What had our funerals been like? Did the whole school attend the teenage tragedy? Had Winter worn black? Did she put white roses on my casket? I loved white roses.

Winter, Aunt Theresa, Nathan. *Winter.*

How would I survive without Winter? How would I make it in a world where she wasn't there to read my feelings and thoughts? Where she wasn't there to understand when no one else could or wanted to? Where no one else knew I liked white roses? How would I live in a world where she *wasn't?*

And how would she survive? Who would get her through college? Who would make her dinner while she studied so she didn't starve? Who would be there for her?

I gave in to another bout of misery and sank down in the water. I cried a long time.

"Summer?" His voice through the door startled me.

I sat up, the water movement echoing off the cavernous bathroom walls. "What?"

"Does your head hurt?"

What a weird question. My head ached. My brain felt like it had been split into a zillion pieces and now those pieces were colliding into one another. "A little." Even that small confession of weakness bugged me, but my head did hurt. Maybe the headache was a side effect of time travel. Maybe every time we jumped, it scattered our brain cells.

"Crying usually gives people headaches."

So he'd heard me. How long had he been there listening?

"I have something that will take the headache away."

"I don't do drugs!" The words came harsh and fast—an automatic response to Theresa's preaching about my mother's addictions.

"No, I don't mean . . . I wouldn't be allowed to administer them if I had them. Soldiers are never given access to those things. We're required to build our own defenses against discomfort. When you come out, I'll show you."

Curiosity and the cooling temperature pulled me from the water. I dried off and grimaced at the clothes—dirty, wrinkled, ripped, ruined. I dunked Winter's shirt in the bath water and rubbed shampoo on it. Carefully, I washed the shirt, working hard to keep it from tearing or fraying further. Much less care was used on the jeans. I hung them both over the shower curtain rod so they could dry, looked at my underwear, and harrumphed. They weren't as dirty as the jeans, but they'd been through a lot. "Yuck." I grumbled, then laughed. I'd likely set a world record. I'd worn the same underwear for over eighty years. I washed those too, unable to bear the idea of putting on dirty unmentionables.

Going out in only a towel seemed like a bad idea, even if he hadn't looked or taken advantage of the bathroom situation, but the priority of clean, dry clothes drove away fear. And a feeling of trust niggled at the back of my mind. Tag hadn't behaved like a monster in any way. I clutched my towel and little glow sticks to me as I opened the door.

The hallway remained empty—Tag likely off in the kitchen. I exited to one of the side rooms hoping to find something to wear for the night while my shirt and jeans dried.

The closet dwarfed the bathroom, to the point of obscenity. As if flaunting the wasted space, not much hung on the rods in the closet—a few odds and ends of shirts and dresses. There were several sets of drawers built into the walls.

One drawer contained silky things that had the look of intimacy. I closed that one immediately. The next one down had regular old underwear. I held a pair up. They were huge and the idea of wearing someone else's unmentionables made me feel queasy, but today was not a day to be picky. I put them on and tied the sides into knots to keep them from falling off. In another drawer, I found a long blue skirt with beaded fringe at the bottom. The beads clicked against each other as I lifted the skirt up and put it against me to see about size—ankle-length and much too wide, but the drawstring would make it fit.

I shuffled through more drawers and found a bra. The thing could have been used to hold bowling balls. *What poor woman had to bear that burden?* I wondered. No knot would make that bra fit me, so I decided to have a feminist moment and go natural. In yet another drawer, I found a grey pullover with nothing weird on it. I tugged it over my head and went back to the bathroom to hang the towel to dry.

I ran into Tag in the hallway coming out of the bathroom as I was going in. He exhaled sharply. "There you are!" He looked about ready to hug me, like a mother would her lost toddler. "I was worried."

"I wasn't trying to scare you. Just needed clothes." Why the need to explain? I didn't owe him anything. If I had run off, he'd deserve it. Of course, running off in an incomprehensible future where I didn't have the legally-required ring probably qualified as a bad plan.

"Food's ready." He nodded towards the kitchen, his eyes never leaving my face.

"Thanks." I shifted uncomfortably. "What?" I finally asked under his scrutiny.

"Nothing." He averted his gaze and went to the kitchen, expecting me to follow.

I did.

EIGHT

The dinner of beans and rice, over-seasoned with salt and dehydrated onions came as a welcome part of the night. Hunger had set in with vengeance. Even though he'd cooked a lot, we managed to consume every rice grain. I stood and started washing dishes. He pulled the pan from my hands. "No. This is my job."

I grabbed the pan back. "Your job? You made dinner. That means you get the rest of the night off. It works that way in most everybody's family. I've been through enough families to make me an expert."

"I'm a soldier. You're my charge. I have a responsibility to take care of you." He tried taking it away again, but I pulled my arm beyond his reach.

"The only person responsible for taking care of me is *me*. And who's dictating that you have to take care of me anyway?" I pointed the pan at him. "Who sent you off to thieve me from my death?"

"I didn't thieve you. You died in that car wreck. I saved you."

I waved my hand in front of my face. "Yeah, yeah. I'm saved. Wahoo and hallelujah." Pain shot through my head as the headache pounded harder. I reached my hand up to my temples and cringed.

"Your head still hurts. I'm sorry. I forgot. Here." He pulled out a chair and tapped the back, indicating I should sit. Feeling wary, I sat.

His hands went to my temples, gently massaging into my skin. I tried to feel apprehension; this was my kidnapper, after all, but my headache almost immediately dissipated at his touch. All the anxiety, fear, and frustration melted out through my toes as his fingers worked over my head. His fingers kneaded their way to the back of my scalp and down onto my neck behind my ears, working to the nape of my neck. By the time he'd finished, I'd nearly forgotten the definition of a headache.

"Better?" he asked. He didn't take his hands away right away, but let his fingers trace lightly back down my neck. After a second or two, he abruptly removed them and stepped away from me.

"Hmm, much better." I felt so relaxed, I could have slept right then and there. "Where did you learn that? Do all *soldiers* have part time jobs as physical therapists?"

"My mother had problems with crying headaches a lot. She—well, with that, I learned how to make them go away."

He stood there for several awkward moments and then patted my shoulder. "Well, I should clean up too." He left me at the table while he fetched the pans from the bathroom and refilled them with water. He placed them on the stove burners and left them to start boiling.

He'd forgotten the dishes, so I went back to washing them. He looked about to intervene again but resigned himself to the idea that I wasn't moving away from the sink.

Tag checked his pans every so often.

"Don't these people have a dishwasher?" I asked.

"The dishwasher would work off the flash heater, which you've already discovered doesn't work. I don't think the electrics have been enabled here either. We can't test the lights, but my flashlight isn't pulling a charge from anywhere. If the electrics worked, the flashlight would be charged by now."

"But they don't even have a dishwasher." I persisted. "You said the rent here was overpriced so that means they're rich people. Why wouldn't they have a dishwasher?"

Tag stood up, his walk to the cupboards more like a tired shuffle. He opened a cupboard full of plates set out on pretty display racks and closed it again, shining his light in it so I could fully see. "When you're done using a dish, you put it away in its racks and close the door.

Intense heat cleans the dishes and then suction pulls the ashes of any debris into the house's compost. It wastes much less water and takes much less work than your clunky machines." He shuffled back to the stove and checked his water.

The cupboards do dishes? Whatever. He may as well have told me that little men jumped out of the woodwork with dish rags and soap. "So back to the other conversation. You've taken me because someone told you to. I want to know why."

"Can't we talk about this in the morning?"

His tired voice should have made me feel bad for pressuring him, but I had to know. Besides, he should've thought about having to deal with me before he kidnapped me. "You have a few minutes while your watched pot doesn't boil." I ignored the funny look he gave me. I swear the guy had no concept of humor. "Seriously, I want to know why *exactly* I was summoned to your precious future. I want to know who's the brilliant mastermind of this fine disaster we're stuck in. I'll finish washing while you explain." I turned my back on him and scrubbed the starchy residue from the rice pan, ignoring that the water felt like it had been surrounding an ice berg before entering the house.

"People can't have babies in the future—"

"I already know that. Let's skip to the part I don't know."

"Things got worse after the Crazy War. Healthy, normal babies were a premium. Once the Crazy Law went into effect, people sort of lost hope."

My hands stopped scrubbing. "What? I don't understand a thing you just said. Crazy war? Crazy law? It sounds like Dr. Seuss."

"Women are sterile in the future. Men too. Childbirth isn't simple like it had been in your time. Entire civilized economies slowed and eventually failed due to the below-replacement birthrate. There was no way to stop the depopulation."

"But you said the world wasn't ending." I waved a soapy hand at him. He'd sat down at the table—likely as tired as I felt. The polite thing would be to let him go to bed, but he'd pulled me into this mess for a reason, and I wanted to understand that reason.

Tag didn't take me with the intent to hurt me. If he had, he'd already passed over a million chances to do so. His making sure I had hot water, that I was fed, that I was safe—all this added up to him being honest when he said he took me away for some other purpose. It felt better knowing I could go to sleep without having to watch my back, but also eerie to know that someone else had pulled the strings to change my future.

"The world isn't coming to an end, not in the way of population. Scientists discovered ways babies could be created and incubated in public nurseries. The parents donate the necessary tissues samples and the public nursery grows them a baby. The brilliant cutting edge technology saved mankind."

"Didn't you say *I* was going to save mankind?"

Tag smiled, his eyelids drooping with the need for sleep. "You will be the crown jewel in the effort to save mankind. The public nurseries aren't stable. And for reasons no one can determine, the brain doesn't develop properly in many cases. But it's worse if the women carry the babies in their own wombs. The public nurseries at least have some success. The couple picks their baby up when its lungs are strong enough to live outside the birthing fluids and they go home. But many of the public nursery babies were mentally unstable, not as many as in natural childbirth, but still too many." Tag's voice cracked, and he wiped at his eyes, dragging his whole hand down his face. No matter how tired my body felt—or his, I needed to hear it all.

"Go on."

"They were allowed to grow up—almost an entire generation of crazies. The world fell into chaos. The government rounded a bunch of crazies up and shipped them off. No one ever saw them again. We assume they were euthanized. The rest of the crazies revolted. There were a lot of them at that time. We went to war with the crazies, and we won. We were completely outnumbered, but their instability made them beatable in spite of their overwhelming numbers."

Tag shifted on his seat, looking generally uncomfortable. "Can we finish this in the morning? It's late. You need to get sleep. I need a shower." He never mentioned that he needed sleep too. "We can finish this in the morning. Maybe we'll figure out the electrics and let the flash heater wash dishes."

"But—" I was almost done with dishes.

He shook his head. "Tomorrow." He led me away from the kitchen down the hall to the room with the big closet. The bed sat like a gaudy centerpiece in the middle of the room. It would take half the night just to remove all those opulent fluffy pillows placed like the tower of Babel at the head of the bed. "You can sleep in here." He pressed the glow sticks in my hands. "In case you need light."

"Where will you sleep?"

"There's a room across the hall." He moved to leave. I snatched at his jacket.

"But what if the people who live here come back?" The question sounded ludicrous even as I asked it. The house carried every appearance of being a vacation home only—a place people paid too much money to spend not enough time. My mind couldn't wrap around that kind of money, not that I didn't dream it one day could, but that I'd never seen that kind of money in my life.

"Did you look in the fridge?" He didn't wait for a response. "No perishables. People who plan to return soon would plan for meals. They only come here on holiday."

I held his jacket tighter so he couldn't leave. "What if tomorrow is a holiday?"

He smiled and gently pried my fingers loose from his sleeve. "It isn't. Go to sleep. We have several days to talk before we have to make the jump to your future." I noticed he didn't say *our* future, or even *my* future in a way that indicated it felt like home to him. He'd simply said *your* future.

He put a hand on my shoulder to give me a little shove towards the bed. The pressure of his hand soaked the cold water still dripping from the ends of my hair through my shirt and against my skin, causing me to shiver involuntarily. He hurried to remove his hand, his smile completely erased from his face.

He cleared his throat. "Sleep will do us both a lot of good."

Before he could get out the door, I called out to him one last time. "Tag?"

He didn't turn. "Yes, Summer?" His voice carried a hint of frustration that I wouldn't let him leave.

"I'm sorry about the volcano."

"You will never have need to apologize for anything to me." His quick strides from the room indicated he would not allow me to detain him any further.

I edged toward the bed, feeling the cavernous room's darkness close in around me. The glow sticks seemed awfully poor substitutes for light switches. I shoved aside the pillow mountain with one great push, and forced myself to climb into the blankets, gripping them tight to my chin.

Sleep wouldn't come. My mind stayed active, alert, and afraid. I searched back through my memory and tried to think of one night I had slept in a room alone. Not one instance came to me. The few times when Winter had left for cheerleading camp, I'd spent the night at a friend's house. Other than that, Winter had never left me. My fingers twitched at the blankets at my chin feeling the foreign texture of cloth. Not once since I'd been taken into state custody and our case worker, Alice, handed us our quilts had I ever slept without mine. Even when I went to sleepovers, the sun quilt went with me.

I rolled over in the bed and tried to force my eyes to stay closed, tried to force my mind to focus on being tired rather than the fact that I was lost in the future, without my sister, and without my sun quilt.

Tag's noise from the bathroom stopped, meaning he'd finished cleaning up and had gone to bed himself. I rolled over again and tried to sleep.

With Tag finally in bed too, the house's quiet added to my distress. Every noise felt like impending doom. What if the house had been vacated because it was haunted? What if ghosts trailed down that long hallway? I snorted. Ghosts? I didn't believe in ghosts, even in the dark when my imagination felt overactive—even when I now believed in time travel. Besides the only time I'd ever seen anything that looked like a ghost, it ended up being Tag.

Several long minutes passed while I mused over ghosts, time travel, and the scary things I truly believed in. I believed in axe murderers and psychotics. My mother had dated enough psychotics for me to have no delusions there. What if the people who lived here came home? What if a spying neighbor turned us in and we got shot for trespassing?

With a grunt, I got up, dragging the blanket off the bed with me as I all but ran across the hall. "Tag?"

"Go to sleep, Summer." His tired, muffled voice came from the mound of covers.

"I can't sleep alone."

He sat straight up. "Well you can't sleep in here!" He all but yelled at me.

"Why not?"

"You hate me. Remember that!"

Surprised by his outburst and his demand that I keep hating him, I turned on a heel and stormed out of the room. "Fine!" Once back in the room and sitting on the big bed, the dumbness of the interchange made me roll my eyes. So what if I hated him? Hating him had nothing to do with needing another breathing person in the same room with me while I slept. Going back in there and trying to apologize and making him scoot over enough to give me room on the bed seemed like it would only end up with him getting pissy again. I waited ten minutes, counting to sixty ten times, like I did when I was little to make time pass quicker. Not that counting actually made time move with any more speed, but that it gave me something to do while waiting. It beat counting sheep.

I tiptoed back in to Tag's room, holding my breath, so he wouldn't hear me. I sat on the floor between the wall and his bed, and wrapped myself up burrito style in the blanket. I went to sleep to the sound of his deep breathing and pretended it was Winter, and pretended the blanket wrapped around me was my own sun quilt.

I awoke sometime in the early morning. The sun hadn't crawled up over the horizon yet, but its stretching rays lightened the sky. I sat up, realizing I felt comfortable. What was I doing in a bed? A quick visual search revealed that I still occupied Tag's room, only Tag was now on the floor. He looked uncomfortable.

Guilt.

I hated guilt.

How had he ended up on the floor? Did I get up and crawl into bed with him in the night—pushing him out? Or had he found me on the floor and put me in the bed, taking the floor for himself?

I tsked softly. *I'm a creep.* The only way to switch places would be to wake him up. Would it be worse to wake him up when he might not be able to get back to sleep, or to leave him on the hard floor? Lying back on my pillow, I closed my eyes. He might be one of those grouchy types if he wakes up too soon. And he really needed his sleep. Tag had stayed awake on the few occasions I'd slept throughout the last two days. The least I could do now was let him sleep as long as he needed.

I allowed myself to drift back into slumber as well, knowing that if the day ahead was anything like the day behind, I'd need every last second available.

The sun shone full on through the window when my eyes opened again. Tag's blanket sat in a neatly-folded pile on the floor. With a deep stretch, I eased myself up and out of bed and wandered out of the room.

"Tag?" I called out once I'd reached the kitchen and found it empty. Fear edged into my heart. Would he have left me here? "Tag?" I called again, louder this time.

I took a deep breath to scream his name when he showed up in the doorway and put his finger to his lips to hush me. I exhaled the breath and frowned, the fear flowing from a trickle to a river. His tensed body with his knees bent for action caused me to take the same posture. I slipped in next to him and whispered, "What is it?"

"Neighbors out taking a walk or something." His hand went to the small of my back as he directed me towards the hallway. "I double

70

checked the door locks and the window we opened to make certain there wasn't anything out of place." His whispers were so quiet I had to put my head right to his in order to hear him. "I was just coming to get you. If they are here to look after the place, we'll need to be ready to move."

I thought of Winter's shirt still in the bathroom drying, and of my jeans. They were all I had left of the world I'd known. Leaving them behind was not an option. "My clothes." I mouthed the words. When he gave me a quizzical look, I put my mouth to his ear and whispered them, my lips accidentally brushing his earlobe. He pulled away as though I'd shocked him with a lightning bolt.

He put his hand out as though it were a stop sign and whispered "Stay!" in a way that made me feel like a bad dog waiting for punishment while my master went and got the rolled up newspaper. He came back with my bundle of clothes. He stuffed them into his back pack and leaned against the wall.

When I stepped closer to him to whisper the question, "So what are we doing now?" He stiffened his whole body as though I had a disease he didn't want to catch.

"We're waiting for the noise of entry." He didn't elaborate and put his finger to his mouth again in a hushing motion.

We stood like statues for several minutes, my own body so tense, my muscles cramped. When the front door opened, I nearly bolted, but Tag put out his hand to stop me, his head giving one violent shake, *no*.

"I don't see why they need a housekeeper for a house no one is living in." A man's voice whined. "No one's here to make a mess."

A woman's voice answered. She sounded patient and used to her husband not wanting to do what she wanted. "They're coming home next week. They don't want to come back to a bunch of dusty shelves"

Cleaning? They were here to clean today of all days? My panicked thoughts raced to the towel and pots on the counter in the bathroom. To the two unmade beds I'd vacated. Even if we tried to hide and lay low until they left, they were bound to notice the disaster we'd left. The owners wouldn't be back for another week. We'd be long gone by then. If they didn't call the police over all the mess we'd left.

"Home?" The man scoffed. "A place you visit two weeks out of every year is hardly something you could call home."

I wholeheartedly agreed with him, though I was pretty sure both of us only felt that way because we were jealous.

The noise stayed in the front room by the door. "Let's start here. Should only take an hour if we hurry." The woman's tone indicated the man had a problem with dawdling.

I hoped they didn't hurry. I hoped that room had cobwebs, and things living in the cobwebs, and layers upon layers of dust. I grabbed Tag's hand and pulled him with me back towards the bathroom. His eyes widened in panic at my taking the lead, but in an effort to stay quiet, he had no choice but to follow me.

With a towel I quickly wiped down the sink and counter to remove any sign of water. The goal was to clean faster than the couple—to stay ahead of them.

We took the pans to the bedroom and stuffed them under the bed. I grabbed the blankets, handing the one from the floor to Tag and threw the other over the bed, not trying to do a tidy job of it. I nodded Tag towards the door. He went to the other room to make the bed. I moved to follow him, but he was back before I could.

We'd cleaned as much as possible. Tag motioned me to the window, sliding it up. I threw one leg over the edge when we heard the man coming down the hall.

There wasn't enough time to get us both out.

NINE

Tag pushed me out the window. I wanted to protest—to scream at him for being stupid. I landed hard on my bare feet, the impact jolting through my spine. I nearly bit my tongue off in an effort to suppress the cry of pain. It hadn't occurred to me to grab my shoes. It hadn't occurred to me we were really leaving the house until Tag pushed me through the window.

I'd left my shoes somewhere in the house. In all that cleaning I hadn't seen them. But worse, Tag was still in the house. Alone. Him being alone meant *I* was alone. I couldn't survive out here in this future alone. "Stupid!" The window had closed right behind me. I tried peeking through the glass, but saw nothing. Sharp needles poked into the soles of my feet, but I didn't dare move to a place that might be needle free.

The man's voice grumbled about having to dust an already clean house. He must not have noticed the window incident, and Tag must have been hiding or there would be very different noises coming from the room. The man scuffed around, moving things, adjusting things, and grumbling the whole time.

It felt as though he took his time on purpose, just so my body could cramp in the tense posture held under the windowsill. I strained hard to listen for sounds of a struggle—of a fight. Would Tag win such a fight? He seemed pretty tough, and he kept calling himself a soldier, but thus far he hadn't done any actual fighting, aside from the wrestling we'd done over the Orbital. And I was pretty sure if he hadn't been so weak and tired, he would've triumphed.

No sounds of struggling came which meant they hadn't found him. Yet. The woman's voice filtered loud and squeaky through the glass. She made a clucking sound. "That's the worse made bed I've ever seen." Her declaration irritated me. I'd definitely seen worse, and it looked pretty good considering I'd only had a moment to put it together. The man replied with something I couldn't hear. He seemed to have moved towards the door—away from the window.

"I told you I wanted to go in order. We aren't even done with the front room yet. Just leave the rest for now. We'll get to it later." The noises that followed sounded as though the pair had gone. I waited, holding my breath, my heart slamming against my ribcage. The room remained silent, every passing second filling me with dread.

What was I supposed to do out here by myself? If he didn't get out, would I be trapped in this time zone with crazies, ID rings, and curfew?

The window finally opened, and Tag's leg swung out. I remembered to breathe.

Tag nearly landed on me as he jumped down. He closed the window and moved us away from the house. The hard pine cones and sharp needles from the trees made it impossible for me to move very fast, but Tag kept us going away from the house, not allowing me time to try to baby my feet. His eyes swiveled everywhere, keeping tabs on our surroundings, ensuring we hadn't been noticed as we evacuated our hideout.

"We can go back in another hour," Tag said.

"Are you crazy?" I had my mouth open ready to spew out all the reasons going back that soon would be worse than walking around barefoot when he interrupted me.

"I am NOT crazy. I've been certified by the best doctors of my time. Never call me that!" He scrubbed his hand over his head making his hair stick out. His outright anger and stormy appearance, along with the newly mussed up hair made him look totally and completely crazy. I had the good sense not to mention that.

Slack-jawed, I stared at him. He could have grown wings and flown off and surprised me less. His little outburst overshadowed my relief at having him outside with me. "Touchy much?"

"What?"

"You're acting a little sensitive, don't you think? I wasn't calling you crazy as in lock-you-up-in-a-padded-room crazy; I was only saying your idea sucks rocks. No need to get all up in my face over it." I tried to turn on a heel and stomp off which would have looked very dramatic considering the way the beaded skirt fluttered at my feet, but the first step landed right on a pinecone. In that moment I'd determined nothing hurt worse than stepping on a pinecone.

I hopped on one foot, while cradling the injured one and trying not to yell. Yelling always made me feel better when I'd hurt myself. "Stupid!" I hissed between my teeth.

Tag chuckled.

"Don't laugh, or I'll call you names that would make a mental patient cry."

Tag sobered up quickly. "Summer, really, please don't use words like crazy, or insane, when talking to people out on the street. Not here in this time, and not in the future that will be your home. It *is* a sensitive topic, one that could get you killed, or tazed at the very least. Most people have children who were, or are, crazies in this time. In the future, most people have lost children to the crazies. No one uses those words the way you just did. No one would dare. To accuse someone of being crazy if they are certified as stable is enough to get you executed. The government has no patience for false accusations. If you call someone out, you'd better be right."

"But I wasn't calling you out." I leaned against a tree to rub my foot. "I was just saying stuff. Don't you just say stuff where you're from?"

He pulled off his backpack after looking around to insure we were alone and rummaged through it. "No, we don't. We say what we mean." He pulled out two empty packages that had contained the dehydrated food from the day before. Their shiny aluminum packages glinted silver in the light filtering through the trees. With his knife, he cut a hole at the end of each, then laced twine through the hole. "Give me your foot."

I felt sort of like Cinderella placing my foot on his bended knee. But Tag didn't have any glass slippers on him. He used the twine to wrap the aluminum package to the bottom of my foot like a sandal.

"Better?" he asked.

I walked several steps, hardly feeling anything through the packages under my feet. "Much better. And hey, they don't look too bad, considering . . ."

The makeshift shoes actually fit my preconceived notions of how shoes from the future might look. "Do you think they'll find my shoes and freak out?" I nodded back in the direction of the house.

"We didn't see them when we cleared out. If we didn't, they might not. Of course, you're probably right about waiting longer to go back. I wasn't thinking. It's been a long few days. I'm losing my reasoning. We should wait until after dark to return, which will make locating your shoes tonight difficult. We might have to wait until tomorrow morning to search for them."

We were walking again, though where to was anyone's guess. It felt like we'd walked a long ways before Tag seemed comfortable enough to halt our little march. From the position of the sun in the sky, I figured we'd hiked several hours. We ended up at a ravine near one of the tributaries. He pulled off his pack and sat down. "We don't have anything to eat. I'm sorry I didn't think to take anything with us. There wasn't much time for packing."

I shrugged. "You will never have any need to apologize to me for anything." I threw his words from the night previous back at him.

He gave me a dry look, but said nothing. I joined him on the ground. For a while we just listened to the water rumble over rocks as it pushed towards the Puget.

"Did you love him?" Tag asked abruptly. He had a way of looking at me that made me decidedly nervous.

I almost asked who he meant, but knew as soon as the question formed in my mind. He meant Nathan. "I don't know." I shifted

uncomfortably, positioning myself so my hand could graze over the water next to us. I didn't love Nathan—not like that. He'd been my friend, my co-conspirator. "He was fun to kiss." I gave over a lopsided smile that Tag did not return. My smile dropped.

"I am sorry for your loss." It seemed to take an effort for him to look away from me and instead fix his gaze on the water. He looked miserable and guilty. He looked as though he'd broken something he couldn't fix.

"We were just dating, you know? It wasn't like we were planning on getting married or anything. I cared about him. I care about what happens to him, and I love him as much as I love any of my friends— maybe a little more, but not love like I love Winter or love like I would imagine loving someone I planned on marrying." *Why the need to make him feel better about Nathan's death?* I shook my head. Nathan's death wasn't exactly Tag's fault. It's not like Tag caused the accident or anything like that. Yet, I didn't think it was Tag's fault he hadn't pulled Nathan out either. That blame fell on whoever sent Tag to me in the first place.

"Yesterday, you said we'd finish our conversation in the morning. Since we've got nothing but time right now, tell me the rest."

Tag stiffened, but finally nodded. "Where did we leave off?"

"We won the crazy war. Wait a minute. Is the crazy problem worldwide?"

He leaned back on his elbows, nodding at the same time he said, "Yes. There are rumors of small groups of people with no HTHBI taint, and no crazies, but no one has ever produced evidence. They say the government is hiding these groups in the center of some mountain, waiting for the rest of us to kill ourselves off. It's a petty conspiracy theory."

"Whose government?"

"The world's government." He sat up and pushed up the sleeves to his jacket as though about to deliver a lecture. "In order for the war on crazies to be won, the countries all had to band together or face annihilation. Each country worried that the crazies would lead us to the use of nuclear weapons, so they went to the United Nations and signed treaties to ban together under one Regent. Each country elected their own official Regent to speak for them under the supreme Regent. After the war was won, no one could see a reason to defect from the rule of the Regents. The system worked well enough, and the voice of the people unanimously voted to keep the rule of Regents until such time as it proves ineffective."

"So you won the crazy war and people still have babies in—what did you call them? Public nurseries?"

"Yes."

I thought about this for a moment, watching where the river disappeared around a bend. The future sounded confused and ugly to me. "I don't see what kidnapping people from the past will do to help the future. Your war is over; the countries are united. It's not like I can do anything to help. You can already have babies in your public nurseries, so why am I here?"

"The people of the world are sick. Their blood holds impurities that they cannot control, or cure. Everyone is born with the HTH infection." His eyes locked with mine with such intensity I was afraid to look away. "Do you know what Crazy Law is?"

I shook my head.

"A baby brought home from the public nursery cannot be named or officially recognized until its third birthday. On its third birthday, they have the baby evaluated. If the child is found unstable, then it is euthanized. It's the law." His voice cracked. "Some parents have a hard time letting go of the child they raised. For the greater good, anyone who tries to harbor an illegal child without testing them is . . . removed."

"You mean killed?"

"You must understand. The government and the people cannot afford another crazy war. If you believe your neighbors to be harboring a possible crazy, you're rewarded for outing them. People fear the government's retaliation if they bond too much with their child and become unable to turn them over. And people fear loving a child they might not get to keep. So many have given up on the hope of raising a child. The Regents have offered incentives—bigger homes, tax credits—things that will entice people to create a child no matter the outcome. But the people are giving up. Fewer people every year are willing to partake of the nurseries. In another generation, there won't be anyone left."

My mouth had dropped open in horror. "Yeah. What did the government think was going to happen when they make people kill their own babies?"

He snorted. "The people don't. The doctors do the euthanizing."

With the heel of my hand, I shoved hard at his shoulder. "Are you crazy?"

Tag caught my hand in his. "Summer, I know it's in your vernacular to utter the word crazy in reference to many different things, but please, for your sake, try to be cautious in its use."

I yanked my hand free of his. "But what you're saying *is* insane! You don't kill your own little toddler just because he might not be as smart as the kid down the street!"

"You don't understand. This isn't about intelligence. It's about stability. It's for the greater good."

"You're right I don't understand. I know a lot of people who aren't mentally balanced, and I *like* them. Good people don't kill their kids. Good governments don't make them. And you want me to go and be a part of all this?" I jumped to my feet, a little wobbly on my makeshift shoes.

Tag was quick to his feet too. "Summer, don't. Don't run away again. Remember you wanted to know the truth. You asked me to tell you, and I am not in a position to deny you that truth you desire."

"Okay, fine, so tell me what your infanticide has to do with me." I still hadn't decided against running. I wanted to. I wanted to stick my fingers in my ears and run away screaming, "Naaaaaaa Naaaaaaa Naaaaaaaa! I can't hear you!"

"Professor Raik created the Orbital so we could seek out those who were untainted, whose blood was clean to make babies that are also clean."

Professor Raik. So the one responsible for my nightmare life finally had a name. "What about you? Are you one of the infected?"

His jaw tightened. "I am."

Tag took a step toward me. For his one step forward, I took one back, almost landing myself in the river. Mud squished up and over my aluminum shoes, between my toes. I barely noticed it.

"Professor Raik had no intentions of altering the past. He's far too clever to unbalance time in that way. He took people who died in their prime, who died before they had a chance to really live—people like you. He's going to build up society by creating a clean, pure-blooded generation—a generation who will never have to turn their children in for testing—one who will grow and develop normally and whose children and posterity can start over with a world gone quite literally *mad.*"

Incredulity filled me. "So what's to keep them from getting the same blood poisoning you guys have? Did you get it from toxins in the air? Or some chemical plant meltdown? Did you get it due to some aftermath of nuclear holocaust? How are you going to keep my blood clean? What's to keep me from getting your diseased blood, Tag?" I took a ragged breath, trying to hold back tears, thinking of all those little curly-headed toddlers being led to their deaths.

"The HTH infection isn't passed through the air."

"Then it's probably in your water—or your food. You won't be able to keep me from getting it."

"It's not like that at all."

"Then what is it?" I took another step back, splashing into the water.

Instead of advancing on me as he had been, he also took a step back, as though purposely dividing us. "It's a sexually transmitted infection."

TEN

I narrowed my eyes. The current unbalanced me. To catch myself, I plopped my other foot down into the water. "Sexually transmitted? What, like AIDS?"

"Sexually transmitted as in it is transferred through sexual relations."

"I know what sex is, Tag."

He waited then, standing back apart from me. He waited while I pieced together the jumbled thoughts.

"But you said something about being able to have babies. How can I have babies if I'll just get your disease?" I hadn't meant to say "your" as in *his*. I meant it as in the collective people of the future. Tag's face hardened and he looked away. "You and I will never be anything more than we are. I am a soldier. While we're together, I am your protector. You are the New Youth, the beginning of a new mankind. You are meant to find one of your own kind to . . ." He turned away and stomped back to his pack.

I grunted. "Don't act all insulted. I was so *not* propositioning you."

He didn't respond. He looked intent on organizing things in his backpack that didn't need organized. I stood in the water until the flash of the Orbital glinted in the sunlight. Without realizing it, I'd slogged my way towards Tag and his Orbital as if the device had its own gravity.

"It needs to be recharged," he said, laying it out in the sun next to several other things that he'd pulled out of the pack. I understood then that he hadn't been organizing things, but setting them out to collect solar power. Tag didn't look at me or turn my direction in any way. It was as if by telling me the future problems, he remembered that we were not meant to be friends.

After a long, hungry look at the Orbital, I wandered off a few feet and sat down, yoga style, crossing my arms over my chest and glaring at Tag and all his future wonders soaking up sunlight. "It's not like I wanted to be friends anyway. I'm not going Stockholm, Wineve." I mumbled the words under my breath, and even though I felt certain Tag couldn't hear them well enough to understand them, I felt better having said them out loud. Out loud . . . and not true. Over the last twenty-four hours, Tag had become the only human I could depend on. A lump of disappointment welled up in my throat as the understanding of how completely cut off I'd become to the world. You had to be cut off when you started to consider your kidnapper your friend.

Alone.

No Winter . . . and now no Tag.

Alone.

They killed little kids, kids who could walk and talk, who were learning to tie shoes and wash their hands before dinner.

Alone.

Crazies.

I pulled my knees up under my chin and wrapped my arms around them. At the moment nothing made sense. Would they consider me crazy just because I disagreed with their actions?

"What did the crazies do that was so bad that they deserved to die?" I asked loud enough for Tag to hear.

"Their crimes are more numerous than the stars in the skies. You could look at a crazy the wrong way and he'd scratch your eyes out with a pencil just to teach you a lesson. They didn't blend into society, but stood apart from it and in many ways considered themselves above it. They were detached emotionally so that it didn't bother them to kill an animal on the street, or another child, or even their own parents. Crazy."

I shuddered and hugged my knees tighter. The confusion of such things battled inside my mind. On one hand, I couldn't imagine living in fear of people who might harm you just because you were in the wrong place at the wrong time. My sense of justice battled with my belief in mercy. Killing little toddlers because they *might* grow up to be frightening? I shuddered again.

How could they know the child tested for instability would be instable in a harmful way? What if they were instable like an eccentric old aunt—crazy but harmless, and maybe even endearing?

I couldn't do this. I had to go back home. "So is the Orbital working now? Will we be able to jump to your future?"

I called it his future in the same way he'd labeled it mine. Neither of us felt any inclination to lay claim on it.

"It seems like it will be fine. It needs recharged, and I wasn't able to do that at the house since their electrics were off. We'll see after it charges."

Tag smoothed out the sides of the wrist band so that every centimeter of the Orbital received full sunlight. He then went and found a place under a tree to rest. As his eyes drifted closed, I shifted to view the Orbital better. Tag was far enough away that I could snatch it and jump out of this time to another one—all before he'd even have time to sit up. I would have to wait a little bit so he'd fall asleep, so it had time to recharge . . .

"Summer?"

I jumped upon hearing my name. "What?"

"Don't."

"Don't what?" The innocence in my voice sounded exactly like the lie it was.

"Don't touch my Orbital. I coded it. You can't make it work. It'll only work when it reads my ring and hears my password, which you wouldn't guess in a million years. And even if you did guess, you'd have to steal my ring off my finger, and my finger with me still attached to it since it needs my living tissue to be effective, and figure out how to make your voice sound like mine."

"I don't know why you're telling me all this. It's not like I—"

"I'm telling you to save you the trouble of trying. Now we can both relax and get a nap. Don't think about wandering off either. Crazy law hasn't been implemented yet. You wouldn't want to run into someone who doesn't like the way you look and decides to rearrange your face. Especially since you can't seem to stop yourself from calling people crazy." He rolled to his side, away from me.

I glared at the Orbital. Stupid Tag and his stupid ring and stupid password. I crossed my arms over my chest, determined to not sleep just to spite him. Imagine him telling me what to do. Who did he think he was?

Not too long after that decision, the sun warming its way to my bones lulled me into drowsiness. I finally succumbed and lay down on the ground, curling into a ball, and giving in to the darkness behind my eye lids. Part of me grateful to not think about the babies being handed over to the doctors with smiles and syringes of poison.

Fitful dreams interrupted my nap. I awoke with a cry, but once awake, couldn't recall anything from my dreams.

"Daysleep must not suit you. You slept far better in the night than you did just now." Tag said. He'd created a little fire pit and had lit a small fire. My first thought was that it was far too hot to be worrying about fires until I smelled the aroma. He was cooking. My stomach rumbled. We'd missed breakfast due to our hasty exit from the house. I edged closer to him, almost feeling like we were starting over from the beginning.

"What are you cooking?"

Without meeting my eye, he shrugged and ground several green leaves between his fingers into the small pan. "Mushrooms. I could only find sage for seasoning. I hope you don't have allergies."

"I don't." Wild mushrooms sautéed in nothing but sage leaves didn't sound like something I'd order from a restaurant, but at the moment, food was food. Anything was fine. He partitioned off a portion for himself and poured it into one of the empty tin foil packets. He handed the pan to me. Handle side out so I didn't burn myself on the metal.

"You didn't split it fairly. Why should you give me more?"

"It's my job to ta—"

"I know. To take care of me." I pushed the pan back his direction, but he refused to take it. "You can tell your Professor Raik that I can take care of myself." I put the pan down at his feet and stalked off, wondering if I could catch a fish in the river with my bare hands. Nathan had a couple of friends who could do it.

"If I divide it evenly, will you come back?" His voice called after me.

Instead of responding, I returned to his little fire and sat down. I divided out the food again and dumped his remaining portion into his packet. I held the pan up by its handle. "Cheers," I said, scooping the mushrooms with my fingers and slurping them into my mouth. The mushrooms burned both my fingers and my tongue, but I felt too famished to care. We'd hiked far to get to where we were—not that I disagreed with putting distance between us and civilization—not when I now knew that civilization had so many issues.

We ate in relative silence. When we were through, I stood and brushed off my skirt. "Let's get back."

We took our time gathering things up and making our way back to the house. And we kept conversation to a minimum. What could we say? With his new passworded Orbital, I resigned myself to no escape. Running away seemed pointless. Where would I run? I was trapped in a life-threatening time with not one friend to my name. Perhaps in the time Tag planned on dragging me to, I'd discover a way home.

Tag's silence seemed to stem from a different source. He held himself rigid, kept himself in check. His silence felt like a billboard announcing that there would be no more socializing between us.

Darkness had fallen before we made it back to the house. I tripped several times, due to the makeshift shoes and my toes jamming into rocks. Once back at the house, Tag jimmied the window open with his knife without my help. I did help with dinner, regardless of his protests. The minimal communication killed me until, during our actual meal, I couldn't handle it any longer. "So how long were you watching me?" I asked.

"Excuse me?" His fork hung in midair, and I swear a blush came over him in the green glow stick light.

"You were there in the cave. But I'd had creepy-being-watched feelings about a week before that. How long were you watching me?"

"Eight days prior to your death." He took a huge forkful of beans into his mouth as though finalizing that discussion.

"What were you watching me for?"

He swallowed and fiddled with his fork on his plate before answering. "There are specifications that qualify a person to be recruited to the New Youth. Your blood had to be tested, obviously. A recruit must be resilient, strong, adaptable to new environments and changes, and . . ." he paused for long enough that I raised my eyebrows at him. "And they have to be of a particular aesthetic beauty—genetically superior in frame, height, that sort of thing."

"Who decides who is aesthetically beautiful?"

He blushed. "Each soldier is trusted to make that determination."

So, Tag thought me beautiful? The notion made me blush as well.

"I'm not dead." I reminded him. "Where'd you get a body to use in place of mine?"

He winced, but seemed resigned to march forward through my questions. "Professor Raik oversaw those details. I merely stopped time and made the necessary changes."

"How do you know he didn't kill that girl just to make her my surrogate body?"

"Summer, Professor Raik is a noble man. He did not murder anyone." He took another huge bite—rice this time—and looked away, pretending to be acutely interested in the swirled blue designs on the table.

"I'm doubting that a whole lot right now. Has this professor of yours been checked for mental stability? Because he sounds insane to me."

"Summer!" Tag's chair scraped back as he leapt to his feet. "Use caution!" He took his plate of food and left.

I didn't think my questions were so reprehensible as to merit him wanting to eat alone in the dark rather than with me by glow-stick light. All of my questions were reasonable. And if he thought moving to a different room was going to stop me . . .

I picked up my plate and the glow sticks and followed him out.

"Don't go walking out of a conversation with me," I said once I found him sitting on the end of the bed he'd claimed as his. His plate sat balanced precariously on his lap. His lips twisted in irritation when he saw me.

"You didn't need a whole eight days to see I was genetically fit. Why were you spying on me the rest of the time?"

"Every soldier is required to view the subject until they feel satisfied that the future will benefit from their presence."

"So if I hadn't passed the test, the car wreck would have been the end of me?"

"Yes."

"That means you think I'm not so bad." I tried to smile as I sat next to him, balancing my plate on my knees.

He scooted away so as to not actually be touching me. I took the challenge and scooted close enough our legs were touching. His body went rigid, he could have been stone.

"What if I get to the future and don't like the boys your professor handpicked for me?"

"Any of them will be far preferable to your last relationship."

"Hey!" I knocked his knee with mine, upsetting his plate. He caught it before it flipped to the ground. "What's your problem with Nathan? Nathan was a good guy. Don't diss on the dead."

"His blood was already bad, already tainted. I checked him as well—to see if he would have been a suitable fit for the future of mankind. He was a level one infected."

"How do you know that?" My mind raced. Nathan—bad blood? He'd had a couple of girlfriends before me, but none of them had been serious, not serious enough for . . .

"He'd injured himself working on his father's vehicle. I tested the cloth he'd used to clean his hand."

I interrupted there. "What's a level one infected?"

"HTHBI, or the *shakes* as people on the street call it, started when several sexually transmitted infections mutated. Human cells mutated. HTHBI is a level five. Level one is a basic infection. Syphilis, chlamydia, HIV, herpes—those are all level one."

That news bothered me. If Nathan was a level one and I wasn't, how had Nathan contracted the infection? Which infection did Nathan have? I almost asked, but didn't really want to know.

Tag must have warmed to the topic because he kept talking. "I actually assumed because of your relationship status that you were poisoned too, but Professor Raik insisted every individual be tested separately."

"So if I'd been a level one infected, you would have left me in the car wreck like you left him?"

"Letting him go was a mercy. A lifetime of disease is hardly one to look forward to." He scooped up more rice.

"I bet if you asked him, he'd feel differently."

"You're angry."

His observation only served to make me angrier. "You think? Of course I'm angry. He's dead! I could be dead too! I'm getting hauled into a world that kills babies and you're sitting here stuffing your mouth with rice, and acting smug and self-righteous over your choice to let Nathan die. And you're judgmental too! What makes you the grim reaper who decides who lives and dies? Nathan was great! You don't know anything about him! You don't know anything about me!"

I moved off the bed in disgust and went back to the kitchen to eat by myself, but not before I heard him whisper, "I know everything about you." The gentle, yet sorrowed, whisper washed over me like an embrace begging forgiveness. I shrugged it off and sat down hard at the kitchen table. I finished off my food quickly, went and found the pots we'd stowed under the bed, and filled them with water. The house still didn't have any electricity, so I'd have to boil my bathwater. I searched the drawers for matches to light the pilot, but couldn't locate any.

Unwilling to ask Tag for a match, I went to my room and dropped down on the bed that was not mine, covering myself in the blanket that was not my sun quilt. This camping out with the kidnapper routine had grown old. Even being in a future with running water and regular normal meals would be better than the nightmare I currently had to suffer through.

Tag could be heard bumbling around in the kitchen. I'd have gone out to help with the dishes and the cleaning up if I hadn't wanted to strangle him. The idea that Nathan could have been here with me, instead of dead, filled me with a whole new loss. Had Nathan been with me, we could have overpowered Tag and his Orbital. We'd be home again in no time. At the very least, I wouldn't feel so entirely lost—so entirely alone.

But Nathan *was* dead. I mourned the loss of him all over again. Crying until my head ached worse than ever before. I curled up in a ball and hugged a pillow to my chest. Everyone I knew was dead. The only way to get them back was to go back to them. And I had no idea how to make that happen.

Tag's dark shadow stood in the doorframe. I felt his presence long before he spoke. "The water's hot and already poured into the tub should you need it." He stayed only long enough to deliver his message and disappeared like the shadow he seemed to be.

I hated him.

ELEVEN

I didn't use the bath water he'd prepared for me, even though every part of me screamed for the relaxation a bath would bring to my body. When he entered my room and asked if my head hurt, I snapped, "It's so none of your business!"

He stood in the doorway for a moment before saying, "Just so you know . . . I had already decided to pull you from the wreck before I administered the test on your blood sample. From my observations of you—your kindness, your generosity to your sister, your ability to endure—you were worth saving no matter what the cost." When I didn't respond, he left to his own room and stayed there, which led me to believe he'd gone to sleep.

For a long while, the sound of my uneven broken breathing mingled only with the sound of my sniffling. What had he meant by, "You were worth saving no matter what the cost?" Would he have really pulled me out if I'd had a disease? Nathan had been worth saving. Why hadn't he seen that? Nathan with his desire to make the world beautiful and his absolute love for life. Nathan would have saved the world if he'd lived long enough. Tag pulled the wrong person out of the car.

For a fleeting moment I wished I could have talked, or even forced, Winter to come with Nathan and me to lunch. If history had recorded her as dead, Tag would've pulled her out too. Going to the future with Winter wouldn't have been any different than moving to a new foster home. Even leaving our sun and moon quilts behind would have been okay so long as we were together.

I slapped my hands over my eyes. Was I insane? Would I want Winter in this future where toddlers were walked to their deaths by their own parents? Where a crazy person could gouge your eyes out just because you looked at him?

No. Not for even a minute would I want her with me in this. Even being alone in her past, she had Aunt Theresa and all her friends, and her amazing talents of acting and her ability to get scholarships, and do something great with her future. And even if Nathan would have passed Tag's "test," I wouldn't have wished this on him either.

Would Tag have really pulled me out? I thought about how careful he'd been with me, how he worked so hard to keep me comfortable— safe. Maybe, just maybe . . . he might have pulled me from that wreck.

Could I blame him for the casual way he discussed infanticide when he'd been raised with crazy people hurting everyone? Could I blame him for taking me out of that wreck when he'd been sent on an errand he believes will save the world?

Tag was a victim of brainwashing, of a society gone mad. And if I looked hard enough at my own feelings, I found myself respecting him for his perseverance. I found myself respecting all those golden opportunities that he'd had to hurt me, that he'd let pass—where he protected me instead. I found myself respecting that he acted more like a gentleman than most of the adult guys I knew—even more than Paul had with Aunt Theresa. I found myself grudgingly grateful to still have a pulse.

I hated that I couldn't hate him.

So I shoved my need to hate someone onto this mysterious Professor Raik. Who snatched teenagers from time to start his own super-race of clean-blooded humans?

Yet, if things were as bad as Tag had said, if people really did refuse to have more children and mankind really was dying out, did the professor's mad methods make sense? And wouldn't it make sense, since I was dead and all anyway, to do something to help?

Questions marched through my mind like battle-weary soldiers as I lay in the dark on a tear-soaked pillow. After I'd exhausted my ability to analyze my situation, and Tag's part in it, the night became suffocating. No matter how much my body needed sleep, sleep wouldn't come. The rhythm and habit of falling asleep to the sound of someone else breathing made sleeping any other way impossible. The house creaked softly in the wind that had picked up outside. My heart rate increased even as I tried to breathe evenly and force it back down to the restful state where I might find sleep. I imagined the shadows playing against the wall from the trees movement outside to be the strange and twisted form of Professor Raik. He was coming to get me—coming to—

With a low growl, I stripped the blanket off the mattress again and hurried to Tag's room. I looked at the floor between the wall and his bed. I moved to lie on the floor, but hesitated. What might be hiding underneath the bed?

You're being stupid! But my body wouldn't budge towards that space between the wall and where Tag slept. *There are no monsters under the bed!*

Repeating that logic to myself didn't change my mind or my ability to lie on the floor and let whatever was under the bed suck me under with it. *What is my damage? I do not believe in monsters, ghosts, aliens, or possessed clowns.*

I wanted to feel safe and protected. Tag would protect me—whatever else. The decision was made before there was time to realize a decision needed to be made. I climbed onto the bottom of Tag's bed, careful not to make too much movement, staying at the edge at the foot of his mattress. Tag rolled over and stretched a little, likely disturbed by my presence. His toe touched my arm. With a sigh of relief, I listened to his breathing, and fell asleep to its cadence.

I awoke to the first patters of rain, realizing Tag was again on the floor. He bolted upright as the first sound of thunder tore open the sky. "Janice!"

"Whoa there," I said, shocked to see him look vulnerable and terrified. I'd have been amused by me soothing him instead of the other way around except his alarm sent a shiver of panic through me as well. "It's just a storm. You're okay."

He took several deep breaths before his white knuckles released the edges where they'd been gripping the blanket.

"Did you have a bad dream?" For him to yell the name of a *girl* . . .

"No." He staggered to his feet and took his blanket into the room I'd vacated the night previous.

No? He was a bad liar. He looked like the boogey man had been after him. Maybe Janice was an enemy he'd once fought. That thought cheered me for only a moment before my face fell into a scowl. I'd heard the caress over the name as he uttered it—the worry that hid underneath that one word for that one person. Janice meant something.

I followed him into the other bedroom to find him making the bed.

"In case they come back," he said as he tucked in the corner.

The explanation made sense. I went back into his room, pushing my irritation with *Janice* out of my mind, and made his bed. Thunder rolled around the mountainside outside the house. Every few moments, lightning flashed white light through the window. Rain pattered over the rooftop and slid down the panes of the windows.

Tag had moved to the bathroom to clean. I went to the kitchen to see if I could find us better food than beans and rice for breakfast. The pantry had everything stocked in those huge sized cans. I found powdered eggs and bacon flavored textured vegetable protein. Aunt Theresa had been big on food storage supplies for when Armageddon fell upon us. I knew that vegetable protein tasted like real meat if you used your imagination. I took out the cans and set them on the counter.

Tag had left his bottle of matches on the stove. I didn't think he'd done it by accident since he seemed pretty aware of his surroundings and his stuff at all times. His leaving it felt like a sort of peace offering to me—as though by leaving the bottle, he offered me a small piece of my independence. I could heat my own water.

Appreciation for the gesture came along with the regret of not using the water the night before. My muscles all ached and a hot bath would have been so welcomed. It probably would have helped sooth my storming headache too. "Stupid pride." I muttered the admonition low enough to be heard by only me, just in case Tag lurked anywhere nearby.

Cold air chilled the entire house. I wished the heating in this place worked . . . *If wishes were ponies* . . . I didn't know exactly what that meant, but it was a favorite saying of Aunt Theresa. It was her way of saying, "You can wish 'til you turn blue, but it isn't going to change anything."

I made breakfast. The heat from the blue flame on the stove actually took the cold bite from the air, making the kitchen preferable to the rest of the house.

Tag followed the smell into the kitchen and offered a cautious smile. He'd cleaned himself up—wetting his hair and slicking it back away from his face. His face shone as though it had been freshly scrubbed and shaved. I wondered where he'd got the razor since I hadn't seen one while snooping through the bathroom drawers. I startled myself when I said the words I hadn't even been thinking. "You look nice."

I bit off the end of the word 'nice' realizing I *had* been thinking he looked nice. I went back to making sure our powdered eggs didn't burn, feeling my own cheeks burn.

He cleared his throat and hurried to pull out dishes for the table. We sat down, each of us acting overly formal and uncomfortable. He picked up the ladle and spooned clumpy yellowed chunks onto his plate. He topped it off with the vegetable protein and a sprinkle of salt. He moved to dish me up a plate, but I hurried to do my own. Any more of his serving me and I'd scream.

"It tastes good." He took several more bites and nodded approvingly. "This spins wild shrooms any day."

"Spins?"

"Yeah, it's good—you know, spins."

I hid my smile at the compliment in my glass of water. The food wasn't bad, definitely better than wild mushrooms and in spite of the headache, I felt better. I took several bites before clearing my throat and asking, "So who's Janice?"

His eyes widened. "No one." He shoved the food in his mouth and looked away. He did that a lot when I started questioning him. I didn't want to end up spending the whole day fighting, so I shrugged and let it go.

We ate in beat to the rain on the roof and the thunder rolling around the bowl of the canyon. We both did the washing up. I opened the cupboards after drying the dishes to put them away and looked at the racks and the hard plastic material the cupboards were made from—like those permanent vinyl decks that are made to look like wood. The dishes were made of the same sort of material. "So if the flash heaters worked, we'd just put the dishes away in the cupboards, close the door, and come back to clean dishes?"

"Yes."

"So every time you close it, it turns on?"

He shrugged as if to say, "Yeah, so?"

I closed it and opened it. "What if I'm only taking out a cup? And everything in there is clean already. That's a waste of energy."

"The sensors know when something is being removed or replaced. It doesn't go on every time."

"But you just said it did."

"Summer, trust that it just works without explanation. Your dishes would be clean and you would only have to put them away to get them clean. Think of all the loading and unloading of your machines your time does. *That's* a waste of energy. This cuts out several interim steps. The whole world lives like that now. In everything, steps are cut out. Life is less complicated, less messy . . ."

"Except for your crazy population going off to their deaths when they're just toddlers. Other than *that*, your world must be as unmessy as a scrambled egg."

He sighed and turned back to the sink of water.

After we cleaned up the place, we lost our feeble grip on avoiding real conversation and so we avoided each other instead. The rain chased out the warmth from the house, so I went back to searching through the closets in all the bedrooms to find a jacket or a sweater. I also did a search to find my shoes. I found them under the bed I was supposed to sleep in at night.

With nothing left to entertain me, staying away from him proved impossible. I wanted to know where he was, what he was doing; I wanted to see him.

Tag sat in a big fluffy sort of chair that looked like a shaggy dog. The shag chair sat in the corner in front of the bookshelves. A book laid spread over his lap. One hand sat on the book, his fingers spreading the pages apart as though in anticipation for the moment he'd be able to turn them. His other hand rested at the back of his neck where his fingers pulled at the short dark hair. The Orbital had been snapped into place on his wrist.

"What are you reading?" The idea of there still being books made of paper and bound covers in the future intrigued me. I instinctively ran my fingers over the dust jackets on the line of books—some of which had familiar and well-loved titles.

"*A Sliver of Midnight*, by Romania Brown." His fingers gave a final tug at his hair before he dropped his hand.

"Never heard of it." I plucked a leather-bound collective works of Jane Austen from the shelf. The heavy volume felt good in my hands. Familiar, normal, like I might just be doing a little reading for my class on classic literature in school. The rain outside felt familiar too, the constant spattering lulling me into complacency.

"You wouldn't have. It hasn't been written yet in your time. Of course, few enough people in my time have ever heard about it. It's a little known classic. I wonder if I'm the only one in the world who's ever read it. Really classics are all we have for decent reading. Not many people grow up with talent in any of the arts anymore."

"Probably because most artists are a little crazy, and you've culled art in all its forms out of humanity."

"Artists aren't crazy."

I snorted. "Van Gogh cut off his ear. Writers are the worst schizophrenics around, hearing voices all the time and writing down

what the voices tell them. Musicians are more tantrum-throwing, drugged-up lunatics than they are anything else. Totally crazy."

"I doubt that." His brow furrowed though as if he'd contemplated my theory and worried there might be some validity to it.

"What's this book about?" Keeping the subject on the book and not on future human conditions seemed wiser. I settled into the chair across from him.

"It's about a man who stands at the point between two days. What's behind him is a mess of misery and despair; what's in front is something unknown and feared. What happens in the day to follow all hinges on that one moment at midnight where he decides how he will handle what he learned from the day prior. It's about our choices and what we learn from our choices. The metaphors of life, betrayal, honor, trust, rebellion—it's all in there—even love." His eyes met mine briefly and flicked away as he nodded to the book on my lap. "You an Austen fan?"

"*You've* read Jane Austen?"

He smiled. "She's a classic too. My mother loved her Persuasion even though Pride and Prejudice remains public favorite."

"She's Winter's favorite. I like her well enough, but she's not my favorite."

His smile broadened. He took a deep breath. "You remind me of—" Thunder pealed and he cut off whatever he's been about to say.

The noise made me cringe as my headache pulsed behind my eyes.

"Does your head still—" He broke off again, likely unsure of whether or not I'd snap at him like I had the night previous.

I nodded to save him from needing to finish his sentence.

"Would you like some relief?"

I felt instantly stupid. He wasn't my butler or servant boy waiting around for me to command him, but I nodded again.

Tag snapped the book closed and got up, setting it over the collected works of Jane Austen on my lap. "In case you want to read something new." He went to work immediately. The swirling motion repeated over my temples and forehead.

The headache dissipated as though he were a voodoo doctor chanting spells over me. His fingers swirled down to the nape of my neck. He murmured something about tension causing headaches too and moved to my shoulders.

As his thumbs rolled over the muscles in my shoulders, his fingers played lightly at the place just behind my ears. I held myself still, willing myself not to shiver at his touch for fear he'd abruptly move away as he seemed to so often do. He retraced his path to my forehead and temples and back down again.

I could sense that he'd leaned in, felt his breath warm on my neck, and so I turned to face him, not sure what I expected to find.

With my movement, he stumbled back as though caught doing something wrong. He inhaled sharply and tightened his mouth. "Does it still hurt?"

"No. It's better now." I felt confused, but the headache was gone. That and all the ache that had tightened itself into my shoulders. "Why do you do that?"

"You asked me t—"

"No." I interrupted him. "Why do you always jump away like that? It's not like I have cooties. I'm not diseased you know."

The words were out before I could call them back. And seeing the flash of hurt in his eyes, I would have called them back, stuffed them in my mouth, and swallowed them down if such things were possible.

His mouth tightened even more. "No, you're not. But I am."

I winced. The problem stemmed from the fact that it was easy to forget. Thinking of Tag as diseased didn't sit well with me. He just looked so *normal*. In my mind, everything he'd described would be for the crazy people only, for the people who drooled, and fidgeted, and gouged each other's eyes out.

Tag was smart, smarter than anyone I'd met. His way of speaking in complete and well thought out sentences amazed me. Give me any ten girls and have him say just five sentences to them and I'd show you ten girls crazy in love. He knew his history—well enough to keep us out of major trouble. He didn't drool. He didn't fidget. He'd read Jane Austen! How many guys in my time zone had done such a thing?

None of the guys I knew had.

So thinking of Tag as diseased, or as a candidate for crazy, irritated my sense of normalcy. And it isolated me again and again. I raced through the spectrum of feelings every moment—miserable to be parted from my sister, horrified at the thought of crazies and dying babies, afraid of the future, angry at Tag for taking me away from my life, grateful to Tag for saving my life. The confusion melted my insides and short circuited my mind. I might be at least half as crazy as the future's craziest citizens.

Trying to think of a way to make peace with the moment, not wanting to end up arguing like we had the day before, I held up his book. "So is this your favorite of the books they have here?"

"Of the ones I've read."

"Then I guess I found my entertainment for the day. A rainstorm and a good book are what Winter used to call ideal circumstances. Once we figured out the library was free as long as you returned books on time, we spent most of our time reading."

He smiled; his eyes warm in spite of the chilled air. "Your love for your sister is part of what makes you shine. I've not seen commitment so deep in many years."

"I do love her." Tears misted my vision. The burn at the back of my throat held down the sob that bubbled up unbidden from my chest. I swallowed it back down. "I'd die for her."

His eyes misted over briefly too and for a brief moment, I wanted him to just hold me and let me cry on his shoulder. He took another step back. "Of course you would. But it is sometimes far better to *live* for the ones we love." He held my gaze for several moments longer before looking back to the book. "I'll leave you to read, then. And no more crying—if you can help it. No more crying will mean no more crying headaches."

I almost made a comment about him fixing any damage but decided he might not offer to help me out again, especially if I made him feel uncomfortable over it.

He left the room, and I allowed myself the shiver I'd held back. The shiver came from more than the cold.

Stockholm. I'd gone Stockholm. I couldn't make myself not like him. Show me any ten girls in the same room with him, and I'd show you ten girls crazy in love . . . even if I was one of them.

TWELVE

I'd read two chapters of *A Sliver of Midnight* and found myself totally transfixed by the words. By the fourth chapter, Tag showed up again with a red lap blanket and a cup that obviously contained something warm since steam curled over it.

"Where did you find lemon and honey?" I asked after taking a sip and finding myself surprised with the flavor.

"There's a lot of honey in the lockdown pantry. The lemon is artificial flavoring."

"Where's the lockdown pantry?" It seemed we'd already searched the entire house thoroughly, and I didn't see any pantry aside from the one in the kitchen.

"In the lockdown compartments under the house." He took a sip from his own mug and beamed to have discovered the new flavors for us. At what must have looked like confusion on my face, he explained further. "Most houses have lockdown rooms or shelters to protect the owners and their families from home invasions. As the crazies grew in power and organization, fewer and fewer people were willing to live in homes without a place of protection within their homes. This is another problem helped by the IDR's. And a problem almost entirely resolved by crazy law."

He settled deeper into his chair with his mug between his hands. As he breathed in and out, the curl of steam danced in front of him. "They have a good stock of food there. We'd have been able to survive here for quite a while."

"You mean until the volcano erupts."

"Yes, well, we don't need to survive that long. We only need another day. We'll be long gone before Rainier feels restless."

His gaze stayed on me, but mine slipped down to the Orbital he kept on his wrist.

"So it works?"

"Perfectly."

I sighed and forced myself to focus on his face and not the Orbital. "We could go somewhere else you know . . . some *when* else. We don't have to go to wherever it is you're taking me."

"I have a responsibility. Rainier's eruption killed directly and inadvertently many people. Disease killed off many more, and since the ability to have natural births has ceased, mankind will be little more than an artifact littering the earth in another century if things are not shifted."

"But they can make more babies whenever they want."

"Yes, but most prospective parents feel reluctant to use the public nurseries. Knowing that crazy testing results in euthanizing over half of the new population makes people fear such efforts. The odds are not in their favor. The government needs babies in real families to keep the few who are not crazy from going crazy. Normal children raised in the nurseries by the nurses turn out worse than the children who were born deficient."

"So I get to be a brood mare? The idea is ludicrous, you know? How many of these *recruits* are going to be willing to become baby farms for you?"

"It isn't like that." He sank lower in his chair. "You'll get all this information properly when you're checked in. Soldiers aren't supposed to spend this much time with purebloods. I don't have all the answers, and I'm delivering the messages wrong. You would have been much better off to have arrived in 2113 immediately, to be assigned to your dorm and to meet your new people. Being with me must be confusing." He took a long drink of his lemon honey water, then frowned into his mug.

"I'm glad I'm not there yet. Your *messages* in the future sound like high-tech brain washing. Being with you at least makes me feel like I'm getting my education honestly. I really don't want to go, Tag. Is America no longer a free country? Does your professor really expect people to go along with this without giving them a choice?"

"He saved you from death. He saved all of them. In return, he only asks that you save the world. You will be the elite—kings and queens. You will have all your needs met, all your wants and desires granted."

I set down my mug and crossed my arms. "Okay. I want my sister."

He smiled. "She's still alive in her own timeline and plays her own part in the history of humanity. Your history ended with your accident. Like a book filled with blank pages. Unfinished and tragic in its lack of completion. Professor Raik has offered you a new pen filled with ink. He holds your book out and asks you to fill those pages rather than leaving them blank. He believes the ability to write your story is a gift. He would not take that gift from your sister no matter how her story may end."

I had to give him credit; his analogy made sense and almost convinced me that I might be acting ungrateful. "But what if her ending *is* tragic? How can I know? If you can tell me her life isn't miserable—if you can tell me that she marries a great guy and has six kids, a great career, and a dog, and dies as an old woman, then whatever you say, I'll do. But I need to know. There has to be a way to look it up. How is this the future and there isn't one computer in this house, or even a TV? You can't tell me no one watches TV anymore. With a little Googling, I can find out what happened to her. Don't you people have Google?"

He flashed his ring at me. "Everything in your day was filled with wires, cables, and complexity. Say what you want about not wanting the future, but once you're there, you'll realize how clunky and cluttered your time is. You'll never want to go back."

"So turn your ring on and hook me up to Google. I need to know what happened to Winter."

"If I connected to the net, it would alarm police because my IDR isn't set up yet in this time. No one in this time would ever believe our story, and we'd end up with the crazies."

I didn't ask if that meant *we'd* be euthanized. Some things were better to not know. I retreated back into the book, closing off any more conversation. Tag picked a different book and started reading as well. We stayed like that for a long time, like an old couple who'd become comfortable enough with each other to not mind silence settling in between them.

The rain let up after several hours, and the sun broke through the clouds for a short while until the rain started all over again. About half-way through my book I found myself dabbing at my eyes and running the back of my hand over my cheeks.

"He just let her die, didn't he?" Tag asked quietly.

I nodded, feeling dumb for him noticing me cry and for being so ridiculous as to cry at all, especially at a book! Even growing up moving from place to place and never fitting into families and schools, I never cried.

But then I'd always had Winter.

And now I didn't. Everything seemed so different without her. It was like I hadn't really known how much real pain hurt until she wasn't there to buffer me from it.

"I cried too—when he let her die. Don't feel ashamed."

He went back to his own book, but I still felt ashamed. I finished the book as the light faded from grey to black outside. Tag had gone to make dinner, but I didn't follow him to help. I finished reading instead, racing the sun to the last word on the last page.

I closed the book and hugged it to me with a sigh and a few sniffles.

"I thought I said no more crying."

Startled, I whirled around to see his shadow leaning against the doorframe. "You scared me." I hurried to stand up.

"I should." He smiled.

"Whatever." My fingers ran over the spine of the book.

"Did you like it?"

I nodded and hugged the book to my chest a little tighter. "I don't think I ever understood the greatness in such—" The word *sacrifice* hung on my tongue, but there was so much more to be learned from the story than simple sacrifice. I'd closed the pages shut and emerged a better person. I shrugged.

"Dinner's ready."

We ate by glow stick light again. "How many of these things do you have left?" I asked.

"Enough. We leave tomorrow. You'll have far better accommodations then. Better company too."

I appreciated that he'd made mashed potatoes and took a healthy serving. "I'm not complaining about my current company."

"Not in the last few hours, but before that . . ." His lip quirked and his blue eyes seemed to be laughing at me. He passed me the pan of soup he'd made. It looked like some sort of vegetable stew and wasn't too bad considering it had come from a can of dehydrated powder and chunks of vegetables.

"Well, don't get comfortable. I might be complaining again later on."

"I don't doubt that." He laughed.

"I've made a decision."

He leaned forward and put his elbows on the table. "Do enlighten me."

"That book, *A Sliver of Midnight,* it made me rethink some things. You might be right."

"Did you just say that I might be right?"

"Don't get excited. You'll probably never hear me say that again. But for right now, at this moment, you might be right. You saved my life. I would have died in that car wreck, and you've given me a chance to do something different, to make the world a better place. I'll give it a chance."

"It's amazing what a little reading will do," he said, though he didn't look as pleased by my decision as I thought he'd be.

We ate the rest of our meal while discussing books and movies. He'd explained that most movies were made by independents and had been that way since before crazy law had gone into effect. Hollywood was only recently making a comeback. He said the classics remained popular and everyone had movies from Hollywood's glory days loaded into their IDR's.

We talked about music. For a while in recent history, keening unaccompanied solos were popular, but big band music had slowly crept in and taken over.

We talked about my mom, growing up, my aunt and her husband, and we talked about Winter.

I found myself listening intently for the things he *didn't* say. He never talked about his own childhood except to mention briefly he'd grown up under the tutelage of Professor Raik. He never spoke about his own family, which made me naturally curious and ever determined to discover why he worked so hard to avoid those topics of himself. His family life couldn't have been any worse than mine, and I was pretty open about the psychosis of my upbringing. Maybe his childhood was one of those ideal types with the mom who bakes, and dad who plays catch with his kids after work. Maybe he just didn't want to rub it in.

I sighed. It figured. Everyone's childhood was decidedly better than the one Winter and I had endured.

We'd long since finished eating when we finally decided to get up, clean up, and go to bed. I was washing dishes when Tag said, "I'll be right back."

I continued on alone, putting the dishes I'd dried away, wondering what it might be like to just put a dirty dish back in the cupboard and open it back up to find it clean. No matter what Tag said, the idea seemed as farfetched as Aunt Theresa's wishes and ponies. Wishes *weren't* ponies, and dishes didn't clean themselves in anybody's world. Tag came back and finished cleaning the sink and wiping down the counters. Paul did that for Aunt Theresa when they did dishes together. It was on my list of cool things a husband should do—argh! What was I thinking? Comparing Tag to my list? *Stupid!*

Tag was one of the *infected*. He had a disease that rendered people incapable of having children. The last thing I wanted was to be waiting in line at a public nursery to pick up my crazy baby.

Besides, Tag had already declared he didn't want anything to do with me in that regard. It seemed like he liked me, but not like that. Every time we were close in any cuddly way, he acted like I gave him a rash. And my boyfriend had just died. Was I so calloused that I was already in the market for a new one? I sighed again.

"What's the matter?" he asked. He rinsed the towel we'd been using then hung it to dry.

"What isn't?"

"It'll be okay. Everything will be fine, and you'll wonder what all the fuss was about."

"Yeah. Tomorrow, my world will change—again."

He smiled and wiped his hands on his jeans, the wet spots looking more silver against the black than they did normally. "Change is all we can count on."

"Too bad mine's all of the spare pocket variety."

He looked confused, but I didn't bother to explain myself. I only shrugged and followed him down the hall to the bedrooms. I moved to go to the room he'd assigned to me when he gently pulled back on my arm. "Not tonight."

"What?"

"Let's both of us get a decent night's sleep tonight." He led me into the room he'd claimed for himself. On the floor next to the bed was the mattress from my room.

I tried hard, and failed, to hold back my grin. "I've got to give you credit. This is brilliant."

"Efficiency is hardly akin to brilliance."

"Who are you kidding? Efficiency is everything like brilliance. So which one is mine?"

He looked offended that I'd even asked. His brows furrowed over those blue eyes, the ones I'd become used to, the ones I spent a good deal of time trying not to think about. "The bed is yours. As has become our custom, I will take the floor."

"Well at least the floor looks a little more comfortable this time." I hopped on my bed, curling my legs underneath me, and spreading my skirt so I stayed properly covered. "When do we leave tomorrow?" I asked.

His face fell from looking pleased to depressed. With only a few glow sticks for light, it was hard to tell if it was only shadows, or if he really was sorry to take me to this obscure future.

"12:13 pm. And barring any more mishaps, tomorrow night you'll be in the New Youth dormitory with your roommate. You won't have to worry about sleeping alone."

"Roommate? What roommate?"

He pulled off his shoes and jacket, setting them next to the mattress on the floor as though he worried he might need them in the night. "I don't know who your roommate is. They don't give me information like that." He slid into the covers he'd placed over the top of his mattress, and tucked his arm under his head as an extra pillow.

I slid under my covers too and then leaned over my bed, resting my chin on the edge of my mattress so I could look at him better. "Tag?"

"Hmm?"

"We're friends right? I mean, you said in the beginning that we didn't have to be enemies. I assume that means we can be friends. So we are . . . friends, right?"

His eyes closed. I couldn't tell if he'd closed them out of irritation or if he really felt tired. "We're friends, Summer." His voice certainly sounded tired. Even still, my stomach flipped a little at the sound of him saying my name so softly.

Stop that! I chastised myself. "Then I have a favor to ask, as a friend."

His chest rose and fell with the deep breath he took. He rolled to his side and propped himself up on his elbow. "Then ask."

"I told you I'd give your future a shot, that I'd try to be part of the solution. But if I hate it there—in your future—if I hate it and *really* hate it, will you take me home? Will you take me back?"

He studied me for a long time. We were close enough I could reach out and touch him, but I didn't move. "Things will go well for you there, Summer. You will have prosperity, wealth, advantages that no one else on the planet will have. There will be many others your age; you will have many friends. You'll find someone you care about. You'll have a family and access to education far greater than anything available in your time. And no one will have you labeled as the lesser half of the Rae twins. You'll no longer have to spend your time figuring out the system and cheating it. You'll have no need to hide your abilities and your intelligence. You'll have no past of an unfit mother to haunt you. No school records stating you to be despondent and unyielding. You won't hate it."

I blinked hard at him calling me the lesser half of the Rae twins, of him knowing how I figured out systems just to cheat them. He must have been watching very closely for those eight days to know so much about my background. "But what if I do?" I pressed, inching farther off the bed to force him to look me in the eye.

"If, after three months, you hate it, come find me. We'll talk again."

"What do you mean, *find you?* You'll be around, right? I mean you're not going to take off on me, right?" Even as I asked, I thought of his calling out the name, Janice, when the thunder woke him up. Maybe he was already married. I had no idea how old he was. Tag looked like he might be twenty, but maybe twenty was like old-maid old in the future. Maybe they got married when they were thirteen. Maybe he had a wife and a couple of little crazies of his own. I glanced at his hand; the only ring he wore was his IDR. But he wore it on his left hand—on the ring finger . . . *stupid!*

The scrolled silver band looked sickly green in the glow stick light he held. It made me *feel* sickly green. Maybe in the future no one wore traditional wedding bands. Maybe they just put their IDR on their married finger and called it good enough. Maybe inscribed on the inside of the band were the words, "True love always, Janice," or some such sappy nonsense.

He didn't answer my question. His eyes were misted, and he focused on the Orbital. "You won't hate it."

"Look at me and tell me where you'll be so that if I have to find you, I can."

He looked at me again, his eyes no longer looking as though tears might fall. In that moment he'd fiddled with the Orbital, he'd composed himself enough that I wondered if I had imagined that he might cry, cry for me, or himself . . . or us.

Stop that!

"I live in the barracks beyond the coliseum library, where all the soldiers live."

I almost asked if he lived in married housing, but bit my tongue. It was none of my business. "So do you promise? If I hate it, will you take me home?"

"If you hate it, come find me." He turned his body and settled onto his pillow so he faced away from me. He did that a lot—just turned away when he felt the conversation to be finished. He stuffed the glow sticks under his mattress, dousing any light we'd had.

"But you didn't promise." I persisted. "Doesn't my free will matter at all in the future?"

"Free will . . . isn't what it used to be. It can't be, not with crazies and disease, and a dying world. Go to sleep, Summer. Tomorrow promises a new adventure."

He refused to say another word to me. I found myself angry all over again at him, angry at him and afraid to lose him. *Stupid!*

I could tell from his breathing he wasn't sleeping. He lay perfectly still. What did a soldier who stole people from their deaths and delivered them to a crazy professor think about before he went to sleep at night? I groaned inwardly. If he hadn't kidnapped me, I'd be dead. Like it or not, that part was totally true. I'd be dead like Nathan. Gratitude for being saved shouldn't have been so difficult to feel.

Of course, maybe dead wasn't such a bad alternative. Aunt Theresa believed in heaven. I believed in . . . something—something would follow life. When I was much smaller, I remember watching one of my foster fathers boil water. The steam rose up from the pan like a ghost. I asked him if it was a ghost. He was a smart man, one of the nice fosters we got to stay with for such a short time.

He sat me down and explained steam and water and the transfer of energy from one form to another. "So is the water dying?" I'd asked, still thinking about how ghostly it looked.

"No, it's just changing to a different level of energy." He was likely frustrated trying to explain something so complex to someone so young, and I had simply nodded that I'd understood and went along my way.

But I didn't agree with him. I thought the water had died, in a way. And the water's ghost went off to do whatever ghostly business it had. Since that moment, I hadn't believed in death as permanent. I would not end in a box under the ground. Somehow energy would transfer and I'd be something else, someplace else. And I'd go along with my own ghostly business. Perhaps my ghostly business would be far superior to Tag's frightening future.

I didn't sleep for a long time. From the sound of Tag's breathing that never seemed to even out properly, he didn't sleep for a long time either. After a while, I reached out and found his hand in the dark. He didn't pull away. After several moments, he rolled my direction and his fingers tightened around my hand. Only then did we both manage to drift into sleep.

THIRTEEN

"Would you pass me the salt?" Tag asked, holding out his hand. We ate a rather leisurely breakfast considering all that the day held for us.

"What if I decided I didn't want to go to your future?" I ignored his salt request.

"I'd make you."

"You can't make me."

He grunted. "Yes. I can." He reached around me and got the salt for himself.

"You and what army?"

"I am my own army." He reached around me to put the salt back. He was weird that way—compulsively putting things back where he felt they belonged. If only he would've compulsively put me back where I belonged.

"Well your army isn't all that effective or I'd already be there. Now that I'm rested and fed, I think I could take you." I smiled and flexed my arm for him.

"You and what army?" His lip twitched at the corner. I wondered how long it would take for me to make him laugh.

"I am my own army." I mimicked back at him. His lip quirked again, but no laugh. I'd grown to like his almost-smiles.

"You should complain to your general about how sloppy your regiments are kept."

I ate my powdered eggs and tried to scowl at him and not laugh at the same time. It took considerable focus to keep my mouth from turning up. We finished breakfast, cleaned the kitchen, made the beds, and readied ourselves for the time change. I put on Winter's shirt and my own jeans. They were stiff from being washed and hung to dry, but it felt good to wear my own clothes. We left no trace we'd ever been in the house.

The temptation to steal the book, *A Sliver of Midnight*, overcame me several times, but I put it back each time I'd eased it out of the bookcase.

At eleven, after all we could do had been done, Tag led us from the house out into the woods. He was careful, watching to make sure no one noticed us, watching to be certain we hadn't been followed.

He led us back up the mountain, not pushing us hard as he had when we'd needed to get some distance while those people were at the house. "Can't we just click the Orbital and have it zap us to the spot we need to be?" I asked.

"We could, but shifting place is different from shifting time. It makes people incredibly sick. Sometimes people don't recover from the shift. I've seen strong soldiers slip into comas they never recover from due to a spacial shift."

"Have you ever done a spacial shift?" I took his hand to steady me while we scrambled up some rocks.

"No. If I died while retrieving the New Youth due an inability to successfully make a spacial shift, I could be responsible for upsetting the entire future."

Made sense. The walk seemed deliberately rambling, and we arrived at the right place at noon exactly. Tag looked at the sky and down to his Orbital several times before nodding in satisfaction. "In another few minutes, we'll be all done."

"I'm scared." I felt an excited anticipation too. The idea of saving the future, of being part of a solution rather than a problem, intrigued me.

"You'll be fine—better than fine. Professor Raik is brilliant. You're lucky to be one of those chosen to work with him." Tag pivoted to keep an eye on our surroundings. I would have thought he might be nervous except his movements all seemed confident and ready for action.

"Should I trust brilliant professors from crazy worlds? And who ever heard of a professor controlling soldiers?" Even if Tag wasn't nervous, *I* was. Whereas all his movements were swathed in confidence and surety, mine were definitely jumpy.

"You only say that because you don't understand. Don't worry."

"I'm not worried." I crossed my arms over my chest and hunched into myself. Terrified was a better word. We watched birds flit from tree branch to tree branch, shaking water from the previous day's rain to the ground. The world smelled clean and fresh.

The minutes ticked by slowly until, finally, Tag took my hand, not roughly like he had in the beginning. There wasn't any force. My thumb pressed in at his wrist. His pulse throbbed, or maybe not his pulse, but mine. Blood pumps through thumbs, and I might have mistaken my heartbeat for his.

He kept his arm up so he could read whatever numbers and messages flashed on the Orbital screen, his left hand moved to the Orbital that sat on his wrist between us. His silver scrolled ring caught my attention. "Tag?" I blurted.

His fingers halted as I said his name. "What?"

"Are you married?"

The immediate grin split his face in two. I'd been wrong before to love his almost-smiles. They were nothing in comparison to the way his entire face warmed and brightened into a real smile. The back of his fingers swept across my cheek as he tucked a strand of hair behind my ear. "I am not married."

My breath caught in my throat at his touch.

He looked away, down to his Orbital and his fingers moved back to press in whatever equation or numbers he needed to enter to make it work.

"Tag?"

He looked up again. "Things between us will be different on the other side of time. I will have to be invisible to you. Be ready for that.

And if we miss our window one more time, I'll likely get executed when we do get there." His voice wasn't irritated, or harsh, merely factual, laced with a touch of—what? Regret?

"It's a time travel thing. We can blink us to the right time no matter when we leave." I tried to insist.

"In theory, you're right, except the Orbital has its own timer. It keeps track of how long it was gone. They'll know we were delayed the moment we return."

"I'm sorry." I said feeling genuinely sorry. "Let's go."

"Ready then?"

I gripped his hand tighter and held his level gaze. He didn't look back to the Orbital so I was caught slightly by surprise when the tugging at my stomach and the compression on my chest heralded the spinning of the world around us. "I think I've decided to like you. You'll never be invisible to me," I whispered. The words were so soft I wasn't even sure I'd said them out loud, but Tag's hand seemed to tighten around mine.

Then the spinning world stopped.

***

We were still in the mountains, only everything seemed dead. The trees looked like petrified stumps sticking up out of hardened mud. Farther down the mountainside, flowers bloomed and wild grasses swayed against the light breeze, but the spot we stood on looked like a bald spot on an old man's head. Mount Rainier's eruption must have tumbled through this area.

There were several hilltops surrounding us with houses still on them, one had a full-on neighborhood. "Do people still live in those houses?" I asked.

He didn't answer me. Tag licked his thumb and pressed it against his ring. The silver band flashed a brilliant red color and Tag aimed his hand to the sky directing a red light—sharp and crisp like a laser beam into the sky.

"What is that?" I asked.

Tag put his finger to his lips to indicate the need for silence.

"Why should I be quiet? No one's anywhere near us."

Tag wiped his hand down his face in frustration and pointed to his IDR.

Oh. So the ring had a microphone, did it? He couldn't have mentioned that before we left? I was tempted to grab Tag's hand and let out an ear splitting scream into his ring, but refrained. Apprehension kept me in line.

Within moments, a bright yellow car with wings that had big fans in them appeared in the sky over our heads. Tag dropped my hand immediately. When I gave him a startled questioning look, he frowned and shook his head imperceptibly.

The car landed twenty feet from where we stood. It looked like a flying taxi cab. Tag walked towards it, showing no fear, apprehension, or any other butterfly-in-the-stomach inducing feeling. He left me with no choice but to follow. He opened the cab door for me, revealing a soft white microfiber interior. Tag inclined his head indicating I should get in, which I did, ducking so I didn't bang my own head on the bright yellow wing. Tag climbed in after me. He tightened my shoulder harness over me so it felt like I'd been cinched into the seat permanently.

A muscular man with dark skin and darker sunglasses sat in the driver's seat. His black hair was slicked back so perfectly tight and molded against his head that it looked like he wore a shiny hat.

"You're late, Taggert," the man said.

Tag didn't respond. His mouth tightened into a grim line, and he looked out the window as we lifted off from the bald patched mountain and into the air. It shot forward so fast, my head jerked back into the seat. I moved to grab Tag's hand in a moment of panic at actually flying—in a car!—But Tag moved his arm out of my reach.

Confused, I nearly forgot about the fact that we were in a flying taxi cab going at speeds that seemed impossible, and occupied my brain by worrying why Tag was acting so weird. I stared at Tag while he stared outside. What had happened to cause such a change? Before we'd left, he'd been small smiles, and hints of humor, along with being vastly overprotective of me.

Now? Now he acted as though he'd never heard of me, as though he was sharing a flying taxi cab with a perfect stranger, and remained quiet and out of reach in order to avoid having to make small talk. He stayed stiff and coldly silent until the space between us felt like a growing chasm—one that I would never be able to cross.

We were in the air for a long time, an hour maybe, and yet landed where I felt we were still in the sky. I looked out the window and could see nothing but clouds beneath me. The clouds stretched around us forming a sort of false bottom to the sky.

"Have we stopped moving?" The sound from hydraulics and machinery along with the jolts and shudders of the car unnerved me. We were definitely not going forward any more, but we were definitely still in the sky. The wings shadowing the windows folded into themselves the way a bird's wings might, allowing the sunlight to shine in. On Tag's side, I found myself staring at well . . . myself.

The mirrored building next to us reflected my confusion right back at me. With a final shudder, the car moved forward again, picking up momentum, a rolling vibration sound came from underneath us. Tracks occasionally broke through the clouds. The building on Tag's side flew past and was gone. No building for me to feel anchored to anything.

I looked to Tag to explain, which he did in a cool neutral tone as though telling a stranger what the time might be. "We're on rails. Flying is prohibited in the city."

And we *were* in the city. As we rounded the building, there were suddenly dozens more. The car followed the tracks, speeding fast enough to make me feel slightly ill. The man in front had turned around to chatter with Tag which meant the man was no longer looking forward.

"What took you so long, Taggert? There's talk that you crazed like your—"

"Enough!" Tag's loud and abrupt interruption made me jump. "No questions. I will answer to no one but the professor. It's the way."

"Sorry." The driver looked sorry too. But he still *wasn't* looking forward.

"Um, hey, not to interrupt your conference or anything but—" I closed my eyes as the car sped along its tracks straight towards a tall building. I felt the swerve as the tracks prevented us from actually colliding with the building. "Don't you guys think the driver, should be *driving?*"

"It's tracked." The driver looked over the top of his glasses at me. His pupils were circled by a rainbow. Like Tag's eyes were blue, and mine were hazel, the driver's irises were *rainbow.*

I must have gasped or something because the driver's lip curled—though whether he was sneering or growling at me, I couldn't tell.

"Tracked?"

"He means it's automated and on rails. We don't need drivers in the sense you're thinking once the cars are tracked. Sensors keep them from colliding with any other cars on the rails, and the rails themselves keep the cars from colliding into anything else. There are no traffic accidents here. If you and your boyfriend had lived in this time, you wouldn't have died. The tracks are actually energy efficient since we've been able to recycle the energy from braking back into the car, like subways. Between the recycled energy and solar energy, we don't depend on fossil fuel anymore."

He must have sensed my raised eyebrows and my glance out the window to the layer of clouds that looked like pollution to me.

"Low storm rolled in. That's not pollution."

"Where do you get the energy to fly?"

"Not everyone has cars with that feature. In fact most people don't. Most people don't have cars at all. Povs can't afford them." He didn't really answer the question, but he made it sound as though only the very wealthy could afford whatever energy made cars fly.

"Are we—" I hated to ask since it would invariably make me sound stupid, but I needed to know. "Are we on the ground?"

The driver laughed. Tag didn't laugh, but seemed irritated with my questions as they forced him to be civil to me by answering. "No. We're on the track system. A lot of crime and Povs exist at the street levels. The Mids voted the tracks to be above street so they had the top-of-the-world view and less chances of being victimized by the Povs. Since they funded the project, they won by majority." He went back to his window with a deep breath that indicated he was done with my questions.

The rest of the ride remained quiet. We circled around buildings until we came to the ocean view. The clouds broke up enough to allow a view down over the ocean to where rain fell and whipped the waves into frothy caps. I focused hard on the space in front of the car, and sometimes the clouds swirled away enough for me to see the tracks in front of us. I tried to look down through the clouds directly beneath us, but could only make out faint lights blinking as we whisked past. The driver leaned his seat back in the reclining position so his head was almost in my lap. He shook his ring finger close to his ear and then rested his hands across his chest. From his ring shone light. When the light touched on the ceiling of the car, I realized he was watching what looked like a homemade movie.

His IDR had provided a movie for him.

I shot Tag an incredulous look, but Tag still refused to act like I occupied the same car, or plane, or train, or whatever the thing we were in was, with him.

The driver's ring wasn't on his left hand, but on his right thumb. His was a fancy gold looking thing with little stones that looked like tiny balls of granite lining the edges.

He laughed out loud at the characters moving on the ceiling, and I scowled. There wasn't any sound. What was he laughing at?

"What—" I started to ask, but Tag interrupted me.

He kept his focus out the window while he interrupted me. "He's hearing the movie internally. The IDR transmits to the drive and plays inside his brain through pulse power. Most people use vid glasses since transmitting in public is rude."

119

I looked back to the driver who'd gone to ignoring me nearly as well as Tag had a moment before. *Pulse power?* "Are you saying he's got a hard drive in his *head?*"

Tag didn't respond. His blue gaze fixated on whatever lay outside the glass window.

The weirdness of his silence mingled with the laughter from the driver while we made hairpin turns on a track leading us around buildings and in some cases *through* buildings made me physically ill.

"I'm going to throw up." I announced, and meant every word.

The driver sat his seat up immediately, apparently not wanting to be in my aim.

"Not in my ride!" He slammed the brakes making metal squeal against metal. The car lifted off the tracks and moved to the side. I opened my door and vomited outside the car into the layer of clouds. I hoped nobody was beneath me at the same time I felt extreme gratitude for the harnesses holding me securely inside the car. Another car flew past us on the track, and I wondered if we had stayed on the track, would we have been run over? Advertisements I hadn't noticed so much before while we were driving scrolled across and down the impossibly tall buildings, making everything seem to be in a sickeningly constant wave of movement, as though the buildings themselves were crawling.

Sensory overload. My brain couldn't comprehend everything my eyes scanned.

The thought of running away again left before it could fully form. Instead, I closed the door to the taxi car-plane-train and closed my eyes so my brain didn't fry from too much information. The future we'd stayed in at the cabin didn't seem half as overwhelming as the future of 2113.

The driver waited to be certain I'd finished before moving back to the tracks, where the car jolted as it connected itself to the track.

I didn't look up again until the car had stopped and moved to the side of the tracks onto a platform. Tag got out his side and walked around the car to open my door for me. I wanted to grab him and insist he take me home to Winter immediately, except my jaw dropped at the building I found myself staring at. The car had parked to the side of the tracks by a huge glass coliseum. A steady stream of people entered and exited the glass building. With every person who went through the doors, whether coming or going, the doorframe glowed green. Most of the clothing seemed normal enough—jeans, loose blousy shirts, skirts on most of the women and many of the men, but the hair colors were as varied as the colors of their clothes. Pinks, oranges, reds, blues, whites, yellows, greens, blacks, and purples bobbed along as the crowd maneuvered around each other. There were even some silvers and golds—a crayon box assortment of heads. A lot of people had swirls and shapes inked between their hairline and their eyes—messages that looked like . . . "Is that a Coca Cola ad on his forehead?" I asked

"Businesses pay a lot of money for personal ad statements." Tag looked at the man in question with mild disgust. "But you have to be willing to be rented for an entire month. Foreheads and backs of hands are prime marketing spaces."

Match your hair to your outfit and run an ad for your favorite soft drink on your forehead. Welcome to the future.

A small group of guys who looked harder and more serious than Tag surrounded us on the platform. They were all younger—late teens early twenties, but they looked old, like they'd seen too much and didn't want to talk about it. They wore black-silvery jeans and black jackets like Tag's. None of them bore any advertisements on their foreheads or hands. Maybe the military didn't allow it. One of the taller guys took a step forward towards us and out of the circle of the others. He looked older, older and meaner than the rest. He had spiky red hair, and not red as in ginger red, but red as though he'd dipped his head in a vat of fresh blood. His eyebrows had been dyed to match and seemed to make his pale skin chalky in comparison. "Soldier Taggert." His voice sounded as though stones had been stuffed in his throat and grated against each other with the movement of his sharp Adam's apple.

"General." Tag bent his head low in respect.

"You're late, soldier."

The "general" didn't even look my direction or acknowledge me in any way. I had a thousand different snarky remarks to make about my being a queen, but bit my tongue and watched with fascination and slight horror. Not to mention the wind buffeted at me, making me feel unsteady as though I might get shoved off the platform where I would fall into the swirling clouds below.

"We ran into some malfunctions with the Orbital, sir." There was a slight pause before the word *sir*. A pause so slight, it went unchecked by the general, but not by me. Such nuances were part of me, testing the pecking order and figuring out where I stood in it. Tag stood below this person, but he didn't *feel* below this person. Interesting. No wonder Tag noticed how I played the system, living in my "self-made mediocrity" as he'd called it. He apparently did the same thing.

"Malfunctions?"

I stiffened, wondering if Tag would rat me out for causing so many problems. The way the man shifted his weight from one foot to the other felt dangerous.

Tag's glance slid to me again, briefly, and was accompanied by another slight shake of the head. "We had a power shortage due to inclement weather. The shortage in power disrupted the electrics, sending us off course. We ended up in the Rainier explosion, which further afflicted the electrics. We had to jump to a safe place and wait until the Orbital could be charged and trusted to bring her here safely. The rest of my report will be given to the professor only, sir."

Again the pause before the title, sir. Tag hadn't been kidding when he said he might get executed if we waited any longer. He might get executed anyway from the looks of things. I wanted to say something that might help, to somehow take responsibility for the problems. Tag tried his best to get me here on time. It wasn't his fault I didn't come easily.

I opened my mouth, felt Tag's body tense, closed it again, and frowned at the standoff between Tag and this "general." My own muscles had tensed as well—tensed and ready for flight or fight. Flight wouldn't get me far, not with the circle of soldiers standing guard at the exit off the platform, and fight . . . well, that wouldn't get me very far either. These guys looked hard and capable, and there were too many of them.

And I couldn't be sure Tag would be on my side if I tried to escape. Yes, he took the heat off me by not implicating me in the blame, but he'd changed so much in the last few moments. His eyes looked cold as they stared down at the ground, his jaw flexing as though he might be grinding his teeth. They were the icy-hard blue I remembered from when I first saw him.

"The professor was concerned, as were we all, that you'd proven yourself to be an unacceptable risk. We'll see if we weren't right." His eyes never left Tag's bowed head. "Report to the professor, Taggert."

Without lifting his eyes, Tag bowed, turned on a heel and without another word to me or another glance in my direction, he strode off with great purpose. Off and away from me. The crowd of soldiers parted for him, and the door to the coliseum glowed green at his entrance.

My breathing shortened with the new panic. Tag was gone. He'd left me with these people I didn't know, didn't trust, and certainly didn't like. The general watched Tag as he went. The general's lips stretched in a thin, calculating line. That man was trouble from spiked red hair to steel-toed boot. He never once looked at me as he snapped his fingers and said, "Take the New Youth to her dormitory. Have her checked in."

Another soldier stepped forward and bowed his head to the general. He took my arm, not roughly exactly, but mechanically. He started to lead me away. I shook off this new person's hold and turned towards the general. "Wait! What's going to happen to him?"

The general didn't turn to me or acknowledge the question. He snapped his fingers again and this time a soldier flanked me on both sides, each of them having a firm grip on my arm as they led me away.

I started to struggle as they swept me along with them, and looked back to see the general still looking towards where Tag had gone. He said, "Unacceptable risk." cleared his throat, and strode after Tag as my new captors pulled me to my future.

FOURTEEN

y new guards never spoke to me. I could have picked up my feet and they likely would've carried me across the platform and to the sidewalk surrounding the glass coliseum. I didn't lift my feet. Instead, my feet moved along with them. We didn't walk far before entering an arched glass tube. The wide tube followed the curves of the building.

Inside the tube was a sidewalk framed on both sides by elaborate gardens. As we walked, I soon realized that the vegetation was all of the edible variety. They hadn't just planted pretty flowers along their sidewalks; they'd planted tomatoes, strawberries, cucumbers and all sorts of other fruits and vegetables. The wide tubes weren't simply a means of keeping the rain off your head, and the wind from pushing you over the edge to fall through the clouds, but they were long and well-planned green houses. Along the lower sides of the tubes flashed digital advertisements, scrolling, changing, always moving, like a million small movies going on all at once. The people in the digital pictures looked like they were talking, but no noise came out of any piping anywhere. I wondered if the sound would play in the hard drives in people's heads. That thought elicited a shudder from me. *Hard drives in people's heads? Ew.*

I had questions, but the men marching me to who knew where didn't look like they'd give answers. Where had Tag gone? He had mentioned he could be executed for bringing me back late. And the spiky-haired guy called him an unacceptable risk. Would they execute him for real? Was he in trouble because of me? Would they punish me too? Or even execute me?

With no other choice, I walked and waited to see what happened next. But my fists stayed in tight little balls at my side. If they messed with me, I fully planned on bashing their noses in. Many people passed us going the other way—teenagers hanging out together, a few people who looked like they were talking to themselves, couples, the elderly, people in a hurry, people who were just wasting time. But no matter who they were, young or old, alone or in a group, no one met the eyes of my guards. No one smiled or offered a casual, "Hey, what's up?" They acted nervous once they realized the guards were in the tubes with them.

We wound through the path of glass and produce, passing by exits into buildings from the tube every twenty or so feet, every once in a while walking through the shadows of some of the buildings. At some point, we walked mainly in shadow due to the towering buildings over us. It was as I took note of the lack of light that the tube ended. An exit and several metal doors stood in front of us. The guards chose the central door. An elevator.

"Going up," a female mechanical voice said, sounding sultry and overly-accommodating.

We went up, high enough my ears popped from the pressure.

The glass tube continued to wind through the city, only now it was doing so several hundred feet above the false bottom of clouds. With the layer of cloud beneath my feet, I'd felt more secure. Now I truly felt like I was walking through the sky. Things were incredibly bright this high up. The gardens continued alongside the sidewalks.

The guards didn't slow down at all. They kept a hold of my arms and dragged me along. I swiveled my head, taking in the ocean off in the distance and the buildings surrounding me. "Are we still in Washington?"

"Naw. We're in the bay," the guard on my right said.

"San Francisco?"

"Ain't no other bay worth talking about."

I looked around and had to admit, the pride in the soldier's voice seemed justified. The view of the city left me astounded and breathless. The clouds rolled slowly out farther over the ocean, leaving the city. I couldn't see all the way to the ground even with the clouds moving away because that far down everything seemed to be hidden by the shadow of the buildings. "Oh!" I exclaimed. "It's beautiful!" And it was. Beauty that slowed my progress, making the guards need to drag at me a little more to make me walk. Sun glittered against the wet-slicked buildings left over from a recent rain.

San Francisco. It certainly hadn't felt as though we'd traveled so far in the car.

In spite of the dizzying height, it was hard to turn away from the view, hard to not look out like some alien tourist. Green dotted the rooftops of buildings smaller than the walkway—more vegetation. Each rooftop was like a miniature ecosystem unto itself. Amazing. And the sunlight gleamed along the sidewalks in the sky. Everything above the cloud level seemed bright, shiny, and new. And even the cloud level with its shifting wisps of white added a delicate beauty to the scenery.

With all the talk about crazies, wars, and disease, Tag had frightened me, but this world didn't look all that much like the things he described. It had beauty and filled me with a sense of wonder I hadn't expected.

But Aunt Theresa used to always say that there were a lot of ugly people walking around in beauty suits. She meant that sometimes crummy people hid behind their beauty. I wondered if San Francisco wore a beauty suit.

We exited one of the side exits into a building and found another elevator. "Going down." The sultry elevator said. It sounded like she was politely telling us we were heading to the fiery furnaces of what Aunt Theresa called "the hot place." I suppressed a chuckle. And go down we did, fast enough I held the bar to steady myself. My ears plugged up, but didn't pop until I deliberately yawned and forced them to.

We walked out onto another level of sidewalks in the sky. This one seemed to line a building that housed businesses and shops. People moved in and out of those shops rhythmically making the entire city appear to be breathing. Farther down the sidewalk tube, the soldiers stopped at a green building that seemed to be at the center of everything else. The sidewalks in the sky all circled around that one building then cut out into their different directions, but it appeared that the city revolved around this one central spot.

The main doors swished open as we approached and the outer edges of the door glowed green. I noted someone else walking past, and saw how his ring glowed red as he came into range of the door. He scowled at the door and ducked his powdered blue head into his powdered blue jacket as he made a sort of snorting noise.

This might be the place all roads lead to, but clearly some of the people living in the city didn't approve of their centerpiece.

As we went inside, I looked over my shoulder to the outside. *Tag, where are you?*

A pinched, stern-looking woman whose wrinkles might have been stretched off her face by her insanely tight bun met us at the front desk.

"Summer Dawn Rae. You're late, dear." Her sweet voice didn't at all match her appearance. She looked like the kind of school librarian who ate little kids when they failed to turn a book in on time. And she'd called me *dear*? The only person who ever called me that had been the waitress at the Corner Café. For a fleeting moment, I wondered if that waitress had gone to my funeral since she'd been one of the last people to see me alive.

Stupid. I'm not dead.

"I'll bet it's been a rough few days from the looks of you." The woman continued. "I'll take you to your room where you can clean up and find something more appropriate to wear to your orientation." She turned a cold gaze to the soldiers. "She isn't a prisoner or a threat. You can go now."

They both inclined their heads, murmuring, "Yes, Kathleen," and bowing back out of the building.

"The soldiers are a little high handed sometimes. I hope they didn't frighten you."

I didn't tell her that she frightened me more than they had. I didn't tell her that by the look of those soldiers, she'd frightened them too. She waved her hand over the door after the soldiers had exited causing the edges of the doors to glow red.

I'm locked in. I thought. *She's said I wasn't a prisoner, but she just locked me in.*

"It's to keep people out while I'm gone from my post." She explained as though reading my thoughts. *Can she read my thoughts?* I repented thinking she looked like a mean spinster who ate kids, hoping she hadn't been able to eavesdrop on me. For all the things Tag had told me about the future, I cursed him for all the things he *hadn't* said.

And who knew what testing they did for crazy people. Maybe they let some people who are borderline crazy pass the test and walk around free as menaces to society.

Stop thinking that! If she was eavesdropping on my thoughts, I was in big trouble. We left the small front entry hall with its singular front desk through a set of double doors made out of some dark wood. The paneling on the doors was carved to look like vines.

Through the doors, I felt like I'd entered another world all over again. Two spiral staircases wound around either side of the cavernous room. The room itself looked like an elegant sitting room. Plush lounge chairs, love seats and sofas were scattered all around. The walls were a pearly blue color that seemed to swirl and shift depending on how you looked it. Books lined the shelves in one nook under the left spiral staircase, and an incredible fireplace sat tucked under the other staircase.

"This is the casual room," Kathleen said.

"Casual?" I let out a pshaw noise. She turned and tilted her head like a hawk might before it swallowed a mouse. I shrugged and tried to clear my mind.

"This is where social gatherings are held. Dances are held on the one hundred and thirteen floor in the ballroom. The dining hall is on the fifty-sixth floor. Your room is on the seventy-second floor. I apologize your accommodations are on lower levels but the upper levels are already occupied."

Lower levels? I looked at the spiral staircase. It went up pretty high, but I didn't think it went up any seventy two flights. And then I noticed the double-wide wooden doors. They sighed open to reveal a spacious elevator. "Going up."

We stepped in and the elevator rocketed us up to the seventy-second floor. Not only did the front doors glow green *and* red for Kathleen, but every door Kathleen encountered glowed green. She was like some sort of traffic cop who figured out how to make all the lights do her bidding.

"You'll find adequate clothing that is your precise size in your closet." Kathleen instructed as we walked down the hall.

Tag must have given measurements or something.

"You'll meet your classmates for orientation soon. And each of you will meet with Professor Raik privately to discuss your new lives here."

Professor Raik. I felt a chill at the very idea of doing anything privately or publically with that guy. "What did they do with Tag?"

"Who, dear?" She walked in front of me, her severe bun bobbing with her every step.

"Tag. Taggert." That was what the general had called him.

"I'm sure I don't know—oh. You mean the soldier who brought you here. You really don't have to worry over him. He's not part of your class. The soldiers are their own class. They take care of themselves and don't mingle in any other society."

"Will they kill him? Because I'm late?"

She turned to face me, slight alarm in her eyes at my question. "I don't know. And you shouldn't care. What happens to soldiers is soldier's business. You're a New Youth, now. You need only worry about things that are New Youth's business."

"New Youth?"

"You're the hope of the future." She said the words, "hope of the future" with the same sigh as Tag had. They really did hope for their future to be better. "Here's your room, dear." She waved her hand over my door, and it glowed green at the edges then clicked open. She pushed it open farther.

"This is my room?" I entered the room with my jaw hanging to the ground. No way would they give me a room like *this*. "There's a mistake somewhere; this can't be my room." I said.

"Why can't this be your room?"

I shook my head and waved my arms at the room. "Look at all this! This is too much for someone like me."

"There's no mistake. The professor doesn't make mistakes. And you remember that no matter who you were before you arrived, you are one of the elect here. So put your past in the past. And don't forget who you are now. The professor demanded nothing less than the best for the world's hope. You will want for nothing here. You'll have the best of everything." She smiled at me, and her face looked far less severe with that smile. "Do you like it?"

"It's . . . amazing." Even on TV, no one had a room that looked like this one. The two canopy beds with the long flowing curtains indicted Tag had been right about me having a roommate, though no one else was in the room at the moment aside from Kathleen and me. The dark hardwood floors glowed against the dim light coming from creamy globes hanging from the ceiling. Cream colored rugs sat under each bed and the curtains hanging down from the bed matched the rugs and the floors with their swirls and patterns. Near each bed stood a desk and chair. The bed on the right looked rumpled as if someone had jumped on it.

"Is my roommate here?" I asked.

"Oh yes. Alison's very friendly. She hasn't been here very long, but she wanted to go see the ballroom straight away after she'd cleaned up. I'm sorry to not be able to introduce you."

Ballroom? Out of all the things to see here, she wanted to look at the ballroom?

There were three other doors besides the one we came in through and a wall that seemed filled with windows overlooking the city. "Your closet is on the left along with your bed and desk. The bathroom is the first door on the right. The other door is Alison's closet. You'll be soon getting an IDR—your soldier explained the IDR, I assume?"

I nodded. "A little."

"They'll also be making an appointment with the doctor so you can get your inoculations."

"Inoculations?" I dropped the edge of the silky bedspread I'd picked up just to see if it was as soft as it looked. My rough fingers had snagged the silk.

"Yes. We wouldn't want you getting sick." She seemed to have missed my alarm at the idea of getting a shot—and not just one. There had been an s on that word inoculation; that made the word plural—as in many.

"So do you think Tag's okay?" I asked again.

"I'm sure he's fine, dear." She said, sounding all kinds of motherly. "I'd better be leaving you to get bathed and dressed so you're clean for orientation. I set your room alarm to give a ten minute warning before you're to meet the professor downstairs, and then again for when you're actually supposed to be there. He doesn't like to be kept waiting, so try to leave at the ten minute alert. You have about two and half hours."

"Will he bring Tag back with him? Since he's talking to Tag right now?"

"I doubt that very much." She moved to leave. I followed her to the door.

"Why do you doubt that? Do you think they've hurt him?"

Her eyes filled with pity until it nearly toppled over in the form of tears. "Don't ask any more questions about him if you don't want to make trouble for him. If he is still okay, the best way to keep him okay is to let it go. The New Youth aren't allowed to socialize with the soldiers."

"But he said we didn't have to be enemies. He said we could be friends."

"I hope you aren't enemies. I worry about the New Youth—" She bit off what she'd been about to say. "If you're his friend, don't ask any more. It'll only make things harder."

I nodded. She nodded too, putting her finger to her lips in a hushing motion. I nodded again. She patted my check and smiled before leaving the room, shutting the door behind her. I waited to see if it would glow red at the edges, to see if she would lock me in, but it never did.

After several minutes of standing and staring at the door, I went and checked to see if it would open. It did. I let out a breath I hadn't realized I'd been holding and went back in my room to check it out thoroughly.

Thoughts of Tag and Winter stayed in my mind which made glorying in the fact that the room I now occupied was posh, comfortable, just a bit fancy, and meant for me, impossible. Winter could have been my roommate. We could've shared this room together. I shook my head. She didn't die in the car-wreck. I had to be grateful for the life she'd been allowed to live, grateful that I still had a shot at my own life.

My closet was a huge cavern of clothing, filled with a vast array of dresses, a few formal gowns, and no jeans. Were they kidding me?

The dresser was inside the closet like the house we'd stayed at in the mountains the last few days. That must be the latest trend in home decorating. I opened the drawers and found unmentionables, which embarrassed me to imagine someone else buying for me. In the other drawers were exercise clothes, yoga pants, a jogging suit, a swimsuit, and one pair of jeans. One. Whose brilliant dumb idea had that been?

The shoes were equally disappointing—only one pair of running shoes. The rest were of the strappy heel variety. I didn't wear heels. At 5'8, I felt tall enough, and I could never coordinate my feet well enough to walk in heels without breaking an ankle. In the future where cars can fly, and sidewalks skimmed the sky, they couldn't come up with something better than girl shoes with heels? Why did society want girls to look like a bunch of baby giraffes learning how to walk?

And all these dresses? Where were all the women to rebel such things? A few dresses—fine, but a whole closet full?

After several moments of looking at my new wardrobe and several moments more of looking in the mirror at my own reflection, I decided what I currently wore was good enough. I touched the glass in the mirror and mouthed the words, "Wonder twin powers . . . activate." It was Winter's shirt in the mirror—her shirt and her face. If I didn't say the words out loud, I could pretend she stood right in front of me. I drew strength from that. Drew strength while swallowing sorrow. I'd find out where she was buried at the very least, and put yellow roses on her grave. Maybe I'd put white roses on my own grave.

I opened the door to check out the bathroom. The tub took an entire wall. The shower looked like an emergency escape pod from a space ship. I washed my face and hands, raked my fingers through my hair and shrugged. I was ready, and it only took four minutes of the two hours and thirty minutes she'd given me. Now what?

I went back into the room and meandered through my roommate's closet, Alison, I think Kathleen said her name was. She had a lot of dresses too. I had just decided to start peeking in her dresser when the door to our room fell open and a very bubbly excited sort of voice squealed out, "You're here!" She said this as though she'd been waiting for days, when Kathleen said she'd only arrived an hour or two ahead of me.

I backtracked out of her closet as fast as I could, while trying to look innocent about sneaking around through her stuff. "Hi."

"Hello!" And she threw her arms around me.

I stood there awkwardly, wondering how to handle this new situation and finally put my hand up to pat her on the back since she didn't seem like she planned on letting go of me anytime soon.

When she did pull away, it was to grip my arms and say through a grin wide enough to be its own canyon, "We're going to be the very best of friends!"

I tried to smile back without looking as bewildered as I felt.

"I'll bet your soldier was completely dreamy, wasn't he? Mine was. As perfect as a dream! But those soldiers aren't half as adorable as the boys in our own class. Just wait until you see them!"

My back went rigid upon her pondering over Tag's looks. "I wouldn't know; I was too busy fighting to stay alive to pay attention to what anyone looked like."

"What are you talking about? Your soldier saved you. You didn't need to fight anything." She plopped down on her bed and used her arm to prop her up. I could easily imagine her in bobby sox and a poodle skirt.

I couldn't stand her.

"We must have had different circumstances." I said.

"I was in a terrible house fire. Smoke everywhere. I really thought I might cough myself to death and then he showed up—like some hero out of a book to save me. How did you die?"

It took me a moment to puzzle out what she'd said. *How did I die?* I wasn't dead. Neither was she, as she herself had already explained. Her "hero" saved her.

"Car accident." *Is this conversation for real?* "What year are you from?" I didn't care what the answer might be. I only wished I could toss her back to her own year to relieve myself from having to listen to her high-pitched, spastic voice any more.

"1957. It was December. My soldier said it was likely an electric fire from the Christmas tree." She sighed. "He really was dreamy."

"By the time you get to 2010, dreamy means you aren't paying attention. Not that you're good looking. Just so you know."

She looked seriously depressed over this news. "Is that true? Oh darn. That's too bad. Dreamy is a great word."

It took all my will not to shake my head. Alison went several minutes without saying anything, but I could tell the silence gap tortured her.

"I'm so excited to be here, I could just bust!" She finally gushed, popping up to a sitting position and throwing her legs over the side of the bed.

It was like she'd come from another planet. "Technically, we were kidnapped. What part of the word 'abduction' are you not getting?"

"My soldier saved me!" She declared, planting both her fists on her hips. "I'd be dead in that fire along with my whole family if he hadn't pulled me out. He saved me!"

I grunted and shoved my drawer closed, standing up straight so I could face her directly. "And it never occurred to you to wonder why he didn't bother saving the rest of your family?"

"He couldn't!" She jumped to her feet. "It was already too late for them!"

I turned my back on her, shaking my head. "Whatever," I mumbled.

She huffed for several moments. "I wanted us to be friends," she said to my back. "You shouldn't be making things so difficult for yourself."

Her comment made me wince. She was right, of course. Making things harder would only . . . well, make things harder. My tendency to sabotage myself was a natural reaction. But I didn't have Winter to make up that difference for my behavior anymore. Yes, I despised my roommate on a snap judgment, not that I thought I might be wrong. In fact, I felt pretty sure I was dead on. The word lunatic had crossed my mind several times already in regard to her, but with Tag's warning about being careful what I called people, I kept my thoughts on her lunacy to myself. Giving her a chance and at least *trying* to be civil wouldn't hurt me. "Look, I . . . We can be friends, okay? I'm sorry if I seemed rude. This is just a lot to handle, you know? So much got left behind. I'm not sure how to make it all okay in my head."

Her eyes misted, and the hands that had been planted on her hips moments before were now clasped tightly in front of her. "I do know what you mean. My mom, and dad, and baby brother were in the house. It was a miracle the way one minute I was choking on smoke and the next minute breathing clean air. I asked him to go get them, and even tried to run into the house to save them myself, but he held me back and said it was too late. I'm glad to be taken here, where I won't have to be reminded of them all the time."

I pitied her. Her whole family gone. But my whole family was gone too. Who deserved the greater pity? *This is not a competition for who had the worst day.* Aunt Theresa used to say that whenever we started whining. "I'm sorry," I said to Alison.

And in the next moment her eyes were tear-drop free. She'd only just come from her tragedy and seemed to be fine with it. I'd had four days to try to deal with mine, and I was still messed up. How could she adjust so well? So quickly?

"When did you leave your time?" I asked.

"Oh, just this morning. We only had a few minutes for me to catch my breath before he whisked me away from that awful smoke and the sight of the burning house. He said he'd timed our window differently so I could have the luxury of a decent bath and the ability to clean up and get myself in order before the other arrivals. I already met one of the others. He was completely drea—" she frowned and brightened in the space of an eye blink. "Anyway, he was nice." She seemed unsure if "nice" was an acceptable term or not.

She spoke of that awful smoke and that burning house with her family inside of it as if they were a paper-cut on her finger.

"And did you see that bathtub?" Her eyes went huge as though she were trying to make them the same size as the bathtub.

She talked about the new clothes as though she'd never seen new clothes. Even I, with no parents, and getting scooted from home to home, had been given new clothes every once in a while. She talked about the size of the room and bathroom. I couldn't argue with her awe on either of those things. I was just as awe struck. Well, maybe not *just* as. She acted as though she really had died, and this was her heaven.

I didn't understand. Not even a little bit. My life had been kind of crummy up until the day of the accident, but it was still mine. I still wanted it.

Alison chattered away like a happy little squirrel, blissfully unaware of the boy standing behind it with a sling shot.

She chattered until the room chimed three long bell tolls—our warning that it was time to go meet this professor. Alison hopped off the bed and smoothed down the skirts of her dress before she looked at me and paused mid-step to the door. She stared as though just barely seeing me for the first time, in spite of the fact we'd been together in our room for two hours. "You aren't really wearing that?"

It was as much of a question as it was a statement. She may as well have told me flat out I looked horrible. I glanced down at Winter's ruffled blouse and my jeans. "What's wrong with what I'm wearing?"

"Don't you want to make an impression?"

An impression. I *did* want to make an impression, but the question was, what kind of an impression did I want to make? The question offered no answers, but Winter's shirt wrapped around me, like armor protecting me. I had no intentions of changing.

"I like what I'm wearing." I lifted my chin a little, like a stubborn child refusing to take off her superhero costume for school.

"Kathleen asked us to clean up and change into something appropriate."

"But who decides what's appropriate?" I continued walking to the door and had it open while she still stood stammering about clothes in the middle of the room.

She caught up in several steps and looked like she might push me back into the room. "*Pants* are never appropriate."

I smiled and closed the door to our room with a resounding slam so she'd know I had no intentions of going back in for any reason. "When I'm from, *everyone* wears pants. And they look appropriate almost all the time."

"Your time sounds terrible. I'm certainly glad to not be there." She wrinkled her nose in dissatisfaction as we walked to the elevator. Well, I walked; she flounced. I'd never seen a real honest-to-goodness flounce before. It was almost cute. Irritating and cute, exactly like a squirrel.

"Going down," the elevator said.

"Isn't this place just amazing?" Alison said bouncing slightly on her toes as though she couldn't contain her own energy. "Talking elevators? Sidewalks in the sky? Cars that fly? And how sleek everything looks? It's amazing, isn't it?"

"Amazing," I muttered.

"Are you not impressed? Oh, did cars fly in your time too?" She moaned. "Oh how I must seem silly to you, gawking like a child at a department store window."

"No. Cars didn't fly in my time. You don't seem silly to be amazed by things you've never seen. If I'm not impressed, well, it's because it takes a lot to impress me." That was true. I'd expected better things of my future than to kill babies and have wars. Alison's soldier probably hadn't told her any of that. Tag had likely said a great deal of things to me that he shouldn't have said simply because we had so much time together where there was nothing to do but talk.

I wondered what sorts of things they might say at our orientation. Would they tell us the truth? Would Tag be there? I hoped with all my might that he was there. *Please don't have killed him for bringing me late.*

The elevator doors opened to what Kathleen called the casual room. People were already there—a lot of people. I blinked several times in bewilderment over how full the room was. It looked like a high school dance with all the suits and dresses. Instead of feeling out of place in my jeans and Winter's shirt, I hugged my arms to myself so I could feel her shirt against me. I'd never gone to a new school without her. And here I was—alone. My clothing was the closest I would get to having my Wineve with me.

I stepped out of the elevator and into the casual room. The people all seemed to be my age. They were in their late teens or early twenties. They all looked like clean cut, upper class kids, the kinds who would grow up to be bankers and lawyers. How did I get mingled into this mess with people who would snub me the moment they found out I was practically an orphan, that my mother had been so drugged out, she forgot to feed her own children?

But as I walked through the crowd, the apprehensive mood struck me. These people had all been ripped away from their homes too. These were all people who'd survived something tragic and terrifying. Alison's flagrant disregard for the tragedy that had befallen her didn't mean that everyone would be like that. These were people with families, and dreams, all gone. And I was one of them. Would my past matter when we shared that bond? Would any of them need to know my past at all?

No one seemed to notice my jeans. They were all quietly talking to each other. Little clumps of huddled, frightened kids. In one group near me, I heard whispers of a boating accident. He'd been swept off the boat in a storm and almost drowned.

In another group, they whispered of a kidnapping. Her abductor had meant to kill her, and would have succeeded if her soldier hadn't come like a guardian angel. Tears trailed down her face, and her lips trembled as she spoke.

I stood with them, eavesdropping on their stories and finding myself, in some ways, grateful to the soldiers who had taken them away from what would have been the final moments of their lives. She'd been kidnapped for real, not like Tag had taken me, but by someone who meant to harm her and then dispose of her. Could I say the soldier hadn't been right to rescue her? Even if she never saw her family again, at least no one would hurt her. Could I argue with that?

I stood with them, wondering if I'd misjudged. I stood with them and waited for proof one way or the other.

"My students!" The voice called over the hum of quiet conversations. Everyone fell silent and turned to the raised platform at the end of the room. The man's long thin fingers curled around the sides of the podium as he gripped it. His short cropped black hair had been feathered back. He was tall, but not so tall as to be overbearing. He looked like he could be running for congressman. He waited until he had everyone's total attention.

"My students. No doubt you all feel bewildered by today's events. No doubt you are all tired and in need of rest and time to think and mourn. I know how hard today is for many of you."

Thus far, he'd pegged my feelings completely. His quiet voice carried strength, and, without wanting to, I found myself nodding as he spoke.

"I know your hearts, my students. And I call you my students, because I have brought you here to learn and to better yourselves. I am a professor, after all, a teacher, a guide. My name is Professor Raik.

I expect to be addressed this way at all times. I've brought you out of the senseless tragedy that would have been the end of your lives so you might yet accomplish great things for humanity."

He let that hang in the air, and I truly felt from the soft kindness in his words that my death would have been a tragedy—that I really did have things to accomplish still.

He shifted and ran his gaze over the room, almost seeming to be picking out every individual and acknowledging them personally. When his gaze fell on me and then moved away, it immediately swerved back. His brow furrowed slightly. I held my breath, wondering if he would call attention to the fact that I didn't belong, wondering if he would yell out that my mother had allowed her boyfriends to try to hurt my sister and me while she got high on the drugs they brought her. He didn't say anything, just inclined his head in a nod and finished his visual accounting of the room without another glance at me.

He talked about the great university where we would attend school. He talked about the importance of self-cleanliness and our accountability to ourselves to maintain standards higher than everyone else we may come in contact with.

"You are the elite. You are the New Youth of the world. You are not to mistreat others for their limits, but neither are you to lower yourself to their levels, or you will find yourself limited as well. But for now, I welcome you. Build friendships with one another. Learn as much as you can from one another. There are no dating restrictions amongst yourselves, but you are not to fraternize with people born naturally to this time. You are above them. You are better. You are my elite!"

A cheer went up. I almost joined in, so moving was his speech patterns and his convictions in the words he said—except the general entered the room. He stayed off to the side and tried to fade into the background, but his red hair drew my eyes to him whether he'd intended it or not. Several others noticed him, but discarded the information of seeing him as though they'd already taken the professor's words to heart and considered themselves much more important than this soldier, even if he was a general.

Or maybe they didn't know he was a general. Maybe they thought him to only be a soldier. Either way, seeing the general made me remember that I wasn't above all the people of this crazy future. I considered Tag to be my absolute equal.

The general's presence made my mouth go dry. Had he executed Tag already and had come to inform the professor of that task's completion? I slipped through the crowd talking with more animation now than they had before. The Professor had used this moment of everyone's need to chatter amongst themselves to lean close to the general.

I eased through a small cluster of girls and wedged myself close to the podium where I could overhear what the redheaded general was saying.

"... has been silenced."

"Does anyone in the barracks know about Taggert's time lapse?" Professor Raik asked.

"No. I've kept it quiet."

"Good. We don't need questions or concerns about loyalty at this critical moment when it all comes together. Get back to the barracks. Keep the soldiers occupied; offer them a bonus for their work. They've earned it." The professor turned back to his podium, and I immediately nodded vigorously at the girl across from me as though agreeing with whatever she'd said.

The Professor cleared his throat, and began his oration anew. More pretty promises of luxury and elitism, more enticing dangling of education, position, popularity, power. He explained the state of sterility humanity faced, the reality of the world's inability to create posterity. But he left out a lot of details, important details. He made the world sound far more needy and sad than Tag had. Tag had spoken things as they likely really were. Professor Raik made it seem as though each of us in the room was solely responsible for the future of mankind. He didn't mention public nurseries. He didn't mention the crazies, the war, the law, the fear. His words were coated with hope and sincerity and promises.

Ugly wearing a beauty suit.

But his words were like static roaring through my ears. I could only think of the words, "has been silenced." *They've killed him*, I thought. *They've killed Tag.*

FIFTEEN

The professor stood down from the podium and invited everyone to partake in the refreshments set up on the opposite side of the room. He crossed the room to where the refreshments were located at a leisurely pace, taking the time to shake hands and welcome his students.

He exchanged soft words of comfort to a few who had voiced concern over their families, and encouraged them with even more words. Everyone he neared seemed to stand taller. His charisma and ability to put people at ease wiped out any of the discordant rumblings that had been evident at the beginning before he'd begun talking.

I'd have likely felt the same way except . . . *they killed Tag.*

Once he'd arrived at the refreshment table, he announced he would be meeting with us each individually to discuss our plans. He poured a drink, handed it off to the girl next to him, and poured another. Of that one he took a sip, smiled, and excused himself from the room.

The room's volume grew immediately. I heard the word "dreamy" and looked around to find Alison talking with another girl. I would have smirked, but was too busy trying to devise a way out of the building without anyone noticing. Without the ability to move in and out of buildings, how could I ever get into the barracks? If only I had one of those stupid rings! I had to find out for sure if he was okay. The speculation—the mere *thought* of them killing Tag drove me to irrationality unlike any I'd ever experienced.

Because if they killed him, then it would have been all my fault. And though Tag and I had shared a rough beginning. He was all I had left in the world.

Kathleen tapped the girl who Professor Raik had given the drink to on the shoulder and whispered in her ear. The girl blushed and stammered and hurried to follow Kathleen out the same door Professor Raik had gone through.

I moved through the room, coming near but never entering conversations as I inspected the windows and how they opened. Tag had mentioned something called entry sensors. He'd said that any unapproved entry was recorded and investigated by the police. That crossed windows off my list of escape plans.

Five minutes later, the girl returned, still blushing, though no longer stammering, and fiddling with a ring on her hand. As she moved through the door, it glowed green for her as it did for Kathleen and Professor Raik. They'd given her an IDR.

Kathleen tapped a guy this time, and he followed her out, only to return a few minutes later with a dazed expression and a ring on his hand. One by one, we would all get our rings, our symbols of belonging here in this future. I moved closer to the refreshment table, and consequently closer to the door, eager to be given access to the world in which I now lived.

"This is all really *wow*, huh?" A blonde guy who stood a whole head taller than me said.

"What?" If my face looked as confused as my mind felt . . .

"It's a lot to take in." He repeated similar sentiments to what I'd told Alison. At least one person here was capable of rational thought.

"Yes. Quite a lot."

He stuck out his hand. "I'm Jay Savage."

Cautiously, I took his hand. "Summer. My name's Summer Rae." I paused. "Savage? Is that your real name?"

He smiled. "The one I was born with. So how did you . . . come to be here?"

At least he didn't ask how I'd died. "Car wreck and a soldier. You?"

"Hiking accident. I was falling—and then I wasn't. I don't know how he saved me. The soldier said wild animals ate my corpse so no one ever found me, until some scout troop was out climbing in the same place nearly half a century later. They identified me through the id in my wallet and old missing person ads." He picked up a glass, filled it with whatever they were serving as punch, and handed it to me. The glass looked like glass, but felt like the weird hard plastic dishes back at the house Tag and I'd stayed in.

I accepted his offering, but didn't drink. "Your mother must have been relieved to finally know what happened to you. After all those years."

His smoothly-shaved face darkened. He bit his lip and scowled as though working through something important in his head. He gave himself a little shake and offered over a tight smile. "I doubt she ever found out anyway. My mom wasn't young. She was forty eight. Forty eight just yesterday and today . . ." He gave himself another shake. "A half a century would make her near a hundred. She would've died without knowing." He nodded as if we'd agreed on his assessment. I nodded too. He needed me to agree—to be on his side. His pain was etched deep on his face. "They had me leave my shirt with the wallet at the scene, like a land-marker of what should have happened. I'm grateful to be alive—don't get me wrong. I just never imagined my life turning out like this."

I smiled sympathetically. "I hear you. This is . . ." I shrugged. Jay looked so lost, that changing the subject seemed the only way to keep him from crying. His worries took the focus off of my own. "So what year are you from?" The get-to-know-you questions we used were weird. How did you die? What year are you from? And yet, we all seemed to be acclimating to those questions as though they were perfectly normal.

"1987."

"Wow. I wasn't even born yet. How old are you?"

"Seventeen. What year are you from?"

"2010. I'm seventeen too." I answered the question before he could ask it.

"I'm still older than you." He smiled and took a sip of his drink.

"Oh whatever! We're the same age. I might even be older, since I'm turning eighteen in a month, or at least I *was* turning eighteen in a month. I don't know how that works anymore." I eyed the table and found that the food looked pretty good. I grabbed a plate and started loading up. If I got my ring and was able to get out and find Tag, there was no telling when my next meal would be. I had agreed to help save the future, but I couldn't do that without confirming his safety.

"Still, I *was* born twenty-three years before you."

I snorted softly. "Well don't go thinking that makes you more mature than me. Chronology and maturity aren't the same thing."

He laughed. His laugh made me smile. It felt good to talk to someone in my same situation who seemed *normal*.

He sobered up a bit and glanced over the rest of the room. "How many people do you think are here?"

I followed his gaze and did a quick estimation, "150 maybe?"

"We're going to be here a long, long time then if that guy plans on taking that much time with every person." Jay's acidic tone made me pause.

"You don't like him?"

"I don't trust him. Let's get our food and find a place to sit down."

I almost protested, believing that by staying close to the door, I'd be picked out among the first and could be on my way. But I had a pile of food to plow through on my plate and would need some time to eat it. I followed Jay to one of the couches.

After a few more minutes of conversing, I determined Jay had exactly the conspiracy theory mind that could be friends with someone like me. If I ever decided to ditch the future, I'd ask if he wanted to come with me.

We ate, talked, and were joined by several others. An eighteen-year-old girl, named Mita Sarin, had been in a biking accident in India. She was stunningly beautiful, but still looked incredibly shaken over her day's events. A twenty-year-old guy named Edward Woodard from London had been hit by a train while listening to his MP3 player. He seemed relieved and relaxed to be included in an opposing option from the train. Apparently several had been the victims of actual kidnappers—people who had taken them to hurt them and kill them. All of those were grateful to the soldiers who'd saved them, grateful to be anywhere but where they'd been, grateful to Professor Raik for giving them a second chance to live.

There were a few more hiking incidents, a few drownings, a couple bombings, many car accidents, motorcycle accidents, and fires. There was even one guy who said he'd been killed in a bowling accident. I didn't bother to ask him what such a death might actually entail.

These were only the ones around me. There were a lot of people I didn't talk to, a lot of stories I didn't know. But I felt torn with every new story.

Most of the people praised Professor Raik for being life and salvation. Others were too traumatized from the day's events to make any judgment, and the very small minority who seemed genuinely ticked off to be where they were. Once Jay put the numbers to how long we'd all be waiting for the professor to talk to each of us, everyone in our circle let out a collective groan.

Kathleen tapped my shoulder. "Miss Rae. Professor Raik will see you now."

I stood, met Jay's eye, and found courage there. I took a deep breath and followed Kathleen out of the room.

She led me down the hall to a plush office filled with extravagant woodwork and lots of oil paintings. I recognized a few paintings and figured they must be copies, since the originals were supposed to be in museums. Professor Raik sat behind a large, imposing desk, his hands folded neatly in front of him. When I fully entered the room and Kathleen closed the door, leaving me alone with him, he stood and extended his hand.

Even more cautiously than I had with Jay, I took his hand and shook it.

"Miss Rae. It's a delight to meet you. The reports of you were excellent. Excellent," he repeated, then pulled his chair in under him as he sat. "Please be seated." His arm waved toward the chair next to me. I sat down.

"Did you not find your new wardrobe to your liking?"

"It's fine, I guess. I'm just comfortable this way." I picked at the loose threads in the knees of my jeans. When he noticed, I forced my hands to sit still in my lap.

"You experienced a lapse in time from the moment you were taken from your time and the moment you arrived here. I'd like to hear about your travels in the interim between times." He settled back, his hands clasped together once again on the desk in front of him.

What if Tag told them something different from what happened? How would I know? If they hadn't already killed him, they might after I say something stupid. My heart pounded so hard, I was sure if I looked down, I'd see the thump against Winter's shirt. "I'm sure Tag can tell you better than I could. He's a lot smarter than I am."

"That's not true at all. Yes, *Taggert* is intelligent, but we know you are also very intelligent, more so in many ways. You are the elite. *Taggert* is only a soldier. Naturally, your viewpoint is valued differently." He emphasized Tag's full name, insinuating that my shortened version, Tag, might be too familiar and therefore inappropriate. And Professor Raik may as well have said outright that a soldier was of far less importance than a pure blooded *student* from the past.

"The weather was bad." I tried to remember what Tag had told the general with the red hair, and thought on how Tag had refused to say anything at all to the driver. Tag had said he would only give information to the professor, yet he had given information to the general too. I wondered if he did that on purpose just so I could hear, just so our stories were the same. "The Orbital didn't work right because of the weather and we ended up in the middle of the Rainier volcano explosion. It was a mess! Tag saved my life for the second time when he got us out of there. The Orbital wasn't working at all then. I thought we were really going to die, but Tag made it work." I used the name

Tag instead of Taggert as much on purpose as Professor Raik had. It was the only power struggle I dared to engage myself in with this man.

"What happened then?" Professor Raik didn't blink, didn't move. A fly could have landed on his nose, and the professor would likely not have noticed it.

"We ended up in another time—sometime in the future. The Orbital still didn't work and we were hungry and tired. Tag took care of me. He found us a place to lie low and get rest and food, while he figured out the problem with the Orbital. As soon as he fixed it, we jumped here." I nodded, more to myself than to him, thinking surely I said nothing too incriminating. Surely my story had to match Tag's enough to clear him of anything wrong.

"Did you get to know Taggert very well?" He no longer put the emphasis on the name, likely thinking I was too dumb to take the hint.

"No. He never would talk about himself." That bit of truth bugged me. He *hadn't* ever talked about anything personal. He never gave any hint as to the person he really might be, except for acknowledging that he'd cried while reading *A Sliver of Midnight*.

"But you like him."

"I respect him."

The professor mulled that over before saying, "So if you didn't talk, or discuss things, what did you do to pass the time?" Professor Raik now leaned back in his big chair, as though merely curious. But his eyes sharpened, and fear shivered through me.

"The house had a library. We read books."

This information took him off guard. "Books?"

"Yes. We read books." I smiled—or tried to. My nerves were so strung out, the smile might have looked more like a wince.

Professor Raik cleared his throat. "I see. Well then, good. A packet will arrive at your dorm room tomorrow for you. It will list classes available, so you can enroll in the university. We expect great things from you and your fellow students. You will have two days to acclimate and get the enrollment forms filled out. School will start Monday."

I waited. He seemed done with me, but I waited. Where was my ring? Surely he'd give me a ring. Everyone else had come back with one.

"That will be all, Miss Rae." He pushed up off the desk to a standing position and smiled his running-for-congressman smile. "A pleasure to meet you." He shook my hand again as he ushered me to the door.

I stopped at the door, thinking fast, trying to stall for time in case he'd forgotten that one important part of this meeting. "But sir? What day is today? If classes start Monday, what day is today?"

"Today is Friday," he answered.

"Oh. Okay then. Thanks." I hesitated, but couldn't think of anything else to say. Frustrated and uncertain what to do next, I grabbed the door handle wondering if it would open for me even if I didn't have the ring. My bedroom door opened, so it might.

"One more thing Miss Rae." Professor Raik turned and went behind his desk.

I tried to contain my desperation for whatever he might be getting. It was so important that he not know I anticipated anything, suspected anything, or *planned* anything. I'd decided no one could read my mind. If they could, I'd be in jail already.

"It's a gift from the Amerio Regent to welcome you to the future." He held out a small wooden box on the palm of his hand.

I reached for the box, working hard to keep my hands from trembling. "What is it?" I hoped the question sounded innocent enough.

"Open it."

I did as instructed. "Oh. It's a ring." I hoped I sounded surprised.

"Yes. Put it on."

I did as instructed and then examined it on my hand. I put it on my wedding band finger like Tag had worn his. Professor Raik didn't say that it mattered what hand I wore it on, but it fit best there anyway.

"It's an identification ring or an IDR. Blood samples were collected from you, and your genetic code was fused with the ring. You cannot use another's ring because it only functions when in contact with the living DNA it's fused with. It's a means of communication, identification, entertainment, it is our monetary system. If you enter a store, you need not burden yourself with a purse, or a pocket full of clunky coin and paper. Your financial accounts are tied to your IDR. Shortly, we will give instructions on how things work here. The ring will be better explained then."

"It sounds complicated. I'm glad we'll get some instructions. Thank you." I smiled and left the room, careful to shut the door behind me. My smile dropped as soon as the door clicked closed.

What he didn't say interested me more than the things he had. It occurred to me that the ring would be traceable. If a door opened for me with the ring, then it stood to reason, there would be a log kept of that door opening. By giving us the rings, they would be able to track us, keep tabs on our comings and goings. The ring was a leash for an unsuspecting dog.

Stupid! And here I'd been thinking the ring would grant me freedom. Where was my brain? I glared at the ring, even the fact that it was possibly the most beautiful piece of jewelry I'd ever seen, I wanted to throw it out the window. Tiny suns and moons chased each other around the wide band.

"All the scroll work and pictures are encoded with data. So it's functional as well as beautiful."

Startled, I looked up to see Kathleen who'd come to collect me and escort me back. "Is everyone's designed differently?" I asked. "How would they know what size to get?"

"While the soldier collected data on you, he sent it back to be processed. They knew the symbols you felt connected to and tried to emulate them on your ring. Personalized IDR's are very expensive, and Professor Raik and the Regents wanted you to have the best." She started walking behind me, herding me forward.

I didn't like having been spied on, but appreciated how closely the ring matched the sun and moon quilts that belonged to Winter and me. Tag must have known how much I would miss them and, in his own way, tried to recreate them for me.

The rest of the day offered no time to escape or plan for escape. Though Professor Raik's time spent with each student became markedly shorter—less than a minute in some cases, it still took forever. After half of us had received our rings, they sent that half to the auditorium. The other half was taken to a day spa of sorts, with pedicures, manicures, massages, and steam rooms. They were much more comfortable while awaiting their rings that way. Eventually we switched places with them, and we got the royal treatment while they learned about their new world.

For all of Professor Raik's understanding that we needed time to rest and mourn, he hardly gave us time to breathe. We were tossed from one seminar to another, learning about the technology of the future, learning we each had what they called lapdesks in our rooms to do our homework on. They didn't mention implanting hard drives into our brains, but they likely would sometime later, after we'd acclimated to our new environment. Jay stayed close the whole day. So did Alison and a guy named Eddie, who seemed to have taken a liking to me throughout the afternoon.

After the spa treatments and the seminars, we had dinner. The dining hall was set up like a fancy five star restaurant in that the room was filled with round tables and real cloth tablecloths. But it also had a buffet style line for us to go through so we picked out our food on the pretty silver trays and sat ourselves down at the various tables.

By the time they left us to ourselves, I was exhausted and unable to think well enough to devise a plan out of the building.

The next day, the packets arrived for Alison and me. The packets were not at all what I'd expected. We each received a slip of paper with a code that granted us access to the lapdesks which were run by the pulse power from our brains and rings. The actual "packet" of information had to be accessed from their internal servers. Everything was digital as far as the "paperwork" they wanted us to fill out.

The lapdesks weren't portable like the laptop from my time. They were permanent fixtures of my room. The portable computer came from the ring, which could be projected to any surface or viewed through a fancy set of glasses Professor Raik provided us.

I chose the classes, ate the meals, attended the lectures, and felt frazzled by the fact that they kept me so occupied, I couldn't focus on how to check on Tag. I could come back and be the dutiful student as soon as I knew he was okay. I kept thinking the words that the general had said, "has been silenced."

In what ways could they have silenced Tag?

SIXTEEN

Three days later, I still had no clue how to get time to myself, and no clue how to beat out the IDR and entry sensors on every building in the world. Inoculations had been nightmarish. They sent us down an assembly line of nurses who held tools that looked like Paul's nail gun. Each nurse slammed the gun into our biceps, forcing dissolvable needles and random cures to diseases I hadn't even heard of into our flesh. The nurses called the needles *inserts*. They said that it worked the same as a regular needle from our times, but that these were far more sanitary. I left the assembly line with a ridge of inserts under my skin that the nurses promised would be gone by morning. It hurt a lot.

Monday morning found me with no ridge on my bicep and rushing along with everyone else trying to find the room for my first hour of university in the future.

"We should go to the library." Jay suggested this during lunch. We had two more classes after lunch and then several hours to ourselves before dinner. *The library!* And a few hours that belonged to me. Tag had said he lived behind the coliseum library. I might be able to get close enough to the barracks to find out what happened to him.

I readily agreed to go with Jay, and Eddie readily agreed to accompany us. Eddie frowned at Jay as though somehow Jay was trying to ease in on Eddie's territory. Eddie's attitude irritated me.

"I'm not your girlfriend," I told him as we walked along the garden tunnels, which I had learned were officially called the sky gardens. Jay snickered. Eddie glared over at Jay, and acted offended I'd suggest that he thought anything different.

"Of course you aren't. We haven't even been on a date yet." He stretched his neck as though his collar might be too tight.

Jay coughed into his hand and smirked at me with an eyebrow raised.

Eddie was from the year 1962. He'd been about to go off to Vietnam and found he'd been too afraid. So he'd shot himself instead. He'd meant to shoot himself in the foot or something like that, nothing that would kill him, but with his inexperience with guns, he made a mess of his face instead. Eddie had a habit of looking at himself in mirrors as we walked by them. I wondered if he was doing it to verify to himself that his face really was just fine. He hadn't actually volunteered the information about dodging the draft to anyone but his roommate, James. James had been the one to gladly share that information with everyone else.

Once we were out several buildings away from the dormitories, Jay took a deep breath and grinned. "Smell that, guys?"

"Smell what?" Eddie asked with a bite to his words, obviously still not happy over Jay laughing at him.

"Freedom." Jay turned his grin on me. "What do you think, Summer?"

A tightening in my shoulders seemed to ease the farther we moved from the dormitories. "Definitely freedom." I had almost become used to the way the ground felt as though it swayed under my feet.

"Did you know the city sells the produce in these sky gardens to the restaurants and grocery stores? They take the profit and do—well, who knows what the government does with profits from anything. I think we should try one of those restaurants out. We should see if the government is any good at farming." Jay seemed to be the type of person who wanted to try everything.

I wanted to argue. The urgency to find Tag, to make sure he was okay overwhelmed me, but would my hesitance look suspicious? Besides, Jay's idea had merit. It might be smart to figure out the workings of the world we now lived in. "They did say in our packets we had a spending account. We could get a fruit bowl or a salad or something. Well, you can get the healthy stuff, Jay. I want a doughnut." I agreed.

Jay wrapped an arm around my shoulder and rubbed his knuckles on my head. "Exactly. If anyone asks, we can tell them it was research."

Jay and I turned right, and started walking toward where we knew shops to be. Eddie stayed exactly where he was. "What about the library?" He called from behind us. His voice had an annoying whine to it; both Jay and I grunted at the noise.

"C'mon, Ed. We're still heading in the direction of the library. We just want to make a stop or two along the way." We kept walking. If Eddie wanted to come with, he could catch up.

Figuring out my spending account was almost as important as finding out what happened to Tag. Figure out the system. That had always been my way. Tag had mentioned I wouldn't have to figure out the system anymore—that I wouldn't have to cheat it anymore, but old habits died hard. Having Jay with me made it seem less like outright mutiny on my part, and more like a prank.

We found a grocery store and went in. I held my breath as I waited to see if the door turned green or red with my approach. The green glow appearing around the doorframe actually startled me. Jay's grin widened.

"Good to know that works," he muttered under his breath.

Eddie scowled as we went in. Future stores were definitely prettier than stores from my past. Everything looked more like a boutique or someone's actual home, rather than a grocery store. The displays were beautiful—organic looking in their colors and set up. There wasn't a lot of actual product on the shelf. The huge and elaborate displays didn't leave room for too much product. Advertisements were more plentiful in the actual stores than they were in the sidewalks—which meant that they were everywhere—little screens advertising products and services flashed at us from every possible place.

"I have never really seen pretty fruit before." I picked up a nectarine. It looked so shiny, it could have been a gift from the queen to Snow White, even if it wasn't an apple.

"Or vegetables either." Jay had a couple of carrots in his hand. We looked around for those little plastic produce bags, but couldn't find any. No doughnuts either. We finally gave up and went to check out, only we couldn't find a cashier anywhere.

"Maybe we should just leave?" Jay suggested.

Eddie hurried to stand in front of the door and flung his arms open wide. "You're not getting Summer in trouble with the law!"

I had to smile at that. It was like having my own Doberman. "Heel, Eddie. He isn't suggesting we leave without paying. As I moved closer to Eddie, a friendly female voice said, "Thank you for shopping with Day's Market, Summer Rae."

I halted in my tracks and looked around. "Who said that?" I whispered.

Jay pivoted, his eyebrows climbing half-way up his forehead. He slowly moved toward us, and when the door glowed green, the same friendly voice said, "Thank you for shopping with Day's Market, Jay Savage."

Jay laughed and looked like he'd applaud if he hadn't been holding the carrots. "Good to know that works too." He pushed through Eddie's still outstretched arms and said, "Let's go, guys."

"You have to pay!" Eddie said.

"We did, Ed. Didn't you hear the nice lady thank us for shopping with them?" With Eddie's confused expression, Jay clapped him on the back. "You did not read enough comic books, Ed. Or all of this would be a little more comfortable for you." Jay held out one of the carrots to Eddie who only shook his head in refusal and looked grumpy in general.

"But how much did we spend? And how much is left in our accounts? For all we know we just bought four-hundred-dollar carrots." I took a bite of my nectarine and smiled at how exactly right it tasted. Gratitude filled me for all the things that hadn't changed. Nectarines still tasted like nectarines. The sky was still blue, and even if there was an overabundance of people whose hair was blue too, I could deal with that, maybe . . . I could deal with it if Tag were still somewhere under that blue sky.

"In my IDR class, they talked about finances and how the IDR's keep track. They said something about Pulse Power. I'll find out how we access the balance," Jay said.

I nodded. We walked along the shops more, noting how the shops all seemed very specialized instead of all-encompassing like the stores of our time. All the shops were in areas like malls, each store catering to one specific need. I did find a Dunkin Donuts and got me a Boston crème.

Jay looked around at all the stores and the people moving in and out of those stores and frowned. "Do you guys wonder what the dark levels are like?"

Sweat popped out on Eddie's forehead as he shook his head violently. "No, I don't!"

"What do you mean by dark levels?" I asked

"The levels lost in the shadow of the sky rises. I've heard them called the dark levels because sunlight never reaches the ground. We can buy things in these shops here where the businesses are doing okay for themselves, or we could go down and spend our money in the stores that are probably struggling. What do they call the people in the dark levels? POVs?"

"It's dangerous down there." Eddie insisted.

"How do you know? You've never been there." Jay's attention stayed pointedly on me. Whether we went down or not would be my decision.

"We could at least look. If it feels unsafe, we can always come right back up," I said.

Jay grinned. "You're outvoted, Ed." And we walked to the nearest elevator, knowing he'd follow along.

In all honesty, a part of me thrilled at the idea of seeing what lay beneath the city, and another part of me cowered in Eddie-like fear.

But I wanted my feet to touch the ground—real solid earth. People weren't meant to live in buildings in the sky like giants out of fairytales.

"Going down," The friendly elevator said. And down we went, Eddie's nervousness reflected in the mirrored panels of the elevator. My ears popped with our descent, and then the elevator stopped.

The doors opened onto another sky garden walk, we were in shadow, but definitely not darkness. Jay frowned and jabbed his finger on the requested level another time. The friendly elevator voice said, "I'm sorry, Jay Savage, but you are not approved for travel to the lower levels. Please make an alternate choice."

"Who says I'm not approved?" Jay grumbled and hit the level he wanted again.

"I'm sorry, Jay Savage, but you are not approved for travel to the lower levels. Please make an alternate choice."

Eddie's relieved sigh served to only fuel Jay's agitation. The elevator doors had stayed open. With a frown, Jay got out. "C'mon, Summer. There has to be stairs. What would they do in a fire?"

We searched for stairs or fire exits for another hour, but could find no way down past the elevator Nazi. Jay finally gave up, grumbling about the lack of safety, and led us to the library.

The Coliseum Library was easily the most beautiful building I'd ever seen. The glass columns reflected light like huge prisms, casting rainbows on everything. Once inside the glass building, I turned to Jay and Eddie. "I've got some research to do, and I'll get it done faster on my own. I'll catch up with you guys in a little while okay?"

Eddie became visibly nervous. "But what if we don't find you again? We don't know any of these people." He cast a quick glance to the rainbow-colored heads slipping around him. He lowered his voice. "They aren't like us."

"I'll meet you right back here in two hours." I pointed down at the spot where I stood. I wanted to disagree with Eddie's assessment of the other people not being like us, but still feared that maybe crazy law might not be as effective as they'd hoped. And the first day of biology class, we'd learned about the disease that brought us to this future.

Every person not of the New Youth was tainted. We were not allowed to associate with them in any way that would allow us to develop relationships with them as they were beneath us. Any sexual relations that might transpire between New Youth and anyone outside the New Youth would end in a trial and the severest of punishments. They never said execution, but they may as well have. No wonder Tag acted so weird around me.

Keeping Doberman Eddie around might make me feel safer, but he'd never approve of the person I hoped to find. He bought into the idea that we were better than the rest of the world.

"Hey, Ed." Jay took a hold of Eddie's arm and spun him the other direction. "Those girls are from our history class, aren't they?" Jay threw a wink back my direction, and I hurried to slip behind the first set of book stacks.

I walked the outer perimeter of book stacks, looking outside the windowed walls to the city surrounding the building. Nothing called attention to itself as being the barracks. I did two laps around the coliseum and had determined I needed to go outside to the sky gardens to search the surrounding buildings directly when something caught my eye, and my heart skipped a beat. *Tag!*

I touched my hand to the glass window, and almost made myself look stupid by calling out his name when I realized the person standing outside next to a sign with a sideways eight on it wasn't Tag. But he had on the silver-black pants and the black jacket. Another person dressed identically joined the first and they walked off together. Not Tag at all, but definitely Tag's people.

I hurried outside, still no actual plan in mind, just a deep and desperate need to see him for myself, to make sure he was fine. My head ached from trying to keep the words, *he's dead; they killed him because you made him late*, from parading through my brain.

I circled the outside of the coliseum until I saw the sign. Being closer and paying better attention, I realized my sideways eight was really the symbol for infinity. Not many people walked this way. The two soldiers previously by the sign had wandered into the building already. I made my way to the door, trying to be stealthy, but needing to get to the actual entrance to see what color it would glow with my ring. If it glowed red and I didn't try to enter, would it record that I'd strayed near the building without permission? Would it glow green?

With a ragged pull for air, I closed the distance between me and the range of the door. It glowed red.

I cursed under my breath and ducked back to the side of the doors where several trees were clumped together as part of the sky garden aesthetics, offering a small degree of shelter since they weren't exactly big trees. As I stepped back, the red glow vanished, but no matter how many times I blinked, I couldn't see anything but red.

Stupid! Now what? I took a few moments to try to control my breathing while twisting my ring around and around on my finger. I finally slipped it off and tucked it between the roots pushing out of the ground. And then I waited.

A lone soldier exited the building after I'd already counted to sixty four times and was halfway through a fifth. I slipped behind him and slid into the building before the door closed.

If my heart had been beating fast before, it now pounded at Olympian speeds. Inside, several hallways snaked out away from the spacious entryway. "Stupid!" I muttered. Which way to go and how to get there without anyone noticing a random girl in a skirt meandering through their halls? And how would I explain why I took off my ring? How would I defend myself if they decided I was a renegade crazy?

Really stupid.

With no other plan in place, I picked a hallway and started walking down it. I didn't try to hide from the first soldier who passed me, but instead acted as though walking through the off-limit barracks was no big deal. I hurried to address him as he frowned in confusion upon seeing me, and as the hand with his ring moved up to his face, likely to call in and report me.

"Could I get you to help me?" I asked.

His hand dropped upon being directly asked for help. "Sorry?"

"Yes. I'm supposed to deliver a message from Professor Raik to Taggert." *Did Tag have a last name?*

The soldier's eyes dropped to my hands, but I bent my head and forced him to look me in the eye.

The confusion on his face filled me with dread. *Please don't say he's dead. Please don't say he's dead.*

"I'm sorry," the soldier said with that voice of finality that made my stomach plummet into my toes.

I'm sorry could mean only one thing.

SEVENTEEN

"You're sorry?"

"I hadn't heard Raik needed him. I sent him to off duty. Taggert's in the game room."

I held in the sob and blinked back the tears of relief upon hearing he really was still alive. Alive! My Tag was alive! I swallowed the information to digest later. "Would you take me there?"

The man's brow furrowed, and he almost looked like he might question my motives, but he finally said, "K."

Stupid skirt with no pockets. There was nowhere to hide my hands and the bare, ringless fingers. Who makes a skirt with no pockets? I missed my jeans more than ever before. Our feet clapped against the tile floor as we wound around the hall. I paid strict attention to detail, noticing every turn we made, mentally memorizing the path to Tag.

I also noted other entrances. Or I should say, I noted the *lack* of other entrances. What would they do in a fire drill? Could the only exit and entrance really be at the front of the building? And to have no way to get to ground level . . . did these people not have any fire marshal standards or safety codes?

He shoved open a door and said in a gruff and suspicious voice, "Taggert, you got a guest." He stood to the side so that everyone in the room had a full view of me. Tag looked up, along with the eleven other soldiers in the room. They'd been hovered over a table of cards. How much I wanted to start bawling and run to him and make him hold me while I cried. *Alive! You're alive!*

His ice-blue eyes widened at seeing me. And his mouth opened as though he were going to say something before he snapped it shut with a click of teeth, the ice in those eyes melting into fear.

I'd crossed my arms over my chest, tucking my hands into my pits where they couldn't be seen. I hoped I looked like Aunt Theresa with my arms folded like that. I hoped I looked about to deliver a king-size lecture. My mind raced with all the things Professor Raik had said. We were the elite. We were better than soldiers. Better than all the diseased people of the future. Elite and they needed to respect us. We were to never feel lesser. We were to never—"On your feet, soldier. A New Youth came into the room. Don't they teach you respect in this place?" Surprised that my voice didn't crack, surprised that it sounded strong and confident when fear raced through my veins.

All of them jumped to their feet, though I'd been only addressing Tag. I heard a couple of them mutter, "Sorry."

"Professor Raik needs you, Taggert." I said his name with a sneer, my heart breaking for acting so stupid and superior when he really was so much better than me, this guy who'd cried when he read *A Sliver of Midnight*.

"When?" he asked, his voice sounding afraid, whether for me, or for him, or for us both, I didn't know.

"Now." I jerked my head towards the door indicating he needed to get a move on and fast. I exited the room, assuming he'd follow, hoping he'd hurry before the rest realized something wasn't right. The questions already formed on their faces with the narrowing of eyes as skepticism dawned on them.

Tag followed me out, shutting the door behind him, the voices rising in the room we'd exited as the others left in there discussed the meaning of my presence. Tag grabbed my arm and shoved me along the hallway. "Move fast." He swept me away from the room like a wave tugging at a sand castle.

We made it down the hall and around the corner before he said, "What do you think you're doing? You can *not* be here!" He glanced behind us. I did too, afraid of what I might find. The hallway remained empty.

"I had to know!" I whispered.

"Know what?"

I nearly tripped we were moving so fast, not running, not calling that much attention to ourselves, but moving fast just the same. "The general said you'd been silenced and then they questioned me about you like it was the Spanish Inquisition. I thought they'd . . ." I trailed off, trying to catch my breath and feeling rather foolish for charging into the barracks without any real reason than my own paranoia.

"The Spanish what?" He waved away the question before I could answer. "Never mind. They could have ex-ed me, and might have, but I assured them you and I are not friends. By coming here, you make me look a bit like a liar."

"Ex-ed you?" We'd come to another corner. Tag peeked around it before pulling me along again.

"Executed."

"So by me coming here, will they execute you?"

"I doubt it, but you can't ever come back here." He stopped and turned me to face him. "Not ever again, Summer." He took my hands in his. At first, the gesture seemed romantic and my stomach fluttered at his touch. But his fingers searched over my hands. "Where's your IDR?"

"I left it outside. The door went red when I tried to come—"

"How did you get in then?" He looked up and down the hall and, seeming to realize we'd stopped, pulled me along again.

"Someone was leaving; I got in before the door closed."

He growled low in his throat. We'd made it to the front door, it turned green as Tag approached. He opened it and shoved us both through. "Get your IDR."

I went to the trees. He followed me, and, for a moment, I thought he meant to come with me. But he waited while I got my ring and glanced back. "I'll have to report this to Professor Raik."

"You're turning me in?"

"You told the others I was going to Professor Raik. There will be trouble if anyone thinks you lied. We'd better get our stories straight because they'll be questioning both of us. Why would you risk coming to see me?"

His face was close to mine; the ice in his eyes had melted into the warmth and concern I'd grown used to for those few days we were together. "I came because I care about—"

"No! Don't say that. Don't ever say that."

"But it's true." I wanted to slap him for being such a jerk.

"Think, Summer. What will happen if you tell Professor Raik that you—" He couldn't even make himself repeat the words as if completely repulsed by the idea. "Think. What would happen if a pureblood were entangled in the emotions of a soldier? The soldier would get ex-ed, and the pureblood would be quarantined until her mind was so completely wiped of independent thinking that she may as well be a toaster." He took a deep breath. "So tell me again, why would you risk coming to see me?"

"I . . . I wanted you to go back and get my sun quilt. I'm having trouble sleeping at night, and I knew you had the Orbital. I knew you could get it for me."

He exhaled. "Good. That's perfect. And what did I tell you I would do?"

"Don't treat me like some idiot kid who needs to be taught the thinking process. Just tell me what you want me to say. We can have our stories straight that way. I won't be patronized by you, Tag."

His half-smile made me waver between wanting to slap him and wanting to kiss him, which wasn't good. A pureblood could never kiss a soldier. The thought made me inhale sharply.

"You really have become a bossy little pureblood," he said.

Definitely slap. Or maybe I'd punch him and leave the little sun and moon imprint from my ring on his forehead. Had I been thinking about kissing him? Yes. And though he irritated me, I still wanted to—still felt a little piece of me die in knowing I never would be able to.

"I told you I'd ask Professor Raik for you, but that the answer would be no."

"Why is the answer no? I think wanting my sun quilt is a reasonable request."

He stepped away from me. "Are you really going to argue a decision made on a fabricated reason for you to be here?" He took another step away and shook his head. "Don't come back here. I mean this. Never come back."

"But how will I know if you're okay?"

His lip twitched up in an almost half-smile. "Be more worried about you being okay. I can take care of myself. I'm a soldier."

"Yeah, well, for a soldier, you nearly got your butt kicked by a half-starved, sleep-deprived girl. I wouldn't go boasting about your strength if I were you." I jammed my ring on my finger and glared at him. But I didn't glare long, that almost half-smile grew into a full on grin. My legs wobbled underneath me upon seeing that grin.

"You are definitely a fighter. Watching you before I brought you here taught me more about true strength than anything I could learn in the barracks. You're something special."

He cared about me too. I knew it at that moment he declared me as special—not in a New Youth elitist way, but special as in important to him.

"You'd better get out of here."

"What do I do if I miss you," I asked, feeling pathetic and needy.

He looked torn before he said in a rush, "If you need anything, I go to the library every Wednesday at five. Leave a note in *A Sliver of Midnight* with any requests or problems." He turned on a heel and hurried off down the path away from the barracks. I'd almost forgotten he had to really go see Professor Raik now.

What a mess I'd made. And yet, Tag was alive. *Alive!* And he could still smile at me. And I now had a way to get in touch with him. That little bit of knowledge filled me with security. Because I didn't think getting into the barracks again was remotely possible. Not only would they likely be put on alert to watch out for some pureblood female making demands, but I didn't think I'd ever dare to go in there again.

With a quick glance around and finding myself alone and unobserved, I made my way back to the library.

***

"I had to die and get eaten by wolves so I could travel to the future and find true love," Jay said as soon as he saw me. His eyes had kind of a drunken look to them.

"What?" With my mind preoccupied with Tag, and Professor Raik, and coming down from my adrenaline high, Jay made absolutely no sense at all.

"I just met an angel named Jennifer. Oh, just wait until you meet her, Summer. She's amazing; you'll totally love her!" He took a deep breath and exhaled as though breathing in an exotic perfume.

Eddie looked alternately pleased with Jay and his new love-struck feelings and irritated with me for being late.

"Are you allowed to be . . . fraternizing?" I asked this carefully, knowing how Jay felt about the system.

"That's the best part. She's one of us."

It had to have been true love, Jay Savage had just referred to himself in the "us" term. Jay thought the pureblood and the disease blood issue was likely a farce brought on to make us feel superior for reasons he hadn't quite figured out yet. He didn't believe in crazies either. I believed our teachers when they told us about the genetics and the diseases. I believed in crazies too. I believed because I saw the fear on Tag's face when he worried over being out after curfew due to crazy law. Tag hadn't faked that fear. And he hadn't been faking when he said he and I would never be together due to his disease.

Jay thought the whole situation we were in was one elaborate scam. But he kept these opinions to quiet whispers when it was just the two of us.

"And get this!" Jay tapped my arm. "She's from the nineties. So she totally knows who I'm talking about when I say U2 is awesome! She knows who Tom Petty is. She's seen the TV shows, *Moonlighting* and

Night Court. I mean, yeah, she laughed at me when I told her those were my favorite TV shows ever and said that stuff was all out of style, but at least she knows what I'm talking about."

"What are her favorite TV shows?" I felt absent in the conversation, my mind lost to the wondering of what Tag might be saying to Professor Raik at that very moment.

He scrunched up his face. "Something weird. *Friends* and *X-files.* They can't be all that good. I haven't even heard of them."

I laughed. "And that wouldn't be because they hadn't been made yet or anything like that, would it?"

"We're going to be late for dinner." Eddie tapped at his wrist, though he wore no watch. The IDR pulsed knowledge to our minds—things like time, weather, information.

I glanced around. "So where is your dream girl?"

Jay sighed dramatically. "She had to go meet her roommate. Ed's right. We ought to get back before they send the police after us." Jay turned and accidentally knocked into a guy wearing a black and white striped pants and shirt set that looked like he walked out of a 1930's prison. His black hat sat crooked on his dyed white head. An advertisement of a chess game glimmered on his forehead. With a flick of his finger, he straightened his hat and shoved at Jay's shoulder with the heel of his palm.

"Watch it!" the guy said.

"Hey, sorry. It was an accident, right? No need to get crazy."

And *that* was apparently the wrong thing to say. The guy cocked back his fist and aimed it for Jay's nose.

And to my surprise, Eddie caught the fist, twisted the guy's arm around and behind his back, and said through gritted teeth. "Hitting a New Youth might be the last thing you do, you punk." He wrenched the guy around so he faced Jay's bewildered face. "Now apologize, you diseased little mutant."

He'd parroted out Professor Raik's words as though taking a verbal exam. "Yikes." I rubbed my hand over my eyes in exasperation. "Let him go, Eddie."

"*They* are supposed to respect *us!*"

"Hey, Ed. C'mon. It was just a mistake. Let him go." Jay tried to gently ease Eddie's hands off the guy's arm, but Eddie maneuvered out of the way, taking the guy with him. A small crowd gathered around us, their various colored heads bobbing close to each other as they whispered about the newcomers and the new violence.

They called us newcomers. Of course we had to stand out with our natural shades of hair and our way of gawking at everything around us. Did they know who we were or why we were in their world?

"He can go when he apologizes." Eddie's absurd insistence irritated me. A lot.

"Eddie Grayers! You let him go right now!" I crossed my arms, tilted my chin, and narrowed my eyes.

Eddie looked torn. "He was going to hit Jay." He explained this as though I was too stupid to have noticed the exchange before Eddie came barreling in. He'd apparently been in a lot of fights in his life and wasn't used to backing down. He reminded me of the bullies who might make a kid say *uncle* in order to get out of a beating. That and his cowardice when faced with going to war seemed at odds with each other. I wondered what his childhood had been like.

"Well?" I said, hoping he let the guy go before other people decided to join in the fight and kick Eddie's butt. And there was the worry about crazies. Didn't Eddie know how unstable these people could be? But when I looked at Eddie, I realized he wasn't all that stable either. Would he pass the future's crazy test?

"Well?" I hated repeating myself.

Eddie released the guy with a great shove so that the black and white outfit flashed through my vision as he fell to the ground. "Next time, you act more civilly to *us*." Eddie stretched his neck and sauntered off.

Jay had my arm as he whispered, "Time to go."

Since the natives were now waking up to the fact that one of their own had been attacked, they seemed to be forming a mob. Time to go indeed. Jay and I hurried out, but not before Jay looked over at the guy sitting in a blob of black and white holding his arm. "Sorry about that, man," Jay said, and hurried us out of the library.

The problem with a glass building after a fight is that everyone inside knows exactly what direction you went. Not too far into our trek down the sky garden path we'd chosen, the noise of a storm gathering behind us became loud enough to make it apparent we were in trouble.

"Nice going!" Jay shouted. "What did you think you were proving back there?"

"He was going to hit you!" Eddie looked surprised to have to be explaining this detail. "You! One of the New Youth!"

"He would have missed. I've got three older brothers. You think I can't duck a punch?" Jay looked dangerously close to seeing if Eddie could duck a punch.

"Must walk faster." I tried to coax them along, but they were too busy arguing to notice that we were about to be overcome by the angry mob behind us.

We'd come to a place where the sky garden connected to landing pads and rail tracks for cars. That was when several flying cars swooped down on us at once with blue lights flashing from both the bottom and the top. The flying cars landed on the platform.

There were flashbulbs going off in our confused faces as people streamed out of the cars. Many of the people had cameras. They were filming us and taking pictures. We tightened into our little circle of three, squinting in the glare of all the light suddenly shining on us. Though we were nearly to sunset, all the new light of the cameras made the day seem like noon. Soldiers in the silvery black pants and black coats streamed out of the cars as well. They formed a line between the mob and us.

"What have you done, Ed?" Jay whispered.

The door finally opened on the last car to have landed. Professor Raik stepped out with Tag right behind him.

Professor Raik glided up to me, his jet black suit crisp and perfect. His hands were clasped behind his back. Tag, walking along behind by several steps, also had his hands clasped behind his back.

"Miss Rae. You've had a busy afternoon, haven't you? Breaking into the soldier's barracks, creating a frenzy in the street . . . Very busy." He said all this quietly enough that with all the other noise of everything going on, the only people who heard were Tag, Jay, and Eddie.

I didn't respond.

Professor Raik swept a knowing gaze over the three of us and turned to face the crowds. All the cameras pivoted so they focused on him. "Friends!" Professor Raik started. He used the same tones he'd used with us when he first introduced himself to the New Youth—as though he were in a pep rally, as though he were a coach offering encouragement to his winning team. The people loved him.

"My friends, we had meant to introduce you to the New Youth at a different time. You all know of the peril our world faces with the declining birthrate . . ."

Jay leaned over to me. "You broke into the barracks?" he whispered.

"We'll talk later."

"But you did it without me?"

I tightened my jaw against the smile. "Later."

Professor Raik announced to the public, with the press present, that a solution had been found to the dying world. He didn't explain where we came from, only said that we were an experimental part of the solution. He told them that we were under the protection of the state, and the Regents. There would be a zero-tolerance policy of anyone interfering with our movements throughout the city, or of anyone harming us in any way. The world was to defer to us, because we were all the world had left to save it.

It was a moving speech. Had I been on the other side of it, I might have cheered along with the group watching. I might have clasped my hands to my chest and thanked the skies for this New Youth coming to save humanity.

But being on my side of things, I merely felt inadequate and stupid. I felt even worse when a movement in the crowd caught my eye. The man in black and white stripes had shuddered when he heard that we were under the state's protection. His face paled to the color of his hair, and he edged himself back, disappearing into the crowd.

Scared. He didn't respect or revere us, he was afraid. That was not how Tag had described my new status in the future at all. The people loved Professor Raik, but feared the state and the power the state had over them. The New Youth were merely an extension of the state's power—like the soldiers. When I'd first arrived, I saw the soldiers made the people nervous and uncomfortable. Now, I was no different from those soldiers.

And though the striped-zebra guy acted like a total creep to Jay, and deserved to get knocked down a peg or two, Eddie's reaction had been way over the top.

Professor Raik finished his oration to much applause and whistles. He posed by the three of us standing lamely next to him so the press could take more pictures. He reminded us to stand straight and smile so we didn't look nearly as lame as we might have without that reminder. Then he offered us a ride back to the New Youth dormitory.

The offer left no room for us to say no.

So we piled into the long black car Professor Raik had come in. It was set up so the two back seats faced each other, much like I imagined a limousine might look. Eddie's head swelled with so much self-congratulation that I feared it might burst. To my surprise, Tag climbed into the car after us, positioning himself next to Professor Raik. Professor Raik waited until the car was in motion rolling along the tracks before speaking.

"That went well," Professor Raik said. "I hadn't anticipated introducing the New Youth to the world quite so soon. But the opportunity seemed as good as any, and I didn't want to hear of any further altercation from New Youth fighting with the people. No. Best to handle it all now. It does seem, Miss Rae, that whenever I hear of trouble anymore, you're at the center of it. You've only been here a few days, yet I hear of your dealings everywhere I turn."

No one spoke. All eyes fixed on me.

Did he want me to apologize? Did he want me to explain? What did this man with the congressman smile and bird-of-prey eyes want from me?

I sat up straight, borrowed the arrogant snippy voice I remembered from one of the cheerleaders on Winter's team and acted like the elite member of society he kept claiming me to be. "I want my sun quilt. I think it's absurd that you brought us here without allowing us to gather a few things that have meaning to us. We should have been able to grab a photo or two, a piece of jewelry that meant something. A quilt that means something. If your little tribe of soldiers can collect our DNA, test us for disease, and learn enough about us that they can personalize our rings, then surely they can gather one or two mementos so we don't feel like abductees."

"I—I don't feel like an abductee." Eddie scooted away from me and cuddled closer to the door as if to prove that we were *not* together.

What a suck-up.

Jay's eyes looked like they might explode out of his sockets at my little request. "You broke into the barracks so you could get a security blanket?" He blushed at his own outburst and fell silent.

Tag's lip quirked to the side—not exactly a smile, or even a half smile, but the gesture was one of approval. That approval gave me confidence. "It's more than a security blanket. It's a symbol of who I am. Why shouldn't I have the things that make me comfortable? Why should I have to forget what my family and friends look like? If Taggert can make electrons jump orbits and change dimensions to pick me up, he can do it to pick up a few of my things as well."

Tag straightened. Professor Raik's eyebrows climbed his forehead. He leaned over to Tag. "Did you discuss how the Orbital worked with her?"

Tag shook his head. "No, sir."

Professor Raik flashed his congressman smile at me. "It seems she should be taking some science classes. You did sign up for some, I assume."

Confused by this turn of conversation, I shrugged. "A few."

He sighed. "Well, it should be interesting to see how that develops. I'm afraid I cannot grant your request. I apologize and understand the things you feel entitled to have, however those items may carry an unforeseeable part to play in history. Many of the students have police searching for them. They would be deemed runaways if important artifacts turned up missing. If the police stopped looking for many of them, they would never have been discovered and we would have had no way of going back and retrieving them. You speak of pictures, but you must remember that those pictures will still have some impact on the living left behind. They may affect decisions and fates we cannot comprehend. What would a soldier return home to find if he were to meddle in the affairs of time?"

I didn't think he meant for us to answer such a question, but even if we could have answered it, none of us dared for fear of giving the wrong answer. The brakes squealed on the tracks, and the car jolted to a halt. "Miss Rae?" Professor Raik said as I stepped out of the car.

"Yes, sir?"

"I trust we won't have any more instances of your presence in the barracks."

"Of course not, sir. I understand your decision." *I saw Tag alive and well. I figured out how to communicate with him. I got exactly what I'd gone for.*

I smiled at the professor and would have turned that smile on Tag since everything worked out okay and neither of us were likely to be executed any time soon, but Tag was gone.

We stood on the sidewalk and watched the car drive away. "He's an amazing man." The worship in Eddie's voice irritated me.

"You are such a suck-up, Eddie," I said.

At Eddie's confusion, Jay jumped in. "She means brown-noser, kiss up, teacher's pet, sell-out—"

"Hey, I saved you." Eddie insisted as Jay moved towards the front doors.

"No, you embarrassed me and caused a riot. Nothing to be proud of, champ."

Eddie fumed, but we'd already moved into ignore-Eddie-mode. Once we'd moved past Kathleen's desk and into the casual room, we realized something exciting had happened while we were gone.

I found a corner to stand in and take several steadying breaths. Jay found a shorter blonde girl and casually put an arm over her shoulder. That must be Jennifer. He whispered something in her ear, and she laughed. She turned to him, explaining something with great animation. I moved to join them when a hand fell on my shoulder. I turned to meet Tag's eyes.

"Where did you come from?" I whispered. He seemed to appear out of nowhere.

"Your room. Your quilt is on your bed—under the top cover. And a couple of pictures. I found pictures that had duplicates of you and your sister in an album that belonged to your aunt. I admit it worried me a bit in returning to see what might have changed, but everything seems as it was."

"Won't you get caught?"

"Not if you're careful. All the New Youth are gathered. No one has reasons to track Orbitals at this time. I know you need those things. I'm sorry I can't do more for you."

"Are you kidding? Thank you, Tag. You cannot know how much that means to me."

His hand was still on my shoulder, yet I felt his fingers lacing lightly in my hair. "I do know. Truly. I'd better get back before I'm missed, but Summer, thank you for worrying enough over me to come find me. It's been a long time since anyone cared or worried—well . . . thank you."

He hurried and left the room before I could say anything else.

When I composed myself enough to talk to everyone else, I joined Jay. "So what's all the excitement?"

"Oh, hey! Summer, you'll never guess. *We* are all the excitement."

"What?"

"It's true," the girl I assumed to be Jennifer said. "It was all over the news. Everyone heard Professor Raik tell the world about us. They projected the news reports on the wall. Crazy stuff."

"Careful using that word." Alison had come up behind us. "Seriously. I've heard people have been killed over calling someone else crazy."

Jennifer just shrugged. Jay, likely thinking about his little experience with calling someone crazy, cleared his throat.

Jay swatted my arm, "Oh hey! Summer, I'd like you to meet Jennifer."

I smiled and we went to the usual questions: *When are you from*, and *how did you die?*

After only a few moments, I decided Jay's love-at-first-sight was perfect for him.

We went to dinner together and told stories about our lives throughout the decades. We also shared things we'd learned about IDR's, the lapdesks, the internet, our access to information and the world around us. Jay had discovered that the Regents all had access to energy coming from a source called the *Tesla's Ether*. That was how they powered their flying cars and vast estates. Alison talked a lot about her nails. I didn't talk much at all. I listened and absorbed what I heard.

They had all decided to catch a movie in the theater. I claimed to be tired and hurried to my room. Relief flooded through me as I pulled my sun quilt around me and breathed deeply into it for a long time. Tucking my hand under my pillow, my fingers felt the edges of paper. I pulled them out. There were three. He'd found the photo of Wineve and me the day we both got our drivers' licenses. Our arms were wrapped around each other. Keys dangled from our hands as we stood between Theresa's and Paul's cars.

The other photo was when Theresa and Paul took us to Disneyland. It was the one and only time we'd ever been to Disneyland in our whole lives. We were fifteen years old and had just come off of Splash Mountain. It was a stroke of luck that Mickey Mouse had come by at the same moment we walked off the ride. We got our picture taken with him in our soaked clothes, our hair clinging to our faces.

The last was a picture Theresa had taken when she very first got us. We were twelve. I barely remembered being that young. Theresa told us to give each other a hug for the picture. When we did, she said words that never left me. "You remember this, girls; remember that no matter what the world does to you, you will always be sisters."

Always sisters. I didn't cry anymore, but instead cuddled into my quilt and tucked myself under the bedspread provided to me by the Regents or whoever got us all our stuff, I carefully placed the pictures into my pillowcase and went to sleep peacefully for the first time in over a week.

EIGHTEEN

L ife as a student settled into routine. The "blackboard" was like a great big computer screen projected on the wall. It had net connection, so the teacher could do research on something we might have questions on right there in the middle of class. And though this was something schools from my time were already establishing, it was outright miraculous to those from older generations and completely boring to those from later years.

Meals, classes, social activities, and little field trips inspired by Jay's curiosity, were all part of the routine. Jay loved the movie theaters since they affected all five senses. If something exploded on screen, the seats in the theater rumbled. If there was a tornado on screen, wind blew in from somewhere. Taste and smell came from pulse power on the rings that coded into the theaters main computer when our rings were scanned. Technology hadn't advanced as much as I would have imagined. Some things felt archaic and clunky like the lapdesks, others incredibly innovated like the IDR's and flying cars. The disparity between dark ages and invention was crazy huge, but when the world goes crazy, crazy things were bound to happen.

The fact that my old phone had more capabilities and apps than the IDR had made me shake my head. People had no idea what they were missing.

And a greater part of my routine became my science classes, specifically biology. The disease that made this future steal me from my death both fascinated and repulsed me. I studied its history, its affects, and its complete take-over of the human body. I wanted to understand the disease, wanted to be more than a brood mare to help humanity, but wanted to solve the problem that currently plagued mankind—to fix the chasm of class between New Youth and the rest of the world.

I'd also become addicted to the library, going whenever a free moment presented itself. Lots of people went to the library as it offered the most versatile gaming and entertainment opportunity, but even more, people went for the books. The sheer volume of books checked out and returned on a daily basis staggered me. I'd never seen such a busy library in all my life and I loved it, though I hated the way people looked down in deference when they passed me.

Books could be downloaded through the IDR and pulsed onto whatever media display was available, but the tactile experience seemed to be the one people wanted. And not all books could be downloaded for public consumption. None of the science books I needed or books on the HTH infection were available for download. They were all hard bound and only accessible through the library.

Though the research I'd done kept me interested in the library, it was the notes that helped me bear the tension between me and the populace when I ventured out. The notes I found tucked into *A Sliver of Midnight* were my private oasis in a world that seemed to be constantly spinning. At Tag's urging, I was careful to never go on Wednesday as that was one of his few freedoms, and, if anyone suspected he communicated with me, he would lose that freedom.

We'd resorted to using code names for each other in case someone ever found our scrawled messages. Tag started calling me Sunny, and as a play on his name I started calling him Yourit as in *Tag! You're it!* Having never played the game of tag as a child, he didn't get the joke, but I thought it was pretty funny.

5-26-2113

Morning, Yourit!

J rented us a flying car and took me and a few others to our childhood homes. It's still there, Yourit,

Theresa's house is still there! I thought it was lost in the mudslide, but it's still there along with all the other houses on Theresa's hillside. They look abandoned though—like full of snakes and spiders abandoned. I wanted to go in, but our driver got a call that we weren't allowed to be outside city limits without special permission. The driver took us back to the dorms where Kathleen gave us a forty-eight minute lecture on taking advantage of our positions as New Youth and explaining that none of us had the funds available to make that journey, but that the driver had been too afraid of saying no to us.

J doesn't think it's about the money, but about control. I can go either way on that argument. But Theresa's house is there! I only wish I knew where Wineve's grave was.

Sunny

Learning to live within the limits of the future took time. I'd never worried about curfew even when Aunt Theresa so dutifully placed curfews on me. News of riots or vandalism, or attacks started by crazies who'd been hidden by their parents was common. Most of the bad stuff happened at the dark levels. It seemed the people who lived in the dark—in that perpetual night—had a far more violent life than the one I lived in the higher levels.

Their pale faces glowed against the light from the cameras. They always turned their heads as though such intense light hurt their eyes. The news also showed the soldiers beating back angry crowds, in the thick of riots with their tazers and sleeping gases. On the news, the soldiers looked like cruel oppressors. It surprised me how many of those soldiers were women. They all seemed so violent and angry. I was always grateful never to see Tag in the riots on the screens.

The news stations replayed those attacks in the dark levels over and over on the net. Such information made it hard to forget that the world was unstable and venturing out at night wasn't safe.

"I found it," Jay whispered over breakfast one morning.

"Found what?" I glanced around to make sure Eddie didn't hover nearby. If Jay whispered, it meant he had something to say that Eddie would tattle on us for.

"A way to the dark level. I went last night."

"What?" I said, my mouth full of cream and crepes hanging open in surprise.

"How?" Jen asked. It was just the three of us sitting at the table that morning, everyone else had either slept in, or had room service taken to their rooms.

"Service elevators." Jay beamed.

Jen smirked and tapped her fork on her plate. "Your IDR works in the service elevators?"

"Nope, but Dennis's does."

"Who's Dennis?" I'd chewed too fast and swallowed hard, making it hurt as the food went down.

"He works in the kitchen. I wanted a burger with onion rings late one night. He made it up for me. I started talking to him, and it took a while for him to warm up enough to be willing to talk much back, but I made a point of going to visit the kitchens every night since then. He's totally rad!"

Jen laughed every time Jay said the word *rad*. She also laughed at *bogus*.

Jay ignored her giggling at his out-of-date expressions. "Last night, he invited me down for a game of poker with him and his friends. It was so cool! Dude, it was the best time I've had since being here. They didn't act all stuck up like lots of the guys here in the dorms. Want to come with me tonight?"

Jen agreed simply because she loved being with Jay no matter where he was going or what he'd schemed up. I agreed out of curiosity. Were the dark levels as bad as reported? Were the diseased riff-raff really riff-raff? Or maybe there were pockets of people with no disease hiding in the dark. Tag had said something about such a thing existing. I wanted to see for myself. So much of our information felt fed to us. I wanted to know if what we saw on the news matched the reality.

"So how did you get down?" Jen asked.

"I took off my ring and left it here in the dining room by the plants where no one would find it until I came back."

"That's how I got into the barracks," I said.

Jay's grin broadened. "I know."

I frowned. "Don't you think that's weird? Why wouldn't they assume people would do stuff like that?"

"Fear." Jen said this before Jay could. "They've made everyone afraid to step out of line. People won't go where they aren't supposed to be because crazies might get them, or the government might accuse them of being crazies. I really don't think people consider going where their rings don't allow. Why would they risk getting caught?"

All excellent points, and ones I'd witnessed firsthand. People in the sky gardens and marketplaces avoided me when they saw me coming. People recognized the New Youth, and steered clear. And all Professor Raik had to say was that we were under the protection of the government. I still stuck to my original thought that killing off all the crazies had culled art out of society, but the longer I stayed within the society, the more I realized it culled out risk-taking and intelligence as well. Very few of the people left were capable of independent or creative thought.

We made plans to meet in the dining hall after lights normally went out—after curfew. My heart jumped in my throat just considering being out after curfew. I wondered many times during the day if the IDR's tracked when we took them off, and wondered many times more if we'd be ex-ed for being out after curfew if we got caught. As we waited for Dennis, Jay imparted his new knowledge of the day. "They don't have fire escapes because the buildings are fireproof. The walls and floorings are all made out of that same stuff they make dishes out of. That stuff doesn't burn." Jay went off for several minutes more about *Tesla's Ether* and how the government was selfishly withholding the one source of energy that would allow people electricity at no cost and with no damaging environmental effects.

Jay quieted his rants when Dennis showed up and led us down into the belly of the city.

What kind of ugly is hiding under the beauty suit?

The elevator doors opened. We stepped out into a world entirely unlike the one we lived in.

The smell hit me first. It smelled dank—the humidity and rot combining to make my gag reflex kick in. The lighting pulsed through green tubes lining the ceilings like huge glow sticks, making the ground floor of the building look ethereal and frightening. Jen huddled closer to Jay, and he put an arm around her in a position of instinctive protection. I crowded in next to them. Dennis, our guide, turned to us and smiled, his teeth bright in the glow of the light.

"Should we turn on some real lights?" Jay asked, trying to abate our nerves a little with something normal.

"Lumes are all we got here." Dennis shrugged like we were dumb for thinking there was anything else and what they had was good enough anyway.

"Lumes." Jay repeated the word and glanced around the littered floor of what seemed to have once been a hotel lobby.

"Some people have leds, but most use lumes. Cheaper. Cheaper's better when the cost of electrics keep goin' up. Cheaper totally spins. C'mon." Dennis waved us to follow him. I was surprised that Dennis's declaration of the electrics costs didn't send Jay into another rant on *Tesla's Ether.*

"Are we on the ground now?" I asked, grateful Jen and I had worn jeans since everything felt grimy. Even the air I breathed seemed dirty down here, though I knew that had to be just my imagination. "The real ground?"

Dennis nodded. "Go outside and see for yourself."

There were revolving glass doors to my right and, after a brief hesitation, I pushed through the doors and found myself breathing in cold humid air—my feet tapping on hard normal cement. The cement had cracks and was obviously worn, but it felt normal and unmoving under my feet, in a way nothing had felt since coming to the future. I'd forgotten how the ground under me swayed above the dark levels until I'd taken those first few steps at ground level.

Plant life existed at ground level, but it was all either a pale sickly green color, or a pale sickly white, rather than the rich deep greens of the sky gardens. Across the street, multi-colored lights spun and reflected from the windows. People had trickled out from that building and into the street—people, music, laughter, noise. The atmosphere reminded me of the few dance clubs I'd sneaked into during the summer with Nathan.

"It's after curfew," Jay said, twisting around so much to take everything in, it made my head ache to watch.

"Is it always like this?" Jen asked. "Isn't anyone worried about the soldiers?"

"Naw. It's July fourth. Time to spin. Soldiers aren't usually around topside."

"Topside?" I asked. This was the ground—definitely not topside.

"Yeah down under, things get pretty rough." When we continued to stare at Dennis like he had ten heads, he said, "You know, in the basement and tunnel apartments. The soldiers spend more time patrolling down there. Anyway, today is a holiday. The Holiday Spins! Tomorrow night, people will go home, watch their nets if they've got 'em, eat their dinners if they've got 'em. People will stay inside."

Jen shook her head. "It *is* the fourth. I can't believe I forgot. And they didn't even mention it in class or anything. Not a word."

Dennis shrugged and nodded to some girl across the street. "Yeah, they wouldn't. The old holidays aren't recognized under Regent law, but down here, we make our own laws . . . at least when the soldiers aren't looking." Dennis maneuvered his way across the street to the girl he'd nodded at. We all followed. I shivered as Dennis introduced us to his girlfriend, Natalie.

"Sorry. The bay's always cold at night, even in summer. I should've told you guys to bring jackets," Dennis said.

How would they know the difference between summer and winter when they lived in the shadows of the city above them? I looked up to see the buildings disappearing into the clouds that had rolled in for the night and shivered again. Which world would be considered the ideal? The one without the ground and the constant shifting of the platforms under your feet being swayed by the winds, or the one without the sky, without the sun? "No stars . . ." I whispered more to myself than to anyone else.

Natalie smiled. "You can see stars if you go out on the ocean. Friends of mine run a star-tour boating service if you ever want to go. I mean, you know, we don't go around advertisin' or nothin' like that. We know how to avoid coast patrols. So this is an offer for you three only. Don't invite anyone else."

Natalie's offer filled me with a degree of relief. So they didn't have to always be in a world without a sky. A way for them to see the moon and stars existed.

"So if it's the fourth of July, will there be fireworks?" Jen asked.

Dennis laughed. "No fireworks. I guess we aren't so tough, huh? We celebrate our holidays, but keep the laws that get us ex-ed. Fireworks are for Disneyland and Regent Day only. But no one's gunna ex us for singing the Star Spangled Banner if we want. It's a free country."

He said that in the same way I used to say back in my own time when I was trying to explain to Aunt Theresa why I should be able to do the things I wanted. "It's a free country!" I'd yell.

"Not in my house," she'd say back calmly. Aunt Theresa seldom yelled back.

I wondered if Dennis believed it was a free country or if he was being sarcastic. His tone made it hard to tell. *It's not a free country in the Regent's house.*

The gritty dark levels were, in a way, hauntingly beautiful. The people didn't frighten me. They didn't act wild or crazy like I thought they might. They acted far more normal than the people living the "high" life above them. Their hair colors were just as wild, many of them sporting several colors weaved and striped over their heads. Their colors seemed to glow in the sick light of the lumes and more of them sported advertisements on their heads and hands. But though they seemed normal as they interacted with one another, they still remained reserved, even shocked, towards Jay, Jen, and me. They'd be laughing with their friends, see us, and duck their heads, hurry back into their buildings casting furtive glances our way until we were passed.

They feared us. The Povs feared us in the exact same way that the rich people did.

I didn't want to be feared.

Natalie and Dennis led us into the place with the strobing lights. It *was* a dance club. The music seemed to have bite, the rhythm and beat unfamiliar and strange. Dennis led Natalie into the fray, and Jay took Jen and went to dance as well. I stood in the crowd of people, locked in my fear of being separated from my group.

I took several deep breaths to calm myself and even considered buying myself a drink except without my IDR, I had no money. I edged over to the wall where I could still keep an eye on Jay and Jen and set myself up for research.

Everyone had the IDR ring, though no one had brain implants as I'd thought. The rings worked off of pulse power from the brain. And the ring could send back pulses to the brain, that technology still startled me. They had the rings and time travel, but so many other things seemed archaic—dusty technologies. The discrepancy confused me more than anything.

The way the door glowed as people neared it proved the use of the rings even down here. But with so many bodies moving in and out, the door constantly glowed, anyone not wearing a ring could leave or enter at their own discretion. It bothered me that no one seemed to notice this flaw in the Regent's ring law. But then . . . a lot of things bothered me.

After several songs, Jay and Jen came back to me, their faces bright from exertion and their smiles huge. "Come join us!" Jay called over the music.

"I should've brought a date," I said.

"Eddie would've been glad to fill that job." Jen laughed at my face souring at the mention of Eddie.

"C'mon! Come have fun for a change!" Jay and Jen each grabbed my hands with the intent of pulling me back with them. As they pulled, the music abruptly stopped. Everyone froze where they stood, all laughter and chatter cutting off as sharply as the music. I turned to see what everyone else had turned to see. The door light glowed red—in spite of all the people standing by it with rings—*the door glowed red*.

The people's faces registered fear. Panic took over the frozen quiet. People pushed and shoved from all directions, working to remove themselves from the area closest the doors. The vast room emptied as people escaped to other areas of the building.

Jen looked at Jay. "Soldiers?"

Jay was about to answer when sirens sounded, loud and unmistakable—soldiers.

We'd all seen the vids. Soldiers raided gatherings with no mercy. We stood there, all three of us holding hands in tight grips, none of us daring to move until I felt Dennis's hand at my back shoving me towards the far end of the room. "Move! Move!" He herded us through the crowd and finally turned us into a doorway where several others were rushing through. "In there!" Dennis yelled as the front doors crashed open.

Screams!

They were the screams of suffering—of pain, fear. The soldiers had arrived. Dennis nearly ran me over in his urgency to make us move. We wound down stairs, and into hallways, down more stairs. Someone in front of us fell, but the press of people didn't stop to help her up. I barely avoided stepping on her as we rushed past.

Another hallway, towards a bookshelf that moved aside. The bookshelf hid a hole that looked like someone had used a jackhammer to create it. I ducked to go through, clipping my ear against the jagged brick edges. Blood trickled down my neck and into the collar of my shirt, but I pressed on, not daring to stop, not daring to look behind.

We wound through several buildings, entering odd little doors that had been hidden by ragged sorts of odd furniture.

The elaborate exit strategy staggered me. These people had tunneled through brick and mortar to create a way out, like mice.

And then it occurred to me, we were no longer what Dennis had called topside. We were in the tunnels, where he said things weren't safe. Not that things were safe where we'd been. Our group of escapees had thinned to a handful of people rapidly following along after Dennis and Natalie. The others had sifted off to different tunnels.

"We should go up." The panic in my voice was evident even to my own ears.

"Can't," Natalie said.

"They've locked down for at least three streets in all directions. We wouldn't be able to smuggle you guys back to the top of the world without all of us getting ex-ed." Dennis's raspy explanation heightened my panic.

"Told you it was dumb to hang with the Regents' pets." Natalie's whispered words were not likely meant for us to hear, but I caught them and felt pretty certain Jay had too. I didn't blame her. It was altogether possible we were the reason the soldiers showed up.

We maneuvered through the tunnels for what seemed forever. Red lumes, green lumes, bright white leds. The varying light colors and strain to adjust to each one hurt my eyes and made my stomach sick. There were some tunnels with no light at all.

Afraid to scrape against a low ceiling, I ducked my head, and kept my hands clenched at my sides. What if there were bugs, spiders, crawling things with poisonous bites and too many legs?

My legs and back ached from walking hunched over and then finally we were at stairs and climbing up—up and out of the earth. I wanted to weep with joy.

When we reached the top, we all stumbled into a dark room.

"We're topside now, we'll find an elevator to get you guys to the sky, right?" Dennis's voice took some of the edge off of my fear of the dark. A noise like a large static charge filled the room as bright lights exploded into our eyes.

I stared down the barrel of a gun aimed directly at my head as the soldier holding the gun smiled and said. "We knew the rats would come up for air eventually."

NINETEEN

A tazer shot out of one gun and directly into Natalie's chest. She crumpled to the floor with a scream as she writhed and wriggled in the electrical current. The soldier aiming his gun at me hesitated as he finger twitched to pull his trigger. "Hey—they're New Youths!"

Dennis took advantage of their hesitation at seeing New Youth in the dark levels and knocked the soldier's gun to the side, then kicked the gun from the soldier's hand altogether, freeing Natalie of the current arcing through her body. The second soldier jerked his gun up, but Jay followed Dennis's example and kicked out at the gun. Jay's kick fell short of its mark and he actually kicked the soldier's arm.

A cry of pain accompanied the crack of a breaking bone. Dennis made quick work of silencing that cry and making certain the other soldier didn't get his gun back. I turned my head away not wanting to see if he'd knocked them out or killed them altogether.

Jen and I each took a hold of Natalie's hands and helped her to her feet. "Can you walk?" Jen asked, looking worried.

Natalie nodded, her pale face sickly. Dennis edged Jen aside so Natalie could use him as a crutch, and we hurried to put distance between us and the crime scene.

Dennis led us across the street, into another building, through it, and out the back door. We crossed several buildings that way weaving a path back to the elevators Dennis's IDR allowed him to use—the ones we'd come down on. Natalie's steps were still shaky, but she kept up. Dennis looked pointedly at Jay. "I need to get her home before I can take you to the sky levels."

Jay nodded. "Absolutely. I completely agree."

Dennis took a deep breath as though it pained him to make these kinds of choices between people. "Stay here, behind the counter over there. The service elevator will take you home, but you have to wait 'til I get back so I can make the elevator work. Don't come out for any noise, right? Don't get curious; just stay down. Curiosity kills in the dark levels."

We all nodded and watched a moment before Dennis gently took Natalie's arm and led her out of the building. He looked back at the door. "Don't just stand there! Get down!"

We scrambled to the remnants of the counter and tucked ourselves into tight little balls where we were hidden from the view of anyone who might enter the room.

Tears slid down Jen's face. "Do you think she'll be okay?"

"I'm sure she will. The effects of the tazer are short-lived. She's likely more scared right now than anything."

It took several moments before I found my voice. "Do you think those soldiers are dead?"

Jay's look was one of resigned rationale. "We'd better hope so, or *we* will be."

I wrapped my arms around my knees and buried my face in my arms to hide the horror such news gave me. People died because of my curiosity. Winter would not be proud of me. Tag would not be proud of me. Were those guys his friends? Would he mourn them when they didn't return to the barracks?

Stupid!

"Do you think he'll really come back for us?" Jen asked.

"Of course." But Jay couldn't promise that. He'd played poker and eaten onion rings with this guy. What did he really know about Dennis?

My legs had cramped, and my butt had gone numb from the cold floor when Dennis showed up again. "Let's go."

Those were the only words he said as we moved up the elevators to the sky levels. When we stepped out of the elevator, Dennis's chalky face was drawn in a tight frown. "I like you, Jay. I'm glad to know you New Youths aren't all purse-puppies for the Regents. But I won't take you down there again. It's nothing personal, right? I just gotta watch out for my own."

Jay nodded his understanding. "I'm sorry we caused trouble for you. And so you know, we're friends. You ever need anything—just let me know. I hope Natalie's okay."

Dennis nodded and hit the button for the elevator.

"Going down." The happy elevator said. It sounded like a warning.

The doors closed on Dennis, and we followed Jay back into the dining hall

By the time we retrieved our rings, exhaustion had taken over the adrenaline rush, depression over whether or not those soldiers had died on the street because of us, replaced fear.

I had played a part in making the world worse. *Forgive me, Wineve. Forgive me, Tag.*

***

In spite of my trip through the dark levels, Tag had been right. At three months, I'd resigned myself to the life I'd settled into. And not just resigned, but in many ways genuinely liked it. As Tag had predicted, I made friends and excelled in school in a way I never had back in my own time. At three months, I didn't ask Tag to take me back. I'd even forgotten we'd made that deal until at four months Tag left a note in our book at the library.

> *08-10-2113*
>
> *I told you. You argued, but when don't you argue? I told you that you would make friends, and be a queen, and not want to go home. It's been four months, Sunny. Four months and you didn't even ask. Yes, I'm gloating.*
> *Yourit*

I didn't know what Tag did with his notes, but felt pretty sure he destroyed them. Paper was difficult to come by due to the digital way of life, so often we resorted to using scraps of packaging. I destroyed all of his notes. Alison liked to borrow my clothes and play in my stuff, not in any snoopy way, but in a chumsy, we-should-share-everything way. I hid the photos Tag had given me of Winter and me inside the lapdesk itself and screwed the back plating back on. My sun-blanket stayed hidden in the layers of all my other blankets, and I demanded to be allowed to do my own laundry. Kathleen had merely grunted at me and let me have my way. I was New Youth. I always had my way.

08-13-2113
Who's a queen? Where's my tiara? I've never seen any crowns on my head. J&J are getting married tomorrow. They're moving out of the dorms and into a house of their own. I hate feeling left behind. I will really miss them.
Sunny

"I can't believe this is really happening!" Jennifer stood in front of a full length mirror, her white dress shimmering in the sunlight coming through the window next to her. She looked beautiful.

I stopped fidgeting with the skirt of my burgundy bridesmaid's dress long enough to say, "What I can't believe is that it took you guys so long."

So long. We never would have called it so long back in my home time. The New Youths pairing off and marrying quickly was incentivized by the Regents. They were showered with gifts. And though they treated us like an elite society, everyone knew that any sexual relations outside of marriages condoned by the Regents would get them in huge trouble. Biological needs encouraged early marriage. We were brought to the future to make babies. They wanted us doing our jobs as soon as possible. I believed that the schooling they put us through was only to give us an environment that felt comfortable to allow us opportunities to flirt and form relationships.

I'd done enough research on crazy testing day procedures. I understood the horrors parents persevered to keep the species alive, and felt guilty that I did nothing to help in the way the Regents expected. It just felt unfair for me to find a mate, get married, and make children I could raise to adulthood when the rest of the population couldn't. I wanted something different. I wanted to cure the disease entirely. If I could do that, the future really would be a better place.

Jennifer turned to the side, still admiring herself in the mirror, her taffeta skirt swishing with the movement. "Can I ask a personal question?" She pointed to her back where a few of the pearl buttons had been left undone so we could keep her necklace from catching in the lace while we put it on.

I frowned, and finished doing up the final buttons. The flowers in my hair made me feel as though someone had hosed me down in rose scented perfume. "No."

Jennifer laughed, making it harder to get the final button fastened. "I'm asking anyway. Why aren't you dating anyone? You've been asked out by a million different guys—"

"Nope. Not true. There are only seventy-three eligible young men in our group. And not even half of them have asked me out. You are grossly exaggerating."

"You know what I mean. Surely one of them . . ."

"I'm not interested in any of them."

"Like you just said, there aren't that many to choose from to begin with. You don't have time and internet dating services on your side."

I laughed. "If things get too bad, I can always use Eddie as my fallback." Eddie remained persistent in his pursuit, and I remained persistent in my deflection of his advances. Thinking of Eddie made me tired.

"I just don't want you to be lonely."

"I'm not lonely." I adjusted her veil on her head so it sat a little straighter and used a bobby pin to keep it in place.

"How can you not be lonely? All you do is read and research and take classes."

How could I explain how the research filled me with purpose, that the classes gave me hope I could really do something to make a difference. How could I explain those little scraps of paper that kept me company as the days turned into months? How could I explain how just seeing the words, *Morning, Sunny*, filled my every need for companionship?

I used Jen's shoulders to face her back towards the mirror. "Don't worry about me. Today's *your* day." I smiled at her, feeling how strange and irrevocably right that Jennifer and Jay were saved from their deaths to be brought together in this future here.

I picked up my flowers from the table near the door to her dressing room. "It's time."

She took a deep breath, picked up her own flowers, and followed me out.

"I don't know if I can do this alone. I wish my mom and dad were here," she whispered as we arrived at the door leading to the gardens where the ceremony would be held.

"I know how you feel." I took her hand and gave it one quick squeeze. "But you aren't alone. You've got your whole life waiting for you out there."

The doors fell open and the bridal march started. Jay waited at the end of the aisle. I went first as maid of honor.

Jay's marriage to Jen was the sixth wedding that month. Our small group from the past had wasted little time in pairing off and moving on. Josephine and Leland were already expecting their first child. They'd been whisked off to some private remote location for observation, since a live birth hadn't been done in over sixty years, and the Regents didn't want anything to go wrong.

And for reasons I couldn't understand, the news of the pregnancy had been kept pretty quiet. I would have assumed such news would be international precisely because they *hadn't* had a pregnant woman walking around on this earth for over sixty years. It should have been huge news. But instead, the nets carried reports of sports winnings, stock market prices, new funding for ocean exploration, and the glitzy life of the Regents.

I passed Kathleen who smiled at me as made my way to the front. Kathleen sometimes watched the nets with me. Her mouth a tight grim line. A few times, I caught her shaking her head. "Why would they take them from the colony of New Youth?" she muttered to herself. "It doesn't make sense." She must have realized she spoke out loud where I could hear because she startled to see me. But I always gave a nod that showed I agreed with her regarding the oddity.

Another oddity was that the Regents had taken the place of fame and fortune over Hollywood stars and musicians. Movie stars were making a comeback, but the Regents were held in higher esteem. I wouldn't have ever guessed that someday a politician would trump a movie star. Many of the Regents throughout the world attended the wedding ceremonies. Professor Raik preened for them and smiled with them. And though I couldn't explain why, seeing them all bunched together at the weddings reminded me of vultures waited for a person to die so they could feed.

I forced a smile as I waited at the end of the aisle for Jen to make her journey to Jay. Everyone looked delighted. Alison positively glowed.

Alison wanted to be next in the matrimony line, but flirted so much with so many different guys, it was anyone's guess who would actually end up walking her down the aisle. There weren't many like me. Most of the New Youth dated and flirted and fell in love. I didn't do any of that.

I frowned as Jay took Jen's hand. What was that emotion that had just bubbled up? Jealousy? I held my breath a moment and contemplated jealousy. What were the chances of me finding anyone worth being with like *that*? Sure, I got along with most of the people in the dorms. They were fun to hang out with, eat dinner with, go to movies with or whatever, but none of them were who I *wanted*.

And the only one I did want, I wasn't allowed to want.

Oh yes. Very jealous.

And the desire to be with that one person denied to me only grew over the next several months.

***

12-06-2113
Did you know that Albert Einstein, the man who made it possible for me to know you, wrote letters to his cousin like we write notes to each other? Every scientist needs a springboard from which to jump their ideas off. I'm grateful for you, Sunny. You make it easier for me to think.
Yourit

Tag's ability with science affected me every day, on more than just the fact he'd made the break-through discoveries on what sorts of forces needed to stimulate electrons in order to give them enough energy to jump to calculated orbits. Were it not for his science, I'd never have been a part of this future. But more than that, he helped me understand my classes. His mini tutorials helped me understand important elements the teachers just couldn't get through to me. And even with all my ability to research the world archives and history chips on the net, Tag's scribbled notes were more helpful.

I did searches on the net for him too—using my classmates' lapdesks so it wouldn't look like I was harboring inappropriate feelings for a soldier. I was sure they could peek at my searches on my lapdesk. But Professor Raik wouldn't suspect anyone else of anything. He wouldn't have a reason to keep tabs of the searches of the other students who so dutifully fulfilled his dream of them marrying and having children.

I was the only misfit of the group, searching for any information about where Tag came from and how he'd been raised. Apparently Taggert wasn't all too popular a name since there was one I found in Amerio Canada, and one in Eurio UK. But I found that most of the pages and news regarding a Taggert in San Francisco were broken links. It was as though someone had systematically erased his existence from the world. He didn't belong to social networks or have an online presence anywhere that could be found. I couldn't even locate records of which public nursery he'd been born in.

I also tried searches for Winter Eve Rae. Many of those links were broken as well. I saw a few news articles archived on the beginnings of an acting career. But just as Tag had seemed to have been erased from the world's digital memory, so had my sister.

12-08-2113
Don't compare our friendship to Einstein's friendships. That man may have been brilliant, but he gave everything he was to science and didn't ever have enough left over for relationships. He admitted he'd failed in relationships. You are not allowed to fail me, Yourit.

Today, Professor Modesitt actually mentioned a young man who wrote the breaking paper on valence electrons, and I knew he meant you. Don't try to deny it. Professor Modesitt asked if I wanted to work a few hours every week at the Public Nursery on Angel Island. He said I'm really catching on, maybe not to physics, but definitely to biology. I didn't mention that I owe it all to you. J.S. is going to have a baby. She wrote me yesterday and told me she's due in July. So it looks like her and I will both be working with babies.
Sunny

"Where are you going?" Alison had the look of disapproval I'd become used to whenever I pulled my jeans out of my closet.

"Angel Island. Professor Modesitt is going to have me work in the Public Nursery."

"And you said yes? Are you cr—" She took a long breath. It had been a trial for many of us to learn to cut that word from our vocabulary. She lowered her voice. "Why would you do that?"

I pulled my jeans up over my hips, buttoned them, and crawled around the base of my bed to find my boots. "I wasn't going to at first, but he said there might be a chance that with further study, they can figure out a way to create less hostile environments for the babies in the birthing fluids. If I learn more, maybe I can help make it so there won't be a need to—" My turn to take a deep breath. "To euthanize the children."

"Having more of them just perpetuates the problem. We're really better off with the decline of their birthrate. Our posterity will breathe life into the world; their posterity only prolongs the inevitable."

I bit my tongue to keep from responding to the daily diet of propaganda fed to us in our classes. The fact that Alison knew how to use the word *perpetuate* was a breakthrough all on its own.

"Would you be able to do it?" I stared at my shoes, tapping the toes together absently.

"Do what?"

I sighed. She'd already moved past the conversation in her mind. "Take your own child to a test they might not pass—knowing that you might not have that child to go home with?"

"Well, that's not a problem we're likely to have, is it?" She laughed.

I clucked my tongue. "Yeah, not likely. Well, I better get going or I'll be late."

"You study too much!" Alison called as I shut the door.

"You don't study enough." I murmured, even though she couldn't have heard me through the closed door. My work at the nursery allowed me access to one elevator that took me to ground level. From there, I had exactly four doors I could enter and exit through with my IDR. All of those doors led to the ferry that would take me to the island.

I still hadn't grown used to the way people let their gazes slip past me as though I wasn't there. No one looked me in the eye or ever said hello. I belonged to the state and although the Regents were beloved superstars of the people, those who carried out the Regent's orders were feared. *I am so not a queen, Tag. Not unless you consider me one of those who got her head chopped off by the will of the people.*

Ignoring those who ignored me had become almost a game. I swept my glance over and around them too. I made a point of focusing on the water, and the waves, and the way the gulls circled and cried in the air above me. I stayed inside the ferry instead of out on the deck due to the cold wind. The world had a blue tinge to it from the ice and snow. So much for the global warming theory.

From the island, the buildings and world created on top of other buildings were really spectacular.

Professor Modesitt stood at the door to the nursery waiting for me. A soldier stood sentry on the opposite side of the door.

"Right on time, Miss Rae. I'd like to introduce you to Mast. He's the guard of this facility, and should you see anything that looks like it might jeopardize our operations, you're to inform Mast immediately."

Mast gave a curt nod.

"Why does the facility have a guard?" I whispered once we were inside.

"Not everyone agrees with this method of bringing children in the world, mostly from parents whose kids didn't pass the test. There are bomb threats, arson threats—well, you get the idea."

"Oh, right." I glanced back towards the doors. "And we only have one guard?" Professor Modesitt hadn't instilled any confidence about my safety working there. The wall behind the front desk was a waterfall. The room smelled like sugar cookies baking, and the soft music soothed like a lullaby.

I smiled. It was a peaceful room; maybe working here would be good for me. My opinion changed the moment I entered the dark cavern called the nursery.

"The cradles are chronological. From day one to forty weeks." Professor Modesitt pointed along the rows and rows of clear plastic baskets suspended three feet off the ground by long metal rails. The room was lit by red lights as though we were in a photo lab. The steady sound of a heartbeat thumped through the room, recreating the experience a baby would feel in a real womb.

I thought of Jen Savage being pregnant and how her notes to me were filled with an over-exuberant love for the child she carried.

With such thoughts of maternal love, I peered into one of the baskets and pulled back immediately. Inside the basket was a small fleshy looking blob. The umbilical cord from the fleshy sac was attached to the side of the basket. As the blob-sac moved, tiny ripples formed at the top of the fluid so that they lapped against the clear lid.

"It's important to monitor the cradles at all times. Their temperature must stay consistent. Nothing must be allowed to contaminate the birthing fluids. Making babies is a precise science."

I didn't remind him that his precise science ended up with a good portion of those babies dead. That was what enticed me to come here. I wanted desperately to put a stop to the crazy problem. I wanted to be a real part of the solution, not just in becoming a little baby farm myself, like Professor Raik, our teachers, and the Regents seemed to be pushing all of us towards, but in figuring out why the babies' brains didn't develop. Maybe, with enough research, I could figure out how to alter the genetic mutations and disease that caused the sterility in the first place.

And then everyone would be equal. Then, I could stop having to ignore the people ignoring me on the ferry. Then, maybe Tag wouldn't stop me from saying the three words that repeated themselves in my mind a million times a day.

Professor Modesitt spent the next several hours showing me my duties, explaining how everything worked, and cautioning me over the dozens of things that could go wrong. It was impossible to focus on him for too long, my gaze kept slipping back to the dark nursery—to where those cradles housed an unknown generation. Which of those cradles would produce healthy normal children? And which of those cradles would represent heartache for everyone involved?

My eyes felt strained after identifying cells in Professor Modesitt's microscope, in spite of the fact that the image had been projected onto the nursery digi-board. We pulled samples from each of the cradles and ran them through tests for variances. I rubbed my eyes at the end of my shift and pressed my fingers against my temples to try to massage the headache away.

Professor Modesitt had accompanied me to the ferry. "It's been a good day's work. I was right about you."

"I didn't really do anything." The water splashing against the sides of the docking area calmed me. I gulped in the sea air, grateful once again for all the things that hadn't changed in the world. Water was still wet; the sky was still blue.

The darkened nursery with its red lights and rhythmic heartbeat sound almost made me forget that normal things existed outside that room.

"You notice; you observe things no one else sees. It's why I hoped you would join me here. I think you have spectacular potential simply because you see when all others are blind."

My face warmed under the compliment. I hoped he was right.

TWENTY

1-24-2114

Morning Sunny,

You've been working the public nursery for two months, and I heard your dedication is unprecedented. I heard a rumor that you ignored the Christmas and the New Year's festivities. How is the year 2114 going to feel about you with you shunning it outright that way? Don't let your other studies fall to the wayside.

Yourit

My other studies *had* fallen to the wayside. I'd become the worst work-a-holic they'd ever seen. The celebration of 2114 had little effect on me or my research and work, but the festivities led to eleven new weddings and a couple of birth announcements.

2-14-2114

Morning Yourit!

Thanks for the Valentine's present. I didn't check out the book you sent me to, but Vomit for Valentines was definitely worth reading! I read it while standing in the aisle between the book stacks. My stomach ached from holding in my laughter. Hilarious! This almost makes up for you missing last week's note. Professor Modesitt has authorized me to work more in the nursery in spite of complaints that I spend too much time there anyway.

I hope all is well with you.

Sunny

The time working in the public nursery had changed me. By venturing out on my own instead of in the social atmosphere of being with friends, the sense of quiet despair from the people settled over me as well. For all the modern wonders of their world, the people feared their government, feared their neighbors, and yet hoped for a better future. In spite of my *elite* status, and in spite of the fact that the general public feared meeting my eye once they realized who I was, I had become one of them—wanting and working towards their same goals—whether they wanted me or not.

I pulled cultures from brain segments that had been stored in the cryogenic freezer and settled in to test the cholesterol deposits stored through the brain arteries in the hopes to find some correlation between the degree of blood flow and the mental capacity in the newborns.

"Do you want to try a live birth today?" Amy asked. She was one of the resident baby doctors in the public nursery.

My heart sped up as my stomach fluttered. "Really? Can I?"

She nodded, her bright pink ponytail bobbing with the motion. She had a bubblegum ad on her hand that matched her hair. "You spend more time with these babies than anyone else around here. You should be there when they take their first breaths."

I put the brain segments back into the freezers and all but ran to the wash station to scrub up. It seemed they did the live births at times when I was out of the nursery. For all the time I'd spent there, the opportunity to witness a child being pulled from the birthing fluids had never presented itself.

I stepped into the dark nursery where Amy had already unlatched the clear basinet from the railings and started to wheel it to the birthing room. I followed her, Professor Modesitt, and a few interns into the birthing room.

In movies from my time, they always portrayed a childbirth as a rushed affair—babies were born in taxi cabs, or women were wheeled into emergency rooms screaming from pain and everyone panicking at the new life about to make an entrance to the world.

Future births weren't anything like that. Everyone treated the moment with reverential awe. They all whispered in hushed tones. Amy motioned for me to stand next to her. She handed me the surgical scissors. "Cut the birthing sac here." She pointed to the end. Once the cut is made, you'll need to help the others apply gentle but firm pressure on the sac."

The sac and the pressure exerted to the sac were the best ways we had to replicate a real birth. It gave the baby the same experience as if they had lived in a real womb. The consensus was that if they simulated the natural birth as closely as possible, then they would have the best chances for success in mental stability. I doubted their methods and on many occasions had to bite my tongue to keep from telling them all how witch-doctor absurd their processes were sometimes. The baby going through a birthing canal had nothing to do with mental stability. Lots of babies in my day were born by C-section and were just fine. The few times I gently mentioned this to the doctors and professors, I was shooed away with a tsk as though I was the crazy one.

For all the new modern wonders of the future, the medical world sometimes seemed to be run by superstitious children.

We applied the pressure and massaged the baby free of the birthing sac. Professor Modesitt pulled the fleshy sac to the side while Amy pulled the baby from the fluids. "Suction her nose and mouth, Summer."

I found the bulbous instrument and cleared away the fluids obstructing the baby from taking a real breath. The baby's squishy eyes opened briefly as the infant mewled a noise of protest.

In spite of all the time I'd spent in the nursery staring into cradles and pulling samples of the birthing fluids, the fleshy blob-like sacs never felt real to me until this baby blinked in the light and released wails from inexperienced lungs. I wiped at my cheek with my sleeve and Amy grinned. "Do you want to hold her?"

DEATH THIEVES

I nodded and took the blanket they had readied for the child and swaddled her into it after Amy settled her into my arms. She was perfect—beautiful in a way I couldn't describe. The HTHBI infection became absolutely meaningless at the sight of this baby girl. Life existed. Real life.

She was *alive*.

Amy leaned down into the baby girl's face. "Welcome to the world, darling."

We brought several babies into the world that morning, and the process made me late to lunch. But I didn't care. I practically floated into the dining hall.

Being late meant no line existed since everyone had already filled their trays and found seats in the dining hall. With a silver tray in hand, I looked over the possibilities of food on display. Eddie showed up at my side as I contemplated the desserts. "Summer." The way Eddie said my name made my skin crawl. "Shall I compare thee to a summer's breeze?"

I refrained from the eye roll, worried that by exerting such force of will to keep my eyes still all the time, I was doing permanent damage to my optic nerve. "It's summer's *day*, and let's not compare me to anything, okay?"

His smile dropped. "Day and breeze mean the same thing."

Avoiding the eye roll took even more effort the second time. "Sure they do."

"You don't like me. You think I'm dumb."

My jaw fell slack at his astute understanding of my feelings. How he could be so dumb, and yet discern my true feelings so well was a puzzle. After an afternoon filled with tiny miracles, Eddie was the last thing I wanted to deal with for my evening. "I like you just fine. I don't think you're dumb at all." The lies grew easier to tell every day. Just fit in, lie low, figure out the system and cheat it. Tag had written this to me on several occasions, and the mantra marched through my mind more often when Eddie hovered nearby.

"You don't think anyone's smart here in this time."

207

"Sure I do. Lots of people are smart: Professor Raik, Professor Modesitt, Jay and Jen, Tag—"

My hands tightened on my tray, and in spite of trying to seem at ease, I felt the blood drain from my face as I strangled on the last word I had not meant to say aloud.

"Taggert?" Eddie asked.

"Who? I didn't say—"

"Taggert," he repeated. "The soldier who rescued you. The one who built the Orbitals." His eyes narrowed as though he knew I already knew this.

"Well, if he built the Orbitals, then he *is* smart." I set my tray on the counter in front of me to try to stretch out my fingers and bring blood back into them. Eddie obviously had no intentions of making this interchange short.

Eddie laughed as though I'd told a joke. "Smart. That's why they keep him, even if he is a crazy."

"He's not crazy!" I couldn't stop myself from defending Tag—even if it did confirm that I'd been thinking about him when listing people I deemed as smart. I'd have blackened Eddie's eye too if it wouldn't have interfered with the "lie low and fit in" mantra. I hurried to think, to save the slip up. "The laws would never allow him to last into adulthood if he couldn't pass the tests. Don't you have any faith in your system?" Shifting the defensive position to him seemed my only hope of surviving this attack.

"The system is flawless. Taggert's only here because his inventions are needed. He was almost ex-ed, you know? There's rumors that he only barely passed the crazy tests. And no one else wanted him after his family got executed. It seemed easier to put him out of his misery and ex him too."

I worked to keep my face smooth and uncaring. *His family executed! What?* "Why? What happened?"

"His whole family traitored the law. His mom faked his crazy sister's death and then hid her so they wouldn't get caught. His dad went home from work early to try to get his family out of the city, but the soldiers got there first. They ex-ed him, and the wife, and the crazy too. Taggert was there when they ex-ed his mom and crazy. He watched the whole thing happen. Whole family of traitors."

"That's horrible!" The declaration burst out of my lips along with the horror that must have been written all over my face. I hurried to cover it up—to appear compliant. "A whole family betraying the law like that. I can't imagine they thought they could get away with hiding a crazy." My own words sickened me. How I had to play their games in order to remain free enough to move around. "If the soldier was crazy, why wouldn't they have ex-ed him with the rest of his family?" I couldn't allow myself to say Tag's name out loud again; I couldn't allow myself that kind of familiarity while confronted with such accusation in Eddie's eyes.

"He could do things, make things work. Like I said, Professor Raik, and apparently you, think he's smart."

My heart pounded, rushing the blood past my ears until Eddie's words sounded like little more than static. Eddie spent a lot of time chasing the heels of Professor Raik, like some dog continually seeking validation from an uncharitable master. Had they discussed Tag in such depth? Had that discussion included me? And if it had, how could such a thing be possible? We'd been careful. I hadn't seen Tag with my own eyes since the day I broke into the barracks. How long ago had that been? Ten months? Had I been here that long?

"Why won't you go out with me, Summer?"

I blinked—the thoughts in my mind hitting the brakes. "What?"

"How's this—this Friday, Professor Raik is having a dinner party. He invited me and a date to join him. I'd like you to come with me." He picked up a plate with cookies stacked on it.

I shook my head in confusion. "I'll be at the nursery on Friday."

"I thought you'd say that. You spend a lot of time working to save crazies. It doesn't look good for you to care so much for an inferior people." Eddie puffed out his chest, lifted his chin and strutted away with a dessert in his hand and a desert in his heart and intellect.

An inferior people? The babies I'd held in my arms were far from inferior.

I didn't bother with adding anything else to the tray. I'd lost my appetite. Tag's family, murdered in front of him. How old had Tag been when his whole family had been taken from him so violently? What would that do to a person? Tag played the part of grateful for his life as one of Professor Raik's soldiers. He acted loyal to the world, and their cause to eradicate the crazies entirely, yet he said things and did things that led me to believe he'd only given me the advice he followed when he told me to just fit in, lie low, figure out the system and cheat it.

Had he figured out the system yet? Would we be able to cheat it? Or was he really not pretending? Seeing your family killed in front of you had to leave some major scars in a young boy's mind. To then have Professor Raik and his flattering words adding further confusion. What did Tag really think? What went on in his mind? Who was he loyal to—if anyone? At that moment I wished I'd saved his notes, wished I could have some tangible proof that Tag was my friend. Thursday, and another note from Tag, could not come soon enough.

"Summer!"

I looked up, realizing I stood in the middle of the dining hall and was holding my tray. "Hey, Alison."

She flashed her dimpled smile at me. "Don't just stand there! Come sit with us!" She waved an overexcited arm at me, beckoning me to their table.

One more chance to practice my ability to not roll my eyes. The whole thing gave me a headache. I took a deep breath and went to their table, settling my tray down in front of me.

Their conversation floated around me until—

"Did you hear what happened to poor LeAnn?" Mita asked.

Gossip. Everyone loved gossip, especially when that gossip involved the marrieds of our group. All eyes turned to Mita, waiting like hungry dogs for a scrap of leftovers.

Mita's dark-ringed eyes showed her dread with the news she had to share. This was not ordinary gossip, but instead something very serious. "She miscarried her baby."

Silence. No one saw that coming. And then the explosion from everyone at once.

"But they were watching her so carefully."

"But she was almost full term."

"But she couldn't have . . ."

Our table seemed full of "But how?" sorts of questions.

"Heather miscarried too." Mita announced, as though she were the grim reaper slicing her scythe through the posterity of the New Youth elite. Heather had been six months along. She'd been carrying twins.

I didn't explain that anything after four months was considered a still born, not a miscarriage. Calling the tragedy by a different name didn't make it any less terrifying—especially for those girls who were on the verge of their own marriages.

Most of the girls dropped their utensils to their trays with clatters. Some of them began to cry. All of them were terrified. The somber mood at the table ruined anyone's desire to eat.

With the meal completed, or at least abandoned, everyone shuffled out of the dining hall with their faces lost to contemplation of how our triumph of repopulating the dying world had faltered.

I went to my historical and current events class feeling not nearly as much pity for Heather or LeAnn as I did for Tag, who had watched his family die. How could anyone expect me to muster the ability to feel more than brief pity for my classmates when my conversation with Eddie was still so raw?

I mulled over Eddie's words, tasting them from all angles in my mind, ignoring the teacher and her digi-board rantings of world events until she played a current news clip.

I sat up straighter in my chair, the hairs on the back of my neck raising as the video footage played on the digi-board. Three of the world's Regents had decided to set examples for their communities by adopting babies from the public nurseries. The footage showed the

Regents going into their local public nurseries and then showed them walking out with an infant in arms.

The news of the Regents adoptions was rebroadcasted over all the vids all day long. Kathleen had a mug of something steaming in her hands as she stared up at the image projected in the casual room as I walked through to the second level to meet a biology study group where I was the only one who would study and the others would flirt and play footsies.

"Strange things," Kathleen muttered.

"What?" I halted my movement toward the stairs.

She frowned, "Nothing, just—" Her frown deepened. "The Regents have never adopted before. Three miscarriages? Three adoptions. Seems . . . never mind. Forget I said anything." She looked horrified that she actually had said anything that sounded as treasonous as her line of reasoning.

"Already forgotten," I said. My heart beat faster as I continued to the stairs. None of the Regents *had* adopted from a nursery—making claims that the people populating their territories were their children. Why now? What changed?

You're being paranoid. I chided myself. *The Regents didn't have anything to do with the recent tragedies of the New Youth.*

But even with my self-chastisement, I couldn't help but shudder at the possibility.

2-26-2114

You've never told me about your family, Yourit. I want to know their names. Who are the people who raised you? Did you have siblings? Did you grow up in Washington, California, or somewhere else? Why do you never talk about you?

Sunny

DEATH THIEVES

2-28-2114
I have no family. I have no last name as is the tradition of the soldiers. To be a soldier is to give up the life you knew before and remember it no more.
Yourit

3-1-2114
You're so irritating. You didn't answer my questions. And don't tell me you remember it no more. You don't forget anything.
Sunny

3-7-2114
My father's name was Shaw. Don't ask any more.
Yourit

TWENTY-ONE

y lapdesk beeped when I entered the room, which meant someone had sent me a message. I liked that the message notification didn't come until the lapdesk sensed my IDR. This kept Alison from asking questions and snooping into my life more than she already did. It had been a few weeks since the news of the Regent's adoptions and the New Youth miscarriages had swept through the New Youth Dormitories—enough time for everyone to move on to their shallow conversations of pedicures and grades on history exams.

I waved my ring over the desk—bringing it to life. Even after all the months of living here, I still felt like a Jedi waving my hand over things to make them work. It seemed weird to not have to touch the screen in any way in order for the programs to open. The IDR and the pulse of my thoughts were enough for simple tasks to be accomplished.

I opened my messages and felt joy in seeing one from Jen Savage.

> Dear Summer,
>
> The pregnancy has been going great. I had my ultrasound today and found out we're having twins! Twins! Can you believe it? I don't remember anyone in my family having twins. Jay nearly passed out when he heard, but you should see him. I don't think he's stopped smiling—even in his sleep! I admit that I'm worried. Margaret wrote me about the miscarriages

from some of the others. I am going on a strict health food diet. Nothing is going to hurt my babies.

Stay in touch. It's lonely down here in southern California. Jay did take me to Disneyland. It's not even close to what I remembered it being. It totally spins! You'll have to visit and come with us.

Miss you.

Jen

I missed her too. Jen and Jay had been moved to Southern California. All of the marrieds had been moved to places where the temperature was far warmer than the icy cold of the Bay area. Some had been moved to other parts in the world, where they were under the direction of different Regents. I thought that was strange. If their goal was to have us create a clean blooded race, wouldn't they keep us all together so our children could grow up and intermarry?

But worrying over the Regents didn't help me get any closer to helping the babies growing in the cradles at my nursery. Jen's pregnancy was going well, which made me happy. But the public nurseries couldn't boast such luck. Some babies were born with the HTH infection so prominently that the doctors euthanized them that same day—though they always waited until I was gone. I understood why the slang term for the infection was the shakes. Those babies quaked and tremored so violently that they wailed over their own lack of control.

I'd become used to the dark room with its rhythmic heartbeat. I found comfort there most of the time, but those wails and shivering, little bodies gave me anything but comfort. They fed my urgency to study longer and harder—to figure out the problem.

But even after arriving at the nursery and logging all the activity of the cradles for the last twenty-four hours, Jen's message still echoed in my mind. She'd had the ultrasound. She'd be having twins. I looked into the dark watery cradle of a child due for birthing in the next week.

Jen had no history of twins in her family. Heather had been pregnant with twins too. I'd heard one of the other couples was expecting triplets.

Odd. Multiple births were rare. Being a twin, this was something I understood intimately. Back in my time, they were becoming more common due to fertility drugs, but what would be the driving force behind so many unrelated multiple births now?

I checked the cradle's temperature, marked it as stable on the digi-chart and moved to the next one. In some ways I thought the instability in the cradles came from the fact that they were just cradles in spite of everyone telling me that a far greater instability existed when they tried to inject the fetuses into real wombs that allowed women to carry their babies naturally. A mother's womb was different. In the womb, the child was embraced by the love fed from its mother every second of the pregnancy. I remembered Aunt Theresa saying that a baby recognizes its mother's voice after it's born. What did the cradles provide in the way of memories for these babies? These babies never had chances to listen to their mothers hum, or giggle, or cry. These babies didn't get the chance to learn how emotions and moods fluctuate. The cradles were cold, sterile things. These babies were vastly deprived in comparison to Jen's twins.

I stopped midway through my inspection of the cradle. Was Jen taking fertility drugs? I snorted softly at myself. Surely, she would know that fertility drugs can create a multiple birth situation. Her doctor would inform her if he were to prescribe her such a thing. Would the Regents, desperate for babies, have included fertility drugs in our inoculations? I scowled into the cradle. *Stop dwelling on things that don't matter. Focus on your job!* With that admonishment and a bit of a shake to jolt myself back into my own reality, I finished checking the cradles.

Once home, I entered the data from the cradles into my lapdesk and spent the next couple of hours analyzing the difference between my data and the books I'd checked out from the library on healthy live births.

"Don't tell me. You're studying." Alison carried several shopping bags. It amazed me that she didn't overextend the credit given her on her IDR

"If you don't study the problem, you'll never find a solution.

"The problem you're trying to fix is obsolete."

Alison used the word obsolete? No matter what she said, she had to be studying a little to have so vastly improved her vocabulary. I didn't argue with her about the problems I wanted to fix. There had been a few dissenters in the New Youth, but for the most part the New Youth loved believing they were better than everyone else. Alison waited for some reaction, but upon getting none, she sniffed in disdain for me and likely for her bad luck on ending up with me for a roommate rather than someone fun. She went to the bathroom, got ready for bed, and slid under her covers. She made a huge show of putting on an eye mask to help eliminate the light from my lapdesk before rolling over in her bed so she faced away from me.

Alison hadn't been able to guilt me into turning out my lights so she could sleep for months. She likely believed I took some demented sort of pleasure in torturing her, and, when I felt like being honest with myself, some part of me did find satisfaction in making her miserable.

After another hour, when I felt certain Alison had gone to sleep, I went to her lapdesk and ran a search for "Shaw, executed, crazy." I used her lapdesk because out of all the New Youth, she was the least likely to be watched for nonconforming behavior.

There were over 58,000 pages with those key words. I narrowed the search by adding San Francisco. 23,467 pages. I narrowed it more by adding Professor Raik's name. 129 pages. My heart pounded as I opened the first page.

Kirk Shaw had worked as a physicist in the research of making long space travel possible. His programs were funded by the university under the approval of Professor Raik.

Kirk Shaw. Tag's father worked, however indirectly, for Professor Raik. The possibility of this being a different Shaw was there, but it fit so well into current circumstances. The article applauded Kirk Shaw for his vast achievements in physics, just like Tag.

There were many more articles on Kirk Shaw, the physicist. All the articles had similar themes; Kirk Shaw had achieved this great goal. He'd solved that great mystery—until page 67.

I read page 67 with an increasing horror. My vision clouded with tears.

San Francisco Times—May 13, 2102
The Regents were forced to take action on one of their own today. Kirk Shaw was sentenced and terminated according to Crazy Law. Shaw worked as the number one physicist under Professor Seaver Raik in the quest to perpetuate human life on other worlds. Shaw had made great advancements in his field when it was discovered by anonymous sources that he and his wife, Joy Shaw, had been harboring a Crazy in their home nine years past the time of testing. Both Shaw and his wife were terminated under Crazy Law. Shaw held police at bay while the Crazy and the Shaw's son escaped the house. The children were missing for several hours, sending police on a manhunt that ended in the park several streets from where the Shaw family resided. The Crazy held a child hostage at knifepoint, but after a forty-five minute standoff, released its hostage and accepted its fate. The Shaw property was confiscated and turned over to the state Regent to disperse throughout the community who suffered from this ordeal. Professor Raik said, "It is a shame that the community lost such a great mind simply because that mind was not strong enough to live within the laws of our great Regents." Professor Raik has assumed authority over Shaw's discoveries and will continue his research.

Who was the hostage? What was Tag's sister's name? Why had the article told so little? What kind of lousy reporter wouldn't want to add all the juicy sorry details of an orphaned child?

Only two of the other pages available under my search included any news of the execution and the Crazy child. But those articles were less detailed than the first. All the others were accolades to Kirk Shaw's amazing mind. I rubbed my eyes, noted the late hour and with a groan, moved to my bed. My fingers rubbed against the worn edges of my sun quilt, safely hidden underneath my sheet and bedspread, and I fell into the nightmarish sleep I'd grown used to over my life. Only in this nightmare, a crazy sister held me hostage, and Tag stood in front of us, not able to decide which of us to save.

TWENTY-TWO

4-1-2114

Yourit, your people are stupid. Nothing personal, and no, this isn't an April Fool's joke. I know you're different. But the scientists of the future have some pretty childish ideas. It's as if the trauma of a dying world and the war you only won due to lack of organization on the part of the Crazies made your scientists infantile and incapable of doing significant work on their own. I've been researching sterility, and mental disorders, and sexually transmitted infections. And guess what? They're all linked. Both Chlamydia and Gonorrhea cause sterility in men and women. And Cytomegalovirus and Chlamydia both can lead to mental disorders. When we pull blood samples and samples of the birthing fluids, we always test positive for these things and several others. But there seems to be a sort of symbiotic relationship happening with these three. The viruses are acting as a retrovirus, integrating their genetic material into the chromosomes of the human cells. The virus is taking advantage of the nerve cells being damaged by the bacteria that causes infertility. And the bacteria are hiding under the cover of the altered cells—feeding and breeding at a cellular level. They've actually altered the cells—damaged genetic code begets damaged genetic code, causing mental disorders and sterility resulting in no babies and crazy people. Professor Modesitt is looking for a cure to the craziness in the birthing fluids, but I don't think the birthing fluids are the problem. The problem is the genetic material donated to create new life. I could be wrong, and I don't have enough training and education to make any announcements to the medical community, but I really think they're looking in the wrong places to find a solution to their problem. The maternal genetic material in the mitochondria can, and has, mutated, causing mental instability. I know you deal with physics, but you've helped with my biology in the beginning. How advanced is your knowledge? Can you take a look at my tests and find anything? I don't know enough to try to find a cure, but at least looking in the right place for the problem might be half the battle . . .

Let me know what you think.

Sunny

I finished writing the letter on the stripped-down cardboard back of a shipping box for aquariums and tried to figure out how I was going to fold it up and stick it in *A Sliver of Midnight*. I hadn't mentioned Tag's family and how I knew what had happened there. If I ever got another chance to see Tag and talk with him one on one again, we might be able to discuss it then, but it seemed cold to bring up such painful memories and not be there to hug him after.

I finally left him a much shorter message in *A Sliver of Midnight* telling him to look in *Australia's Ancestry* for the real note. *Australia's Ancestry's* huge size made it possible to hide the note without needing to fold it.

After an hour of perusing medical books on genetics and sexually transmitted diseases and infections as well as books that specifically studied HTHBI, I stacked my armload of new research and prepared to leave.

"Quite a heavy load, Miss Rae."

I peered around the stack of books to see Professor Raik leaning against one of the glass columns and grinning his congressman smile at me.

"It's not that heavy." My heart quickened with the fear that he might have been following me. Had he seen me leaving notes in books?

"Not in literal weight maybe, but it is heavy reading, wouldn't you agree?"

I did agree. Only an idiot would look at my stack and think I'd picked out fluffy bunny books. I shrugged noncommittally, not sure of his intentions. "You did say I should take some science classes."

"So I did. Mind if I walk with you?"

I shrugged again and offered over an awkward smile. We passed under the sensors at the doors where the computerized female voice agreeably thanked me for my book selections and reminded me to return them in fourteen days. Professor Raik hadn't offered to help carry my books home proving once and for all that chivalry in the future was dead.

"Are you happy here?" he asked finally.

"Happy, sir? Is anyone really ever happy?"

He raised a perfectly shaped eyebrow and cleared his throat. I shifted my books so they didn't topple onto the sidewalk and waited for him to initiate a more specific conversation.

"Eddie invited you to a dinner party."

So that was the problem. Eddie was always the problem. "Yes, he did."

"And you declined?"

Well duh! That's what I would have said if it had been anyone but Professor Raik. "Yes, I did."

I turned down the sidewalk to go toward the garden tubes, but Professor Raik stopped me and motioned toward his car. I swallowed hard, but got into his car, settling the books on the seat next to me.

Once seated across from the professor, I remembered the note from Tag still in my pocket. The message carried nothing incriminating. Just idle chit chat from someone named Yourit. But if he already suspected . . .

"Eddies worries about you." He started again.

"Does he?"

"I'm trying to understand why you would reject him out of hand."

The car jolted forward, speeding along down the rails. Honesty might be the best policy. "Eddie has all the intelligence of lunch meat. Any discerning female would reject him, and I'd hardly call it out of hand."

"Intelligence. So you're looking for an intellectual equivalent." Professor Raik mulled this over a moment before he said, "Young Taggert is quite intelligent."

I willed myself not to blink, fidget, or shift with my sudden nervousness. Playing stupid with Professor Raik would, in fact, *be* stupid. *You have the right to remain silent*, policemen used to tell suspects. I wondered briefly if they still did that, or if they just ex-ed them and let the clean-up crew handle the rest.

"You've been running some interesting searches. And frankly, I'm curious."

"Curious about what, sir?" They'd checked my searches. Stupid, stupid, stupid! How had they checked my searches?

"Curious about your relationship with Taggert."

I snorted. "You think because I find Eddie repulsive that I have a relationship with a soldier I haven't seen in a year?"

The car jolted as the locks holding us to the rails released. We didn't slow our speed, but instead accelerated and lifted off the tracks altogether, taking to the sky. Professor Raik viewed the landscape as it swished past. *Where were we going?* He took his time in forming his answer.

"When was the last time you saw Taggert?" he asked. He still kept his gaze toward the window, but I knew he wasn't missing anything.

He likely had a vid-cam recording me so he could rewind and analyze our conversation later.

"The day I broke into the barracks."

"And yet you've dated no one while here. Doesn't that strike you as out of the ordinary?" He briefly flicked his eyes my direction, and offered an assuring smile. I hated his smile. Some of the girls thought Professor Raik was handsome, and they'd have made a play for him were it not for the directive that we were not to fraternize with anyone who had diseased blood. That put the professor in the off-limits category. Still, I wouldn't have been surprised if any of them had tried to seduce him. They loved him. I was terrified of him, even more now that I knew he'd been involved in the executions of Tag's family, and even more now that I was trapped in a flying car with him miles above the ground whisking off to who only knew where.

"I had a boyfriend at home. Nathan died in the car wreck I should have died in." I willed myself to look weepy, which wasn't hard. Nathan hadn't deserved his fate. He could have been amazing if he'd had the chance to live.

"So you abstain from romantic interests out of mourning?" His gaze settled on me—locking me into place.

My breath felt erratic; could he see that? Could he see how my blood raced through my veins out of sheer panic? "Survivor's guilt is painful. Besides I'm learning. You said we should learn. I've—"

"Oh I know." He waved away my protest. "I see those searches too. You're on a quest to cure the disease you don't understand."

I opened my mouth to tell him he was as stupid as his scientists, but bit down on my tongue hard enough to taste the blood. Insulting the man who scared me to tears didn't seem all that smart. "Lots of us aren't in relationships. My roommate isn't serious with anyone—"

"You know your situation is different. None of your classmates are investigating their soldiers, even the ones who had Taggert. None of the rest of your classmates worry about the commoners."

He said commoners as though he weren't one of them—as though his heart didn't pump HTHBI through his body too. I held his gaze as levelly as possible, my muscles hurting from holding still.

"How did you locate his name?" Professor Raik asked.

I shrugged, wondering what the driver thought of our conversation. I hadn't admitted to actually running a search because of Tag, and I hadn't used Tag's name in my searches for a long time. Kirk Shaw was not the same thing as Tag. Playing stupid might be the smartest option yet. "Can you be more specific? Whose name? I do lots of research."

"Taggert's father." Professor Raik very nearly growled the two words.

"I didn't research Taggert's father." Incredulity and the righteous anger of the wrongfully accused filled my voice. Having been raised in the foster care system, this was a voice I'd used a lot in my life. "How would I know who some soldier's dad's name was? I don't even know who *my* dad's name was. I've only done research on my sister, which there isn't any information on, by the way, and science stuff. What do I care whose related to who?" I added the part about my Winter searches because I knew he already knew and by making him look guilty of withholding information, it might make me look more innocent.

I held my breath. The denial hovered between us.

He made a noise in his throat, like a self-deprecating laugh. "Hmm. Well, we shall see what we see."

"Where are we going?"

"We're going to my estate for dinner." He turned his smile all the way up to "beaming."

"Eddie's going to be there?" It smelled like a set-up.

"Yes—and several others."

And how could I say no? He'd corralled me into the car, accused me of stuff I was actually guilty of doing, and I had no way of getting home again short of walking—past curfew—in the dark where crazies might still lie in waiting. "I'm not really dressed . . ." I had at least worn a skirt today, but not one I would have picked for a night out.

"You look . . . perfect."

I froze. I may not have dated a lot of different guys in my life, but knew that leer and recognized that tone.

My pulse quickened, and I drew myself back into my seat as deep as I could go, as if by moving those couple of extra millimeters, I'd be able to put myself out of his reach.

He didn't reach.

The rest of our flight was taken in silence. And though I'd looked away—out the window, pretending to find interest in the topography below me, his eyes never strayed from me. I could feel them roving over every inch of me and had to quash the desire to throw open the door and jump to my death.

When the car touched down, I was surprised to find we didn't hook into a rail system, he had a little landing pad in his side-yard. No rails led to his home.

As soon as the engine cut, I sprang from my door and moved several feet away from the car. If nothing, he grinned wider as if he enjoyed having unnerved me. I followed several paces behind him as he approached his palace-sized house. "Where do you keep the moat?" I muttered.

"We have several ponds in the back."

His answer surprised me since I'd kept my voice intentionally low so he wouldn't hear. "Oh, that's nice." His door glowed green on our approach, and we entered into a marbleized hallway that opened into a room with ceilings high enough to be mistaken for the sky. The many couples were all dressed formally, women in floor-sweeping gowns, men in dark-suited attire. Relief flooded me upon seeing Eddie— anyone was better than Professor Raik for company. I very nearly fell into his arms in my desperation to get away.

Eddie smiled. "You almost look happy to see me." His arm went immediately around my shoulder and no amount of shrugging and shoulder jostling removed him.

I was wrong. Eddie wasn't better than Professor Raik, stupider, maybe—but not better.

"I'm glad to see you changed your mind about joining me." He murmured in my ear, his lips intentionally brushing my ear lobe.

I went from shrugging to shoving. "I didn't change my mind, meathead. I was tricked into coming. You—just stay away from me." I put my hand out to stop him when he moved forward, knowing I was sending major mixed signals and not caring at all. I stepped in close enough to make myself heard by him only. "You mess with me, Eddie, and I will make that little accident you almost had while dodging the draft seem like a better alternative than what I can make happen to you. With my study in the labs, I have no problem *accidentally* injecting you with HTHBI. You'll be crazier than the worst of them, and you'll get the shakes so bad, you'll look like a human earthquake."

Eddie's jaw fell slack, and his eyes widened. I turned on a heel, and, feeling a bit like Alison, flounced away. I grabbed a glass from the table, poured myself whatever they had in the punch bowl, and let my anger simmer down from the boil. The corner provided an excellent place to fume and take in my surroundings. Most of the guests were Regents and Regent Advisors. These were the people in the futuristic limelight. These were the movie stars of the new world.

And they were watching my searches—even the ones not made on my lapdesk. The ring. The IDR must link somehow to wherever the searches are made—no matter whose lapdesk is used. These people killed Tag's family. And they'd taken me away from mine.

I didn't eat anything during dinner, my stomach soured by the company. Professor Raik's gaze followed me like a searchlight everywhere I went. He slid in beside me towards the end of the night while other people danced.

"So you really don't prefer Eddie?"

I narrowed my eyes to where Eddie danced with one of the other girl's from our dormitory. "The intelligence of lunchmeat."

Professor Raik's smile went from congressman to predator. "So do any of the young men we picked for you seem suitable?"

The impropriety of the question disconcerted me. Was this his way of seeing if I was a lost cause to furthering mankind and therefore available in some way? Maybe it was nothing and Eddie's advances mingled with my own paranoia had finally got the best of me. I didn't respond.

Before Professor Raik could ask anything else, a small eruption of excitement came from the far end. Regents clapped and let out cheers. Soldiers, dressed in what I supposed to be soldier formal—long silver black dusters over their silver black pants and shoes shiny enough to be black gemstones, marched into the room. They circled the entire perimeter. My breath caught when I recognized Tag as one of the soldiers. His concentration on his performance for the Regents meant he hadn't noticed me.

"They're magnificent!" One of the Regents declared. She turned to Professor Raik. "Really, Seaver! You've outdone yourself with this group!"

Professor Raik nodded in recognition of her compliment. And I couldn't help but agree with her assessment. *He* was magnificent. My Tag—magnificent. The near year we'd spent apart had only helped him to fill out more in the shoulders. His hair was a bit longer in the back. I couldn't help but smile while looking at him. The soldiers turned their heads towards Professor Raik as part of the program. Once facing him, they saluted. Tag's eyes widened when he caught my glance, and he stumbled over his next few steps of marching. The soldiers all passed us bringing their weapons to their shoulders. Tag jerked his head, glancing back at me once before returning to the drill.

Professor Raik's eyes followed Tag's line of site to me. Professor Raik's expression darkened briefly, but smoothed out as the Regents burst into applause at the soldiers' performance.

Professor Raik knew.

He didn't know about the notes, or the friendship, but he knew emotion bubbled up in us when we were faced with each other. He knew feelings existed where feelings should not. And no amount of denial on my part would convince otherwise.

Oh Tag . . . I wish I'd stayed away from the library tonight rather than getting trapped into this dinner. But in reality, it wouldn't have mattered.

Professor Raik didn't go to the library ever. His whole purpose in being there at the same time as me was to get me to this party.

And I was lying anyway. The joy at seeing Tag overrode my fears of what might come of this moment.

"Magnificent, Seaver!" The Regent repeated as she clapped energetically with the crowds. I briefly wondered if she'd been one of the Regents who recently adopted a baby from the public nurseries, but shook my head. It didn't matter. While she and several other Regents had Professor Raik otherwise occupied, I caught Tag's eye. *Library,* he mouthed. I nodded, slipped behind and past Raik and his Regents, heading for the staircase leading up to the library. Several people commented through the evening that Professor Raik's was one of the finest home libraries they'd ever seen. They all held this as a credit to Professor Raik's outstanding brilliance.

In the library, I pulled out a book on the history of Einstein, and settled myself on the couch, prepared to look innocent in case anyone else showed up. My toes tapped against the plush carpet impatiently while minutes ticked away from me. I thought about checking out the window to see the ponds Professor Raik had mentioned, but worried my ring getting too close to the window would leave evidence of my presence.

I turned pages absently and didn't read a word, my gaze slipping towards the door that remained stubbornly closed.

It startled me when the door did finally open. I averted my eyes back to the book to look like I'd been reading.

"What are you doing here?" Tag's voice. The book tumbled to the floor in my hurry to get up. I couldn't help it. I threw my arms around him. The act must have surprised him, or he would have likely pulled back, but he let me hold him a moment and even returned the embrace before he untangled himself from my arms.

"Why is it that the first thing you ever say to me is 'what are you doing here?'"

"Because wherever I get to see you, it's in places you shouldn't be!" He stepped back to put space between us.

"Why shouldn't I be here?" His attitude irritated me. In all this time it'd been since we'd seen each other and the only thing he could think to do was lecture me?

Tag backed away a few more steps. "Yes. I guess you should be here. I guess I should offer congratulations. I'd heard you were with Edward."

"Who? And congratulations for what?" Surprise filled me. There were rumors about me among soldiers?

"Edward. I don't know his last name. He trails after the professor like a dog. Professor Raik said you two were to be married."

"Eddie?" I laughed. "Eddie married to me? Do you really think I'm that desperate?"

Tag looked confused. "So you're not?"

"I'm not what? Desperate or marrying Eddie?"

"Don't confuse me. Just answer the question." He looked frustrated, annoyed, and worried.

I tried to sit back on the couch as I said, "Neither. I wouldn't marry Eddie if my life depended on it, and I'm too busy to be desperate."

He took hold of my hands making it impossible to sit down. He pulled me over to the desk. "Duck down under there."

I lifted my eyebrows at him. "You want me to what?"

He grunted and rolled his eyes. "If anyone comes and sees us together, it would be bad. Especially Edward. He'd make a big deal about it, and we'd both be in a lot of trouble, me especially. If you're already hidden, we can have a few minutes to talk without being worried."

I ducked down, admitting to myself that Tag was right and this set-up made sense. I sat cross-legged under the desk, hating how it diminished my view, I finally get to see Tag and end up only staring at his black shoes. "Why would Professor Raik tell you Eddie and I were getting married?"

Tag sat on the desk and faced the window, which irritated me since I really could only see his shoes then. But his sitting there and looking out would make him appear innocent to anyone coming in. "I think it has something to do with your searches."

"You know about those too?"

He leaned over enough to look me in the eye. "Searches that seem suspicious or overly questioning of the current political system mark you as a dissenter—even if you do those searches on someone else's lapdesk. The IDR pulses to any device used. The pulse leaves a digital fingerprint."

I figured it had to be the IDR to rat me out. "So you're saying the freedom of information act is no longer valid?"

"That's what I'm saying."

I caught his swinging foot before it smacked me in the nose. "What about freedom of speech?"

He sighed. "I told him getting women from any year past 1980 was a bad idea."

"Why, because we can think for ourselves?"

"No, because you aren't subtle."

"What kind of dumb man would want a subtle woman? He'd always have to remember things like her birthday and anniversary on his own because she wouldn't be in his face reminding him. Subtlety just gets men in trouble."

He leaned over the desk and grinned at me. "Yes well, the lack of subtlety gets questions asked when you're trying to keep a low profile."

"I'm sorry about your family." Changing the subject so abruptly and to such a brutal topic could be considered heartless, but I had to say it. I'd thought it almost as many times as I thought about telling him how much I loved him. Since I couldn't say the one, I had to say the other. Who knew when, or if, another chance would come?

His grin froze and then slowly faded into pain. His fingers curled over the lip of the desk gripping it so tight his fingertips went white. "I'm a soldier. I have no fam—"

"Don't!" My shout surprised even me. I crawled out from under the desk enough so I could face him. "Don't do that Tag. You have a family. Being gone doesn't mean they don't exist and that they don't belong to you. Winter is gone. I'll never see her again, but she's still my family. She belongs to me. Now more than ever since my memory of her is the only thing that exists. If I decided to forget, then I really would be erasing her forever. You can't do that to them, Tag. They belong to you. If you kick them out of your memory, they're really gone."

He didn't answer. His jaw flexed and his eyes shimmered as though he might cry, but he didn't cry. He stared at me and took deep breaths. I unlatched his fingers from the desk and took his hand.

"They broke the law by hiding—"

"Don't tell me you believe in that crap? Not being willing to turn their kid over to the government to kill doesn't make them lawbreakers. It makes them heroes."

His eyebrows creased into each other as though the conflicting emotions were colliding inside his head.

"She didn't hold me hostage," he whispered. "No matter what you might have read, she didn't. She was trying to protect me. My mom yelled at Janice and me to run. She yelled out to go and protect each other. It was the last thing I heard her say before I heard her body hit the floor. Janice was just trying to do what Mom told her and protect me from them. She would never have hurt me. She wouldn't have hurt anyone."

Janice. The name he'd cried out when we'd been together in that house.

I opened my mouth to offer him sympathy—something that might take the ache from his voice, but the door burst open.

TWENTY-THREE

Tag's hand released mine with a shove. I scooted back into the darkness under the desk, my heart thudding hard against my chest.

Tag stayed on the desk, but I could tell from the way his feet shifted that he'd swiveled to see who'd come in.

There was a thin gap between the lip of the desk and the backing that hid me. I peeked out the gap to see what Tag saw.

A soldier with his weapon drawn and trained on Tag stood next to Eddie. Both Eddie and the soldier looked confused as their eyes roved over the room. With them backed away by the door, I had a clear view.

Tag's voice sounded calm. "Does the professor know you've got your weapon drawn around one of his pets? He won't like that, Rhett."

The soldier's look went from confusion to dismay. He pointed to Eddie. "He said there was a soldier in here fraternizing with one of the New Youths. Raik wouldn't like *that* either. How was I supposed to know he wasn't playing straight with me?"

The soldier, Rhett, turned a lever on his gun that made a slight hiss as he powered down. "Sorry, Tag. We didn't mean to—"

"Where is she?" Eddie's interruption made Rhett grumble about New Youth stupidity.

"Give me a name, and I might be able to help you." Tag's even tone and casual unconcern carried over to his soldier friend. Rhett allowed himself to chuckle at Eddie too.

"You know very well who! She's not with everyone else!"

"Did you lose your date?" Tag asked. "It's hardly a compliment to yourself to think she ditched you to make with a soldier."

"Where is she?"

"You still haven't told me who we're talking about. Regent Amber was in here a few moments ago. So was Mrs. Thornburg. But I don't know where they went, so I don't know where they are."

"I'm talking about Summer!"

I flinched at the mention of my name. Eddie had stormed right up to the desk so that all I could see of him were the pressed creases of his pants.

"You mean the girl with Professor Raik?"

"Don't play stupid with me!" Eddie's manic voice had taken on a dangerous edge.

Tag laughed and slid off the desk. His legs moved away from the desk, and he wandered over to the bookshelf where I had a better view of him. "Play stupid? With you? I hate to play games with people who clearly have the advantage."

Eddie must not have realized he'd been slammed, but Rhett hid a chuckle in a cough. "Everyone's watching you. You kept her away for almost a week all alone. No one trusts you. You just stay away from her. She's my fiancée, and I won't tolerate her being damaged by a low-life, diseased-ridden—"

"That's enough!" Rhett cut in. "You've seen for yourself. Your girlfriend's not here. Go look somewhere else."

Eddie stomped out of the library.

Tag waited until the door whispered closed. "Saving that guy was the biggest mistake I ever made. His blood might be fine, but his intelligence is . . . lacking."

Lunchmeat, I thought to myself.

"I'm sorry I came in here loaded. He seemed so certain. And the rules—"

"Must be obeyed." Tag finished the sentence for him.

"I'm glad she's not in here. You know our orders. The gun wasn't set to taze."

"Yes. I noticed that."

"I wouldn't have ex-ed you, though." Rhett looked uncertain.

Tag smiled and shook his head. He looked tired. "Yes, you would've."

Rhett shuffled his feet a moment before brightening. "No, really! You owe me money! I can't ex you 'til you pay up!"

Tag laughed outright. "If that's all it takes, I'm going to borrow money from all the guys."

"You stumbled during drill when you saw the girl Raik's pet is searching for. That's why I believed him. There *is* something there, isn't there? You care about her; don't you?"

Tag's eyes slid to my hiding place. "Of course not," he said, his voice still casual. He settled himself on the couch and put his feet up on the coffee table.

He lied. I knew he lied by the panic that raced over his features in his easy denial.

"I don't love her. I don't even know her. How could I?"

"I didn't say anything about love." Rhett grinned knowingly and dropped himself on the couch next to Tag.

Tag's face froze in that half smile, the panic shouting from every frozen muscle. He laughed. "Well, you implied. But be realistic, I haven't seen her for almost a year."

More lies. They were my same lies—the ones I told Professor Raik. And yet, they hurt to hear—each denial a dagger paring off slices of my hope.

"Four days of life threatening accidents are enough to bond any two people. Anyway, it's not like I care," Rhett said, yet he looked like the entire conversation interested him more than anything in the world.

Don't trust him. Keep lying. And yet I wanted to hear something different. I wanted him to confess that he cared for me the way I cared for him. I needed to hear it like I needed air.

"Four life-threatening days that were a lot more trouble than they were worth." Tag stood up. "We ought to get back to the party. I'm obviously not going to get any reading done with people coming in with thoughts of ex-ing me." Tag laughed to show he was joking, but

235

Rhett stiffened anyway. Tag held the door for Rhett and shot me a meaningful look. Only I had no idea what the look actually meant.

Did he want me to stay? Did he want me to leave? I counted to sixty once preparing to do it nine more times when I realized Tag wasn't coming back. The danger involved in him returning would simply be too great. I crawled out from under the desk, straightened my skirt and raked my fingers through my hair so I didn't look suspicious. I hesitated at the door, worried about what might be on the other side.

With a deep breath, I cracked the door open and peeked out. The hallway seemed empty. I hurried out of the room, down the hall, and to the bathroom.

The bathroom was a good place to hide out since, when I finally came out, no one would question what I was doing. Anything done in a bathroom was an off-limit topic for polite conversation.

I stayed there for a long time. The knock on the door startled me. "Summer? Summer are you in there?" It was Brianna's voice. I'd seen her earlier on the arm of Brian. They were likely to be the next set of marrieds from our group.

"Yeah, I'm in here."

She made a noise that could have been either relief or exasperation. I couldn't tell which. "Everyone's been looking for you. You've got all those soldiers on edge and looking like they might start tazing people."

I pinched my cheeks to make me look flushed and opened the door. "I'm sorry. I don't feel very good and that stupid Eddie wouldn't stop following me around. This was the only place I could think of to hide out."

Brianna felt my forehead. "Well, you don't feel hot . . . maybe you're coming down with something though. Sorry about Eddie. You can ride home with us if you want."

"I'd like that."

She put an arm around me and led me back down the stairs to the party. Worried faces watched me descend the stairs, but many faces more never turned my way to look. Most seemed not to be looking for me, or to even care that I'd been missing. That made me feel better.

Not nearly as many people cared as Brianna had made it sound so the disturbance upon my entrance remained slight. Tag cast a cursory glance my way, rolled his eyes, and went back to the soldier he'd been talking to.

His apathy felt like a blow to my stomach, but I couldn't blame him. He had to act like I'd been an inconvenient part of his day. I turned my eyes away from him. Professor Raik finally swiveled from where he'd stood in heated discussion with Eddie. Eddie looked physically ill to have been receiving a tongue lashing from the professor.

Good. Serves the little punk right.

I could feel nothing but loathing toward Eddie. He'd stolen precious time away from Tag and me—time I didn't know if we'd ever get another chance at. Brianna walked me straight to Professor Raik and Eddie.

"She was in the bathroom. She's obviously sick so I'm going to see her home. Thank you, Professor, for a wonderful evening."

I was grateful for her explanation. She shook the Professor's hand. Jeremy held out a wrap to put over her shoulders and during that distraction, Professor Raik said softly, "No interest in him at all?" His head inclined in Eddie's direction slightly.

"Would *you* be interested in someone like that?" I asked.

He didn't respond, and I didn't continue the conversation, simply feeling grateful to be led away to the car waiting for Jeremy and Brianna. It took every ounce of will to not turn once more and look at Tag. My neck muscles were caught in a battle between what my heart wanted and what my brain knew to be stupid.

"One moment." Professor Raik's voice called out. "I brought you here. I should see to it that you return home safely."

Brianna released my arm and smiled at Professor Raik with utter adoration. "Why, that is very kind of you, sir." Brianna gushed and fawned over the professor a moment more before Jeremy dragged her off.

They were gone before I could think of anything to say to keep them with me.

Professor Raik made hurried goodbyes to a few select guests and took me by the elbow, leading me back to the front of his house where his car waited.

His driver was already seated in the front, appearing to have not left in the few hours we'd been inside. Professor Raik looked at the driver and an opaque divider went up between the front and the back.

Panic.

The car took off into the air. Professor Raik sat across from me, his eyes sharp and hungry like a bird staring at a worm. After several minutes, I almost relaxed, thinking he only meant to intimidate me—which he had. But surely he couldn't touch me. I was a New Youth. He was diseased. It was his own law. Of course he wouldn't break his own law.

I told myself these lies until he moved from sitting across from me to sitting next to me.

"You have no intentions of marrying," he said.

"Of course I do. I'm still really young. I have lots of time to decide on stuff like that." The tremor in my voice revealed my fear.

He smiled and reached up to tuck a strand of hair behind my ear. "I make you nervous." A statement—not a question. I didn't respond but automatically inched away towards the window. Really, if I jumped, would it kill me? Maybe I'd only break my legs. Or maybe I'd fall on something soft.

His arm wrapped around my shoulder while his other hand went to my leg.

I kept my knees locked together, wishing I'd worn jeans instead of a skirt.

He used my leg to pull me away from the door and closer to him. "I won't hurt you," he whispered.

I wished desperately for that to be true. *Don't hurt me. Don't hurt me.* I wished Aunt Theresa was here in this time with me. She'd kill any man who even allowed the thought of anything inappropriate to cross his mind. And if anyone ever had hurt me, she'd have hunted him down and killed him a hundred different ways.

But Aunt Theresa was dead. And Tag was too far away and entirely helpless when it came to the professor. I had no protectors.

Professor Raik's lips fell upon mine. My teeth ground together hard—my entire body clenched tight like a fist. His hand moved up my thigh, demanding, claiming. *NO!* I screamed inside my head. *Please No!*

Winter and I protected each other from this sort of thing. And yet here was the very man who had managed to separate us. He'd managed to get me alone where I had no protection, where no one would save me.

No one could save me but me.

I bit down on his lip, hard enough that when he yanked his head back in reaction to the pain, his lip tore in my teeth. I spit and almost threw up at the metallic taste of blood—like I'd been sucking on a dirty penny. I tried to scoot back toward the window, but his hand on my leg prevented me from moving. "No!" I said.

"I promised not to hurt you," he said, pressing a clean white handkerchief at his mouth. He lowered his face to mine again, his breath hot against my cheek. "I should've made you promise not to hurt me."

My breath stuttered out in spurts; my eyes tracked his every move so that I was prepared to block any further advance.

Professor Raik smiled, the blood giving his teeth a pink shine. "Of course, you can't hurt me. Not really. I am powerful Miss Rae. You need to understand that. I hold the nations by a chain. They all want what I have to offer them in the New Youth. I have wealth greater than anyone in all the nations because of my arrangements with the Regents. Why should I not get for myself what I've given them? I gave them futures in the New Youth; why deny myself a future?" His eyes searched over me as if I was a possession. "But I won't force you, Summer."

He called me by my first name, stripping me of the politeness in referring to me as Miss Rae.

"Just remember the power I have—the world and future I could offer you." He breathed in deeply at my neck before straightening. "But I won't force you. Someday—someday soon I'd imagine, you will come and ask me. You want to save this people. To save them, you'll need power. Power I have. You'll need me. You will desire me. All you have to do is ask."

He removed his hand.

I scooted back as soon as he released me. He smiled, taking note of the blood staining his handkerchief. He folded it neatly and put it back in his pocket before straightening his tie. He moved to sit across from me again.

I tucked myself against the door, keeping a wary eye on him, while trying to see how far it would be to the New Youth dormitory.

He didn't say or do anything else the rest of the ride—just smiled at me in that smug and satisfied way.

I hated him.

As soon as the car came to a stop on the rails in front of the dormitory, I jerked on the handle to open the door.

It didn't open.

In panic I turned back a questioning gaze to the professor.

"Eddie won't be allowed to bother you again. His claim on you is obviously misplaced. You need an intellectual equal. You belong to me, now." He reached across me, not bothering to keep his fingers from grazing over me as his ring glowed green and he opened the door.

I leapt from the car and ran into the building. Not even caring that I left a stack of books behind.

Kathleen was at her desk and stood immediately upon seeing me. "What happened?" she asked.

Could I tell her? Who could be trusted in this lunatic world? "Nothing," I said and tried to edge my way past her.

"You've got blood on your mouth and chin, and you just exited Professor Raik's car. That's quite a bit more than nothing."

"Do you think I'm infected?" I blurted. "Do you think I'm diseased now? Will I get the shakes?" Why would such a thought be the first to come to mind? I'd pretended to be too good to be elitist about the diseased people, but I felt terror at the thought of having caught the disease from Raik.

"What happened? Did he—"

"He kissed me, and I bit his lip. I spit the blood out as soon I tasted it, but what if I'm diseased?"

She took me up in her arms and held me tightly for a moment before tugging me into the back room behind her desk. "Let's get you away from prying eyes and clean you up."

The back room was more like a little break room complete with a small bathroom, probably so she didn't have to leave her post for very long. She handed me a water glass. "Wash your mouth out and spit into the sink. Do it until you feel like you don't need to anymore."

Would such a time ever come?

But I did as directed. I drained three glasses of water before sitting heavily into a chair, my whole body trembling.

"He broke the law," I said. "And I can't do anything about it. I can't tell anyone because he owns the whole world."

She smiled. "But you have the satisfaction of knowing he's going to have a sore mouth for a while. Lip wounds take a long time to heal."

I smiled too, though the action felt thin.

"Seriously, dear, good for you for fighting for yourself. He probably never imagined you were capable."

"Do you think I'm infected?"

"I don't know. You work in the labs, Test yourself tomorrow. I'm sorry he did this to you. I'm sorry I can't help more, but let's get you to your room." She helped me to my feet and kept her arm around me the whole way to my room.

"You're different from the others, Summer. You have a spark I've not seen for a long time. I have so little power, but I'll see what I can do to keep anyone from snuffing that spark out."

I nodded as my door glowed green. She turned and left me to enter on my own. I scrubbed in the shower for over an hour trying to get the feel of him out of my skin. *Stupid! Stupid! What had I been thinking getting into a car with him?* And yet, how could I have said no? Who really ever said no to Professor Raik? And for him to think I would someday choose him? On purpose? That's an old man with a healthy dose of ego. I would need to be on guard from now on. Could I buy a gun in this future? Did they have permits for things like that? Or maybe they still had pepper spray. I sank to the tub, letting the water run over me and down the drain.

***

On my way to bed, I noticed my lapdesk flashed with messages, sleeping would be impossible until I was certain none of those messages were bad. When I saw the first one was from Jay and knew that Jen was so close to delivering, I felt sick. *Please let the twins be okay.* The thought repeated itself in my head as the message opened.

Dear Summer,

I'm in the hospital right now with Jen. I am proud to tell you that I am the father of twins! I know, I know. I'm taking all the credit when Jen did all the work. We had a boy and a girl. Their names are Erica Dawn and Scott Michael. They are so tiny that I am terrified to hold them. Jen is exhausted and is sleeping now, but I figured she would want you to know immediately.

It was a little scary there for a while. They wouldn't let me in the room with her while she delivered due to the complications the others had faced. So I sat outside that room panicking. During one part of the delivery, nurses came running out and told me they had to put her under so they could take the babies because her stress levels were too high. I have no idea what they were talking about (and still don't). But they sure caused my stress levels to go up.

Anyway, when they finally let me in, there were two bassinets with babies in them. Jen was still sleeping. She woke up for a minute, smiled at the babies, and went right back to sleep.

I'm glad the babies are okay. I don't think she'd have been able to handle it if something bad had happened to them during the delivery. Visit us soon. We're asking you to be their godmother, so you have to come soon.

Love you, kiddo,

Jay

Relief flooded me. It wasn't like the last few moms. Everything turned out fine and all the suspicions that had crawled into the back of my mind slinked away invalidated. And I was a godmother!

I had no idea what that meant or what that required of me, but the honor of it thrilled me and overpowered some of the horrors of my night. There was a couple of messages from Alison—one informing me she'd borrowed my silk skirt, and another telling me that she found the cutest little puppy and wondered if I'd mind a pet in our dorm.

I looked around our room, and shook my head. If she had a dog, I'd end up being the one to take care of it.

Definitely no dog. Except . . . A dog would be good for protection. I wrote her back and told her to go ahead as long as the dog grew up to be one of the large breeds with big teeth. I wrapped myself entirely in the sun quilt and curled into the fetal position like so many of those babies in the public nursery after we'd taken them from the fluids and placed them in incubators until the parents came to pick them up. I wondered if they slept that way because they felt so completely unprotected.

***

Tag hadn't communicated since Professor Raik's little dinner party. I tried to tell myself he was just being careful, that he wasn't angry with me—or worse—dead because of me. If Professor Raik really suspected anything, he would definitely get Tag out of the way. I wrote several notes to Tag, but didn't mention the incident with the professor. The shame of being in such a position making me want to hide.

I didn't have the shakes—no HTH infection, which gave me great relief and guilt. Relief because I still remained pureblooded and guilt because the disease shouldn't have mattered so much to me. Was I just like the others in my group? If Tag came and asked me to marry him, would I deny him for fear of becoming tainted? I'd never inspected my feelings toward the disease on a personal level, and now didn't like what I'd discovered about myself.

Alison decided not to buy the dog.

Another Regent adopted from the public nurseries. Professor Modesitt felt that the Regent's example was a good sign for society. He said if we continue our work to make the fluids stable, we might be able to get all the Regents to adopt.

I ignored his excitement. The Regents were stuck up morons who spent more time claiming equality for everyone than practicing it. And the fluids weren't the problem. I was sure the actual sickness in the cells caused the insanity. But Professor Modesitt waved away that theory as one that had already been studied and turned out to be inconclusive. Professor Modesitt firmly believed the birthing fluids were the trouble.

It had been almost four weeks since I'd heard from Tag. I fumed and worried over this on my way to the nursery when I realized there were many families with small children on the ferry with me—children who all appeared to be around the age of three.

My gaze, accustomed to slipping away from the people around me, focused.

The woman sitting across from me clutched her squiggling daughter tight. "Down!" the child insisted as she tried to squirm her way free.

The mother murmured in her daughter's ear; the child relaxed and turned to stare at her mother pointedly. The child brushed the mother's lavender hair away from her face. "Are you going to cry?"

The mother was, in fact, already crying. Her husband kept a protective arm around her shoulders and tears fell from his eyes too.

The mother never took her eyes off the child as though each second might be the last she'd see of her.

And so it might be.

All of the parents seemed to be in a pre-mourning state—regardless of dress, hair color, skin color, or age.

Some of them didn't cling to their children so tightly, but allowed them to play and hold the railings as the wind from the sea swept across their faces. Children pointed out seagulls and clouds. Some of them looked down, hoping to see a fish jump from the water. Angel Island grew on the horizon as we neared its docks. All the parents remained focused on their little ones. As the ferry shuddered into its dock, small cries erupted and were quickly hushed by a few of the women.

No one noticed me, the New Youth, as I stared at them whispering words of comfort to each other and silently saying goodbyes to the children who didn't understand. And for the first time, I felt guilty— guilty that I could have children without worrying that I would one day have to ride the ferry.

I'd never come to the island on the day they did testing. Almost a whole year without ever having to witness this heartbreaking scene.

Once the ferry docked, and people unloaded, walking up the ramp, not knowing their fate, I stayed seated watching them go.

Every one of those adults would come back to the ferry crying. Some would come back and be crying out of sheer relief. But others would weep for the loss.

Nearly two-thirds of those children would not leave the testing center. They would be the unnamed—the lost.

A guard, not one of the soldiers, but a regular day-job guard approached me nervously. "You need to exit the ferry. If you want to go back to the mainland, you can get back on by reentering the turnstile."

My eyes met his. He shifted nervously under the direct gaze of a New Youth. I looked back to where the last of them disappeared up the ramp. He followed my line of site.

"I am not getting off the ferry today." My eyes burned with the tears I held back.

The guard eyed me a moment before nodding his understanding. "No. I don't suppose you are."

The guard went back to the captain manning the ferry where they exchanged heated words. "Then you go tell her!" the guard said before stomping away.

But the captain never did tell me whatever message he wanted relayed. After several passengers got on, the ship pulled out of the dock away from the weeping mothers, and fathers, and children who would not live to see another sunrise.

TWENTY-FOUR

I waved my hand in front of my dorm room door, making it glow green for me, and bit back a sob. Some days, the green approval glow reminded me of the glow sticks Tag had used for light during the time we had between my world and this one. Thinking of the lights reminded me of how uncomplicated that brief moment in my life had been. It had seemed complicated at the time, but in comparison, it had been like a moment of weightlessness before gravity pulled me to the ground and sucked me into the crust of the earth until I suffocated.

I pushed the door open and dropped my stuff just inside the room. Alison hated it when I did that, but I didn't care.

"I didn't think you'd ever come home."

The unexpected man's voice in my room made me jump and curse at the same time. He stepped out of the shadows, and my moment of startled fear turned to surprised relief. I needed a friend today. I needed someone to cry with me and understand my horror. "Jay! What are you doing here? Is Jen with you?" I crossed over to him and gave him a hug. Only when I had my arms around his neck did I realize his arms stayed rigidly at his side, and he hadn't smiled when I'd greeted him. I pulled away. "What's the matter? Where's Jen?"

When his eyes stared at me like glassy pools of dark water, I gasped. "What happened to the babies?"

His face crumpled at the word *babies*. He covered his face with his hands as tears leaked out his eyes. And then he reached out for me and clung to me like I was the only handhold on a sheer rock wall. "The babies are gone." His words broke into a sob.

Gone. Not sick, or hurt, but gone. I pulled him over to the bed and made him sit down. "Tell me what happened. Where's Jen?"

"She's at home. I can't tell her. She'll be so . . . so *broken*. I don't know what to do. I don't know where to go, or who to trust."

"Wait. What do you mean gone? How would Jen not know that her babies are gone?"

He stood up and faced me, his face twisted in grief and rage. "They *said* the babies were ours. But they aren't. Summer, they took the babies, and they lied to us. They stared at us, looking all happy and thrilled with us for providing the world with children who would never get the shakes at the same time they were lying to us about what they did. Because those babies—*those* babies are not mine!"

I tried to reach out for his hands, to make him sit back down, but he stepped away and started to pace in tight circles on the floor in front of me.

"Are you saying that Jen cheat—"

He whirled on me. "No! I'm saying the hospital took my babies and replaced them with those mutants they make in those nurseries!"

I flinched at hearing Jay call the nursery babies mutants. The babies I'd come to love, the babies who would grow to be children on the ferry someday. "That's quite the conspiracy theory, even coming from you." I stood up since he refused to sit again

"I'm not cra—well I'm not! When Jen went into labor, they took her to the hospital. They wouldn't let me in with her because they were afraid I'd contaminate the room or something. They were gone for a long time. It seemed like forever, and the doctor came out and told me they'd had to put Jen under. They said they had to in order to make the delivery happen without any complications. But they put her under so she wouldn't know. They wouldn't let me in so I wouldn't know. They tricked us. They stole our babies."

"Why would they do that?" Reasons of 'why' swirled in my mind. Instinctively I knew, before he opened his mouth to tell me—I knew.

"They gave them to a Regent." He gripped his hair in his fingers as though he needed something to hold onto, but couldn't find anything else. "No, not gave. Gave is the wrong word. They *sold* them to a Regent. The Regents don't want crazies. They want perfect babies. And they don't care if they have to steal them to get them. As far as the Regents are concerned, all of the New Youth is their property anyway."

"How do you know? How do you know the babies aren't yours?"

He pulled out a sheet of paper with graphs on it. "I took blood samples."

My head hurt. The day had been so horrible already; this was too much. "You put a needle in your own babies?"

"They aren't mine. Get it? They aren't right. I just couldn't seem to bond with them. Neither can Jen—not really—though she tries hard. She cries a lot and said it's likely just the 'postpartum depression,' or whatever, but it's not. Those babies don't act right. Scott cries all the time—I mean *all* the time. And Erica never cries at all. She turns away when anyone tries to look at her. She doesn't even cry if she's been too long without eating. And they don't seem to like even each other. Wouldn't twins feel comfort when they're together?"

That hit a nerve. Having Winter around always comforted me.

Jay continued, his pacing kept in tiny manic circles. "So, yeah, I tested them. And they aren't mine. And they aren't Jen's. I don't know who their tissue donors are."

"You've gotta tell Jen."

Jay shook his head. "I can't tell her until I have her own babies to put in her arms."

"So what? You come tell me? What do you think I can do?"

He stopped pacing, grabbed my shoulders, his fingers gripping so hard, it almost hurt. "I need you to get your soldier's help. I know which Regent has my kids. He and his baby-stealing wife haven't gone back to their own country yet. I need a way into the apartments where they're staying, in and out again. And I want an Orbital. I want out."

I shook my head and held up my hands in protest. Panic seized my chest. "My soldier? I don't—"

"Don't lie to me, Summer. I know you still communicate with him. And I know you care about him. I knew it the minute I found out you'd broke into the barracks when we first got here. The way he looked at you when we drove back with that crazy professor. You guys are close. Don't deny it. You can't think I'd turn you in, or whatever, for fraternizing with the *diseased riff raff.*" His tone oozed with sarcasm as he repeated the propaganda. "If I were going to do that, I'd have done it a year ago. I need his help. I want my kids back. And then I want out of this insane asylum. I'm taking Jen and *my* twins, and we're getting out of here."

I was still shaking my head and had jerked my shoulders out of his grip. "Why would you think I have any way to communicate with him?"

He looked at me like I was stupid. "You go to the same book all the time at the library. The same book and you never check it out? Do you honestly think you're sneaky?"

Well, I had until he put it that way.

My legs gave out from under me, and I sat on the bed once again. Jay wasn't making up stories. Every time there had been a misfortune with the marrieds' babies, there were Regents adopting. Of course the Regents couldn't keep claiming miscarriages and stillborns. They had to offer replacements for the infants they stole from Jay and Jen, or the marrieds would get suspicious, or depressed. Either way, they'd stop reproducing.

They needed my help. I looked Jay in the eye. "Tell me what you want me to do."

Alison came back long after Jay and I had finalized the details of the plan. "You still here?" She asked looking mischievous. "Will Jennifer be upset to know you've been in our room for this long?"

Jay smiled. "I'm here for her." The smile looked forced and didn't sit right with his eyes dark with so much rage and pain. Alison didn't notice.

"But you're right." Jay stood heavily from where he'd been sitting at my desk. "It's late, and it won't look good if I'm here all night. Thanks for letting me in earlier, Ali. I appreciate it. Waiting in the hall all night would have sucked."

Alison flinched at what she considered crude language, but her smile came right back on again as Jay stretched and moved toward the door.

"See you soon, kid." Jay gave me a hug, smiled once more at Alison, then left.

See you soon. Soon meant two days. He wanted me to meet Tag at the library tomorrow—Wednesday—the day Tag normally left me messages. Then he would meet us both the next day back here at the dorms.

I tried to explain that Tag had been silent for almost a full month; I tried to explain that Tag could very well be dead, but Jay wouldn't listen to the possibilities of things not working out right. Jay had a plan and intended to carry it out, no matter what.

There was so much ache in my bones that I pulled apart my lapdesk once Alison had gone to sleep and pulled out the pictures of Wineve and me. The one of when we were little, when Theresa first got us was the one that commanded my attention. "I wouldn't wish this world on anyone, Wineve. But I'd give anything to have you here with me." Between Professor Raik and his little attack, Tag seeming to have turned up missing, the children on the ferry, and now Jay, I wondered if it were possible to truly die of a broken heart. I had no one to help shoulder my burdens, and they suddenly seemed too heavy to bear.

***

The library wasn't particularly busy, but I cringed when the doors flashed green, "Welcome, Summer Dawn Rae." I'd never really cared that the computer announced my comings and goings to the library, but today it felt as though the announcement was heard around the world. I didn't slow my stride, and headed straight to the book. "Please be there," I whispered under my breath.

I almost broke into a run when I saw him standing among the stacks putting our book back on the shelf. His other hand was stuffing the three small notes I'd left into his jacket pocket. I picked up my pace so he wouldn't leave the stacks before I got to him. It would look weird if we both went in there together.

"Tag." My voice cracked with the sob—the sob of all the pain of the last month, and worse—the pain of the last 24 hours.

"Summer!" His eyes darted around to see who might have witnessed my arrival. "Summer, you shouldn't be here. You can't keep doing this. If they catch you, they won't hesitate to take action. They won't care that you're one of the New Youth."

I glanced around, feeling paranoid enough on my own, but with him acting freakish too, I felt like I might jump out of my skin. "I had to come. I need your help. So much has happened."

"What? What's happened?" Caution edged his voice.

"Professor Raik . . . all those toddlers in the public nurseries . . . my friends. The Regents are evil disgusting people."

Footsteps echoed on the marble floors of the library, and I jumped, but they were echoing away from us, not towards. Even so, I grabbed Tag's hand and pulled him deeper into the stacks. Even with all my fear, with all the conspiracies raging through my mind, my stomach still flipped upon holding his hand. I wanted nothing more than to lean my head on his shoulder and weep while he held me.

"To say such things is traitorous. Please, Summer, use caution."

"They took her babies." I hadn't meant to blurt it out like that, but panic, and fear, and the need to have someone on my side, someone who could help me, overcame the need to explain properly. "The Regents kidnapped Jay and Jen's babies. They took the babies from the other marrieds too. None of those babies died in childbirth or were miscarried. They were stolen."

He stepped back, trying to distance himself from me, but I gripped his hands tighter. He shook his head. "You can't say things like that. No doctor has done a live birth like that for decades. They weren't prepared. Those other babies died. Next time they'll have better training. And your friends have their children."

"Jay took blood samples. They switched his children with babies they got from the public nurseries."

"That's impossible—"

"Tag! Listen to me! Impossible? Both of her babies are missing—replaced by babies from the nurseries, and out of the blue a week later a Regent decides to be good examples to his country and adopts two babies from the public nursery? Every time one of the married couples had a baby die, another Regent gets the grand idea to adopt? That doesn't seem suspicious to you?"

Tag darted a quick look around and hunched in closer to me. "Could you keep your voice down? You're acting—"

Heat flamed over my face. "I am *not* crazy! I'm telling you something is wrong here. Something bad is happening."

He let go of my left hand and gently brushed his fingertips across my cheek and tucked my hair behind my ear. Professor Raik had done that too, only when Tag did it, the feeling made me feel safe instead of preyed upon. "I'm sorry. I shouldn't have said that. Not after I worked so hard to get you to stop calling people that. It's just . . . this is a lot to digest right now. I'm sure Professor Raik would never—"

"What do you owe that guy?"

"What?"

"You defend him like you're his personal bodyguard. He's the villain here, Tag."

Tag's free hand rested on my shoulder and with his other hand, his fingers tightened on mine. "He took me in when everyone else would have had me ex-ed. He gave me a home, gave me an education. He's been like a father to me. I owe my life to him." His fingers traced along my neck as he pushed all my hair behind my shoulders. His eyes locked onto mine—pleading for understanding.

"You don't owe him anything. He was there when it all happened because he made it happen. He was the one who ratted out your family and got your parents and your sister killed. Taking you in wasn't an act of mercy. He took you because he wanted you—wanted your brain. How many of the ideas that make the Orbital work were yours, Tag? The *Tesla Ether*—who figured out how to pull energy from the ether? He killed your family and used you. And he's a snake. And now he's stolen my friend's babies and sold them to the highest bidder. He told me he controlled the nations. And I think he really does. He said he gave the Regents what they most wanted—babies with no complications. This is a huge money scheme for him."

Tag's whole body froze, his eyes hardened into the cold blue ice that were both familiar and frightening to me. "You're wrong."

"I'm right. And I need your help."

He shook his head. "I can't help you. Not with this."

"What do you owe him?" I wanted to shout the words. I wanted to scream until my lungs dried up.

"I don't owe him. I owe her. Janice gave up so I could live. She's dead to protect me. I owe it to her to keep living."

"I see." And I did. His whole life centered on the guilt of that day. He likely truly believed that he brought New Youths into the future to save the future. He likely did it all in Janice's name, but he'd been wrong. They were selling the babies to Regents who didn't want the mess of crazies.

"Have you told Jennifer? Have you told her any of this?" he asked.

"Oh yeah, because I want to tell her that her babies are still alive and being rocked to sleep by total strangers and the kids she's been trying to mother will have to be euthanized when they turn three, and probably before that since they're already displaying signs. I'm just running around breaking the hearts of the people I love. Oh wait. No, I'm not. You are!" I dropped his hand with a shove of disgust and turned my back on him.

"Summer, don't—"

"Don't tell me one more time to fit in, lie low, figure out the system and cheat it, because you're a hypocrite, Tag. You know the system, and instead of cheating it and making things better, you're standing to the side and watching the system eat away at everything. You think you're doing it for her, but I think you're doing it because you're a coward. I'm done watching. You do what you want." I hurried away then, not running like I wanted. Not doing anything to attract attention. Running would have to be done some time, later on when there would be nothing left to do but run.

I stomped into the elevator.

"Going down," the elevator voice said.

"You're absolutely right," I said back. "You're all going down."

TWENTY-FIVE

There was only one option left. Professor Raik wanted me to ask. Well he'd get his wish. He said I'd come to him, and he was right about that, but he was wrong about my reasons. The two Regents who'd adopted the babies hadn't yet gone back to their own countries. They wanted to wait until the babies had been properly immunized. Raik would know where they were staying. He would have access to them; I had access to Professor Raik. Jay needed that access.

I'd need to hire a car to take me there and wasn't sure of the protocol so hurried back to the dorm first. Besides, I'd need to collect any of my belongings that I wanted to keep, in case things turned out bad, making returning impossible.

I packed an extra pair of jeans, Winter's shirt, some underclothes, the pictures of Winter and I, and the sun quilt all into a big backpack. I glanced around the room, but couldn't think of anything else collected in my year in the dorm that was important enough to take with me.

With a deep breath and a tight grip on my back pack strap, I went downstairs to find Kathleen.

Her hair was tied back in that ever tight bun that stretched her wrinkles across her face. She turned, her black skirt swirling with the motion when I cleared my throat and said her name.

"Yes, dear?"

"I need to hire a car." I tried to sound confident. People who hired cars had to be confident. I'd already been yelled at for the little adventure with Jay and hiring cars.

Kathleen lifted an eyebrow and set down the tray of flower arrangements for the dining tables she'd been holding. "A car, Summer? Where will you need to go that you would need a car?"

My plans had to sound important and had to be truthful because they could track where I went with my IDR anyway. "I'm going to visit Professor Raik."

She took in a small sharp breath, and her head barely moved in what might have been a shake of disapproval if she hadn't caught herself. "What is your business with Professor Raik that you should need to see him without him sending for you?"

I tilted my chin in defiance. I was the New Youth after all. I didn't need to answer to anyone. "It's personal."

She stiffened. "Of course. Why don't you come back here with me while I make the arrangements? That way you'll have somewhere to sit and rest."

I followed her behind her counter to her break room. She motioned me to sit at a red plush chair in the corner by a small table. I sat. She maneuvered to her lapdesk and continued to cast cursory glances my direction before muttering under her breath, scraping back her chair and standing abruptly. "No, I won't!"

"What?" I stared at her in disbelief. Did she really just tell me no?

"This may get me ex-ed, and I just don't care. I think I know what you're doing going to see that man. You won't accomplish anything—not that way. And you'll lose yourself there. That man'll never let you go. You won't help anyone by going like this."

My heart raced and I stood too, trying to slip towards the direction of the door. *She knew? She knew what my plans were?* "I don't know what you're talking about. What do you think I'm trying to accomplish?"

She placed herself between me and the door and crossed her arms over her chest and scowled. The scowl along with that severe bun made her almost as frightening as a soldier with a charged weapon. "Don't play the fool with me. I've been on his orders to watch you since you got here. He almost sent you back like he did a few of the others in the beginning. They weren't submissive. They weren't vain or desperate enough to live to take part in this scheme."

My mouth had dropped open. "Sent me back? They were going to send me back?" My chest tightened around the pain in my heart. *I could've gone back.*

Her eyes softened. "No, dear, not like that. No one goes back and gets a second chance with their lives. Going back means they send another soldier back to just before whatever accident took your life. The second soldier informs the first that the mission is to be aborted. Whatever happened to take your life will happen on schedule. Those sent back weren't to be considered lucky."

"But they didn't send me back." I shook my head realizing there was no way around her. I'd have to play the part of a New Youth so she would drop her suspicions. "Because I deserve to be here. I'm the elite. I—"

Kathleen let out a grunt of disapproval. "Oh stop! You don't believe that. I told you I've been watching you from the beginning, keeping track of where you go, who you talk to. Professor Raik doesn't trust you. He lets you stay because you're intelligent and strong and those are attractive traits. If you go to him like a sacrificial lamb, he'll have no problem slaughtering you. You already know he's capable."

She crossed her arms over her chest. "I saw Jay Savage come to your room the other night. Are my assumptions right about why he was there?"

"You haven't told me what your assumptions are," I said carefully.

"The marrieds were all separated, secreted away, and then they lost their babies. Why wouldn't they keep these people together so that any offspring they create would grow up together, intermarry, and create more offspring? Why would they all lose their babies when nothing was wrong with any of them? Jay knows about the babies, doesn't he?"

Careful. I had to be careful. But I was also so afraid, and her questions jumbled my senses. I stared at her black skirt.

Her hand went to my chin, and she forced me to look at her. "You're not like them. Your heart is good. If you want to help Jay and Jennifer, then you can't face him directly. He's crazy, you know."

The word crazy made me jerk my chin from her hand.

"Don't act surprised. You know it's true that man walks an unstable line. You go to him and you will lose yourself."

I threw my arms up in the air. "So what am I supposed to do?"

"Every fine home has a service entrance. And I happen to know the people who take care of that house." She smiled. In that smile, I made up my mind to trust her.

I told her my whole plan. "Tonight's too soon!" She insisted when I tried to get her to go with me immediately. "The only servers in his house after dark are cooks, and not a one of his cooks are friendly enough to help you; plus, he'll be home. You don't want him home while you snoop about. Wait until morning. Be patient."

Patience wasn't my best virtue if I could count it as a virtue at all. Sleeping was impossible, and I had to pull out my sun quilt after Alison had started snoring. That did the trick and soon it was morning. I acted sick so Alison would get ready and leave without me. Then I hurried to dress myself, repacked my backpack, and waited for Kathleen to fetch me.

Part of me feared she was setting me up, making it take every ounce of effort not jump up and run away on my own.

When the door glowed green and Kathleen appeared, I half expected a small army of soldiers to be with her.

She was alone, and looked as nervous as I felt.

"I've done some looking into things, just in case he keeps things in his office here. I didn't find anything, so it must be all at his house. I know some people handy with the IDR access who broke into his lapdesk. He doesn't keep anything much there except student schedules and other things that don't help. That means everything you need is physical—real paper and the like. That man may be crazy, but he's smart enough to know how vulnerable the lapdesk access is to anyone with a whit of skill. I'd hoped we could keep you out of his house altogether, but it looks like you'll have to go in."

I nodded, anxiously awaiting her to lead the way, but she stopped me. "Leave your ring here. The IDR won't grant you access to the dark and will alert to those watching that you're trying to go into unauthorized areas."

I yanked the ring off my finger, placed it under my pillow, and followed her to the dining hall. We didn't go through the doors I typically used—the ones all the New Youths used. We went through the door that led to the kitchens. Dennis was there.

"Den, I got a package for you to deliver to your girlfriend's mum."

Dennis wiped his hands on the front of his food-stained white smock and looked up to find me there. He immediately shook his head and backed away. "Last time I took her to the dark levels, Natalie got tazed."

"Yes, well this time, you'd better be more careful because if anything happens to Summer, you'll wish it was a just a good tazing you'd get."

"What's Natalie's mum got to do with her?" He'd picked up a chopping knife and deftly sliced a carrot into little orange coins. He'd started another one when Kathleen grabbed his hand away from the chopping block.

"She needs into the professor's house. She just needs information. It's not like she'll be taking anything he'd notice was gone. No one will know she's ever been there. No one will get caught or into trouble."

I didn't mention that I'd gathered my things in case I couldn't come back, in case I did get caught and needed to run. Dennis looked skittish about the whole idea as it was.

When Dennis consented, Kathleen turned back to me. "Good luck."

"Why are you helping me?"

A shadow fell over her face, and her lower lip tightened against the upper one. "I lost two little girls to testing day."

I nodded. The words, "testing day" said everything that needed saying. That very first day Kathleen had indicated a great hope in the

New Youth. If she now knew the professor was using that hope to make his own life more comfortable, she must be really angry.

Dennis took off his apron. "I'd better hurry. If we're gone too long, you'll be wrong about no one being in trouble—*I'll* be in trouble."

I threw my arms around Kathleen's neck. "Thank you for helping me. You know, you remind me of my aunt Theresa."

She smiled as though she understood the compliment I never thought I'd place in such words.

*****

"Keep up!" Dennis called as he led me deep into the dark levels. I felt like I'd walked down enough stairs, we should've reached the earth's core.

We entered a wide cobbled sort of street off a narrow alleyway. It felt like we were in a neighborhood at nighttime, not in some weird underground sewage system. He knocked on the third door to the left. The knock made a tinging noise since the door was made from a thin rusted tin sheeting. Natalie opened to his knock and nearly bowled him over in an embrace. "Did you tell them you were sick? How did you get off work?" Then she saw me and dropped her arms so she could fold them over her shirt that glowed an odd bluish white in the light over their door. "What's going on?"

"We need to talk to your mum." Dennis looked genuinely sorry to be standing there making such a request.

Natalie eyed us both before widening the gap of the doorway and let us in.

Natalie's mom, Maggie, shook her head to say no and shook her fists to say absolutely no. At least until I told her about the babies.

"Babies born naturally . . . And here I'd thought the world was about to end when you're telling me it's just starting over." She grabbed a bright white apron and placed it over my head. "Raik's housedressers always wear these. You'll stand out showing up without it." She also made me wear a hat to cover my natural brown hair.

Dennis had gone as soon as he'd relayed his message to Maggie. I silently wished him well as he made his way back to the world in the sky.

Maggie gathered a few other things and set off. We took several derelict elevators going to various degrees of up. She'd apparently had better clearance than Dennis because he hadn't had access to very many elevators at all. Like Dennis, Maggie barked out orders to pick up my feet and keep up. "If I'm late, there'll be questions!" She insisted. Once we reached a level she called topside, but still seemed like the dark hallways of the cities under the earth, we caught a train.

"He's almost always gone until five on weekdays." She coached me on how many precious minutes I'd have. How I should keep my head down and not speak to anyone if I ran into them. "And don't touch anything you don't need to, and absolutely don't take anything out of the house. I can't have trouble for my family, understand me?"

I nodded and agreed and tried not to catch her paranoia.

We exited the train and entered a "for hire" car. The car took us to Professor Raik's mansion, settling in the back close to some sheds. A couple of men moved in the garden area beyond the pond, but they didn't bother to look up beyond a passing glance at the car arriving.

Once the car had taken off, Maggie set off for a small door at the back of the house. "Stay close to me. You aren't getting in without me and my IDR," she said in a low voice. "Once we're inside, I'll take you to his office. I won't come back for you for forty-five minutes. His office is the only door in his house that requires an IDR for entrance and exit. You'd better be ready when I come for you because I won't be giving a second chance." I nodded even though I walked behind her and she couldn't see me. I hoped it wouldn't take forty-five minutes to find where the Regents' apartments were.

We crossed the main hall, where his big party had been held, to a hallway with several doors, his office was the last door straight back. I bounced on my toes a little as Maggie swept her hand over it and it glowed green. "Remember," she said for the tenth time. "Don't touch anything you don't need and don't take anything! None of the other housedressers have access to this room, so my entire family will be at risk if you get caught. Don't get caught." She gave a short nod to indicate she meant business and closed me inside.

I turned to face the office and grunted. The huge room would take hours to search. There were as many shelves in here as there had been in his library upstairs. And they were all full. The shelves seemed too daunting, so I made for the desk first.

The long top drawer held nothing interesting. An old fashioned fountain pen and ink pot sat in a thin marbled case. I snorted at that. Who did the guy think he was? King George? There was a keychain with a chunk of amber dangling at the end. A couple of real keys also dangled from the amber keychain. No one used real keys anymore.

I sifted through his belongings: the letter opener shaped like a dagger, and the odd paperweight shaped like an Egyptian scarab beetle, cough drops, packs of gum, and a few electronic things that could have been anything.

Nothing.

I cursed under my breath, furrowed my brow and went for the second drawer. He had real paper files here. I opened a few of them, but nothing looked interesting except the one at the back which had a patent seal. It looked like an invention of some sort and had Raik's name at the top. So was the man a frustrated inventor? I shoved the file back in the drawer. Who cared who the man was or what he wanted. I made a vow to not get lost in anything else I might find until I found the information Jay needed.

I kept that promise through the third drawer, ignoring the files with several names of marrieds and not quite yet marrieds that I knew personally. I kept that promise right up until at the very back I found a file with my name.

I forgot the promise immediately.

"What's this?" I lifted the file out of the drawer and spread it open on the desk. It had Tag's report of my life, all the information about who I was, what I liked and didn't like, my test scores, my grades, my blood type, my physical exam records, news clippings of the accident and the coroner report. Tag had said many times to me in those few days we were together, "When you died in that accident . . ." But I hadn't really felt dead until reading the news clippings of the accident, my obituary, the coroner's report. "I really am dead," I whispered.

In the background of the picture they'd taken of the accident, I could see Winter with her head buried in her hands. I traced my finger over her picture. "I should have stayed in school like you asked, Wineve. I'm sorry. I didn't know." I sniffed and blinked back the stinging in my eyes, and flipped over the newspaper to uncover the papers behind it.

I blinked again, but in confusion this time. It was a report on Winter. I read through it entirely. The report listed a series of dates with boy's names and the level of infections they carried next to them. It listed her blood type, her physical health stats. There were words like Low Ovarian Volume, Low Antral Follicle Count, PID, and the words fatal ectopic pregnancy with a date.

Fatal ectopic pregnancy.

I looked down to find the next paper in the file was her coroner report.

The paper seemed to be shivering as a result from my shaking hands. "She dies!" I started pacing, having entirely forgotten my reason for being in Raik's office, having entirely forgotten everything.

What else mattered?

I'd done enough studying over the last year on STD's and STI's. I knew what PID meant—pelvic inflammatory disease. Chlamydia caused PID and had the potential for ectopic pregnancies. My sister died as a result of the same thing that was slowly weeding out all of mankind.

"She can't die!" I yelled. "Not her!" If Jay was getting Jen and the twins out of this time zone, he was taking me with.

I was going home.

TWENTY-SIX

I still searched for the information Jay needed, but couldn't find it anywhere. There was nothing on the Regent apartments. I took out the files on Jay and Jen and was starting to read them when the light glowed green at the door. I stood up—puzzled. Had it already been forty-five minutes?

The puzzlement drained into horror when I saw Professor Raik's surprised expression. He took several awkward steps into the room. When his eyes fell on the open files on his desk, his surprise turned to anger. His face contorted into rage.

Three soldiers came in behind him—one of them the red-headed general. They too looked surprised to see me there, but none of them looked as surprised as Tag.

"What is the meaning of this?" Professor Raik shouted.

His anger alerted the soldiers that my presence here was unwelcome and the first two snapped their weapons to attention. They were like fine-tuned machines answering the push of a button.

I stood frozen to the spot, a few errant papers still dangling from my fingers. From behind Professor Raik and the soldiers, I caught a glimpse of Maggie's pale face before she turned and sped away from the scene. I hoped she got her family moved and hidden before anyone realized how I'd gotten in.

"What are you doing here? Who sent you?"

I didn't answer. My legs were tight and ready to spring into action. My heart pounded so hard that the blood rushing past my ears almost drowned out Professor Raik's question.

Professor Raik didn't wait for an answer. "Taze her."

I should have been grateful he didn't say, "Kill her." But before I could even duck, I felt two tiny impacts—one at my chest, and another one at my collar bone. My body seized up like a huge single cramp. My arms curled inward, and I was on my toes as the shock arced through me. Pain coursed up and down my spine, but I couldn't cry out. My forehead felt like it was being squeezed like a lemon, and my shoulders hunched into my ears. The whole moment felt like an eternity before my seized-up and cramped muscles released and I was on the floor, breathing hard. I yanked the tazer clips off me.

Professor Raik was shouting something and there were other shouts too. I crawled out from behind the desk so I could see and know where to run, my muscles rapidly getting over the shock of the tazing effects. None of the soldiers had their guns anymore. Tag had a fistful of the general's red hair and was using the general's head to ram the other soldier in the chest. The one being rammed was knocked to the ground. The one doing the ramming toppled over, apparently knocked unconscious by the blows. The soldier on the ground pushed the general off and kicked out at Tag's legs. Tag almost missed jumping the kick and danced back several steps to avoid another swipe. The soldier jumped to his feet and swung at Tag's face. Tag ducked the punch and came up with two successive blows to the chest and one to the face.

Raik grabbed my ankles and pulled me back behind the desk. He was sitting on me now, pinning my legs to the ground. His hands reached out and pinned my arms down too. "Always trouble with you. I should've sent you back."

Instead of answering, I grabbed the lapels of his shiny black suit and used his weight to roll him. I got my leg out from under him and slammed my knee up in between his legs. I straightened my leg and brought it in twice more before daring to try to stand and get away. Raik grabbed for my leg, but I pulled myself up to the desk for leverage and slammed my foot into his nose. His head hit the floor, and he stopped moving.

Tag still fought the soldier, dodging as many punches as he caught. His face had several cuts. The soldier pulled a knife from one of the many pockets in his jacket and Tag punched the soldier's wrist. With a terrible snapping noise, the soldier's hand flopped to the side, the knife falling to the ground. Tag turned so his back was to me, swept up his leg and kicked the soldier in the face with his boot, knocking the soldier to the ground.

His chest heaved as he stood over them. His back rising and falling as he struggled for breath.

Raik woke up, moved to his feet, and dragged his hand across his nose, smearing the blood over his cheek. He glanced at the blood on his hand and growled as he lunged for Tag.

"Look out!" I screamed.

Tag turned in time to be caught by the sheer force of Raik's momentum. They both fell to the floor in a tumble. They rolled and struggled, Professor Raik gaining the advantage, using his hand to keep Tag's head against the floor so Tag couldn't roll him the way I had. Tag bit into the fleshy part under Professor Raik's thumb. Although Professor Raik screamed, he didn't release Tag.

I grabbed the paperweight of the beetle and, using Tag's example, in my other hand grabbed a fistful of Raik's hair. I slammed the beetle paperweight into Raik's face several times before he released Tag's head and caught my hand, saving himself from another crunching blow. He twisted my arm, forcing me to cry out and drop the beetle. Pain shot through my shoulder.

Tag maneuvered out of Raik's grasp, brought his hands together and slammed them into Professor Raik's chest. Professor Raik buckled under the blow. Tag punched him hard in the face, knocking Professor Raik unconscious.

Tag jumped to his feet and grabbed for one of the guns in the process. He then grabbed my hand and said, "Are you okay?"

I nodded dumbly, my hands running over my body to check to make sure I really was okay.

He kept the gun trained on Professor Raik in case he decided to get up again. "Did you get what you needed?"

"Winter dies!" I said, my voice the horrible shriek of the inconsolable.

"Everyone dies sometime, Summer. Did you get what you needed for Jay?"

I'd forgotten about Jay—forgotten about Jen and their babies. I shook my head.

"What are you looking for; I probably know where it is." He went behind the desk, still keeping the gun trained to where the soldiers and Professor Raik lay unmoving on the floor. "We can't stay here; there was a housedresser out there, and she's likely called for help by now."

"She's running by now. She's the one who let me in."

Tag nodded. "We still need to hurry. What do you need?"

"I need to know where the Regents are. The one who recently adopted is staying in town. And I need two Orbitals."

"Why two?"

"One for Jay and one for—"

"One for you. So you were going to leave me?" His jaw muscles flexed as though he were grinding teeth.

I shrugged lamely. "You said you wouldn't help me."

"Well, I've obviously changed my mind." He handed me the gun. "We need to get these guys tied up. If we leave them, they'll be able to sound alarms and cause trouble. If they move while I work, shoot them." He removed the rings from all three of the unconscious men and put the rings in his pocket. He tied them up, grabbed the other guns on the ground and said, "Let's go."

"But we didn't—"

He rolled his eyes. "You're in the wrong place. The soldiers are given orders to guard the Regents when the Regents are in town. We have a schedule in the barracks, and any of us who've pulled guard duty . . ." Tag pointed at himself. "Knows exactly where we're going, because we've been there before and won't even have any trouble getting in."

"What about the Orbitals?"

"Kept in Raik's office at the barracks."

"Oh." I felt stupid. I broke into the wrong place. All this drama and Tag had all the answers. I also felt angry. If he had all the answers, he should've helped me yesterday when I asked for help.

But I didn't regret coming into Professor Raik's house. I grabbed my file and stuffed it in my backpack. "Then let's go."

Tag tazed and knocked out the driver of Raik's car and dragged him off into the bushes before we could leave.

"I've always hated that guy," Tag said as he lifted the car from its parking place by the house. We tracked on the rails near the barracks and Tag pulled to the side. He turned to me. "You have to stay here."

"Why?"

"Because you kind of stand out, and there are more than two soldiers in the barracks. We'd be dead before you could say, 'bad idea.' So stay here. I mean it."

"I'm not a child. You don't need to repeat yourself."

He made a face at that and got out. He leaned his head back in. "And stay down. If anyone sees you, they'll wonder why Raik left you in the car."

I agreed and slid down to floor where I scrunched in a ball to keep myself out of sight.

Tag was back relatively quickly with three Orbitals. He threw them in my seat and hurried to track the car and get us moving. He didn't even glance at me beyond a quick verification to make sure I was still there.

"I don't know where to find Jay." I hated the admission. It made me look stupid and disorganized. But Jay had said he'd meet me at the dorms and I didn't think we could go back there. That would be the first place searched when Raik woke up and got himself out of his office.

"Don't worry. I know where to find him."

"How?"

"I looked up his IDR location."

"Oh." Again I felt stupid. "You know you could have helped me yesterday and saved me a whole lot of trouble."

"Yes. I could've."

"Why didn't you. Why today and not yesterday?" I climbed up into the passenger's seat, no longer able to stand being curled into a ball on the floor.

"Yesterday, you weren't getting shot at. It made a difference."

"Oh. Well, I'm still mad at you."

"I know."

I wanted to hit him for that. Instead, I stared at the window to the beauty suit of San Francisco. It was beautiful. A whole lot of beautiful hiding a whole lot of ugly. I opened my mouth to try to apologize for being willing to leave him, to yell at him for making me make that choice, to tell him once and for all that I loved him.

But he was braking.

And I looked around to see where we were. We were at a little restaurant. Jay was sitting at a seat by the window staring out into the world.

"Stay!" Tag ordered again.

"Yeah, 'cause you ordering me around's going to make it happen. I don't think so." I got out to the sound of him cussing under his breath.

I tapped on the glass, startling Jay to attention. He saw me standing with Tag and jumped out of his chair, nearly toppling it over to get to us. He rushed out of the restaurant. As the door of the restaurant closed, the computer voice thanked Jay Savage for dining with them today.

"Get in the car," Tag said, pointing to the car we'd stolen.

Jay stopped short. "That's Professor Raik's car."

"Yes, which is the best vehicle to be approaching the Regent's apartments in, don't you think?"

Jay nodded and moved to get in the car.

Tag stopped him. "Ditch your IDR. If anyone watching sees you going near those apartments, you'll be ex-ed before you can blink. Regents don't mess around."

Jay took off his ring and tossed it in a recycle bin. He got in the car.

Tag lifted from the tracks and flew us down the coast line until we reached a place where the housing areas were all on the ground. He tracked and turned to Jay. "Getting babies from the arms of a woman who has loved them for the last several months is going to be impossible. All she knows is that she is the child's mother, and you are coming to kidnap her kid. Moms fight for their kids."

I snorted. "You never met my mother."

Tag shot me a look that made me shut up all other sarcastic remarks.

"Dads fight for their kids too." Jay's level tone of calm anger left me with little wonder on who would win this battle.

The car braked. "We don't have much time, Jay. I don't how long Raik and the guys will be out. They'll know where his car has gone. They can see where I'm at, even if the two of you stay in their blind spots."

"You didn't kill him?"

"No, I didn't kill him. Do you have a problem with my method of help, Savage?"

Jay looked like he'd bitten off what he'd plan to say and gave his head a single, sharp shake.

"When I say this woman is the mother of these children, I mean it. She loves those kids."

"So will their real mother."

"You mean like she loves the ones she's got?"

Jay glared at Tag. "Those aren't hers."

"But they're still babies. They're still babies needing a mother and father and someone to love them and show them how to grow up normal. When you go, what will happen to those babies? Will you just leave them there?"

Jay's anger turned to shock. "Of course not! We're not going to leave helpless babies to die!"

"Then what will you do?" Tag whispered the question.

Jay stared at his hands, seeming for the first time since he showed up in my dorm room, confused. "We'll have to take them with us. That's the only way, isn't it? They'll die if we leave them here—even if

we leave them with someone—they'll only have until they're three."
Jay looked up, his eyes glistening with tears.

"So you do love them—those babies that aren't yours?"

Jay inhaled sharply. "Yeah. I guess I do."

"Good." Tag nodded to the guns in the back. "Take one of those."
Tag got out of the car and looked at me. He opened his mouth, but I
stopped him before he could order me to stay.

"Save your breath." I pulled a gun from the back seat too.

"Fine. Great, take a weapon. Do you have any idea how to shoot it?"

"No, but neither does Jay, and you gave *him* one."

Jay shrugged, indicating I was right about his weaponry skills.

Tag tightened his mouth into a thin line, and reset each of the guns.
"None of them are on taze. We don't have that kind of time. So don't
pull the trigger unless you plan to down someone forever, got it?"

We nodded and followed him towards the buildings.

I glanced around me. This was one nice neighborhood. "Wow," I
muttered. "They could've been rich babies." Jay glared at me. "What?
I'm just saying . . ."

"Summer?" Tag said.

"Yeah."

"Shut up."

I did as instructed.

Tag had his gun held ready as he approached the door. He didn't
allow the door to decide if it would glow green or red, he simply shot
out the doorknob and kicked the door in.

I hadn't expected the gun to be so loud and nearly dropped my
own gun in surprise at the staccato beat of each bullet flying from the
barrel. We stormed the house.

Tag took out the two surprised soldiers. I wondered if he knew the
soldiers—if it hurt him to down them. It hurt me to watch happen.
Real people—really gone.

The woman inside of the room the soldiers had been guarding held
one of the babies. Her eyes went wide with fear as she glanced down
towards the cradle where the other baby was.

I heard a muffled crying, my ears still feeling stuffed from the deafening sound of the gun. The babies were crying. The woman was crying, her sleek red hair sticking to her face as she shook her head.

Jay lowered his gun, unable to hold it steady while she held one of the babies. "I want my children."

His hard voice left no room for argument. Yet, she stood there clutching the child and shaking her head. "They're mine! I'm their mother!"

Jay walked right up to her. Tag kept his weapon trained on the woman. I couldn't, afraid I might accidentally shoot her or the babies. I didn't think I could do either and live with myself after. The Regent's wife rushed to the cradle, but Jay slid in between her and the cradle obstructing her path. She nearly ran right into him.

"Summer! Get the baby." Jay directed, not taking his eyes off the woman. She panicked at his words and tried to lunge around him to the cradle. He maneuvered and stayed in front of her. She held the child in her arms so tightly, I feared she'd crush it.

I picked up the one in the cradle. The little girl had a green bow in her feather fine hair. She smelled like fresh flowers as if she'd just come from a bath. She was heavy and much bigger than I'd expected. The babies in the public nursery were always so small that the size of this baby surprised me. She was still crying, likely terrified from the sound of the guns. I backed away behind Tag with her in my arms.

"Give me the other one, and no one else will get hurt." Jay slung the gun over his shoulder and held out his hands to the woman. She began backing away towards the windows which I realized, after a moment, were doors.

"Jay! The doors!"

He lunged for the woman, catching her up in his arms and pinching at her shoulder. A cry escaped her lips, and she released the baby involuntarily. Jay caught the baby before it could fall too far and pulled away from the woman. Her hands clawed at his face, but he fended her off and pulled back, lifting the gun back up to target on her.

"My babies!" she screamed. "He's taking my babies!" Someone must have heard the gunfire and seen the damage because outside, sirens blared. The noise startled me. I hadn't heard sirens except for on the vids and nets and that one time in the dark levels. I'd almost forgotten what they sounded like.

"Soldiers coming." Tag said. "Time to go." Tag looked at the woman as if struggling to make a decision. He finally shouldered his weapon, strode to the woman, and grabbed her hand. He jerked the ring from her finger leaving a trickle of blood where he'd scraped across her knuckle. He left her in her room with the empty cradles and kicked the door closed. Tag took my gun from me and pulled one of the Orbitals from his jacket pocket. He strapped it to Jay's wrist. He indicated Jay should give the baby he had over to me.

The one he held had a yellow bow in its hair. Another girl. I briefly wondered if he'd noticed his twins were both girls, but he didn't seem to be focusing on that. He focused on the Orbital and the wonder if we'd all get out of this building alive.

Tag readjusted the strap so it didn't cut off the blood to Jay's hand. "Right about now, they're suspecting the New Youths, Jay and Jen Savage, of an insane act of attacking a Regent. Soldiers will have already been dispatched to your house."

Tag started calculating numbers on the Orbital screen. "You'll never get to her in time. She'll be implicated and ex-ed before you ever get to LA. So you're going to have to do this in steps. You have no other choice if you want to have a happy ending. I've set this to get you to 1986. You'll need a babysitter. This is close to your own time which I did on purpose so you wouldn't stand out, but don't call a relative, that's the first place the soldiers will be looking for you. Call a babysitting service, call clergy of some kind. Just make sure it's someone you don't know, but feel okay leaving the kids with. You won't want to keep jumping time with the twins in tow, so don't even look at me like that."

Jay smoothed out the scowl on his face and listened as Tag explained how to set the date timer and the jump calculations. I listened intently thinking of how nice such information would have been back when I

DEATH THIEVES

was trying to escape with the Orbital. The babies made listening hard, since they were still crying, but I rocked them back and forth, thinking my arms might fall off from the weight of them. They settled down into whimpers.

Even the Regent's wife pounding on the door didn't seem to bother them once I rocked them.

Tag stayed focused in spite of all the noise and distraction. "You'll want to get back to Jen at least three hours ago. From the way the windows look, you'll be gone before they can get to you. They won't expect you to plan so well because, frankly, most of the soldiers don't understand the windows well enough to calculate that many steps ahead. They can't play chess either. You want to jump with Jen and the other twins to the exact time you leave 1986. You'll be kind of stuck at that point. The Orbital isn't exactly made to hold the figurative weight of that many people. I honestly don't know that you could take all four babies and the two of you without losing someone. So you'll be stuck in that time, got it? Don't contact people you know and love because it will get you caught. Your lives depend on it. The soldiers have Orbitals. Orbitals can find other Orbitals. You'll want to destroy yours as soon as possible. There's money in your pocket." Tag placed a wallet in Jay's shirt pocket. "Move to a different country with the kids and have a nice life, okay? It was great knowing you for this last hour or so. I hope I don't see you again."

Jay didn't seem to take offense to Tag's abrupt directions and dismissal, but he looked at me as if realizing he wouldn't be seeing me again either. "Thanks, Summer. You saved us, dude. You are the coolest person I know. We won't forget you. You're leaving too, right?"

"Yeah. I'm leaving."

"Then I won't worry about you. It's too bad they did this to us. It's too bad they didn't mean it when they said they were making the world better, because they really could've, you know? You could've saved the future once you graduated biology school and all that."

I smiled. "Or I could've made it worse. Who knows? Anyway . . . take care of your family."

275

"Yeah. I'm all over that. Hide yourself somewhere awesome, with a beach and yacht, right?"

"Right."

He hugged me. Since I was holding two squirming babies, the hug was a bit awkward. Jay took the babies from me, looking relieved to be holding them and seeming like someone practiced in balancing two kids in his arms. He smiled as he tapped the screen. He and the babies faded into the background.

Tag took my hand. "Let's go."

"We've gotta go see Winter."

He was shaking his head before I finished the sentence. "No way. Did you not hear what I told your friend?"

"Yes, I heard." Pounding at the door had finally resulted into splintered wood. The Regent's wife was making an exit. I tried to talk over the noise and the noise of the sirens getting louder. "But Tag, she dies because of an STD. If I warn her, she'll be careful, she'll have a full life."

"And you'll be changing the future! Isn't it bad enough we sent six people to the past who don't belong there? I would have sent them to the future if I thought they'd have a chance of surviving there. Who knows what kind of damage we've done? And you want to do more? You can't save the world! Hasn't everything you've seen over the last day taught you that? I thought you could. I really did. But we can't save the world!"

"I'm not trying to save the world. I'm trying to save one person. Take me to my sister!"

He took a deep breath as though about to yell at me again, but the squeal of brakes outside cut him off. The Regent's wife splintered the door enough I could see her eyes glaring with fury at us. "I'll have you ex-ed!" she yelled. "We'll find you wherever you go!"

Tag set the screen and said to the Regent's wife, "I'm sorry."

The room spun around us until it blurred into obscurity.

The tightening at my chest accompanied the pull at my stomach. I closed my eyes and gripped Tag's hand. When my chest stopped feeling like someone was trying to squeeze out all my oxygen, I opened my eyes again. The sun was high in the sky, and my feet were planted firmly in sand. Gulls cried out in the air. The Regent housing hadn't been built yet. I smiled at Tag and threw my arms around him. "Are we really in her time? Tell me I'll really see her."

"You'll really see her." He let me hold him and even seemed to be holding me back.

"I love you, Tag."

He didn't tell me not to say those words, but he didn't say them back to me either. I shrugged off my disappointment.

"It's a long way to Washington. We'd better find a place we can rent a car." He pulled away.

I halted. "You mean steal a car. I don't have any money." I almost suggested we try to shift place, but remembered he'd said most people didn't survive it. What good would coming all this way do us if we killed ourselves upon arrival?

He opened his jacket pocket. "When I took the Orbitals, I took the liberty of financing us as well. We have enough. And I have several driver's licenses from several different decades just in case." He tried to move again.

I tugged his hand back. "Can we just sit a minute? We're safe, and I need a minute. My legs feel like water."

"Orbitals can track Orbitals. And we're in the same year you came from. They'll expect that. We're not safe." He brought me in and held me a moment longer. "I know you're tired. So am I. But we're not done. You can rest in the car. It'll be several hours before we get to Washington." He pulled me along and this time I let him.

We took turns driving and made good time to Washington. It took just over nine hours and the sun had already set on the city of Orting. I was driving, the roads familiar and yet dreamlike at the same time. Was this really my home? Was Winter really here? Had I changed over the last year? Would her face still be my mirror, or would the stress of what I'd seen and been through show in my face?

I shut the car off in front of Aunt Theresa's house and stared at it for a time before the lack of movement in the car woke Tag up.

He stretched. "We're here?"

I nodded. "Let's go."

We exited the car, Tag a little slow as he tried to wake himself up. It was late and the house was dark with the sleep of its occupants. I put my hand on the door to knock, but Tag seemed to have awoken enough to realize what I'd planned and pulled my hand away. "You're dead as far as these people know. You'll give your aunt a heart attack if she sees you." He tapped on his screen and then wrapped his arms around me. I melted against him, loving the feel of him as things shifted around us. I opened my eyes and found that the world looked grey as it had the day of my accident. Grey, because we were outside of time as Tag had described it all those months ago. Tag was the only thing that had color. He let me go and went to the hide-a-key inside the little garden gnome by the porch.

"How'd you know that was there?" I asked.

"I was watching, remember?" He used the key and entered the house. He bumped into the entry table and let out a yelp. "That's the second time that thing's done that to me."

"Shh!" I waved my finger in front of my mouth.

"We're outside of time, Summer. No one can hear us."

"Oh. Right. I remember that." I took a moment to breathe the house in, to feel the hominess and rightness of it. Aunt Theresa had pictures of us on her wall and on the mantel over the fireplace. She had the ceramic handprints we'd made in second grade, and carried around with us from home to home until we ended up with her, hanging by the TV. And I knew if I were to look in the kitchen, there would be report cards and more pictures on the fridge. "She really did love us, didn't she?"

"Your aunt?" Tag looked confused. "Of course she did. Would she have raised you if she didn't?"

"Right. You're right." I smiled and went to the stairs taking them two at a time, hurrying to get to my room, where Winter was sleeping.

I opened the door and found myself face to face with Winter's wide frightened eyes staring at me. Her eyes widened even more upon seeing me—the surprise evident. Her mouth had been gagged. She sat on the bed right next to Professor Raik.

TWENTY-SEVEN

Winter!" I moved to go to her, but Winter let out a squeal through her gag as Professor Raik tightened something he held to her side. A knife. I halted.

"Hello, Summer. Taggert. Nice of you to finally join me. I've been waiting a long time. We were starting to think you wouldn't come here after all, and it would have been such a bother to have to include the soldiers to hunt you down." When he smiled, the dark stain of blood under his nose crusted and flaked in spots. His head had several large purpled lumps from our earlier battle.

I realized that the room was grey, but Winter was filled with color and so was Professor Raik. They were outside of time too. That was why Aunt Theresa wouldn't have known to help Winter.

"What do you want?" I asked.

"I should think it obvious. I want the babies back—it's bad business to have to offer refunds. Mr. and Mrs. Savage . . . well, we can work the rest out later. Hand over the Orbital, Taggert."

Tag held my gaze as he undid the bindings at his wrist. "I'm sorry, Summer." He said as his hand moved to the last latch. With a quick flash of movement, Tag pulled a small knife from his jacket sleeve and flung it at Professor Raik.

In Raik's distraction, he had released his hold on Winter. She threw herself to the side to avoid the knife. Tag and I both dove at the same time—Tag diving at Professor Raik—me diving at Winter. I grabbed her arms, pulled her free from the bed, and yanked her to her feet, racing from the room with her. In the hallway, I ripped the gag from her mouth.

She fell into me, her shoulders convulsing with sobs. "An angel. I'm seeing an angel!" She repeated over and over. Her embrace tightened around me so much that I could barely breathe, but I didn't pull away.

"I've missed you, Wineve. I'm sorry I left you. I would take it all back if I could. I'm so, so sorry."

"Who's that man in there?" She asked, her voice muffled against my shirt.

"He's evil, Wineve. Pure evil. Go and hide somewhere. Don't come out until I call for you or until Tag calls for you. Tag's a good guy. But go hide. I have to help Tag." I shoved at her. "Go! Now!"

Without waiting to see if she'd done as I told her, I went back into the bedroom. Tag and Professor Raik were gone. One of the Orbitals lay on the floor half-shoved under the bed as though it had been kicked in the scuffle. I hurried and picked it up, my heart hammering against my chest. "Tag!" I screamed.

Winter's face popped into view from the doorway. "What happened?" she asked.

"I told you to hide!" I said, trying to think of what could have happened. Who was winning the battle between them? Who had won? Would the winner return? And if so, would I have to prepare for a fight or a reunion?

"Is the evil gone?"

"I don't know. He is for a while, anyway. Let's go downstairs. We need to be ready."

"Ready for what?"

I gripped the Orbital in my hands. "For anything. We need to be prepared for anything."

I put my arm around her shoulders and led her downstairs and to the kitchen. I pulled out a few knives and settled them on the counter for easy access, but did so quietly, remembering that the things I touched would make noise, even if I didn't. Aunt Theresa couldn't help us now, not when she couldn't see us, not when she couldn't see the enemy. And for reasons I didn't understand, I wanted desperately to protect Aunt Theresa. I turned to face Winter, not knowing how long we had before someone came back, not knowing if I'd have time later to tell her what I came to tell her.

"Wineve, you look terrible," I whispered, wanting to cry at how thin she'd become, how sunken and dark her eyes looked.

Those dark eyes filled with tears. "That's not a nice thing to say to the person who shares your face. But your face, it's so different. You look *older*."

I laughed. Laughed, cried, and grabbed her up in a hug. "I've missed you! You've no idea how much I've missed you over the last year."

"You've only been dead for three months," she mumbled.

I let her go a little so she could breathe. "Yeah. Well . . . Time's been a little different for me." I felt her relax against me, and we both sat, simply crying.

"I came back to tell you something." I moved out so I could look her in the eyes when I told her my message, so she could see my sincerity.

And I told her about the future and how she would die and how much it hurt me to have her go in such a tragic mindless way—much like my own passing had been. I told her about the future where people were desperate to have babies, but were sterile due to diseases and genetic mutations that no one seemed to be able to cure. I told her about the public nurseries and the sorrows involved in testing day.

She listened, her pale face and dark sunken eyes, horrorstricken at my news.

"Promise me," I said at the end of my narration. "Promise me you'll be careful, and smart, and that you'll grow to be an old lady with purple hair who shakes her cane at people."

She promised.

And some of the weight that had been sitting on my chest lifted, and I started crying all over again. She took the Orbital I'd been twisting in my hands and put it in the pocket of her bathrobe so she could hug me without anything hindering us.

I held my sister and wept.

Tag entered through the kitchen door, his presence eliciting a scream from Winter and a cry of relief from me. I released Winter and ran to Tag, who looked like a ghost. He was covered in ashes, his lips bright red and his eyes a stark white against the grey filth covering him. "What happened? Is he coming back?"

Tag smiled, the ash dripping onto the floor with his every movement. "He's not coming back. He just met up with a mudslide on Mount Rainier."

I swallowed the sob and grabbed Tag around the neck, laughing and crying some more. "How? How did you get him to Rainier?"

"I took a chance and place shifted. The good news is I'm one of the lucky few who can place shift without dying."

I laughed more and hugged him tighter.

Tag realized Winter stood outside of time with us. He explained to her that she had to "change" in order to be part of the world again. Tag told her she had to be quiet once the change took place so as not to wake Aunt Theresa and Uncle Paul. She nodded her understanding. Tag took my hand, I took Winter's, and the world shifted around us, seeming suddenly bright and filled with colors.

"We have to go now, Summer. The Regents are going to demand blood after what's happened. I have to get the rest of the Orbitals, and we don't have time. You know you can't stay. They'll always come here to find you."

"I know." I hugged Winter again, knowing this would be the last time, and feeling like I was dying all over again. I hugged her and breathed in Aunt Theresa's kitchen. I had been right about the fridge. It was still littered with pictures of Winter and me, still littered by report cards and papers that had A's on them. My stuff still existed there. The mug I made in pottery class as a sophomore, as wobbly and weird as it looked still sat on the counter, the hand towels I'd made in sewing class still hung on the stove handle. I'd been gone for three months according to Winter, and yet Aunt Theresa still kept my things.

"Be nice to Aunt Theresa and Uncle Paul," I said to Winter as I pulled away. "Tell them—"

Aunt Theresa's voice came from upstairs. "Winter? Winter honey, are you alright?"

Tag gave me a look and said, "We need to go!"

"I know."

Tag made some calculations on the Orbital and took my hand.

"Wait!" I said, stopping Tag from pushing the screen that final time that would pull us away, knowing that Aunt Theresa would be rounding the corner to the kitchen any moment and wanting with all my heart to see her.

When she showed up, I smiled at her shocked face. "I just wanted you to know, Aunt Theresa. I wanted you to know I love you, and am so thankful for you taking us in the way you did. You saved us. Thank you."

I squeezed Tag's hand, letting him know I was ready, and called out, "I'll love you forever, Wineve! Wonder Twin Powers!" as Tag touched the screen and the world around us blurred.

Winter's answering call of "Activate!" spun around us over and over and over.

The world snapped back into view in the year 2114. Tag stepped aside, looking truly horrific, covered the way he was in ashes and dirt. Tag pivoted several times, looking worried. "I left it here."

"You left what here?" I asked.

"The car. After I dropped off the professor into the mudslide, I spun myself a little forward and left a car here so we could get into the city faster to get the Orbitals. I'm not about to try place shifting with you."

I glanced around the mountain meadow skeptically. "Well, I don't see a car."

He turned and was likely glaring, but it was hard to tell under all that crap on his face. "I noticed that. Thanks." He spent several moments frowning at the Orbital. "I can't get any readings on any of the other Orbitals, but one."

"One? Where's that one?"

284

"In Orting, Washington. It's been there since 2010, but hasn't been activated since then. It's dead." He looked as confused by this as I felt.

"What does that mean? Did someone else go back to Winter? Is this a trap? What does that mean?"

He shook his head. "Not a trap. The thing hasn't been accessed in all this time." He snapped his fingers and looked at me in wonderment. "The professor. He had an Orbital too. We must have left it there." He took my hands to calm me down before I flew into a panic over leaving Winter vulnerable to soldiers tracking the Orbital to her. "I can't track any of the others. They don't exist, Summer. Let's not panic yet. Let's just see what's going on here before jumping back there. Winter will be fine. Trust me."

And so it was that we found ourselves walking into the city, Tag acting incredibly paranoid about who would have taken the car and how he knew they were waiting in ambush somewhere, but continuing to offer me comfort about Winter's well-being. How he thought he could act comforting when he was acting like a paranoid lunatic defied all reason. We came across a stream where Tag cleaned himself up as best as he could.

It felt like we'd walked half the day before we came into the city. I was exhausted and wanted nothing more than to sleep, but Tag was as alert as I'd ever seen him. "Something's wrong."

"Yeah, something's wrong. Our ride is missing, and my sister is trackable because we left an Orbital at her house."

"No, I mean look around." He stopped me and lifted his chin in the direction of the city sidewalk.

"Yeah, people, and . . ." Were these people undercover soldiers? A degree of his paranoia for our present circumstances rubbed off on me.

"The hair, the clothes, the way they walk; look at all the children!"

And I looked again. He was right. The entire feel of the street and the people was different than the world I'd lived in for the last year. And there were *children*. Lots and lots of children.

"Something's happened," Tag said. He passed by a doorway of a shop and waved his hand in front of it. A little boy inside the shop saw Tag wave and waved back. Tag frowned and waved again. The little boy waved again, too, but I realized what Tag meant. No light glowed around the door, neither red nor green even though Tag still had his ring.

I frowned at Tag's ring after offering a smile to the friendly kid inside the shop. "Do you think it broke in the ashes?"

Tag shook his head. "No. The future's shifted." He checked the Orbital and frowned some more. "And I still can't get a reading on any of the other Orbitals. We need a library."

"If the future shifted, are we different?"

"I don't know. We were outside of time during the shift. I don't know what we are."

We asked around until we found the public library several blocks down. Tag sat at a computer terminal, where the computer asked in a friendly voice, "What would you like to search?" Tag had to voice all the commands to the computer, seeming frustrated that he had to use his voice rather than pulse power from his brain, since his ring no longer worked. He did several searches for the Crazy War. Over sixteen million search opportunities showed up, but none of them on *the* Crazy War. He ran searches for Public Nurseries and ended up with a million possibilities for day care services. He ran search after search after search until he finally shook his head in defeat. "The world's changed."

His eyes filled with wonder and fear, he faced the windows that led to the street outside. "Everything's different."

I scooted him out of his seat and ran a search for Winter Eve Rae. There were over eleven million searches available. I clicked the first one and read until the words blurred due to the tears stinging my eyes.

Winter Eve Rae was a few steps ahead of the beat as she took to the red carpet for the premiere of her new movie, Iron Gate. Rae, who costarred with Allen Lucas was reported as being taken aback by the size and enthusiasm of the crowd as she returned to the red carpet for the last time. Rae is best known for her academy award winning movie The Revolution which started a revolution all of its own . . .

"We did it." I whispered. "You said we couldn't, but we did." I tapped the screen. "We saved the future, Tag. She became a star, and she told people the message I gave her. She shared it with the world!"

"I can't believe it." Tag scowled. "This isn't real."

We clicked on several links moving through Winter's rise to fame and her fabulous career, to the clinics she opened around the globe to help teens get the medical care and advice they needed as they moved into sexual maturity. She began a foundation that researched level one infections and found cures—cures that happened before the infections mutated. Winter spread the message and changed the world.

"What does this mean?" Tag asked. He turned to face me directly. "Are there Orbitals still out there? Are the soldiers still there, the New Youth? What does this mean to *us*?"

His questions spawned one of my own. "Do you still have the HTH infection?" I asked slowly.

He tensed. His eyes flickered with hope. "I can test myself. I have the test strips I used for when I was collecting the New Youth." He scraped back his chair. "I'll be back."

My heart filled with hope like never before. *We can be together.* While he was gone I ran a search for Kirk Shaw and Taggert Shaw. According to the news, Kirk Shaw and his wife lost their son Taggert in a drowning accident when he was nine years old. So there was no other Taggert running around this time. I wondered how Tag would take that news when I told him.

To take my mind off of Tag and his test, I went back to the search on Winter. Someone wrote a biography called *One Long Winter*. In the article I read, the writer mentioned a dead sister's ghost coming to Winter and warning her about the future. The devil was also there fighting her angelic sister, and Winter knew at that moment that she had a purpose in life and she owed it to her sister to live a great life.

"Wineve, you sound crazy." And I laughed at the computer screen. Laughed at the irony and perfect beauty of my sister changing the world.

Tag strode purposefully to me. "Time to go. We need to see the barracks. We need to be sure everything is really gone and fixed."

"What about your test?"

He didn't look at me, but placed the test strips with his blood samples on the counter in front of me. "I'm the same. Nothing's changed." I picked them up and followed him out, wishing I could make the test strips in my hand magically change. I finally shoved them in my pocket.

He managed to use some of the cash he had to buy us train tickets to San Francisco. Neither of us spoke on the ride there which took only three hours compared to the nine it had taken by car. Tag seemed lost in thought as he fiddled with the Orbital. I was exhausted and slept for a good part of the time.

We arrived in San Francisco at street level. The street was clean and well cared for. And it wasn't so dark it felt like night. No one avoided my glance. Cars were still tracked but the tracks were street level *and* sky level. I looked up to the sky levels where I'd lived. There were structures up high, but they were built to allow light to the street.

Tag interrupted my moment of awe. "I need to go somewhere. Will you stay here? You can maybe go to a restaurant and find food. I just, there's something I need to see."

"Um, no. You are so not ditching me in a strange city."

"You lived here for over a year."

I snorted at him. "I lived in a totally different here."

"Fine, then come on."

I assumed he was taking me to the barracks, but we walked a long time until we were in a residential area. He walked down a tree lined street and then backed up behind one of those trees. He watched a brick house for several moments before I asked, "Whose house is this?"

At that moment a little girl and boy spilled out the front door and into the yard. They were wrestling. A woman followed them out, her

288

hands on her hips as she scolded the kids. She looked half-amused with the kids so her scolding was only half-hearted.

Tag straightened when he saw her. "Janice," he whispered.

"Taggert! I mean it! Give that back to your sister now!" The mother finally interrupted in the argument.

He jolted a little at hearing his name, but realized she addressed the child. "She's alive, and grown up like she should have been." Tears rolled down his cheeks as he watched. "Grown up, with kids of her own."

Janice looked our way and Tag ducked behind the tree. We stayed out of sight until we heard the kids go inside, all thoughts of arguing gone as their mother asked if they wanted to help her with a puzzle.

"My sister's all grown up, and she named her kid after me." Tag's head leaned back against the tree. "Does that mean there is another version of me somewhere, walking the streets right now in this time? Or did I disappear from their lives somehow. Am I a missing person?"

I reluctantly told him about the drowning accident from the news feeds I'd read.

Tag lifted his head. "So, where do I fit in the world now?"

"Where do *we* fit in the world now?" I tossed his question back at him.

"You're right. I need to figure that out for you. Come on, let's go. We've seen what I needed to know here." He smiled at me. "You saved your sister. Then your sister saved my sister."

"I save her, and she saves everyone else. I told you that's how we work."

Our walk back from the barracks, which didn't exist, was slower, less purposeful. He stopped at a restaurant and took me inside to get us some food. Once we were seated in a booth, Tag said, "I've called in on all the Orbitals. We can't track them. I think . . ."

"What?"

Tag focused on the tracked cars zipping down the road. "I think we didn't change because we were outside of time when the change took place. We're still the same but the world shifted from under us.

Everything else after the moment we left your aunt's house is different. That means that the New Youth never happened. All those kids we saved still died in whatever tragedy came to them. That means—"

"Jay and Jen?" I took off my Orbital and placed it on the table.

He frowned. "I don't know. They weren't outside time, but they weren't in its path either. They were behind that time, so maybe they're okay. Maybe not. Maybe the fact that the New Youth never happened means that they got erased from the past because they would have still died in their accidents."

We scooted back in our seats as the waitress brought us glasses of water and menus. "But we didn't. We didn't get erased. I'm still here. You're still here with your soldier's uniform and Orbital."

"Like I said, we were outside time when time changed." His eyes searched mine, then looked down at his menu.

We ordered, got our food, and ate to the sound of idle meaningless chatter. Tag wouldn't focus on real conversation, instead he asked me weird questions about my favorite foods, music, and animals in the world. By the time we'd finished eating, I was ready to slap him. We were in an alternate universe and he wanted to know what animals I liked?

"I can't stay with you, Summer," he said finally.

"What?" I looked around. "Where are you going to go?"

"I don't know. But I can't stay with you. You have your whole life still. You can get married, have kids, become a biologist. I can't be part of that. I'm still . . . If I stayed, I'd be like poison to you."

"Don't be stupid! I don't have anyone else!" I waved to the restaurant around me. "Look around, Tag. I don't have any family or friends. I don't have any skills. I don't know how this new future works. I don't know what their technology is. You leave me here alone and I swear I will hate you forever."

He threw a wallet to the table and slid out of his seat. "But you'd hate me more if I stayed. You'll be fine. Just know this means I love you more than anything. I've loved you from the first time I ever laid eyes on you. I love you enough to keep you safe from the poison that created me." He then took a book from out of one of his many jacket pockets and put it in front of me on the table.

A Sliver of Midnight.

Him saying the words I'd wanted to hear rooted me to the spot. He'd told me he loved me. I was so stunned, it took me a moment to get over the words and realize he was already out the door to the street. I scrambled out of the booth and shoved open the door. I turned in circles to try to see all directions.

Tag was gone.

Numb with shock, I stood in the middle of the sidewalk, like a lost child in the park. Some part of me just knew he'd come back if I waited long enough. *Stupid!* He wasn't coming back.

With a sharp intake of breath, I remembered the book and things left on the table. Maybe he left some clue . . . something . . . My shaky legs carried me back into the restaurant to our booth. I scanned the table and through the contents of the wallet and the book. I lifted the napkins and plates. Nothing.

I slid back into my seat and leaned my head on the table. He left money, enough to get me started in a new life. He wouldn't leave me with nothing. But by leaving, he *had* left me with nothing. And I remembered how I felt after reading *A Sliver of Midnight.* I'd never felt such sacrifice.

And that's what Tag had done. He sacrificed his happiness. But he got it all wrong. By sacrificing his happiness, he sacrificed mine too.

I couldn't cry. It felt like my tear ducts had dried up, and besides if I got a crying headache, who would massage it out again?

"Stupid jerk!" I said out loud.

"Oh, don't say things you don't mean."

I bolted upright, expecting Tag, and instead faced a young teenage boy, maybe fourteen years old—fifteen tops. I glanced around the restaurant.

"Are you lost, kid?"

The boy smiled. He looked like Winter a little bit, which in a weird way meant he looked like me. "Nope. Not now. I did get lost today and ended up somewhere that totally nicks, you know?" He lifted an eyebrow at me. "No. I guess you wouldn't know."

He reached over and helped himself to Tag's leftover fries. It was then I noticed the Orbital strapped to his arm. "Where'd you get that? Did you steal that from Tag?"

He smiled. "Nope. It's mine. I made it myself. One of my better moments. Dad was totally proud."

I gasped. "You're a soldier."

He laughed. "Yeah, like any military would take me, though Dad threatens to send me to military school all the time. Nope. Guess again."

I stood up. "Look, you little punk, you would not believe the year I've just had. You can't come in here, eat my friend's food, and freak me out. I have no problem ripping out your tongue and stapling it to the wall as an example to other idiots who think I can be messed with!"

He didn't look at all phased by my outburst. I reached over to make good on my threat, but he put out a hand. "Whoa there! Take a good look, my Orbital is green, my favorite color, by the way, which you never remember when you buy me clothes. Dad's was black . . . so boring. Mine is cool, Dad's nicks. Mine—cool. Dad's—nicks. Got it?"

I grabbed his arm and looked at the Orbital strapped there. His was green. Tag's was black. But he'd said *Dad*. I sat back down, confused. "What's going on? And quit talking in circles."

"I'm your son." He grinned wide for me then. "Ta-da!" He grinned wider, if such a thing were possible.

I stared at him.

"What, that doesn't fill you with joy? Any mother would be thrilled to find she has a kid like me, and you stare at me like I just grew a zit on my forehead while you watched. Hello? That was a big announcement. You should be, well, something . . ."

"Is this a joke?" My mind was tired. My kid? He had to be messing with me. I was nineteen years old. I didn't have kids. I didn't even have a boyfriend because mine just ditched me to who only knew when and— "You're my kid?"

He nodded.

"And you've got an Orbital?"

He nodded again.

"Tell me your dad's name."

He laughed. "What? You don't know the guy you made kids with?" I shot him a look that shut him up.

"Sorry, Mom, just messing around. Taggert Shaw is my dad, though he doesn't always like admitting to it, and has actually denied it on an occasion or two if you can believe it." The kid stole some more fries and shoved them in his mouth, continuing to talk around the fries so that he sounded garbled.

Do we never feed him or something?

"You told me you'd be here at this exact moment, sitting in this exact booth and feeling kind of bad because Dad dumped you. Not one of his finer moments. Sometimes Dad totally nicks, but you love him, so what do we do? Anyway, you told me this was your worst day ever. You told me you almost gave up. I just wanted to come cheer you up and let you know you've got several great reasons not to give up—me being among those reasons. Also, me being here will hopefully prove to you I'm not a total lost cause. In the back of your mind as you raise me, you'll know I cared enough to visit you on your worst day ever. I think this should make me your favorite."

He slid out of the booth. "If you think about it long enough, you'll know what you need to do." The kid mopped up the rest of the ketchup with the few remaining fries and stuffed them in his mouth. "I'll see you back at home."

He moved to leave, but stopped. "When you find Dad, will you let him know that when his son comes home escorted by the police. It really wasn't his fault. And he's really sorry for what happened to the car. Thanks, Mom. Love you." The kid actually planted a kiss on my forehead and then disappeared from where he'd been standing.

Did that just happen? I blinked, then groaned. No! He left with the Orbital! I let him leave with the one thing I needed more than anything. *Stupid!*

I pondered everything he said, trying to piece together the puzzle. *If I think about things long enough . . . I'd know what I'd need to do?*

The restaurant felt stifling, I paid the bill from the money in Tag's wallet and left, walking the streets and wondering what I needed to do next. Where would I go? Was it safe to carry around all this cash? Should I open a bank account? Did they have bank accounts?

I found myself feeling suddenly wistful for the days when Winter and I hid money in the closet under the floor—our own little pot of gold.

I stopped short.

Tag said he'd tracked a dead Orbital back to Orting, Washington.

I needed to get back to Orting, Washington.

***

The trip to Orting took no time at all. The rare flying cars from Tag's time weren't so rare in this alternate time and pretty cheap to rent, all things considered.

Unfortunately, Aunt Theresa's house had new owners.

"Hi." I said to the woman who opened the door.

She had a baby on her hip and had the look of a woman in the middle of a full and busy day. She waited for me to get more articulate.

"Hi." I tried again. "My great, great aunt lived in this house a long time ago. And we think she left an old watch in a secret hiding place upstairs."

"You want to come in my house?" The woman asked, shifting the baby to her other hip.

"No. I don't need to go in." I thought about crazy people and crazy wars. No one would let a stranger in their home under the best circumstances. "I definitely don't need to go up, but I would be willing to pay you if you would go up while I sit here on the porch waiting. If you could look for me and see if it's there, I'd be grateful." I smiled, hoping I looked in some small way sweet and trustworthy.

She let my request hang between us before saying, "Pay me how much? If the item's valuable, it's in my house which makes me the owner."

Why did people always play hardball? Why couldn't someone say, "Oh hey, let me be nice and do you this tiny favor that will take me less than two minutes?"

I kept the smile pasted on my face. At least I hoped I did. "The item is an old broken down watch. I'll pay whatever you think it's worth. You name the price." If I named a price and she felt the price was too low after finding it, she might lie to me and say it wasn't there.

She shrugged, shifted the baby again, and said, "Where is it?"

I told her and then sat on the porch to wait. I heard the door lock engage and sighed. So the world wasn't sunshine and roses in the future, but it wasn't crazy wars and dead toddlers either. I could live with that.

Less than two minutes later, the woman was back. "This what you're looking for?" She held out the Orbital.

I sucked in breath hard. "So it was there." I tried not to look too excited. "How much do you want for it?"

She looked skeptically at it. "It doesn't look like it's worth much."

"No. It doesn't." I agreed.

"Eh. Take it. I don't know what I'd do with it." She handed it to me.

Not believing my luck, I accepted her offering. I pulled a few bills from Tag's wallet and held them out for the woman anyway. "Buy your baby something special—something that'll last for a few years, past his third birthday."

***

I laid the Orbital out in the sun, letting it soak in power for the rest of the day. Once it had charged, it was time to go. I finally bound the Orbital to my arm and pressed the screen to make it show me where, and when, Tag had hidden himself.

He wasn't very original. He'd only moved a few years into the future from when he'd left me. I traveled to his location in my current time, took a deep breath, and pressed my screen.

Then, the tug at my stomach, the tightness in my chest, the blur of the world spinning around me.

When the world snapped into vision again in the same place only a few years later—2121. He was in the park sitting on a bench, just down the street from the diner he'd left me in. I smiled at Tag's surprise. He shook his head as if trying to clear his vision from this mirage he had in front of him. He jumped to his feet. "What are you do—"

He was going to ask me, yet again, what I was doing there. Honestly, the man could never just be glad to see me. I shut him up by throwing my arms around him and planting my mouth firmly over his. He tried to break away at first, but the attempt was feeble and after the initial moment, he was kissing me back, his mouth tracing kiss after kiss over my lips. The heat between us felt desperate, melting all the pain of the years away until it was just us. Us in time—any time—it didn't matter *when* so long as we were together. His hand went to the back of my head, his fingers lacing through my hair, pulling me closer.

His warmth and energy filled me with life and the waiting seemed to unload itself into that one moment of heat—like a flashfire— brilliant . . . beautiful.

It was almost physically painful when he came to his senses and broke away, sticking out his arm to put me at a distance and trying to fumble with the Orbital at his wrist—trying to run away from me again. "No." He mumbled that several times while trying to make his hands work at the Orbital. "I won't . . . I can't."

I grabbed his hand firmly and shoved him back down onto the bench. I scooted next to him, making certain to keep hold of his hand in mine so he couldn't jump away to somewhen else. "I've seen the future," I said. "I've seen our child. *Our* child, Tag. And he's beautiful! And he eats like a horse. I hope we make good money, because he's going to be one expensive kid. And he's beautiful!" My voice cracked. "That means that we find a cure for you. That means we have a future together. But we have to *stay* together to make that future happen. Between the two of us, you with your brains and me with my research, it probably won't even take too long. I love you, Tag. And this is our sliver of midnight—this very moment we're standing in. This is the sliver of time where we make the right decisions for our lives. The first time you spoke to me, you told me I was dead. Now, I've got a message for you—"

I gripped his hand tighter. "You're still alive, Taggert Shaw. And it's time for us to live."

ACKNOWLEDGEMENTS

There's a sign above my desk that reads: "Writing is hard work. Do it only if you have to." It's a bit of a joke... and also not. Writing is hard work. But luckily, there are people in my life who have made the load a little lighter.

First, thank you to Heather Moore, who's always in my corner, cheering me on and cheering me up. You were one of the first to dive into Death Thieves, and your feedback, advice, and example have kept me going—and kept me relevant! Jessica Day George and Josi Kilpack, thank you for taking the time to read and offer your invaluable thoughts. Your insights sharpened this book in ways I couldn't have done alone. Amy Jameson, your belief in this story and your knack for brainstorming titles better than mine helped me push through a dark patch in my writing life. I'm forever grateful for that.

Paul, thank you for your sharp content editing that made me question things I didn't even realize I should be questioning. Jeff and Jen Savage, and James Dashner, thanks for years of friendship, advice, and unwavering support. You guys rock.

And to my own Mr. Wright—you are my constant. You support every wild dream I chase, holding the ladder steady while I climb. I love you more than words can say. To my three amazing kids: thank you for enduring take-out and ramen while I wrestled with this story. You can't possibly know how much I love you.

Lastly, to you, the readers—thank you. Every time you pick up a book, every time you share it, you give the story new life. Writing is tough, but absolutely worth it!

www.ingramcontent.com/pod-product-compliance
Lightning Source LLC
Chambersburg PA
CBHW021209250626
47155CB00008B/2741